ZERO DAYS

A CYBER THRILLER

IAN WILLIAMS

Red Door

Published by RedDoor
www.reddoorpress.co.uk

© 2019 Ian Williams

The right of Ian Williams to be identified as author of this
Work has been asserted by him in accordance with sections
77 and 78 of the Copyright, Designs and Patents Act 1988

ISBN 978-1-913062-02-6

A CIP catalogue record for this book is available from
the British Library

Cover design: www.dissectdesigns.com

Typesetting: Tutis Innovative E-Solutions Pte. Ltd

Printed and bound in Denmark by Nørhaven

A mound was mistaken to be a pagoda and worshipped – until the lizard came out

Old Burmese proverb

Chapter One

The Buddha Head

Bagan, Myanmar

There was something almost hypnotic about the small blue blob on her computer screen; its steady pulse drawing her in and not letting go. Her laptop was propped up on pillows, and she sat cross-legged on the bed in front of it, tapping gently on a red stud above her right nostril, her finger matching the rhythm of the blinking blob. At the same time she explored the two silver rings that pierced the left corner of her upper lip with her tongue. It was something she did without thinking, the way others tap or swing their feet, spin pens or drum a table with anxious fingers. She'd known hackers who did them all, while popping endless pills to get through the long hours at the keyboard.

At first she didn't hear the gentle tapping on the door. When it came again, louder and more persistent, she moved quickly and silently across the room. She held a hammer tightly in one hand, a heavy slab of metal on a thick wooden handle, made for stone carvers in the market. With the other hand she peeled back a square of dark tape covering a small spyhole she had drilled through the wood herself.

The server took two steps back as she opened the door, staring first at the hammer, then at her. His mouth tried to form words that wouldn't come, eventually stammering, 'Big sorry, Miss Vika. Big, big sorry.' Because they'd run out of beer and had to send out for it, because it was warm beer, because he had taken such a long time. So long, that Miss Vika had completely forgotten placing the order, and she glowered at him, while he stared back, like he always stared, like a startled rabbit in the headlights, as if she was a creature from another planet.

Vika snatched the bottle of Mandalay beer, with its logo of a golden pagoda, and a glass of ice from the server's tray, replacing them with two one-dollar bills as crumpled as the kid's uniform. The ice cracked as she poured the beer, the froth racing up the glass, and only a quick and hungry slurp prevented it from spilling on her bed, on which she resumed her vigil in front of the blue blob.

A ceiling fan creaked and wobbled above her, as if it might come crashing down at any moment. It struggled to cool the room, the humid air reeking of mosquito repellent laced with smoke that seeped in from nearby piles of burning garbage.

She leapt from the bed.

Smack, smack, smack.

The punches hit square and hard.

The heavy duffle bag shuddered under her blows. *Smack, smack, smack.* She'd found the bag in the market and filled it with rice. It wasn't ideal, not like the punch bags she'd trained with, but it served its purpose, another way of relieving the tension. *Smack, smack, smack, smack.*

When the explosion came it was so loud it shook the window. It was the signal she'd been waiting for, thunder marking the arrival of the afternoon rain. She parted the sagging brown curtains, which she had permanently drawn. A gecko leapt to the floor and she took a step back, showing respect for an ally, at least in the fight against mosquitoes.

Palm trees bent and swayed as they were whipped by the intensifying wind, black clouds sucked the light from the afternoon sky while a curtain of rain advanced from across the river, scrubbing out the distant bank. The rain might last less than an hour, but it would provide her with the cover she needed.

She pushed aside a shower head with permanent dribble that hung limply from the mildewed wall of a bathroom described as a super deluxe en suite, and examined herself in the cracked mirror. The multiple piercings – eyebrows, a pin cushion of an ear, tongue, as well as the nose and lip. The hair – long on one side, shaven on the other, and purple. Appearances didn't matter in the online world, her world, where you could be whoever you wanted to be. In the real, offline world, anonymity was more difficult.

She stuffed her hair under a cheap red 'I Love Myanmar' baseball cap. Her blue eyes, wide and intense, vanished behind a pair of large Gucci sunglasses, before she pulled on an oversized rain jacket with hood.

She stole one last look at her laptop.

The gently throbbing blob hadn't moved. He was still in the museum.

She left through the veranda door of her ground floor room, glancing nervously at the windows above her own, curtains drawn, dull lights beyond. They were still in their rooms. The rain was now hammering hard on the roof of the guest house, the palm trees shrivelling under the intensifying onslaught. She stepped into the storm. Nobody in their right mind would set out on a walk now, and that made it ideal.

The dark sky rumbled and flickered as her feet sank into the waterlogged lawn. She pulled her hood tightly to her face, and in a few quick strides was under the cover of trees leading to a muddy path along the bank of the river. The driving rain stung her face each time she looked up, the river just a frothy grey nothingness.

The modern archaeological museum was a sprawling pavilion-like building with a tiered roof topped by golden towers. There were a series of broad pillars and arches with ornate carvings, somebody's fantasy of past imperial glories, but the cheap concrete was already cracking. A clock inside the entrance showed five o'clock. A woman at the ticket office said the museum closed in half an hour but sold her a ticket anyway.

Vika left a trail of water across the cavernous atrium. She quickened her pace, ignoring the display cabinets, instead concentrating on her phone. It guided her towards the blob, directing her to the far corner of the atrium, up two flights of stairs, and to a heavy door marked, 'PRIVATE WORKSHOP. DO NOT ENTER'.

It was not the sign that stopped her. She needed to be sure he was alone.

She stepped into another exhibition room to one side of the workshop. Display cabinets containing Buddha statues. A large laminated board explained the hand gestures. Touching the earth, preaching, meditation, compassion. The last was protection against danger. She lingered longer on that one. The glossy board let her see everything behind her. An elderly attendant, his head slumped, was asleep in a chair. A door leading to a terrace was ajar, blown open by the wind, a pool of water seeping in, though the rain had stopped as abruptly as it started. She stepped silently onto the terrace. Beside the workshop, the terrace was littered with heavy metal cabinets, battered and rusting. She stopped close to an open window.

She'd not known what to expect. Until that moment the professor had been just a beating blue blob on her screen. Click once and it was on a map so they could track him. Click again and it became a moving line, jumping and falling with the beat, the vital signs of life they could manipulate at will.

He was elderly, with a dishevelled head of grey hair and thick beard. He sat at a cluttered desk, leaning forward and gently brushing the long dangly earlobe of a Buddha head. She watched as he blew it gently, moving his mouth right up close, as if he was sharing a secret. She'd read his biog – explorer, acquirer of antiquities, benefactor to the world's top museums, a man who collected academic chairs like others collect stamps. But this was no Indiana Jones. His movements were slow and deliberate, stooping as he stood to fetch a pair of magnifying spectacles, a light on top, which he used to read the squiggles that made up the ancient words of an inscription carved into the four sides of a plinth-like stone on which the Buddha head was sitting.

The professor looked up sharply and then fixed his eyes on a backpack at his feet. He leaned down and dug around in the bag, emerging with a cell phone, holding it between his forefinger and thumb, keeping it at a distance at first, as if it was something dirty or contaminated. He looked at the screen, hesitated, and then jabbed his finger clumsily to take the call, succeeding at the third attempt.

'Yes, I hear you,' was all he said. The words slow and taut. Then he listened.

The call was no more than thirty seconds, after which he placed the phone on the table and sat staring blankly at the Buddha head.

Was the call from them? Playing with him, one last demand perhaps, one last order before this master of the ancient world was shut down by a weapon from the future.

Vika knew she had to move, and she had to move fast.

But she stopped abruptly and retreated behind one of the cabinets as a boy approached the professor. He was tall and gangly, dressed in traditional Burmese skirt-like longyi and check shirt, a mug in his hand, which he held out in front of him. The professor's hand appeared to be shaking as he reached to take it, the two of them stepping out to the terrace. Neither spoke.

They stood looking out at a vast plain beside the bloated Irrawaddy River. The temples seemed to have burst into life, glowing under the late afternoon sun. The plain bristled with them, some short and stubby, others soaring above the plain, multiple terraces topped by conical spires of ornate brick and gold.

Coaches raced towards them, throwing up water from flooded pathways. Tourists poured from their doors, cameras and selfie-sticks in hand, following tour guides with little flags, climbing up the temple terraces for the sunset. The retreating storm clouds were replaced by hot air balloons, adverts for a 4G cellular network on their sides, offering a better sunset view to those with deeper pockets. The professor turned, a look of disgust on his face, slowly shaking his head, before he and the boy stepped back into the workshop.

Vika jumped as a hand gripped her shoulder, spinning around, instinctively clenching her fists. It was the attendant from the exhibition room, who barked a series of disjointed instructions in broken English. 'No. Must not. Here forbidden. Go, please. Close now.' Two security guards stood behind him, and the three of them walked her to the museum entrance, allowing her to stop at a small gift shop.

'Two minutes please. Two minutes.'

She bought a card showing an engraving above a temple entrance, a dog, a snarling three-headed dog. That should get his attention, she thought. 'This is a friend,' she wrote in the card. 'You are in grave danger. You MUST disable the transmitter.' Then a series of instructions, as clear and precise as she could make them. 'This will take you offline. It will save your life.' She sealed the card in an envelope, on which she wrote the professor's name in bold letters. '*Please*,' she said, pressing it into the hand of the attendant. 'You *must* give this to Professor Pendelton. He has to have it today. *Urgent*, you understand?'

She handed the attendant a twenty dollar bill, to help with the understanding.

He looked bewildered and then smiled, a smile she found impossible to read, and said, 'Sure, yes, fine. Urgent,' before steering her to the door.

She ordered a bottle of water in a small café opposite the museum's main gate, and then sat waiting and hoping.

Nightfall comes quickly in the tropics, and the light was rapidly draining from the sky when the museum door swung open and the professor walked onto the steps in front. He struggled to get his backpack over his shoulder. It seemed unusually heavy, but he waved away a security guard offering him help.

He was carrying the envelope in his right hand as he walked down the steps.

Vika rose quickly, crossing back towards the museum compound, wanting to be sure, but by the time she reached the gate, the professor was climbing into the back of a battered museum car, which spluttered as it swept past her through deep puddles and onto a rutted and potholed road. She watched as a single rear light flickered and bounced before it disappeared into the gloom.

* * * * *

A chorus of frogs welcomed Vika to the small restaurant opposite her guest house, where she sat at her usual corner table, the server bringing her a fresh coconut with a straw without asking.

She jumped between her cell phone and laptop, searching for the blue blob.

The restaurant, all bamboo and wood, a thatched roof as leaky as a sieve when it rained, was popular with backpackers. It had the musty smell of the rainy season, the damp air laden with stale beer and tobacco. The yard out front was a jumble of bikes and a refuge to never fewer than a dozen languid dogs, tourists being more generous with their scraps than the locals. During her time in Bagan, Vika had made the corner table her own. It was private and had a strong Wi-Fi signal, but no matter how many times she booted and rebooted, connected and reconnected, the blob would not respond.

It was unreachable.

She glanced nervously at the guest house, spotting Yuri as he crossed to the restaurant. He was tall and muscular, with the rolling walk of an athlete, and he made straight for Vika's table, sitting opposite her. She kept her eyes firmly on her screens, ignoring him at first.

'The lobby. Why the fuck weren't you in the lobby, ready to leave, like we told you?' he said; the words spat rather than spoken.

She reached for the coconut and sucked on the straw, searching for the last dregs of milk and making a loud slurping sound. Then she slowly looked up, staring at Yuri, cold and hard, sucking again on the straw, louder this time.

Yuri stared back. His face reddened, and so did his scar, a scar that ran from high on his forehead to his eyebrow, then started again below his eye, a deep crevice down his right cheek. On his right arm he had a tattoo of a spider, its thick legs emerging from under his T-shirt, reaching down towards this wrist and wrapping around his forearm. He had another tattoo on his chest, an orthodox church, a cupola poking out above the neckline of the T-shirt. He was wearing a thick gold chain and was chewing gum.

'The boss wants you in the car, like now,' he said.

She answered with another long slurp.

He reached and tugged at one of the rings through her upper lip. 'I don't hear you Vika. Maybe I should just rip this out. Help you talk better.'

She slapped his hand away, stood up and leaned across the table, bringing her face right next to his. 'Do us all a favour Yuri and get yourself a stud. A fucking big stud. And stick it in your arse. That way *you* won't be able to talk at all. Because, you know what? You're full of shit.'

She grabbed her laptop and bag and pushed past him.

She pulled open the rear door of a black pick-up truck that was parked in the shadow of a dark temple wall. 'My brother. I want to speak to him Dmitry. That was the deal, now we're done here, now you have what you want.'

'Get in,' was all Dmitry said at first, flicking back his hair with his right hand, talking to the back of the seat in front of him.

Vika hesitated.

'My brother. Now. I need to know he's OK,' she said.

'Everything's good,' Dmitry replied. 'Let's get away from here first, then we'll make the call.'

He was still looking straight ahead, the contours of his angular face highlighted for a moment by the headlights of a passing car. His thick brown hair hung limply over his forehead, partly hiding his small sunken eyes.

She climbed into the back beside him, Yuri driving. He pulled the truck onto the road that led out of Bagan.

Dmitry flicked his hair again and then rested his hand on a Buddha head that lay on the seat between them.

They drove for five minutes and then turned onto a bumpy track, the truck weaving to avoid potholes and stray dogs that refused to move.

'Where the fuck are we going?' Vika said.

'Shortcut,' said Yuri.

A few minutes later they reached a small clearing where the remains of three small temples – little more than piles of stones – and two white, bell-shaped stupas, were illuminated by an almost full moon. A steep wooded bank led down to the Irrawaddy River.

The truck stopped and Dmitry said, 'You like the rain, do you Vika? Big nasty storms, a walk on the wild side?' His words, cold and slow.

Vika said nothing, suddenly very alert, a tightness in her stomach, glancing at Yuri sitting motionless in the front, cutting the engine. Then back at Dmitry, a white envelope in his hand, the envelope she'd left for the professor.

He pulled out the card, looking at the front, tracing the outlines of the snarling dog with his finger. 'Nice temple,' he said, opening the card. 'Horrible spindly handwriting. Never liked it. Always was hard to read.' He flicked back his hair. 'Pity the professor never got a chance to look at it.'

He tore the card into small pieces and threw it from the window.

Still not looking directly at her.

For a few moments they sat in silence. Her heart was pounding, and she felt the sweat dripping down her cheek. She lunged for the door handle, but it wouldn't open.

'Central locking. Even in Burma. There's progress for you,' Dmitry said, caressing the Buddha head as he spoke.

Her door was opened from the outside, Yuri standing beside it, a gun in his hand, pointing at her head. 'Get out,' he said.

The noise of cicadas seemed to grow as they walked, Vika in front, Yuri a few steps behind, gun trained on her back. The cicadas echoed and were amplified by the temple walls, the noise broken only by the barks and yelps from scrapping dogs, launching their nightly skirmishes and battles amid the temple ruins. Mosquitoes buzzed around Vika's ears, and she slapped at her neck, where they were beginning to feast.

Yuri told her to stop. 'Give me the computer.'

Vika slowly turned, clinging to the laptop case, clutching it to her chest as if it was her frightened child.

Yuri stepped forward as if to grab it, but then stopped, both of them looking down the path, towards the sounds that were getting louder and closer. A rumbling mix of jangling bells, creaks and strains. A voice, talking in bursts. Soothing, but firm. Giving instructions. A wooden cart was approaching along the path pulled by two big white bullocks with humps swaying rhythmically from side to side. The driver of the cart was buried beneath a big straw hat. Yuri lowered his arm, concealing his pistol behind his back as the cart got closer. He was in no hurry. He had the gun. Vika wasn't going anywhere.

As the cart drew alongside, Vika saw her chance, swinging her right leg with all the force she could muster, her shin crashing into Yuri's ribs. He doubled-up in pain. She swivelled, her hands clenched, a leg striking him around knee-height this time, sweeping his legs from beneath him and throwing him into the path of the bullocks.

And then she ran, slipping and stumbling down the steep riverbank, grabbing at trees and bushes for support.

Yuri fell awkwardly on his gun, which fired. The bullet whizzed harmlessly into the bushes, but the sound echoed around the temples like a thunderbolt. The startled bullocks strained violently at their yoke. Their loud, explosive grunts of terror rose to a horrible roar. They pulled in different directions at first, and the cart strained as if it might be ripped apart at any moment. Then it leapt forward violently, and the bullocks bolted, dragging the lurching, bouncing cart behind them along the bumpy path. The old man yelled. With one hand he gripped the side of the cart to avoid being thrown off; with the other he pulled with all his strength at the reins, trying to restrain his panicked animals.

Yuri had rolled away before the bullocks bolted. He stood, rubbing his ribs, as the cart disappeared into the distance.

Dmitry was quickly at his side, a gun in his hand. 'Let's go,' he said. 'We need to find her.'

They followed her down the bank, muddy and slippery but with plenty of trees and bushes to cling to, becoming steeper and rockier until they reached a point where there didn't seem to be a way through. Then, a few metres ahead, they saw a flash of light, as if Vika was trying to find a way through using the torch on her cell phone. The two men moved slowly towards a thick cluster of bushes from which the light had seemed to come. The bush rustled and Yuri fired. Then fired again. Emptying the magazine into the bushes. Thirteen rounds.

But when they reached the bushes there was nothing there but shattered branches.

'Nice job,' said Dmitry, flicking back his hair.

They climbed further down towards the river.

'Hey,' said Yuri, shouting to make himself heard above the rising noise of the rushing water. 'Take a look here.'

He was holding his cell phone a few centimetres from the ground, the phone's torch shining on several spots of crimson red.

'Blood,' he said.

They followed the spots towards the river, where they became more frequent and bigger, until they merged into each other becoming little pools. Right up to the water's edge.

They looked at the river rushing past them, bloated from weeks of heavy rain.

'She won't survive that,' said Yuri. 'She's dead.'

They turned and walked slowly back up the bank.

Chapter Two

Cerberus

Berlin, Germany

'What the *fuck* is that supposed to be?'

'It's a visualisation of the online world. Data as art.'

'Meaning what exactly, Anna?'

'Meaning whatever you want it to mean, Chuck. Come on, it's art and it's cool.'

'Oh yeah?'

Throbbing circles swam around the screen. Multicoloured lines hopped and wriggled. Others shot like rockets from side to side. Fat graph-like columns jumped up and down like deranged yo-yos.

'How is that *not* cool, Chuck?' She bent forward to read the label. 'It's a visualisation of live data from airline traffic and Facebook updates, combined and then superimposed on a spatial mapping of online news events. That is so, like, *unbelievable*.'

But Chuck Drayton was no longer listening. His attention was elsewhere: on his cell phone; on the server crossing the old factory building with a tray of drinks; on another carrying canapés. On the sad geeky crowd, mostly men, rubbing their stubbled chins and nodding profoundly beneath whitewashed brick walls hung with enormous video screens.

By the time he looked for her again, Anna Schulz was waving to him from the other side of the gallery.

'Will you just look at this one, Chuck?'

Bursts of purple static flashed across the screen, fluorescent dollops roamed and jostled like cells under a microscope. Then they burst like an erupting volcano.

'It's data from North Sea weather beacons superimposed on the ebb and flow of text messages from cell phones all across Berlin. Can you believe it? It's like *unreal*,' Anna said.

'That must have been one hell of a message,' said Drayton.

'This is *so* amazing. It's a Michel Bandini.'

Anna spoke as if she was describing an old master. A Goya or a Constable. Imploring some sort of recognition from Drayton.

There was none. 'It looks just like the other one.'

'Oh, come on Drayton. What is there not to like about this?'

'I preferred the popcorn.'

'The popcorn is just a bit of fun.'

'I like fun. Art should be fun.'

They walked towards the entrance where a glassed-off room had been furnished like an old East German apartment, with the addition of a large popcorn machine sitting in the middle. The machine was popping corn kernels relentlessly, the rat-a-tat sound relayed via speakers to the main gallery. A powerful ceiling fan spread the popcorn, which had already buried part of a fading sofa and a boxy television. It would keep going until the entire room was full.

Anna put her face close to the glass. 'I don't even know what it's supposed to represent.'

'Does it matter?'

'Well, since it's my gallery it would be useful to know. The art critic of the *Berliner Morganpost* said it showed the old East Germany subsumed by the consumer society. *Die Welt* said it showed how ordinary lives were being overwhelmed by data.'

Drayton placed his nose right up against the glass, sniffing, but was disappointed to find the glass did a good job of containing the smell. 'Popcorn as data. I like that angle. I could live with that. What does the artist say?'

'Whatever.'

'Whatever?'

'Yes, just that. Whenever he's asked, the artist just says, "whatever". Like it means whatever you want it to mean.'

The gallery was beginning to fill.

'Will you please at least *look* like you're enjoying yourself, Chuck. *Please*. It means a lot to me,' Anna said, waving at people she'd recognised and then crossing to the entrance, playing the host, each greeting an elaborate ritual of kisses, hugs and hand-holding.

Drayton snatched a glass of red wine from a passing server. Another screen showed a moving line, rhythmically jumping and then falling. The background pulsated with light, like storm clouds at night, the intensity matching the movement of the line. The label below said 'Palpitations. The rhythm of life'. It was another Michael Bandini.

More data as art, except to Drayton this one had a chilling familiarity. He froze, staring at the line. He felt his own heartbeat rising and then outpacing the beats on the screen. He felt the beads of sweat on his face and neck, a tingling in his hands. He turned and moved quickly towards the exit, pushing through the growing crowd, hardly registering the angry grunts as he left a trail of spilled wine and scattered canapés.

He was breathing heavily, sucking in the cool air, as he steadied himself against a wall in the cluttered factory yard outside. The yard was littered with rusting machinery, most of it overgrown. A series of rail tracks buried by weeds. Squat red-brick buildings surrounded the yard on three sides, almost all their windows smashed, walls crumbling. Tall chimneys looked like they might topple at any moment.

It was a large, sprawling complex, and he struggled to find his bearings, following a cracked path that might once have been a railway track. It led to a side exit to the street, partially blocked by a broken wall on one side and a collapsed overhead arch. Only one section of the factory had been refurbished and turned into offices – or 'spaces,' as Anna called them, and that was where she had her gallery.

He stepped gingerly around puddles and broken glass and into a large hall, dark and damp, shafts of light cutting though the gloom from smashed windows high on one wall. He used the torch on his cell phone to guide him around discarded beer bottles, cigarette butts and a pair of syringes.

In the centre of the hall were several stained mattresses and an old disintegrating sofa. He sat on the sofa, which sank under his weight. A steady beat broke the silence, the dripping of water in a distant corner of the room. All he could think about was the line from the screen, and in his mind it was long, flat and lifeless, below it the faces of the dead, rigid arms raised, and all of them pointing at him, accusing him. Then in the gloom he imagined he saw the face of the snarling dog, the dark three-headed dog, ridiculing and taunting him.

He wasn't sure how long he sat there, but was startled by her hand on his shoulder.

'Hey, you OK?' said Anna, sitting down beside him. 'I thought I'd lost you.'

'Not that easily,' he replied, making a joke of it as he always did. 'I needed some fresh air.'

'Fresh air. In here?'

'What was this place, anyway?' he asked, as they walked back across the yard.

'The building on the far side was a railway repair place. Over here was a brewery. We think it might have made soap at some point as well. There are derelict factories like this all over the old East Berlin.'

'There you go. Soap, beer and trains. The basics of life in the East.'

'It will be amazing when it's all done. I've seen the re-building plans.'

'*If* it's done.'

'You really don't like him, do you Chuck? Is that what this is all about? Why you've got such a downer on the exhibition too, because Efren Bell's the sponsor? He's planning to sink millions of Euros into this place. He's a visionary.'

'He's a fraud. A self-promoting charlatan.'

'Oh, for fuck's sake.'

She turned and started to walk briskly back to the gallery.

'Look, I'm sorry Anna,' Drayton said, catching her and then reaching for her arm, pulling her gently towards him before she could re-enter the building. 'I've got a lot going on right now. Efren Bell's a genius, a pioneer, the future of tech. There. Does that help?'

He went to kiss her. She turned her head away, but then turned back and returned his kiss, holding him tight.

'But he's still a charlatan.'

She ran her hand through his thick hair, studying his face. 'You sure you're OK?'

'Sure. Yeah. Just a little tired. Let's get to lunch.'

They left the factory hand-in-hand, Anna insisting they walk, and laying down conditions for the meal. 'This is a computer-free lunch. Right? I know what you're like when you get together with Milo and Holger. Beer and computers. The beer I can put up with. But not the computer and hacking talk. It's boring. *Boooor-ring*. You get onto that, I'm going home. Deal?'

'It's Holger's birthday.'

'I don't care. So a computer-free birthday. Deal?'

'Deal.'

'How old is he, anyway?'

'Forty.'

'He looks older. Weird couple, your friends.'

'How do you mean, weird?'

'Well. There's big happy harrumphing Holger with that sing-song Danish accent, and Milo the mouse who seems incapable of communicating with anything that doesn't have a screen. How weird is that?'

'Milo's nerdy, that's true. And Holger's Norwegian. He told me he can order beer in fourteen different languages.'

'I don't doubt that.'

They walked along a shaded path beside a canal through the Tiergarten. It was a warm autumn afternoon and the path was busy – cyclists, joggers and walkers weaving and jostling. Others lounged in the sun beside the water. There was a carpet of leaves in reds, yellows and browns on and around the path. A cyclist hurtled past them and through a puddle, splashing mud onto Anna's dungarees.

'Shit,' she said, moving to one side of the path and swiping at the mud, which merely smeared it further. Drayton handed her a tissue. Her dungarees were light denim with designer rips across the knees, the trouser legs stopping just above bare ankles. She was wearing blue trainers and a striped T-shirt;

scruffy, but in that casual, edgy way he thought Berliners did so well. He thought it suited her. The new hairstyle too. Short, blonde and spiky, ideal to prop up her big round sunglasses while she worked at the mud.

They walked in silence for a while, past an old pumping station and under a bridge daubed with graffiti. A group of children ran yelling and pushing into the narrow space below the bridge. A dog walker, chaperoning half a dozen dogs of all shapes and sizes, struggled to control his yelping pack as the kids hurtled past.

It took them an hour to reach the beer garden beside the canal, a sea of bikes out the front. The place was busy, but Anna quickly spotted Milo Müller and Holger Norgaard in a far corner of the garden, a pair of large cloudy wheat beers on a table in front of them. Norgaard greeted her with a big hug; Milo with a handshake. Fist bumps from both men for Drayton, who then handed Norgaard a Checkpoint Charlie beer stein he'd bought that morning.

'Sorry, no time to wrap it. Happy birthday.'

Before Norgaard could answer, a server arrived with a plate piled high with sausages, a pork knuckle, sauerkraut and fried potatoes; 'Sorry guys. We were hungry so went ahead and ordered.'

Drayton eyed warily the mountain on the plate. 'What you gonna do with that Holger, eat it or climb it?'

'It's my birthday treat.'

Norgaard laughed. He braced himself, theatrically holding a knife high in one hand, fork in the other. Contemplating whether to tackle it from the north face or the south. Anna was right. He did look older. He was overweight, a tight blue shirt straining to contain his beer belly. His hair was grey and thinning. But Drayton also knew that behind that sloppy and gregarious exterior was a mind as sharp as a razor. He'd never met anybody who could find their way around a computer quite like Norgaard.

Milo was much younger. In his early twenties, Drayton guessed. Another computer genius in his own way. Though a genius of the darker arts. He was tall and wiry, with a mop of unkempt black hair. He was wearing a plain crumpled white T-shirt and jeans, and had the pale and emaciated look of a gaming addict at the end of his third full day in front of his console. He picked at a sausage with one hand, working his phone with the other.

'Hey Anna, I can't wait to see the exhibition,' he said, his eyes never leaving his screen. 'How was the opening?'

'Reception was good. Big crowd.'

'I can't wait to see the popcorn. Sounds so cool.'

'Oh, wow. Thanks Milo,' she replied, talking to the top of his head.

Drayton had texted ahead. "No computer talk. No hacking talk. Please!' And that's mostly the way it went, at least at first, as the server ping-ponged back and forth between the bar and their table, carrying rounds of sausages and beer. From time to time a light breeze blanketed them with smoke from the sizzling barbecue, Norgaard making a big show of sniffing the sausagey aromas, as if he was sampling an expensive perfume or rare wine.

'I could sit here all day,' he said.

'You have sat here all day,' said Drayton.

Norgaard talked about the price of beer in Norway, 'Man, I'd be bankrupt now if this was Oslo.' Milo about his local bar, built on a rooftop in the gritty Neukölln neighbourhood he called home, 'They're like planning to accept Bitcoin. Can you believe that?' Anna on the plans for the factory, 'It'll be the biggest start-up hub in Berlin. That's so *wow*.' Drayton trying to sound supportive, 'And Anna's got some pretty incredible start-up ideas of her own.'

Then, as the sinking afternoon sun crept across tables clogged with empty plates and beer glasses, Milo looked up from his phone and broke the uneasy truce. 'They hacked a rhino's GPS. Can you believe that?'

'Who did?' said Norgaard.

'Chinese poachers. There's a story, like, here online. The GPS tracker was attached to the rhino in this African wildlife reserve by conservationists so they could, like, keep track. But the poachers hacked it and ...' He raised his hand to make it look like a gun, two fingers pointing ahead, the thumb raised. 'Bang. No more rhino. No more horn.'

'Did you read the story about the connected toaster that got hacked and burned a house down?' said Norgaard. 'It happened in California. Was called Bud.'

'A toaster called Bud?' said Milo.

'Yeah. Bud wriggled when it thought it was time for breakfast. But ideal weapon for arson. Like I've always said, connected home equals hacked home.'

They all laughed, except for Anna. Drayton could see her glazing over. Looking away. Plotting her escape.

'You know there's a site on the dark web, called "The Grim Reaper",' Milo said. 'For a fee they'll destroy anybody you want. Online, I mean. You know, hack all their stuff and put out real shit about them.'

'Identity theft and character assassination for hire,' said Norgaard.

'Real assassinations too.'

Drayton could see Anna fidgeting, her face darkening, looking as if she might just log in, find this grim reaper, and have all three of them taken out. He made a stumbling attempt to change the subject. But it was too late. Norgaard had started a game of spot the hacker.

'Here, right now, in this beer garden, there's maybe eight, nine people on laptops. All using the beer garden Wi-Fi. *Unsecured* Wi-Fi, like all public Wi-Fi. Any of them could be sniffing, harvesting the passwords and logins of all the others. Doesn't take much skill for that. My money's on the guy with the beard and the baseball cap on the far side there. Gotta be a hacker.'

Milo wasn't convinced. 'He's too old and in a group. They don't operate in groups. More likely the woman on the table next to him. The one in the yellow T-shirt. What do you reckon, Chuck? You're the expert.'

Drayton didn't reply, since Anna was standing up and slinging a small backpack over one shoulder. 'Well guys, I could stay all afternoon, but I have things to do. Happy birthday Holger.' She high-fived Milo and Norgaard, air-kissed Drayton, and then left the beer garden.

'Sorry,' Norgaard said, 'Got a bit carried away.' He waved to attract the attention of the server and ordered more beer and another plate of sausages. 'Is she still pissed about the breakfast thing?'

'No. We're over the breakfast thing. She just gets a bit bored with all the hacking talk.'

'What's the breakfast thing?' asked Milo.

Norgaard took up the story, enjoying Drayton's embarrassment.

'Anna's been trying to reform our dear friend Chuck. No easy task.' He leaned across the table, placing a sympathetic hand on Drayton's shoulder. 'Their day used to start with a single slice of organic banana bread and a glass of fresh orange juice. Isn't that right?'

'Organic, gluten-free and sugar-free banana bread,' Drayton corrected him.

'Until one day Drayton here leaves a book in the café. So Anna chases him, catches him as he enters McDonalds, that house of sin. "What are you doing?" she yells as Drayton's about to place an order. "Just grabbing a coffee," he says. And you know what the guy behind the counter says? "Hi there Mr Drayton. The usual?" Then he fetches a double sausage and egg McMuffin, hash browns and a large coke.'

They all laughed. Even Drayton. 'I needed some nutrition,' he said.

Norgaard raised his glass. 'Let's face it, you're a lost cause, my friend. The sooner Anna figures that out, the better. *Prost.*'

'Well, yeah. Maybe she already has. Cheers,' Drayton replied, making it sound like a joke.

Then Drayton's phone rang. The smile drained from his face which became serious and alert. He listened in silence for a few moments and then said, 'Now? Are we sure? The entire network? Crippled? The same image? They're with me, Milo and Norgaard … We're on our way.'

He placed his phone back down beside his beer. 'Herr Schoenberg. He needs to see us now. The U-Bahn's being hacked. The entire metro system's down.'

'Is it them?' Milo asked.

'It looks that way. The same calling card. The same image of the dog – the same snarling three-headed dog.'

* * * * *

The image had become the hacker's signature. The dark, pointed face and narrow eyes. The raised ears, the jagged teeth and a snarl that seemed to say, 'I'm coming for you'. It was black on a white background, one of the heads looking straight ahead, the other two in ghastly profile. Drayton called it Cerberus, after the grotesque three-headed dog from Greek mythology. The guardian of the gates to the underworld.

The ransom note beside the image was written in broken English. 'You hacked. ALL data encrypted,' alongside a demand for US $100,000 in Bitcoin in exchange for a digital key – a passcode – to unlock the files. There was a number, an anonymous Bitcoin address to which the cryptocurrency should be transferred.

'This is what the U-Bahn ticket agents found when they went to log in this morning. The ransomware froze their payment system and crippled the ticket machines,' said Schoenberg. 'At first they kept the network running, opening the gates so people could ride for free. But they became worried about the safety systems and shut down the whole network this afternoon.'

'Will they pay?' asked Norgaard.

'They say they won't. Though they probably will. They've no back up.'

They were sitting in the spacious living room of Wolfgang Schoenberg's elegant villa close to Lake Tegel in the north-west of Berlin. It was a large building dating from the 1920s, with white-washed brick walls and a sprawling dark red roof, which looked like an outsize winter hat pulled low over the face of a chubby child. It stood beyond tall bushes and a rusting metal gate at the end of a quiet cobbled street. You'd hardly think you were in the city at all if not for the distant rumble of aircrafts taking off from Berlin's main airport to the south and ever so slightly shaking a large chandelier hanging from the ceiling above them. The living room had an austere feel to it, like its owner. It was sparsely furnished, mostly dark and antique, a large and musty Persian rug in the middle of the room. The only concession to modernity was the large video screen on which Schoenberg displayed the ransom note with the image of the three-headed dog.

It had taken an hour for Drayton, Norgaard and Milo to reach the place. They struggled to find a taxi, which after the shutdown of the U-Bahn had become as endangered as Milo's GPS-tagged rhinos. It was a route they knew well, since Schoenberg preferred to hold private meetings at Lake Tegel, no longer trusting the office.

He was in his late sixties, and struck Drayton as more bank manager than cyber sleuth. Even on a Sunday he still had that formal look, though he'd discarded his usual dark suit and tie for a brown checked jacket. He was polished and courteous, carefully weighing his words to the point where it was sometimes hard to know what he was really thinking, though Drayton had learned to recognise the clues. If he massaged his bald head, or pulled at the short tufts of grey hair that remained above each ear, it usually meant he was getting agitated. That your loan was about to be turned down. A thumb and forefinger through his short moustache signalled interest. If he removed his glasses, round with tiny wire rims, then it could go either way.

At that moment, he was polishing his shining crown with big sweeping movements of his hand. Then his fingers moved to the tufts above his ear. 'Let's take stock. What do we really know at this point?'

'It's spreading, and it's spreading fast,' said Drayton. 'That's all we can really say for sure. The targets are big, the ones that are supposed to be the most secure. It's as if they're showing off, telling us that's nothing's immune. And everybody's being hit, none of the major cyber powers are being spared.'

26

'More than twenty countries so far,' Norgaard said. 'The biggest attacks have been in the US, Russia, China and Britain. The latest attacks that we know about are on water companies and healthcare in Britain. Four cities without water, fourteen hospitals crippled. In the States, it's hit banks and air traffic control, ATMs are out of action, and it's the biggest shutdown of air space since 9/11. And the entire city of Boston, all its servers are frozen. In Russia, the St Petersburg power grid's down and two nuclear power stations are offline. The Moscow transport management system too, lights all messed up and digital signs spouting nonsense. Satellites targeted, though that's an unofficial source. In China it's oilfields and transport, the bullet train network paralysed.'

'This is just the beginning,' said Schoenberg, as thoughtfully, slowly, he walked to a small drinks cabinet from which he collected a bottle of wine and four glasses. 'Red? It's a Württemberg. Fruity, but light, if you're good with that.'

They were good with that.

He poured four large ones, draining the bottle. Then Drayton said, 'At a technical level, we're dealing with two things here, the ransomware itself and the weapon that gets it into computer systems.'

'The ransomware is a pretty basic, off-the-shelf piece of kit,' Norgaard added. 'No surprises. Hunts down the files, encrypts them, freezes the system. Locks you out. And the price of the key for unscrambling your system is always the same. One hundred thousand dollars, whatever the target. The real mystery still is how it's getting in and how it's spreading. We know ransomware usually comes in attachments or links in phishing emails or else it's on websites you visit. Click and you're done for. But not this one.'

'Here's the thing,' Drayton said. 'This bug's smart. Really smart. Most malware targets a specific operating system or type of software. This one can break into them all and at the same time seems tailored for each target. And it can hide, change its appearance, cover its tracks. It can adapt to its environment. That's why it's so difficult to map its behaviour.'

Schoenberg pulled at the hair above his right ear, as if he was trying to pluck the final tufts. 'And the sewer, anything in the sewer?'

'The chat rooms, the hacker forums, they're all buzzing,' Milo said. 'It's a big deal on the dark web. Lots of excitement. Lots of chatter. Boasting. Bullshit. The usual. But I'm not seeing patterns or clues.'

Schoenberg fetched another bottle of wine. The light was fading fast, and he turned on a pair of small table lamps, which cast an arc of light on the paintings immediately above them. One was a twisting river, a castle above it; another a striking portrait of an older woman, her grey hair meticulously pinned up. She was sitting stiffly to attention and staring into the middle distance, with a look that was difficult to read. Schoenberg's mother? Grandmother perhaps? There was certainly a likeness in those enigmatic features. A third was of Albert Einstein. Schoenberg said the Nobel Prize winning physicist had lived in the house in the 1920s, when it was owned by the Prussian Academy of Scientists. It was a particularly dour portrait, and Drayton felt the great man's silent reproach for their lack of progress.

He noticed a photograph beside one of the lamps. It showed two young children, perhaps eight or nine years old, sitting side by side next to a lake. The boy was dark haired and sombre looking; the girl, his sister perhaps, was blonde, with blue eyes and a precocious smile.

Schoenberg walked to the window and for a few moments stood and watched the rustling trees beyond. Then he walked slowly back to the table. 'That's not encouraging,' he said. 'And right now we have no way of stopping it.'

* * * * *

Anna was working on her laptop when Drayton arrived back at their apartment shortly before midnight. She was sitting at a table beside an open window, below which a passing tram screeched and rattled, the sounds mixed with laughter and shouting from the bars and cafés lining the street. The late night Prenzlauer Berg chorus.

'You're late,' she said. 'Must have been quite a party.'

'Work. Something came up.' He stood behind her and then leaned down and kissed the back of her neck.

She was typing manically, switching between several documents she had on the go and a messaging app. 'It's *so* exciting. It's happening. He's coming to Berlin.'

'Who's coming?'

'Efren Bell. He wants to launch the project. At the factory. It's big. Big. Big. And there's so much to organise.'

'I'm sure there is …' He was going to say more. Starting with the challenge of finding a space big enough to accommodate Bell's ego. But he stopped himself. He was too tired and had drunk too much to argue. Instead he pushed the straps of her dungarees off her shoulders, which he began to massage. She turned slightly, pushing him away and replacing the straps. He sat on a large fading leather sofa and turned on a television. The midnight news leading on the U-Bahn hack, a caption across the bottom of the screen described it as 'Berlin's biggest ever cyber-attack.' There were images of empty stations, and then the ransom note with the snarling three-headed dog.

Anna joined him on the sofa, looking at the screen, at the dog, and then at Drayton. She watched him, watched his eyes fixed on that snarling image. She hesitated, but all she said was, 'So that's why you're late.'

She pulled him towards her, cupping his cheeks and then tapping gently on his forehead. 'So when you gonna let me in, Chuck? When you gonna let me in?'

'When you gonna let *me* in,' he said, toying with the straps of her dungarees. This time when he pushed them back she didn't stop him, nor when he undid the side buttons and slipped his hand inside. They kissed and she climbed on top of him, pinning him to the back of the sofa. 'Sometimes you can be such as arsehole, Drayton.' He mumbled an apology as he worked on removing the dungarees, which had always struck him as poorly designed for moments of spontaneous passion.

When they were finished, they both slept, holding each other tight on the sofa.

* * * * *

It was early the following morning that she said to him, 'By the way, your wife called.'

'My ex-wife.'

'She still calls herself your wife.'

'Debbie called here, to the apartment?'

'Yes, she said you don't reply to emails and won't answer your cell phone when she calls. She says you owe her money, something about repairs to the house.'

'Great. And who did you say you are?'

'Your girlfriend. I wasn't going to lie. She asked me if I was living with you.'

'And you said?'

'That I am.'

'Terrific. And what did she say to that?'

'She said, "poor you". She said she enjoyed Berlin when you were here together. When you were a diplomat. Nice town. Before you started screwing the wife of a German minister.'

'She told you that?'

'Why not? Is it true?'

'Like I told you, my last marriage was complicated. Messy.'

'Like screwing a minister's wife complicated?'

'Debbie's got a vivid imagination.'

'Well, whatever. I've got to go.' She kissed him, the inkling of a smile on her face. Then she put her hand on his head and ruffled his thick hair. To Drayton they seemed like gestures of pity rather than anger. 'I have a *tonne* of stuff to do.'

She left the apartment, blowing him a kiss from the door, smiling. He watched her from the window, opening it slightly, wanting to shout after her, but not quite sure what to say. He sat for a while, watching, listening. A clanging tram, the rumble of a delivery truck on the cobbled streets, a brush cleaning the sidewalk as the café below prepared to open, a local anarchist launching his morning anti-capitalist sermon from a window of a graffiti-covered squat across the street.

He'd found Anna's smile infectious from the moment they'd met. That was shortly after he moved back to Berlin. He laughed when she called herself an artist, because so did half of Berlin. She cringed when he told her he worked in computers. That he was a cybercrime investigator. When she told him he was 'fascinating,' he wasn't sure whether to be flattered or concerned. 'You're a mess, but there may still be hope,' she said, only half joking, studying him like one of her paintings.

She was ten years younger than him, bubbly and enthusiastic. 'You've got potential,' she'd laughed, but that

31

potential was hard to spot in the forty-four year old face that now stared back at him from the bathroom mirror, pale and hungover, streaks of grey accelerating through his thick black hair. His dog-eared toothbrush lay on a shelf beneath the mirror, its brush splayed as if it had been crushed under foot. Anna's pristine electric toothbrush looked down from its charging cradle nearby in silent disapproval.

The living room was hung with large splodgy paintings. Anna's modern art replacing what she'd called the dreary old photographs that had come with the apartment. Drayton let her have her way, though he liked the photographs because he liked the history. It was why he'd chosen to live in Prenzlauer Berg. Last time, as a US diplomat he'd had to live where he was told; charmless modern places bristling with the latest security. Now he could choose for himself. The Prenzlauer Berg tenements had largely survived the war. It had been part of old East Berlin, home to dissidents and artists, writers and intellectuals, and their legions of watchers from the secret police, the Stasi. He often sat by his open window, beer in hand, imagining what it would have been like to live in that Orwellian world amid the run-down tenements. When the wall came down the developers moved in. It was now one of most hip places in the city to live.

His cell phone rang. The *Mission Impossible* ringtone, the one he'd set for his ex-wife. It must be the middle of the night over there. He ignored the call, and then for a while sat on the old sofa, thinking about Debbie's conversation with Anna. Anna had a right to be angry. He had screwed the wife of a German government minister. It had been four years ago while he was stationed at the US Embassy in Berlin. As a result, he'd lost his job and been sent back to Washington DC in disgrace.

It had ended their marriage. He hadn't been frank with Anna, but he felt he had a good reason for that.

The woman's name was Maria Schoenberg. She was the bored wife of the Energy Minister, who was twenty-nine years older than her. The minster's name was Wolfgang. And Wolfgang Schoenberg was now Drayton's boss.

* * * * *

The offer of the Berlin job had come as a surprise to Drayton, though the bigger shock was that the phone call came from Schoenberg himself. It was three months earlier, and Drayton was angry and surprised that he'd been found. The call came through on an old landline he never knew existed, buried behind a dusty bookshelf in the corner of the remote cottage he was renting, and where he had tried to take himself offline. No internet, no cell phone. He needed time alone, time to think.

'I need you,' Schoenberg said.

Drayton demanded to know how Schoenberg had found him, told him to get the fuck off the line and leave him alone, but the German cut him short. 'It's hard to go off the grid these days, but then I guess you know that better than most.'

When Drayton didn't respond he said, 'The attacks, they're like nothing we've seen before. I need answers – and so do you.'

Drayton slammed down the phone and pulled the lead from the wall, but he knew Schoenberg was right. And three days later he was on a flight to Germany, the Atlantic Ocean 36,000 cloudless feet below, a third glass of champagne in his hand, laptop open in front of him. He'd spent weeks without looking at a computer, trying to escape that world, but the images from the hospital haunted him, and deep down he'd known all along that it would be impossible to stay away.

Schoenberg sent his car to the airport, a big black chauffeur-driven Mercedes, which waited while Drayton checked into his hotel and then drove him to the Lake Tegel house. All the German had told him was that he was to head a small team of cyber investigators with a simple mission: to find Cerberus and put it out of business. As the car cut through the late morning Berlin traffic, Drayton looked at his phone, at the notes and news clippings he'd gathered on Schoenberg. It didn't take long to read; he was embarrassed by how little he really knew about his new employer. An online search had turned up a barebones résumé. A string of top German government jobs. The energy ministry sandwiched between technology and security roles. Drayton had called in a favour from a State Department staffer, now on the Europe desk, who added more, but not much, in an email that read like a stream of consciousness.

'Hey Chuck. Couple of conversations. Gossip mostly. Seems he was once some sort of liaison for the intel folk. Technology. Cyber. That kinda stuff. Smart, lot of respect. Hard to fathom though. Smooth. Pretty weird ideas on cyber arms control. Like he believes in that stuff. Been pushing it at the EU, UN and a bunch of other acronyms I won't bore you with. Big no-no here. We're busy tearing up treaties, not signing new ones. America first. Fucking madhouse. You got out at the right time. Cheers.'

The only personal information Drayton had gathered was four years old: pillow talk mostly, with Schoenberg's wife, none of it flattering. Mean. Aloof. Obsessive. Secretive. A cold bastard. They were some of the milder descriptions. She was hardly objective, but it put Drayton on guard.

Schoenberg met him at the door of his house with a firm handshake and a smile that was impossible to read. The first thing the German said was, 'Welcome back to Berlin.' He placed a hand on Drayton's back, guiding him as they walked side by side towards the living room. It was a warm sunny day and the room was humid and stuffy, windows flung open to capture an almost non-existent breeze. Mostly it captured flies and the noise of aircrafts. Schoenberg poured wine. A dry white Riesling. A mousey housekeeper served pork schnitzel and salad.

Drayton was determined to clear the air, to start things off on a good footing. 'About your wife, about Maria, I just want you to know...'

Schoenberg raised a hand. 'She was my third wife and not the best. You probably did me a favour, though I could have done without the publicity.' He paused to sip his wine. Slowly, lingering. Drayton wasn't sure how to respond. It wasn't the reply he'd expected. He let the silence hang, before Schoenberg said, 'And how's your ex-wife? Debbie isn't it? She didn't take it well.'

'Not at all well,' Drayton replied, trying not to show his surprise at the question. Drayton had struggled to find information about the German; Schoenberg appeared to have had little trouble digging into the American's past.

Drayton tried to steer the conversation towards Schoenberg, towards what he'd done after the energy ministry, after Maria. But the German swatted away the questions like the flies hovering over the table. A faint grunt and a shrug to tell Drayton it wasn't something he regarded as interesting or relevant.

'*Prost*,' he said, raising his glass. 'You took down the Black Viper syndicate. More than 200 hackers in seventeen different countries. The biggest cyber bust of all time. Quite an achievement.'

'I was proud of that,' Drayton said, and he meant it. A year-long investigation. Black Viper was the name of malware that could remotely take over a person's computer, even recording the strokes on the keyboard. It picked off online banking passwords, or just about anything that was personal and sensitive and could be used for extortion. Drayton set a trap, a honey trap he called it, and he lured in the viper, tricking and turning it, until it led him back to the hackers.

'Agile defence, isn't that what you call your system?' Schoenberg asked.

'I never called it anything. That was the newspapers. It's not rocket science. More like common sense. There's a big shortage of that in the tech industry. You have to understand the mentality of the hackers, what drives them. It's more about psychology than technology.'

'Yes, an entomology of hackers you called it. I like that. Treating them like insects.'

'It was an attempt to classify them by motivation. Fun, money, anger, patriotism. That sort of thing. And by who they are. Kids, pros, the hired-guns. And the coders who craft the malware, because that's how a lot of them see it, like a craft. There are loners, firms who run it like a business, intelligence agencies. And every combination and variation in between. You've got to understand them before you can hit back. Sometimes really silly things give them away. We located a cyber espionage ring in China because they were working nine to five and took weekends off. They were predictable. Bureaucrats.'

'And the Russians, what are they?'

'The Russians are smarter. Work with criminal syndicates. Keep it deniable. Once you've figured out what you are dealing with, once you've ticked the boxes, that's when you can turn the bug around. Treat it like an agent, a secret agent, and make it work for you.'

'Turn it into a double agent?'

'Yes, if you like. Feed it plausible stuff at first, win the confidence of its controllers, make them think the bug's still working for them, until it leads you back to their computers, provides you with their secrets.'

'Impressive,' said Schoenberg, refilling their wine glasses.

He pulled a photograph from the inside pocket of his suit jacket and placed it on the table. The thing Drayton noticed first was the purple hair, long on one side, shaven on the other, and the piercing blue eyes, showing little sign of emotion. A stud through her nose, the rings through her lip and eyebrow, sparkling under the light from the camera's flash.

'Do you know her?' Schoenberg asked.

'Should I?'

'What does the photograph tell you?'

Drayton picked it up. 'That she's confident. Arrogant, maybe. I'd guess she's good. Plenty of attitude. A rebel. A dangerous combination in a hacker.'

'She was all of those – and more,' Schoenberg said, putting the photograph back in his pocket.

'Who is she?' Drayton asked.

Schoenberg ignored the question.

'And of course you were there at the beginning, weren't you Chuck? The first known attack by Cerberus, at the Mountville Memorial Hospital in Washington DC.'

Drayton froze, a slab of schnitzel hanging in limbo, halfway to his mouth, his mind back in the dingy control room they'd set up at the hospital, from where he'd watched as the bug worked its way into the hospital's computer system, making relentlessly for its target. Single-minded, avoiding his traps, getting ever closer, until he'd shouted, 'Shut it down. Shut the fucking thing down.' But the system would not shut down, the bug had taken control, and by the time Drayton reached the wards, running, yelling, ripping plugs from the walls, fourteen people were dead. And on the crippled computer monitor above them, the jumping lines and flashing lights, the vital signs of life, had been replaced by a single flat line beside the image of the snarling three-headed dog.

'What happened at the hospital Chuck?'

Drayton struggled to regain his composure. The whole thing was supposed to classified. A CIA operation, and the official explanation for the deaths was contaminated drugs, the doctors blamed.

'The bug got through. People died,' was all he said in reply.

'And that's why you went off the radar. You blame yourself. Your defences failed. That's why you hid yourself away?'

'I wasn't hiding,' Drayton replied sharply. 'I needed time.'

'Hard to imagine, isn't it Chuck, that this crime-filled cyberspace was once so full of utopian promise.'

'Cyberspace doesn't exist,' Drayton snapped back. 'It's not some abstract force, some magical kingdom, some fucking Narnia. It's real people at keyboards and screens, doing real things, bad things. You have to understand those people, you have to get inside their heads, go through and tick the boxes, figure out what drives them before you can shut them down.'

'And what drives Cerberus? Which of your many boxes does it tick?'

Drayton thought for a moment, sipping his wine. Then he said, 'Sometimes I think it ticks them all. Sometimes none at all.'

* * * * *

Schoenberg's organisation was called simply the Berlin Group. It was a bland and meaningless name, which was precisely as he liked it. It had been set up under the authority of Interpol, the international police organisation, to coordinate the investigation into what was already being described as a grave threat to the world's computer systems.

That didn't make cooperation any easier. The world's big cyber powers were already riven by mutual suspicion. The German government acted as a sort of honest broker, providing support and an office in Berlin, often known as the city of spies – an irony never lost on Wolfgang Schoenberg. It was his show, and he'd personally chosen Drayton, Milo Müller and Holger Norgaard to be his inner circle, figuring that only a small and tightly focussed team of investigators, working in secrecy, could defeat Cerberus. And that suited Drayton just fine.

They called on outside help when they needed it, tapping into a cast of international police, spies and analysts – which Schoenberg called his outer circle, his itinerants, who came and went as needed. They were drawn from throughout the world, from tiny Estonia, which punched well above its weight in the dark cyber jungle, to the big cyber beasts of US, Russia, China and the UK.

The Berlin Group occupied four rooms on the tenth floor of a new building overlooking the main intersection at the glistening heart of Potsdamer Platz. They were the only occupant of that floor. The building was made of red brick and glass. Lots of glass. The architect had won a city award for ergonomic design, but Norgaard warned that on hot days it was like working in a microwave oven.

The rooms were linked by a meandering corridor. Schoenberg occupied a corner office, though his occupations were brief and cautious. He preferred the privacy of his Lake Tegel home for any conversation of consequence.

In another office, Milo, Norgaard and Drayton had desks and computers, rarely used. Their workspaces of choice were the gloomy corners of trusted bars and cafés. Drayton's favourite was the Control-Delete Bar, around the corner from the office, so-called because the owner repaired computers when he wasn't serving beer. His name was Fritz, which was also the name of his dog, an elderly and flatulent Dachshund. With its short, stubby legs and long body, it bore more than a passing resemblance to its owner.

Drayton took an instant liking to his two new colleagues, if not to flatulent Fritz. They had a boyish enthusiasm for computers, and an almost mawkish fascination with the dark cyber world. And he liked their attitude, the eagerness with which they went after hackers.

Norgaard had been the youngest head of the Norwegian Cyber Defence Force before his call to Berlin, and he never missed an opportunity to remind them of that. Not in an arrogant way but in a way that said, 'I may be the life and soul of the party, but I know what I'm talking about.'

He knew computers the way a neurologist knows a human brain, down to the smallest misfiring neurons, but he also knew how to explain the digital grey matter in something approaching plain English. That was unusual in the computer world, and Drayton admired him for it.

Milo was one of those geeks who had trouble communicating with anything that didn't have a screen, but he was a master of the sewer that was the dark web, home to criminals, perverts and predators of every possible size and shape. Drayton had him trawling the hacker chat rooms and forums looking for patterns and clues that might help lift the cloak of hacker anonymity and lead them to Cerberus.

In the early days, long beer-fuelled evenings had a habit of lapsing into child-like reminiscing about hackers they'd known and busted. Anna, on the evenings she'd joined them, had quickly grown bored, and Drayton couldn't blame her for that, especially when they began to recycle the same old exploits and Cerberus remained as elusive as ever.

Norgaard boasted of his operations in Oslo, how they'd busted an international cybercrime outfit which called itself the 'Lords of Mayhem'. 'They were selling all kinds of malware. Good stuff. Powerful stuff. We traced their server, but instead of taking it down, we hacked them. Hacked the fucking hackers. Took it over. So all the orders came to us. Not only were we able to bust the hackers, but the big customers too.'

Drayton told them about China, where he'd been assigned after Berlin, how they'd cracked the computers of a cyber spy ring by infecting the online menu of the takeaway place they used. 'When they clicked on the dumplings to place an order they got a whole lot more than soggy flour and chewy meat.'

'The dumplings, the fucking dumplings, that is just so neat,' said Milo, hanging on every word of the other two men, both almost twice his age, as if they were battle-hardened veterans recounting epic tales of war.

'It's why I love this job. The buzz when you take down a hacker,' Norgaard said. 'What about you, Drayton. What made you take the job?'

For a few moments Drayton said nothing. 'You're right. We have to keep the hackers from winning,' he said, but he lacked conviction. It's personal. I'm here because of what happened in a grim hospital ward in Washington DC. Because I fucked up and people died. Because I want to sleep at night. Any of those would have been a more honest answer.

The third room was set aside for the itinerants, available to them should they need a place to log in, which mostly they didn't. Most would never dream of going online via a connection that had not been vetted multiple times.

41

The fourth space, the biggest, was a conference room. The room was stark, its decoration minimalist. White walls, a large rectangular table at the centre. A coffee machine in one corner. Three large screens hung at one end of the room. The biggest, in the middle, carried a graphic, an attack map, purporting to show live cyber-attacks, data firing around the globe like missiles. It looked like a scene out of *Star Wars*, and Drayton thought it would make a good addition to Anna's gallery. It was Schoenberg's way of injecting some urgency to the meetings that took place below.

Schoenberg had hung a series of photographs alongside the picture windows – the room's only artwork. An image from the 1920s, when Potsdamer Platz had been Europe's busiest intersection, location of the world's first traffic light. Another of the place in ruins at the end of the war. Then as a desolate wasteland, the Berlin Wall running through the middle of it. A kill-zone between east and west, where East German guards took out anybody trying to cross.

Now it had been reincarnated, restored to its former glory – or so the developers said. Drayton watched as flocks of electric scooters, the latest additions to Berlin's sharing economy, scurried back and forth, doing a pretty good imitation of the East German guards.

The conference room was the busiest of the four rooms, where Schoenberg and his team sat down with the men he called the Cardinals. They came from US, Russia and China and were described officially as 'liaison,' a title as bland and meaningless as their official biographies:

Ric Cullen. American. Aged 41. On secondment from the FBI. Career details: cybercrime analyst. Forensic officer. Previous roles: blank.

Igor Strykov. Russian. Aged 53. On secondment from the Russian Foreign Ministry. Career details: Senior analyst, cross-border crime. Previous roles: blank.

Wang Yang. Chinese. Aged 54. On secondment from the Cyber Space Administration of China. Previous roles: blank.

Drayton was introduced to them at the end of his first week in Berlin, when Norgaard whispered in his ear, 'You're about to see international cooperation in action. Surly, bad-tempered and paranoid.'

A ransom note carrying the image of Cerberus, the snarling three-headed dog, was displayed on one of the big screens.

'Broken English. Interesting,' Cullen said, running a thumb and forefinger through a short goatee beard. He spoke in a sharp, aggressive tone. 'Our analyses suggest the hacker may be a native Russian speaker.'

Strykov laughed. A cynical, wheezy laugh. '*Niet, niet, niet.* Your analysts are wrong Ric. Hackers use crap English to disguise themselves. It's hacking 101. A smokescreen. The worse the English, the more likely the hacker *is* English. Or American.'

Cullen sat back in his chair, which creaked under his large and athletic frame. 'That's very helpful Igor,' he said, his words oozing with scorn, running a hand over his closely cropped hair. 'Perhaps you can share your analyses. Or those you promised last week. What are your thoughts Mr Wang?'

Wang sat stiffly in his seat, focusing on something beyond the window. He spoke rarely, and when he did it was in a dry, stilted monotone, as if he was making a political speech to the Politburo.

'My government is committed to full disclosure and the full sharing of data on the criminal enterprise,' he said. Then stopped without providing either.

They circled each other warily, liking scrapping dogs. Over the weeks it would become a ritual. From time to time one of them would throw a few cyber morsels on the table to try to draw the others out, but always careful not to do or say anything that might reveal their techniques or capabilities.

Schoenberg filled the blanks in their résumés.

'Strykov's GRU, Russian military intelligence,' he told Drayton. 'for years he ran their cyber operations.'

'But the GRU *runs* cybercrime groups. I mean 'Fancy Bear'. Isn't that the GRU?' said Drayton.

'It is, and they hacked US elections. Elections in Germany and France. The World Doping Agency, banks, journalists. The governments of Georgia, Ukraine, Estonia. Fancy Bear's got quite a record. Mostly politically motivated.'

'And now he's here.'

'Yes, intriguing, isn't it?' said Schoenberg. 'Then there's Wang. He was, and possibly still is, deputy head of cyber command of the People's Liberation Army. I'm surprised you didn't come across him while you were in China. Perhaps you should bring him some dumplings.'

Drayton smiled. He was impressed, but not surprised by what Schoenberg told him. Not after the way the German had stripped bare his own past. He assumed he tapped into a network of diplomatic and intelligence contacts built over a lengthy career in and out of the shadows. He knew how to play their game.

'None of them are hands-on computer people,' Schoenberg said.

'Isn't that a problem?' Drayton asked. 'This is a cybercrime investigation.'

'Oh, they understand very well the power and importance of computers – to espionage and warfare. That's what matters to them. They don't press the buttons, don't need to, they run the operations.'

'And Cullen,' Drayton said. 'What do we know about him?'

'His background is in the military, special forces. Though his résumé has been scrubbed pretty clean. Now he's CIA. I'm pretty sure of that.'

Drayton didn't need to ask. He was absolutely sure. He'd recognised Cullen the moment he set eyes on him. In the hospital he'd been using a different name. He rarely did small talk, not now, not back then. He rarely did conversation at all, but he did do patriotism, an aggressive exaggerated patriotism. Drayton remembered that. In the hospital he'd been a brooding presence, slipping in an out of the control room, but always in the background, always watching, just as he was watching now.

* * * * *

They called it a breakthrough, but it just confirmed what they already knew, that Cerberus was like nothing they had ever seen before. They were working at their usual table in the corner of the Control-Delete Bar, beer and a plate of fries alongside their laptops. Milo was sharing the fries with Fritz the dachshund, while keeping a wary eye out for Fritz the bar owner, who took a dim view of customers feeding his overweight dog.

Norgaard had isolated the bug used against the Berlin metro in the same way a medical scientist might isolate a deadly virus, neutralising and then examining it. Drayton watched the Norwegian at the screen of his computer as he disassembled, re-assembled, poked, prodded and generally did everything you could with a piece of malware, concluding that the snarling three-headed dog might never be stopped without rethinking the way computers are built.

'It's got to be the chip, it's got to be the chip,' Norgaard said.

Drayton agreed. There was no other explanation. The malware was getting into computer systems through a flaw in the very fabric of microchips, the microchips used in most of the world's computers. That was why it was able to infect all operating systems and roam across all devices.

It was a startling conclusion, and one they needed to share, so Schoenberg immediately called a meeting of the Cardinals, who lined up as usual on one side of the conference room table, Schoenberg and his team on the other. Cullen doodled in a notebook; Strykov pulled at the sweaty, stained collar of his shirt and ran a cloth along the inside; Wang pulled at his ear, but mostly sat looking blankly out of the window, as Drayton laid out their conclusions.

'But *how's* it getting in?' hissed Igor Strykov, affecting an air of cynical indifference, slumped in his seat, while his fat fingers rotated a coffee mug on the table in front of him. He was a broad bear of a man, with hooded eyes like sagging awnings over dark shop windows, offering little hint of what lay beyond. Norgaard gave him the nickname Muttley, after the snickering, sneaky and slightly menacing dog from *Wacky Races*. He reckoned the Russian's wheezy smoker's laugh was spot on.

'And *where's* the flaw?' barked Cullen, in a rare demonstration of solidarity with Muttley. He was sitting bolt upright in his chair. Always did. Enormous hands on the table, fingers tapping impatiently, his broad, square, military shoulders poised like a boxer's challenge to the others. Norgaard called him Captain America.

Drayton said they didn't know. He said they hadn't found the flaw. 'But it's the only plausible explanation.' They'd arrived at their conclusion by a process of elimination, he said, since the malware didn't appear to be getting into computer systems by any other route. 'It has to be directly attacking the chips.'

'So it's just a hypothesis,' mumbled Wang to nobody in particular, addressing the Politburo again. He pushed a pair of heavy black-rimmed spectacles up his nose and smoothed his hair, which was dyed the regulation black favoured by Chinese apparatchiks. Norgaard had given him the nickname Winnie-the-Pooh, since he bore a striking resemblance to the rotund honey-guzzling cartoon bear.

Though Norgaard never used the nicknames to their faces.

'A dangerous hypothesis,' said Schoenberg.

After their initial burst of questions, the Cardinals said very little. But there was an edge in the room. At first Drayton thought it was because of the morning's news – more deaths blamed on Cerberus. Ransomware had frozen the traffic management system in Boston. Traffic lights stuck on orange; others changed and flashed randomly. There was mayhem. Multiple accidents, and a family of four died in a collision with a truck.

But Drayton sensed another reason for the atmosphere. Could it be that their own agencies had reached much the same devastating conclusion? A flaw in software can be patched. But not a flaw in a chip – a chip used across the world from weapons to the giant servers controlling industrial systems, to phones and connected toasters. Computer chips themselves might have to be redesigned. The disruption would be unimaginable.

* * * * *

The Cardinals found names for the latest attacks on their computer systems. Wang Yang called the ransomware that had crippled several Chinese oil fields Northghost7. The shutdown of the city of Boston was attributed by Ric Cullen to Charlie32. Wheezing Igor Strykov blamed the St Petersburg power grid shutdown on what he called Treptower5. British cyber experts blamed the attack on British water companies on Glienicke12. They all bore the signature of Cerberus, the snarling three-headed dog, but there were subtle variations between each of them.

Then one grey morning, rain lashing against the conference room window, traffic gridlocked below, Cullen announced that the NSA had cracked Charlie32. 'We found a kill switch,' he said, a look of smug satisfaction on his face. Boston was back online. Cyber sleuths from Britain's GCHQ cracked Glienicke12. The water was flowing again. It seemed like the first genuinely good news in weeks.

Then after a few moments hesitation Wang said, 'The oil is flowing again.' His English was slow, sometimes faltering. 'Our experts have also cracked the code.'

'Ours too,' said Strykov. 'The lights are back on in St Petersburg.'

They had all found what they called a kill switch. Essentially the key to unlock the ransomware. Drayton assumed they'd all discovered it hidden in the code, but nobody was volunteering details.

Schoenberg stood and walked to the front of the conference room, hands behind his back, looking less the bank manager this time and more the learned professor addressing a hall of slightly dim students. He removed his glasses. Well done. You've made a good start, top marks for effort, but there's a long way to go, and don't forget this is a *collaborative* course.

Strykov said the St Petersburg investigation was on-going and he'd provide more details of the breakthrough when he could.

Cullen said, 'There's simply not much more we can say right now.'

Wang nodded in agreement. 'Our investigation is at an early stage.'

Then Drayton said, 'Think of it as a jigsaw puzzle. And you've each discovered a piece. We can't tell a lot from an isolated piece, but put them together and there's a broader picture.'

Cullen stood and walked to the coffee machine. Wang blew his nose. Strykov's dirty handkerchief was back at his sweaty neck. Nobody spoke, the silence only interrupted by gurgling and hissing as the coffee machine delivered Cullen's Americano.

'Perhaps you all just paid the ransom, and none of you *found* the kill switch,' Drayton said, not even trying to hide his impatience.

Cullen glared at Drayton. 'Which means *what*, exactly?'

'Which means, why don't you share your great discovery, Ric? Unless there never was one. Maybe you just paid the ransom. A bunch of Bitcoins paid to the three-headed dog.'

Cullen winced. 'With respect, Chuck, I don't think you can expect any of us to provide operational detail. Let's just say we're all maybe getting better at our jobs.' He smiled, but not from good humour. It was a bitter and hostile smile.

Schoenberg coughed and raised a hand. Schoenberg the diplomat. 'There are of course operational considerations to sharing data. I understand that. But I don't need to remind you all about the urgency – and the threat we are up against.' Then he proposed another break.

Cullen grabbed Drayton's arm as they left the room, steering him into one of the nearby offices they never used, pushing the door closed behind them and pinning him hard against the wall, a fist full of Drayton's shirt in his hand.

'Who the *fuck* do you think you are Drayton? Calling me out like that,' he hissed, tightening his grip, Drayton struggling for breath. 'You forgotten about the hospital already? Maybe you should just have kept running, kept hiding, because you know what, you fucked up, you fucked up big time. And people died because of you.'

He released his grip.

'But I'm gonna give you a chance to redeem yourself, to make things good. Because you know what? We're on the same side, Drayton.' Pushing him down into a seat, and leaning close. 'I expect you to tell me what's going on with Schoenberg and with the others. Strykov and Wang, in particular. You're working for me now, you understand?'

And in case Drayton didn't understand, Cullen said, 'I'm giving you a chance to put things right. Or to make them worse. Because I can destroy you, Drayton. Never forget that. It's your choice.'

* * * * *

Outside, the rain had eased, but it was still drizzling. Drayton bought a coffee and sat on a damp bench close to a mock-up of the world's first traffic light, a strange contraption, set on five solid pillars and hand-operated.

'Maybe that's what we need to beat the hackers,' Schoenberg said, taking a seat beside him.

'Maybe,' Drayton replied, his mind elsewhere.

'Ric Cullen doesn't really like you, does he?'

'It's mutual. He, or people like him, are the reason I left government service.'

'But the Mountville Memorial Hospital, that was a government operation. CIA, was it not?'

Drayton didn't immediately answer. He sipped his coffee, watching the old traffic light turn green, no longer surprised by Schoenberg's knowledge of what was supposed to have been a classified operation.

'They were a client. Just another client. I quit working full-time for the government after China.'

'So what did happen, Chuck? What went wrong at the hospital?'

Drayton raised the collar of his coat against the cold, and for a while neither of them said anything.

Then Drayton said, 'There was a Russian, a double agent, he'd defected to us about a year ago, and he was being treated in that hospital. There'd been a tip-off about an assassination attempt. The GRU, Russian military intelligence, wanted to make a point to anybody else thinking of betraying the motherland. They were planning to hack the hospital computer systems, target the syringe infusion pump. Take control, hit him with a killer overdose. Wham. Right into his veins.'

'And you tracked it. Followed the bug. The CIA wanted to learn about it, turn it round.'

'That was the idea. It was powerful and unknown. We followed it, right into the computer system. The plan was to isolate it, sandbox the thing, and all the time let the Russian controllers think they were still in charge. Long enough to do the analysis. But it seemed to anticipate our every move. It learned. Changed its behaviour, hid. I told them we couldn't let it get any further. We had to destroy it, destroy it quickly. I keyed in the code to kill it. But nothing happened. Nothing.'

Drayton warmed his hands around his coffee cup, speaking slowly now, looking into the distance.

'By then it was too late. It was already controlling the pumps. The Russian was the first to die. It was very quick. But it also infected other pumps. Collateral damage, I guess you'd call it.'

'And you blamed yourself?'

'Who else is there to blame. I was the guy at the controls. I'm still not exactly sure what happened. But it should never have got through.'

'And Cullen was there?'

Drayton nodded.

'It was the first time hackers had used the image of the three-headed dog. Does that make Cerberus a Russian weapon?' Schoenberg asked.

'The hit was contracted out. That's the way the Russians work. Keep it deniable, keep it at arm's length. And look at the Cerberus attacks since then. The targets have been everywhere, including in Russia.'

* * * * *

It began to rain more heavily, and they took shelter in a glass-covered atrium off the main Potsdamer Platz intersection. It was large and airy, lined with cafés and designer boutiques. There was a gallery to one side, and around a dozen protesters had gathered outside. They were outnumbered by bored-looking police, who stood in front of the gallery's glass windows and large revolving door.

The protesters were chanting and holding screaming banners and placards. 'STOP GENOCIDE IN MYANMAR BURMA', 'STOP KILLING MUSLIMS IN BURMA', 'SAVE MUSLIM ROHINGYA'.

Other placards showed an image of Myanmar's leader, an elegant woman with a flower in her hair, to which had been added fangs and a splattering of red paint. Words below read, 'Aung San Suu Kyi. Shame on You!' On another placard, the Facebook name and logo had been doctored to read, 'Hatebook'. Red paint oozed out of the Facebook thumb, 'Delete Facebook', and 'Delete the lies and hate', daubed across it.

The gallery's walls were hung with large Buddha images. Buddhas among trees and on hillsides. Another in a field. One dominating a small island in a river. A poster advertised an exhibition, Buddha and the Landscape, opening today, and sponsored by the Myanmar embassy.

Drayton and Schoenberg walked deeper into the atrium.

'You don't do social media, do you Drayton?'

'Used to. Deleted most of my accounts. Don't like what they do with the data. And you?'

'Never,' the German replied. Sharp, emphatic, as if it were obvious, and the question itself was pointless and unnecessary.

They reached the far end of the atrium, which was dominated by a large video screen showing rolling news headlines, a strap below carried the latest currency rates and share prices. The Berlin office of one of Germany's main news agencies lay behind the screen, which was filled with images of a man walking briskly through the arrivals hall of Berlin's Tegel Airport, surrounded by cameras. Bodyguards clearing a path through the pushing and jostling mass. The images were wobbly. The man at the centre of the scrum had slicked back grey hair in a ponytail. He smiled, waved and climbed into the back of a waiting Mercedes. A caption said, 'Efren's hundred billion dollar dream'.

Drayton and Schoenberg stopped at a fussy and over-priced ice cream kiosk with a long Italian name. Drayton ordered a large cone with three scoops. Belgian chocolate, caramel cookie crunch and a raspberry cheesecake gelato.

Schoenberg ordered a small cone with a single scoop of vanilla. 'You trained as a lawyer, didn't you? Picked up the computer skills later?'

'I've never pretended I was a computer geek. I'm an investigator who knows computers. I've never bought the idea that cyberspace is somehow beyond the law, or even needs new laws. We've got plenty, against fraud, extortion, theft. Murder even. The computer's just another way of doing it. It's just a matter of getting the person at the keyboard.'

'Tell me about New York,' Schoenberg said. 'The New York Attorney General's office, 2006 until 2009. Isn't that when you worked there? Before you joined government service.'

'I did. It was my first big break after law school.'

'So you were there through the financial crises?'

Drayton nodded. 'It kept us busy.'

'But still, nobody was jailed.'

'The figure is one. One solitary banker, last time I counted.'

'How do you feel about that?'

'How do you expect me to feel? Nobody was held to account for the biggest man-made economic disaster since the great depression. You don't have to be a card-carrying socialist to think that stinks.'

'You worked on the Efren Bell case?' said Schoenberg, nodding towards the video screen.

Drayton waited as a loud cry went up at the other end of the atrium. Shouting and angry chants. The Myanmar ambassador arriving for the exhibition opening.

'The case was never prosecuted,' he said.

'Not enough evidence?'

'Oh, there was plenty of evidence. He traded on inside information. He knew what was coming. Sold the market short massively and made billions.'

'He says it was all down to algorithms,' Schoenberg said. 'Clever trading algorithms that kept him one step ahead and predicted the fall.'

'That's what he says. The evidence says otherwise.'

'So why was he not prosecuted?'

'That's a question I still ask myself. It was a political decision, and Efren Bell was always generous with contributions to our elected officials. I thought we'd nailed him. I pushed hard to indict him.'

Schoenberg took off his spectacles and wiped the lenses. 'Maybe too hard. They forced you from your job and accused you of leaking details to the *New York Times*. You blew your legal career on account of Efren Bell.'

Drayton didn't immediately reply, sculpting his ice cream with his tongue, stunned again by what Schoenberg had learned about his past. 'There was pressure, yes, but it was my choice to leave.'

'Not good with officialdom, are you Drayton?' the German said. Again there was that faintest of smiles, unreadable as always, and then yet more questions.

'And Bell's Russian partner? Dmitry, wasn't that his name, Dmitry Gerasimov? What happened to him?'

'He fled,' Drayton replied. 'And Efren Bell denied they were ever in business together. To East Europe. The Balkans maybe. There were a lot of rumours, none of them good.'

'It was Macedonia,' Schoenberg said. 'Dmitry set up what he called a financial services company. You didn't hear about that?'

There was another cry from the far end of the atrium as police dragged away a protester who'd thrown something at the gallery window. It came as a welcome distraction for Drayton. Of course he'd heard about Macedonia. But he was beginning to resent the questions, especially as Schoenberg seemed to already know the answers. What was the point? He wanted to push back, to steer the conversation away from his past and demand answers of his own. But the German's manner wasn't that of an inquisitor, more of a gently curious old uncle.

'Like I said, there were rumours,' Drayton replied.

'Macedonia was essentially a boiler room operation, at least in the early days,' Schoenberg said. 'Selling shares that didn't exist to gullible American and European investors. Then Dmitry diversified into fake websites and bogus social media accounts. They looked legitimate, but were full of inflammatory and outrageous stories.'

'A click farm?'

'One of the first.'

It was a simple business model. People love to click and share that sort of material, the weirder the better, and back then advertisements blindly followed the clicks. So it wasn't unusual to see ads for top brands beside stories about the Pope in a Vatican orgy, aliens kidnapping Queen Elizabeth, or Obama eating children as a midday snack. A whole industry grew around it, and it was lucrative.

'Dmitry was one of the first to discover its political power,' Schoenberg said. 'That people actually *believed* a lot of that stuff, or at least wanted to. It generated anger and hate, and not just money. And that realisation attracted a whole new set of clients.'

Lawless Macedonia became a hub for click farms and then the new political influence operations until, under enormous international pressure, the government started to crack down, a new anti-corruption commissioner taking her job seriously.

'The commissioner was shot dead a month into her job,' Schoenberg said. 'Dmitry was accused of ordering the hit.'

'And did he order it?'

'He didn't need to. He pulled the trigger. After she turned down his bribes and ignored his threats, it became very personal. Dmitry cashed out and moved on soon after that. He had little choice. And Macedonia was in any case becoming too crowded. Cybercrime offered a brighter future elsewhere.'

'Where did he go?'

Schoenberg didn't answer directly. 'To friendlier shores. Where his skills were in demand.'

Then the German asked, 'What kind of character was Dmitry?'

'Vengeful, vindictive, though technically very smart. Very determined. That's how he was usually described. Though I never met him in person. Didn't meet Bell either. Though during the investigation I felt almost part of the family.'

'And you'd recognise Dmitry if you saw him again.'

'He's hard to forget.'

He watched Schoenberg, who had turned away from Drayton and was standing with his hands behind his back, looking again at the big screen. He appeared to be deep in thought. The American found him impossible to read.

'And Efren Bell is now the toast of Wall Street,' Schoenberg said, turning back to Drayton. 'He used his windfall from the financial crises to set up his Digital Pagoda Fund, now the biggest single investor in start-ups. If he succeeds in raising his latest tranche of money, another one hundred billion dollars from investors, it will be the largest pool of private cash ever raised.'

Drayton crunched at the last piece of his cornet, an aggressive crunch that launched a dollop of raspberry cheesecake gelato down his trousers.

Schoenberg handed him a paper napkin and said, '*Time* magazine calls him the most influential person in technology today.'

Chuck Drayton's Sundays with Anna had taken on a routine. Mid-morning out of bed. The gluten-free and sugar-free vegan banana bread breakfast at the café beside Eberswalde Strasse U-Bahn station. A short walk to the Mauerpark flea market to join the crowds squeezing between tables straining with old trinkets and tacky souvenirs. Maybe buy one or two. Perhaps a walk up the nearby hill to one of the remaining stretches of wall to watch graffiti artists daubing over last week's splodges. Then to a bar beneath their apartment for lunchtime jazz and enough beer to more than offset any benefit from the banana bread. Back home mid-afternoon and usually back to bed, scattering clothes on the way, to take up where they'd left off mid-morning.

This Sunday Anna had other things on her mind. She was out of bed early, telling Drayton to keep his hands to himself, and when he joined her in the living room late morning she was at her laptop at the table by the window.

'Twenty-four hours to go and so much to do. It's *so* exciting. But the security, the catering, the stage and lights, the screens. Cleaning up the factory yard. It's been a nightmare.'

'Is he bringing the Rolling Stones with him or something?'

'Come on Chuck, you promised. No bitching about Efren Bell. *Please*. This is big.'

Drayton left the apartment. He was determined to stick to the routine. At least the lunchtime bar and jazz part of it. By the time he got back to the apartment, Anna had gone to the factory, but she'd left her laptop open on the table. He messaged her: 'Hey, Anna, you've forgotten your computer. You want me to drop it by later?'

She messaged back: 'Don't worry, I have the files I need. I can survive without it today. Thanks x.'

He pressed one of the keys and a screensaver of changing Alpine photographs was replaced with a busy desktop. No password protection. Not smart. He set up a password, acting almost out of instinct and keeping it simple. *AnnaBerlin.* Thinking she could change it later. She should have basic security.

Then he was distracted by a phone call.

It was Milo Müller.

'I need to see you.'

'I can be at the office in half an hour or so.'

'Not the office,' Milo insisted.

Drayton found Milo and Norgaard at their usual table in the corner of the Control-Delete bar, Fritz the dog sleeping at their feet, Fritz the owner trying to explain to a French couple in the corner that the beer was supposed to be cloudy. 'It's Weissbier. *Weissbier.*'

Milo was excited. He'd spent weeks trawling through the hacker forums of the dark web, posing as a hacker himself. Gaining trust and invitations to closed and more exclusive groups, deeper down, where forums and chats could quickly grow, split and then disappear, re-emerging under different names. Like hydra-headed monsters. Some needed passwords, ever changing. It was a paranoid world, and Drayton had urged him on, urged him to look for patterns and clues. And now he thought he'd found one.

'He goes by the hacker name Neo. The thing is, like, he's in your face. And the anonymising. Usually they multi-anonymise, depending on the forum. But Neo, you know, he's uni-identity.'

He was gabbling, his brain moving faster than his mouth, which tended to happen when Milo got excited. He was spitting out rapid chunks of jargon.

Norgaard translated. 'What he's saying is that this Neo doesn't switch around identities like other hackers. And he's boastful and sloppy.'

Milo said he had an instinct. 'It's the way he brags about the Cerberus hacks, as if he knows more about them. There's a German hacker forum, and he told them there'd be free travel on the Berlin U-Bahn. And this happened before the hack. *Before* the hack. Like he knew it was coming. Like he *knew* it was coming.'

Drayton called Schoenberg at his Lake Tegel home. He said the dark web was all smoke and mirrors, but he trusted Milo's instincts, and Schoenberg said they should brief the Cardinals. A meeting was set for the following morning.

*****

They lined up as usual on the two long sides of the conference room table. Schoenberg, Drayton, Milo and Norgaard on one side, the Cardinals on the other. Schoenberg began with a round-up of the latest Cerberus attacks: A Brazilian dam shutdown, several hospitals crippled in Singapore, which counted as a relatively quiet week. Then Milo began to talk – excited, nervous and struggling with his words as he repeated what he'd told Drayton and Norgaard.

'All hackers brag,' said Strykov dismissively.

'It means nothing,' agreed Wang.

'We'll need more than that Milo,' said Cullen, in that slightly patronising way a teacher might talk to a small child who's come up short with their homework. 'What exactly are you saying anyway, that this Neo somehow *is* Cerberus?'

Milo kept his eyes firmly on the desk in front of him, his right hand spinning his cell phone. 'Well maybe not Cerberus as such... But like... He like... You know... He seems to know a lot.' He was speaking to the table, struggling with the words.

Milo wasn't good at presentations. He wasn't good at anything that wasn't mediated by a screen. He could spend hours in the anonymous world of the dark web. Entrance only via special software. Bouncing between hacker forums and brushing shoulders with the darkest of the dark, but he struggled with real people, and was visibly wilting before the baying Cardinals. He repeated that Neo seemed to know in advance about free travel on the U-Bahn.

Strykov began to tease him over his heavy use of 'like'. 'The U-Bahn's *like* shut down *like*. But, hey, nobody's travelling, free or paid, *like*.'

Norgaard stepped in for Milo. 'That's true, it's shut down, but it didn't straight away. The hack hit the ticketing system and station gates, and for the first few hours they decided to leave the gates open, people travelling for free. It was the afternoon before they got worried about safety and shut the whole thing down. So it does fit with Neo's prediction about free travel.'

'Anything more?' said Cullen, impatiently.

'Neo's joined a couple of forums, talking about Bitcoin and other cryptocurrency stuff,' Milo said, sounding clearer, bolstered by the support from Norgaard, 'Like he might have a chunk to spend.'

'And?' said Strykov.

'And the cryptocurrency chat rooms he's been entering, they are mostly hosted here in Berlin.'

'That means nothing,' Cullen said.

'He seems familiar with places they talk about,' Milo said. 'And the times he comes online, it fits with this time zone. At first it looked as if he was in the Far East. Then he moved here.'

'This is a big time zone Milo. And hackers work weird hours,' Strykov said.

'Is this the best you can do?' Cullen sneered.

Milo's reply was faltering and barely audible. 'Like I said, it's… You know… An instinct.'

'Well, we'll need more than an instinct,' said Wang, standing to leave.

'Next time you call an emergency meeting, Herr Schoenberg, please make it for something worthwhile,' Strykov said, his words punctuated with a wheezy laugh.

Schoenberg ignored the taunts. He began to massage his head and pull at a tuft of hair above his left ear, the signs Drayton had come to recognise as agitation, but keeping it under control as ever. 'That's good work Milo. Thank you. Though it does sound as if you've got a little more digging to do.'

Drayton could barely contain his anger as he watched Milo getting mauled. He wanted to hit back. What had the Cardinals ever brought to the table that was any use? And he probably would have told them that and a lot more if his attention had not been grabbed by his cell phone, increasingly panicky messages from Anna filling the screen. 'I can't get into my laptop,' 'It's not letting me in. All my stuff,' 'Urgent stuff,' 'FUCK!!' 'What should I do?' 'I seem to be locked out.' 'It's asking for a password,' 'I don't have one.' 'FUCK, FUCK!!'

Drayton replied with '*AnnaBerlin*', the password he'd locked it with.

'Really sorry. I meant to tell you.'

She shot back, a series of short angry outbursts. 'What the FUCK Drayton?', 'You fucked up my morning. Today is

SO important', 'Don't you dare touch my fucking computer. EVER!'

He messaged back saying he was only trying to help, that she had to be more aware of security on her computer.

'Drayton, you are paranoid. FUCKING paranoid,' was her response.

* * * * *

'There you go, Milo. Uncle Holger's medicine. You'll feel better after this. It's a craft beer. Eight per cent. They brew it out the back.' They were back in the Control-Delete Bar, trying to calm Milo.

'They gave you a tough time,' Drayton said. 'But you did well.'

'Didn't feel that way,' Milo said.

'You know what?' Norgaard said. 'They all seemed almost *overeager* to ridicule you. It was a performance. For each other. For us. A show to give the impression that Neo is a waste of time, and not worth taking seriously.'

'And you think they did – take him seriously?' Milo asked.

'Very seriously,' Drayton said. 'These are people who've made a career out of deceit. They lie for a living. Doesn't just happen online, Milo. Muttley stopped wheezing, at least for a while. Winnie-the-Pooh was no longer looking out the window. Even Captain America was fully tuned in. When was the last time you saw that?'

Norgaard asked Fritz to turn up the volume on a television that was mounted on the wall close to their table. CNN had cut to a packed senate committee room, senators sitting in a horseshoe in front of a witness table. There were two people at the table, a man in uniform and a woman in a brown business suit. There was a strap across the bottom of the screen with the words, 'THE BOSTON HACKING HEARINGS'.

'I don't know what annoys me more,' Norgaard said. 'The creepy witnesses or the ignorant senators. The senators are all in their sixties and seventies. Makes you wonder if they've ever used a computer in their lives.'

One senator leafed slowly through papers in front of him before theatrically removing his glasses and addressing the witness table. 'So what exactly is a zero day, General?'

'It's a vulnerability that is unknown to those who would want to mitigate it and open to exploitation by a zero day exploit,' said the witness in the uniform.

'Whoa! Whoa! Whoa!' shouted the senator, raising a hand, a look of mock horror on his face, while a bank of cameras clicked manically beneath him. 'Hold up. Hold up. Can we have that in plain English, General?'

'Well it's an unknown vulnerability. At least to the vendor.'

'Please!' yelled the senator. 'Imagine you're explaining to your mom and dad. Right? And mom and dad think surfing the web is something spiders do on wet days. And a hard drive is a tough journey back from work. You get what I'm saying? Now please let's try again.'

The woman in the grey business suit beside the General raised her hand. 'Maybe I can help out here.'

And the senator said, 'Maybe you can. Talk to your parents.'

'It's a computer bug. A flaw in a computer system. But one that the owner of that system doesn't know about, so they've not yet found a way of fixing the flaw.'

'Because they don't know about it?' the senator said.

'That's right. But the hackers do know about it. Maybe they've discovered it, or bought it from somebody else. And the weapon they use to get into the computer system, to exploit that bug is the zero day exploit.'

'Well, I'm still not sure my mom and dad would get that, but we're making progress.' said the senator. 'Why zero day?'

The General said it referred to the time between a bug being discovered and a patch being made for it. The patch being kinda like a repair. And zero days meant just that, zero days. Because the computer owner couldn't develop the patch because he didn't know about the bug.

The senator was scratching his head now.

'So let me make sure I've got this right,' he said. 'I'm running the city of Boston. Somebody has discovered a hole in my computer system that I have no idea about. That's the zero day. He fires a bunch of ransomware through that hole and cripples my computers, locks me out. That's the zero day exploit. Yeah?'

'Well in broad terms.'

'I don't want broad terms. You're the cyber experts. You're the CIA. The NSA. The guardians of our nation's computers. Yes or no.'

'Well yes, basically.'

'This hearing's looking at what happened in Boston, but we could be talking about the power grid, the water supply, transport, air traffic control. Anything run by computers. Correct?'

'That is correct,' said the General.

The senator pressed on. 'So in the arsenal of cyber weapons out there, these zero days, they are the most deadly? Like nukes?'

'I'm not sure that analogy is quite correct,' said the General.

'Why not?' said the senator. 'You're talking of potentially massive destruction. And there's another thing. What happens when *we* discover a zero day. Do we announce it to the computer industry, to the world, play the good guy, so they can fix it and everyone can sleep safely in their beds at night? Or do we keep it to ourselves, squirrel it away, stockpile it, like nukes, just in case we might need it to attack somebody else's systems?'

When there was no immediate answer, the senator said, 'Well? Talk to me. It's a simple, question, and I'd like a simple answer.'

The General leaned and talked to the woman next to him. He drank some water and shuffled some papers in front of him. Another two uniforms approached the table and they all conferred. The camera cut to a wide shot of the committee room. It cut to the senator who'd been doing the questioning and was now rubbing his nose and looking impatient.

Then the General said, 'With respect senator, it's not so simple, and it's not something we are able to discuss in a public forum.'

The Senator threw his hands in the air and then called a recess. CNN cut back to the studio.

Drayton turned away from the television and cut back to his beer. 'You know why they won't discuss it?'

'Sure,' said Norgaard. 'Because the US intelligence agencies, and those in Britain, France, China and Russia are the biggest buyers of zero days on underground markets.'

'And they'll pay millions of dollars for the most destructive. It's big money,' Drayton said. 'The new arms race.'

* * * * *

Drayton called up Anna's number as he left the Control-Delete bar. It went straight to voicemail, and he began to leave a message. 'Honey, I'm sorry about the computer...' But then stopped, deciding it was far better to talk to her in person.

An app on his smartphone located a scooter, and fifteen minutes later he was at the hulking Ostbahnhof, one of old East Berlin's main railway hubs, where he dumped the scooter and walked to the Spree River. Along the river bank, the longest remaining fragment of wall was now an open air gallery plastered with paintings and graffiti, pride of place given to the former Soviet and East German leaders, Brezhnev and Honecker, giving each other a smacking big kiss.

He hardly recognised Anna's factory complex, set back from the river. The place had been tidied up, the junk removed, the yard now full of cars, nice cars. A well-dressed, geeky crowd lined up at a desk, waiting to squeeze into the gallery beyond, from which discordant noises came in waves, first the heavy base beat of dance music and then what sounded like a million manic birds trapped in an aviary. Heavy security with squiggly earpieces roamed around the entrance, eyeing new arrivals with a look of boredom and menace. A young woman ticked names off a list. She was wearing a tight green dress, which looked as if it had been sprayed on, and a permasmile to match.

'I'm a friend of the gallery owner,' Drayton said, when she couldn't find his name.

'You'll still need an invitation,' said the woman, eyeing his shabby black bomber jacket, over dark blue shirt and dark jeans. Looking at him like he'd just swum across the Spree to get there, via a couple of large bushes.

Then, from close to the door, another woman said, 'Chuck! Chuck! What are *you* doing here?'

It was Brigitte, one of Anna's partners, and she agreed to add him to the guest list, a bit too reluctantly for Drayton's liking, and then said, 'Sorry, but Efren Bell takes his security very seriously.'

'I'm sure he does. Where is the great man?' Drayton asked.

'Anna's done a fantastic job, Chuck. You should show her a bit more appreciation.' She paused and then added, 'She's really pissed at you. The computer thing.'

'Yeah. Bit of a misunderstanding,' he replied. 'How's it going?'

'Good. It's going good. Efren Bell's investing twenty million Euros in the factory. *Twenty* million. He's going to refurbish the place and turn it into Berlin's biggest incubator for start-ups. He really believes in this city Chuck. He's going to make it his main base outside America. He's *such* a visionary.'

The gallery was packed. A long T-shaped stage ran down the middle, big posters around the walls. Bell with an OmniX, his futuristic electric car, soon to be fully self-driving. Bell with a mock-up space station, another project. Bell with a bunch of robots. Drayton took a red wine from a server, then another since he figured it might be a while before the server next returned, the place being so busy.

'He's such a cool guy,' said Brigitte.

'His autonomous car hit a cyclist. Killed her. It happened during tests last week in the States,' said Drayton. 'That's not cool.'

'It was a statistical inevitability. That's what Efren told us while we were showing him around. It was the cyclist's fault.'

'Efren told you that too?'

'Yes he did. The cyclist cut in front of the car in a really unpredictable way.'

'Isn't that the point? Humans are unpredictable. They're different from computers. They're impetuous, not always rationale. Driverless cars are programmed to follow the rules. Humans don't always do that. Humans can do weird things, which only other humans can anticipate. Human drivers and autonomous cars will never work well together.'

'Efren said the cars can learn, and it just shows why we need to get rid of human drivers as soon as possible. They're a menace.'

'Well, here's to Efren Bell's brave new world,' said Drayton, raising his wine glass.

'Do you realise he's also developing levitation technology for his cars, so they can skip over traffic jams?' Brigitte said.

'And how's that gonna work?'

'I'm not entirely sure. Some sort of elevated magnetic overhead lane they can switch to. Come on Chuck, have a bit of imagination. Look at his plans for space. Elon Musk wants to colonise Mars, but Efren wants to build towns along the way, sort of way stations hanging in space.'

'Kinda like a motorway service station? To pick up a room and a Big Mac en route?'

'Oh, come on Chuck. How is he not inspiring? The man's bold. He's a visionary. He's working on teleportation. Like Star Trek!'

'Kinda like 'beam me up Scottie'?' Drayton said. 'That's not gonna do much for his electric car business. Because why would Scottie drive to the office when he's got a teleporter in the garage?'

'Chuck! The guy's ahead of his time. He's visualising the future. The *Leonardo* of our time. How can you not see that?'

Drayton thought he spotted Anna across the other side of the stage. Short spiky blonde hair, big glasses, black T-shirt. That had to be her. He waved and shouted. She looked across. Then looked away. She was with Efren Bell, leading him to the back of the stage. They were smiling at each other, sharing a joke. Bell putting a hand on her shoulder, before the great visionary bounded onto the stage like an overexcited Labrador.

He was dressed in a black suit over a grey turtle-neck. He looked tanned, his greying hair slicked back in his trademark ponytail. He wore a pair of tinted glasses with round lenses. Designer stubble. A wireless mic so he could roam around the stage, parading and preening like a model on the catwalk.

There was wild applause. Flashes from cameras. A video camera-operator followed him around at a respectful distance. Two remote cameras were attached to runways above him. All relayed onto big screens at either side of the stage.

The future was about vision. Courage. Imagination. Youth and energy. He said he'd found it all in Berlin, the most edgy and exciting city in the world to be an entrepreneur. The capital of creative people. It would be the centre of his European operations.

Drayton watched him work the stage, work the crowd, telling them how he'd made his fortune from the 2008 financial crash, but wanted to give back, to invest in the future.

'I didn't come out on top because of what I knew about finance. It was clever mathematics that predicted the market. Algorithms made my fortune. And they will shape the future. Those who write them are the real Masters of the Universe.'

He started pointing, picking out random faces below him.

'You. And you. And you. You are the future. The pioneers. Algorithms drive artificial intelligence and artificial intelligence will drive everything. AI is going to transform everything we do, everything we are. Everything is now a computer, and computer code is the new universal language. Powering a digital future. Zeros and ones. And those with the vision, those who speak that language will make our future. The Masters of the Universe.'

His last words were drowned out by fevered clapping and cheering.

But Drayton was no longer paying attention. He was trying to cross the room, to the far side of the stage where Anna was now standing. He squeezed and pushed through the crowd, wishing that Bell had brought along a teleporter or two.

He then tucked in behind a server, who parted the crowd in front of her with biblical efficiency. The geeks showing a good deal more respect for the server's tray of wine than for Drayton.

He was now behind Anna, stretching his hand, tapping her arm. She turned, looking surprised and then plain angry.

'Chuck. Not now!'

She turned back to the stage, smiling again. Smiling at Bell, who was standing directly above her and was smiling back. Then he moved back to centre stage. The lights went down and he stood in the crosshairs of several spotlights, raising his hand to calm the applause. He looked like an evangelical preacher calming his frenzied followers.

'One hundred billion dollars. That's what the Digital Pagoda Fund is raising to invest in the future. One hundred *billion* dollars to back smart ideas. Smart people. Smart systems. *Secure* systems.'

He waited for the cheers and whoops to subside again.

'*Secure* systems,' he repeated.

Bell's picture on the big screens was replaced by an aerial shot from a drone flying low over a vast plain at sunset, the plain dotted with red brick temples, golden towers and stupas. All accompanied by music, a heavy base beat growing in intensity.

'You know, we can learn a lot from Buddhism. And like the ancient Buddhist temples, I want the fund to be a focal point, around which we can gather. I want it to be a point of inspiration, enlightenment and support.'

The screens faded to black and the aerial video was replaced with a single image of a golden bell-shaped Buddhist stupa, which was then framed by a computer screen and superimposed on an image of a padlock, the online world's symbol of security. Letters appearing below, in capitals, one by one as if they were being typed.

It spelt the words THE DIGITAL PAGODA FUND.

But Drayton missed the grand finale because he was fighting his way to the back of the room. He'd received a call from Norgaard. It was hard to hear him clearly above all the clapping and cheering, but he heard enough, the big Norwegian saying, 'We need to meet, and we need to meet now. It's about Neo.'

* * * * *

Chuck Drayton met Norgaard and Milo at a sausage stand under a railway line in Kreuzberg, where the Norwegian was tackling a big hot dog, his coat splattered with mustard and tomato sauce like he'd had a bad afternoon at paintball.

'There's a meet-up in half an hour at the bar across the road,' Milo said, pointing with his sausage at a graffiti-daubed five-storey building. At ground level it was covered in big bulbous letters and contorted comic-book characters. In some places the graffiti climbed up the wall like ivy. In its midst was the entrance to a bar called Wizard's Brew. There was a Bitcoin symbol in the window.

'The meet-up's about cryptocurrencies and it happens every month,' Milo said.

He said this area of Berlin had the highest density of places in Europe accepting cryptocurrency. 'Maybe even the highest in the world. Even my local bar, a rooftop place, down the road. In Neukölln. Not much to look at. It's taking Bitcoin.'

During the Cold War, Kreuzberg had been in West Berlin, but surrounded on three sides by the wall. The place had been a ghetto for hippies, squatters, anarchists and impoverished

Turkish immigrants. Back then, nobody else had wanted to live there. Rioting was a popular pastime. Since the wall came down, a lot of new money had flowed into the area. But it retained its libertarian buzz, and had embraced cryptocurrencies with gusto.

'I think Neo is coming to the meeting,' Milo said. 'He's been in a chat room run by a group organising the Wizard's Brew meeting, and he said he's coming along. He's been asking a lot about Initial Coin Offerings, to invest Bitcoin in business start-ups. He sounds like he's got a lot of Bitcoin to invest.'

'So how do we identify this Neo?' Drayton said.

'I think he may be an old guy. I mean more than thirty. Maybe forty. And English. Maybe Scottish,' Milo said.

'Yeah, that's really old,' said Norgaard. 'How do you arrive at that?'

'Neo was the name of the computer hacker in *The Matrix* movies. Remember them?' Milo said. 'And they were made between 1999 and 2003.'

'Yeah, I remember,' Drayton said. 'Weird movies. But maybe our Neo here just likes the name. And why do you think he's a guy? And why English or Scottish?'

'A guy because most of them are. English because of the slang he uses. When he joins a chat he says "hiya". He talked about having to break away from the chat to get some "grub". Another time when he signed out he said he was "knackered". Then he described the Initial Coin Offerings as "the dogs bollocks".'

'The dog's what?' said Norgaard, spilling another dollop of mustard down his coat.

'Bollocks,' said Milo. 'It means really fantastic. I like looked it up. Comes from the fact that dogs lick their bollocks so much, they must taste really great.'

'Oh, for fuck's sake Milo,' said Norgaard, throwing away the remains of his sausage. No longer hungry.

'And the Scottish bit?' said Drayton.

'He talks a lot about whisky. All Scottish brands. Like he's pretty familiar with that stuff.'

'Or just likes whisky. Thinks it's the "dog's bollocks" maybe,' said Drayton.

'You'd better get over there,' Milo said, looking at his watch.

'You not joining us?' said Drayton.

Milo said that might not be wise since he lived in the area and might be recognised.

It was dark inside the bar, a series of antique-looking lamps built into black walls more for decoration than any light they provided. The bar lined the far wall, craft beer on tap, shelves well-stocked with spirits and wine. There were a couple of overhead fans, not operating, and a pair of big tired-looking plants near the door. Some kind of electronic trance music in the background. Drayton reckoned there were perhaps thirty people. He ordered two beers.

The language switched between English and German. The crowd seemed to be divided into three broad groups. Three tribes. There were the Kreuzberg originals, the libertarian revolutionaries. They were scruffy, but cool scruffy. Then there was the academic tribe, who were just plain scruffy. The third tribe were the techies and the geeks, the type he recognised from Anna's factory, seeing Bitcoin as a cool new way of financing their start-ups.

'So prices have crashed. Who gives a fuck,' said a bearded Kreuzberg original, by way of introduction. He was sitting near an open window smoking a joint. A black Labrador at his feet looked more stoned than its owner. 'So speculators get burned. Fuck them. We don't need them. Cryptocurrencies are the most important invention since the wheel, man. We're gonna make the corrupt old banks squeal.'

As a warm up act, it served its purpose.

'Too fucking right,' agreed an academic.

'Fuck the banks,' said another.

The bearded original went back to his Labrador and joint.

'That's Hans,' whispered Norgaard. 'Quite a Kreuzberg legend. Spent five years in jail for selling explosives online. Now he thinks cryptocurrencies are a better way of blowing up the system.'

The geeky crowd, not averse to a little speculation, and giving somewhat more than a fuck about the system, examined their drinks and exchanged awkward smiles.

'The cryptocurrency economy is still fifty times bigger than it was a year ago,' said another of the academics, who launched into a roll call of all the new businesses in the area now accepting Bitcoin. There were shouts for him to speak up, since the Labrador had fallen asleep and was snoring loudly.

'There were always going to be booms and corrections. We were never going to build a new economy overnight,' said an original.

An academic launched into a jargon-stew of a lecture about smart contracts and traceable tuna, decentralised economies, the purity and equality of an economy without rent-seeking and parasitic intermediaries, where citizens were empowered by the immutable truth of cryptocurrency.

Norgaard whispered to Drayton, 'It's an immutable truth that my beer glass is empty, and so is yours.'

Then tribal warfare broke out.

The libertarian tribe, inspired by the academic's stirring speech, decided Initial Coin Offerings, using cryptocurrencies to finance new businesses, might not be such a good thing after all, because instead of striking a blow against the capitalist system, it might just prop it up, further postponing the arrival of their crypto-anarchist utopia.

One geek thought that was ridiculous. 'You guys need to get real.'

Which tested the limits of libertarian tolerance.

'Shut the fuck up!'

'*You* shut the fuck up.'

'Let him speak.'

'He's got nothing to say.'

But the geeks were finding their voice and their confidence. Progressively they got the upper hand, the originals and the academics taking time out to refuel on craft beer and freshly rolled joints. The geeks had already filled up on coffee, and now took possession of the floor, focussing it on business, talking start-ups with hunger and enthusiasm because of course as any right-thinking person knew, cryptocurrencies were about making money, lots of money. What was the point otherwise?

Nobody identified themselves, names never given or asked for, that was one thing the tribes all had in common.

So who was Neo?

Drayton and Norgaard assumed he was among the geeks, since investing his Bitcoin was what had brought him along.

Norgaard focussed on three people drinking what looked like whisky. Though one seemed too old, and another spoke with a French accent. The third was a younger woman with long red hair and big round glasses, who had entered the bar on her own. She was a possibility.

Drayton was focussing on two men in their early twenties, who were sitting among the geeks, though not quite fitting in. The others mostly knew each other, but not these two. They were drinking beer, not saying much, but listening hard and occasionally taking notes.

'We do have to make sure it's the people who benefit,' said a revived Kreuzberg original, trying to wrench back control from the geeks.

'It's got to enable businesses that are shunned by the banks,' said an academic.

'People's finance,' said another.

The discussion was calmer now and seemed to be winding down.

Drayton had an idea. He raised a hand and said, 'I think it's the dog's bollocks.'

There was silence at first. Most not getting it, giving him looks that said, 'You what?'

The Labrador stirred, maybe thinking it was about time to stretch down there, but was so stoned it could hardly raise its head.

Only two people laughed. The woman with the red hair said, 'He means it's really fantastic.' She spoke with a broad Scottish accent.

And one of the two guys on Drayton's radar said, 'Too right.'

He spoke with a London accent.

Drayton and Norgaard looked at each other. They watched as both paid, using their smartphones, most likely in Bitcoin. It was 8.42 p.m.

'I'll follow the guy,' Drayton said to Norgaard. 'You take the girl. Let's see where they end up.'

The guy was clean-shaven, boyish looking, with short curly hair. He was wearing a plain blue T-shirt over faded black jeans, and what looked like a new pair of red and white trainers on oversized feet. He put on a black jacket as he left the bar.

He crossed the road, passing under the overhead railway line and then deeper into Kreuzberg's graffiti-lined streets. Five minutes later the man that might be Neo entered a building with a contorted metal sculpture out the front and daubed with anti-capitalist slogans. A squat.

Drayton found a small bar opposite, where he ordered a beer, took a stool at the window and phoned Norgaard, telling the Norwegian where he'd ended up and saying he'd hang there for an hour or two and watch the place. Norgaard said he'd followed the woman to some high-end restaurant and she was in there now. He said he doubted she was Neo. 'So looks like he's with you.'

Norgaard joined Drayton in the bar. 'How do they live in those places?' he asked, eyeing the graffiti with distaste. 'They call it art. Vandalism, if you ask me.'

Drayton didn't answer. He was looking at his phone, at missed messages from Anna. Two of them saying, 'Let's talk,' and suggesting they meet at a place close to their apartment.

'I need to run an errand. Give me half an hour,' he said to the Norwegian.

He opened the scooter app and found one parked a couple of blocks away. It took him ten minutes to reach the bar, which was attached to one of Anna's favourite theatres. Wooden floors, big fading leather armchairs. Fans overhead. The server told him he'd just missed her. She said there were still a few tickets left for the late performance of a dance show she described as an 'interplanetary, post-dystopian, trans-disciplinary cabaret.' Drayton said thanks, but it sounded too much like his day job.

He drove the scooter to his apartment, where he ran up the stairs, taking them two at a time. He called for Anna, but there was no reply. He walked to the bedroom. The wardrobe doors were open and her clothes were gone. Then he saw the yellow Post-it Note on the pillow, on which she had scrawled, 'I'm sorry Chuck. I'm moving out. Need time. I can put up with a virus or two in my computer. Maybe even a worm. But not with you. Sorry xx'.

* * * * *

Drayton pushed a grainy photograph across the table. It was from the bar, Wizard's Brew, taken on his cell phone, and it showed Neo glancing across the room shortly before he left for the squat. He then showed a second photograph to which he'd matched it, the same short curly hair and slightly mischievous face.

'His name is James Timothy Edwards, a twenty-year-old unemployed Londoner. He arrived two days ago on a flight from Bangkok, Thailand. He left the UK eighteen months ago, skipped probation, which he'd been given for hacking. Sold software for crashing computers. Ran the business out of his parents' attic. One of the conditions of probation was that he wouldn't touch a computer.'

Norgaard said he'd spoken to Neo's mother. 'She was cautious when I phoned. I told her I was an old friend, who'd met her son travelling. She said he'd gone first to what she called "one of those old communist countries." The last time he'd been in contact was four months ago from Bangkok, saying he was travelling in the Far East.'

'Social media?' asked Schoenberg.

'Facebook, Twitter accounts. But largely inactive since he left the UK,' Drayton replied.'

And Milo said, 'He's kept most communications anonymous. Mostly through dark web forums and chat rooms, and the pattern fits his travels.'

They were sitting drinking coffee in a spartan café with peeling linoleum floors and table tops, yellow walls and dim fluorescent lighting. It had once been a canteen for Stasi spies, where East Germany's secret policemen would take a break from their surveillance of the entire population. It was now part of the Stasi Museum, and the museum had retained the café's drab décor, though Drayton was pleased to see that at least the coffee machine was of a more recent vintage.

Schoenberg sat on one side of a long table; Drayton, Milo and Norgaard on the other. It was the morning after the discovery of the person that might be Neo. Milo had the pale look of a gaming addict after a night in front of the consul; Norgaard, usually so decisive when it came to choosing food, struggled to concentrate on the café's menu. Drayton was riding a caffeine-induced high, anxiously swinging a foot under the table. They had taken turns to monitor the squat until Schoenberg could arrange what he called a 'watcher' through his police contacts. Then they'd been up most of the night following leads, Milo burrowing deeper into the dark web, Norgaard and Drayton working their contacts, crunching the data from police and news archives, trying to pin a real identify on Neo. If Neo was involved with Cerberus, he had to be good, but he was also young and sloppy, leaving the trail to Berlin that Milo had picked up. Drayton was convinced they'd find something in his past. Hackers didn't just emerge from nowhere. And there it was, Neo on the front page of a London newspaper after his conviction.

If any of them thought there was anything unusual in Schoenberg calling the meeting in the old Stasi headquarters, they kept it to themselves. They knew better than to try and second-guess him. The German said the place was private, said it without a hint of irony, that he liked to come here from time to time 'to remember'. To remember what, he never said.

He looked fresh and rested. He always did. 'What else have you got?

'8.42,' Drayton said. '8.42 is when Neo paid for his drinks in Bitcoin in Wizard's Brew. Bitcoin is anonymous, but it's not private, so we were able to pinpoint the transaction, and we now have the address of Neo's wallet.'

'But don't they use multiple wallets, and mix up the Bitcoins?' Schoenberg asked.

'They do, and they can. Which makes identifying a wallet harder,' Milo said. 'But Neo's sloppy. He keeps using the same one, the one he used to buy his drinks in the Wizard's Brew.'

'Whatever he was doing in the Far East, he was making some *very* good money,' Norgaard said. 'There were a series of six big monthly payments into his wallet, totalling around twenty thousand US dollars a time, almost like a salary.'

'Six months in the Far East,' said Schoenberg. 'One hundred and twenty thousand dollars. Nice work for a twenty-year-old unemployed Londoner.'

'And he's cashed out twice, I'm guessing through a cryptocurrency exchange,' Drayton said.

'Do we know the owner of the wallet that was paying him or the exchange?' asked Schoenberg.

'That's what we need. That's what we're working on. That's what can lead us to Cerberus,' Drayton said.

Drayton's phone rang. 'Hello Ric, what can I do for you?'

His listened for a while, Ric Cullen on the line, trying to sound friendly. Then Drayton said, 'Don't worry about it Ric... We all lose it from time to time... Neo? We're still looking into that... No, nothing new at this point... Sure, you'll be the first to know.'

'Ric Cullen?' Schoenberg asked.

'Yeah. Wants to know, "Any more news on Neo?".'

'They didn't sound like they cared the other day,' said Milo.

'Oh, the Cardinals care,' said Norgaard. 'I've had calls from Wang and Strykov asking the same question.'

And you said?' asked Schoenberg.

'We're working on it.'

Then Schoenberg said, 'It's very important we keep this information to ourselves.'

He paid the bill, pushing a handful of Euros across the table's stained linoleum. 'I think we should perhaps have a conversation with James Timothy Edwards.'

They left the Stasi canteen down a long, dark corridor to a lobby with a bust of Karl Marx and a statue of Felix Dzerzhinsky, the founder of the KGB, the Soviet secret police. Drayton checked his phone as they walked, looking for messages from Anna. He'd heard nothing since last night, since the Post-it. She wasn't returning his calls or his messages.

A man greeted Schoenberg with an enormous bear hug. Schoenberg introduced him as Heinz and said that if it hadn't been for Heinz there would be no Stasi museum. 'This man had done more than anybody to keep these horrible, but necessary memories alive.'

Heinz was a small, compact man of Schoenberg's age, with thinning grey hair and a laugh that belonged in a bierkeller.

'It's certainly been a struggle at times, he said. 'We've always been grateful for what you did for us, Wolfgang.'

Heinz took Schoenberg by the arm. 'The new exhibition is fantastic. Let me show you, very quickly. Two minutes.'

Norgaard said he had to make a call. The others followed Heinz up a broad staircase at the back of the lobby. Heinz told them that deciding what to display was always tough since there were so may files. 'If you placed all the Stasi files side by side, they'd stretch for a hundred miles.'

The museum occupied building number one of the sprawling complex that once housed the East German secret police. It was the building where the long-time head of the Stasi, Erich Mielke, had his office and from where he ran the country's largest employer, with 100,000 full-time staff and nearly 200,000 informers. Drayton studied the old spymaster's solid old desk with its bank of clunky phones, a quote on the wall saying, 'Comrades, we must know everything'.

Heinz showed them a series of newly framed documents, pointing at one that looked to Drayton like a deranged game of snakes and ladders.

'It shows a Stasi investigation.' Heinz said. 'In 1985 they decided a computer scientist who'd become a playwright should be investigated. It took them six months to come up with this, with seventeen full-time spies and countless informers, including the man's then wife, as well as friends and neighbours. This is the result: a map of all his friendships. Every relationship. All his movements. Everything he does and everything he likes. All his connections.'

'Creepy,' said Drayton.

'But you know what?' said Schoenberg. 'Today you could learn this, and more, simply by accessing a Facebook profile. Or Instagram. Or even a Google search. The Stasi could only have dreamed about that kind of access to personal information. That sort of power.'

Drayton looked at Schoenberg, still finding it impossible to figure him out, an old spymaster worried about privacy and surveillance. Maybe it was a German thing. The history, the Nazis and then the Stasi. Most of the spooks Drayton had met didn't give a rat's arse about privacy.

'Wow, is this for real,' said Milo, standing in front of a display cabinet containing cameras hidden in belts, tree trunks, a worker's hard hat, even in a watering can.

'All rather quaint, don't you think? said Heinz. 'But in their day, the Stasi was considered the most effective and ruthless of East Europe's secret police. Only they failed, didn't they Wolfgang? Because for all their power, all their toys, they didn't foresee their own demise, and the collapse of their own country.'

Drayton guessed that Heinz could have talked all day. He had an almost morbid fascination with the Stasi's secret world. They left him still musing over how best to display that tyranny. A few minutes later they were in Schoenberg's black chauffeur-driven Mercedes, driving back along roads lined with soulless communist-era apartment buildings of pre-fabricated concrete. The old East Berlin. The blocks had been given a facelift, maybe several facelifts, since unification, but that still couldn't disguise their grim monotony.

'I have a cell phone number for James Timothy Edwards,' said Norgaard, who was squeezed in the back between Milo and Drayton. Schoenberg in the passenger seat. He explained that Neo had bought a local SIM card when he landed, and registered it using his passport. Norgaard obtained the phone number from the service provider.

He rang the number.

'Hey James,' he said, sounding friendly and familiar.

A hesitant voice at the other end didn't identity itself, just saying, 'Who is this?'

'A friend of a friend. I'm told you may have some cryptocurrency to invest and I may be able to help you... Can't say more on the phone... Where are you staying? There's a coffee shop... That's the one... I'll explain when we meet.'

Norgaard ended the call. 'That was surprisingly straightforward,' he said.

They drove to Kreuzberg, the car stopping a couple of blocks from the squat where Neo was staying, and around the corner from the coffee shop in which Norgaard had arranged to meet him.

The Norwegian left the car. 'Let me talk to him alone. At least initially.'

'The more we learn the less sense it makes,' Drayton said to Schoenberg. 'Let's assume Cerberus *has* found a flaw in the fabric of computer chips that we don't know about. That's a big deal. That's the mother of all zero days. But he's just using it to deliver ransomware. Basic ransomware. And as far we know only a fraction of the targets are paying up. If you had that capability, surely you'd do more? Once you've broken in, a system is wide open, everything's possible. Theft, spying, sabotage. Take the banks, they have some of the best cyber defences outside the military. If you break in there, you can manipulate the markets. Make a lot of money that way. Plunder ATMs, empty their vaults. It's like you develop a super-sophisticated nuclear missile and use it to deliver balloons.'

He paused. Looking for a reaction from Schoenberg. There was none, or at least none the German was showing.

'It makes no sense,' Drayton continued. 'Unless this isn't about extortion at all. Unless it's all a show. A performance. A sales pitch. Unless Cerberus is just demonstrating a weapon. Showing what it's capable of.'

'Showcasing it for potential buyers,' Schoenberg said, running a thumb and forefinger through his short moustache. 'I'm hoping that perhaps James Timothy Edwards can provide us with some answers.'

But Neo never showed up at the coffee shop, and Norgaard returned to the car looking agitated. There was urgency in his voice. 'The squat,' he said. 'Let's get to the squat.'

First they saw the flashing lights. Then two police cars. An ambulance. A police woman telling people to move back as she taped off an area in front of Neo's squat.

'What happened?' asked Drayton.

'Who knows what goes on in there,' said the police woman.

An older man standing nearby pointed towards the top of the building. 'Somebody jumped. From up top there.'

It was then they saw the body on the sidewalk. It had been covered by a blanket, but blood was oozing from underneath. One foot was sticking out from the bottom of the blanket. It was wearing a bright red and white trainer.

Chapter Three

Digital Futures

Yangon, Myanmar

He checked his cell phone. First the battery, which was almost full. That was good, though he'd brought along a portable charger, just in case. The camera was hungry on power, especially when he was shooting video, and he needed plenty of video.

He looked at his Facebook news feed and Twitter. The latest photographs were spreading fast: grisly images of burned and mutilated bodies, burning homes, the head of a dog superimposed on the body of a Muslim cleric. A pig's head on another. Alongside the photographs were the denunciations: Rapists! Murderers! Animals! A rising tide of poison, each hate-filled post seemingly trying to outdo the last. And most ending with the time and place for revenge.

He smiled as he scrolled.

He took the train. It was slow, but probably still the quickest way of reaching Thaketa Township in the east of the city. The police would close roads to help smooth the passage of the main convoy of trucks from the Organisation for the

Protection of Race and Religion, but he wanted to be there ahead of them. To see them arrive.

His home was in Insein Township on the other side of the city, a scruffy first floor apartment in a run-down tenement block he shared with his parents and two sisters. The block was close to Insein Prison, its watchtowers visible beyond a wasteland strewn with smouldering rubbish and patrolled by scrawny dogs, rummaging for scraps.

His father had once told him it was a place of immense cruelty. But mostly, those living in its shadow preferred not to acknowledge its existence. It was something dark and unspeakable. For the older people especially. They wouldn't even look at it. Wouldn't walk anywhere near it. It seemed to have a curse-like hold on them. He could sense the fear inside his father if he was forced to pass anywhere within sight of those watchtowers.

He was twenty-one years old and too young to remember those days, at least not in any detail. The military had run the country for five decades, but The Lady was now in charge. She'd spent time *inside* that prison. And she was a patriot, building a new Burma for the Burmese and defending Buddhism.

He squeezed along the narrow station platform, around makeshift stalls and ground sheets overflowing with food and drink, a rising clamour of voices as the train approached. The six decrepit carriages of the Yangon Circle Line train were dragged slowly into the station by an ancient diesel engine. The outside of the carriages were daubed with hand-painted advertisements for a new 4G cellular network and a Red Bull energy drink.

A young woman stepped off the train and waved. 'Ko Win, where are you going?' He pretended not to hear and boarded the packed train through another door. The engine wheezed and spluttered to life, sending dense clouds of smoke into the air. The carriages strained and then jerked forward, crawling out of the station and through a vast yard littered with rusting locomotives. Groups of people criss-crossed the tracks ahead.

Ko Win squeezed onto one of the hard blue benches, which lined the carriage. He was wearing Western dress, faded blue jeans and a T-shirt. There were others dressed that way too, alongside men and women in traditional dress, the women's faces covered in a cosmetic white powder. Most sitting on the benches, legs folded beneath them. Almost everybody had a smartphone, mostly cheap Chinese models, like his own. Windows and doors were all wide open, providing some relief from the stifling heat. A child next to him stood on the bench and leaned out of the window, grabbing at trees. Hawkers moved up and down the carriage, selling fruit and snacks, yelling as they passed. A big woman selling watermelon sat on the floor in front of him.

The train moved in fits and starts and it took an hour to reach Myittar Nyunt station, the closest to his destination. The station was little more than a cracked and overgrown slab of concrete beside the track. Ko Win put up his umbrella as he left, a sudden torrential downpour coming as if from nowhere.

At first sight there was little to distinguish Thaketa Township from most other townships that made up the outer suburbs of Yangon. Stained and crumbling tenement blocks beside small, squat homes with corrugated metal roofs. Strips of overgrown wasteland with more piles of smouldering rubbish.

What was different was the silence, and the almost complete absence of people on the streets. Perhaps they knew we were coming, he thought. He walked slowly down one of the wider roads, avoiding potholes the size of craters, and passed a police post. Nobody was on duty. The police had melted away, as they always did before the trucks arrived.

He took cover in a doorway, checking his cell phone for any last minute change of plan. The only sounds were barking, yelping dogs and the battering of rain on metal roofs.

Thaketa Township was home to Yangon's small Muslim population, though that wasn't immediately obvious. There was a mosque close to where Ko Win was waiting, a pair of stubby minarets obscured by trees that were growing out the roof of an adjoining building. The loud speakers at the top of the minarets had not been used for weeks, the call for prayer stopped at the request of the police, who said it was 'provocative'. Prayers now took place in homes or else a small madrasa, a religious school a couple of doors from the mosque. The Organisation for the Protection of Race and Religion had now demanded the prayers stop altogether, because that was provocative too. Today they were coming to enforce their demand.

The Muslims of Thaketa Township had always regarded themselves as first and foremost Burmese. Most were not particularly devout. They went to Burmese schools, had Burmese friends. Most had been in Myanmar for generations. They heard about the barbarity in the remote areas of the country bordering Bangladesh, hundreds of thousands of Muslims forced from their homes and expelled across the border, but still they thought Thaketa was safe. That it would never happen to them.

The intimidation and attacks in Thaketa Township were sporadic at first, but then grew in intensity. Buddhist friends and neighbours stopped talking to them and then grew openly hostile. Shops stopped serving them. Children were expelled from school; their parents sacked from their jobs. But it was the hatred on social media that frightened them most. Community leaders had seen the angry calls to protest that day and many people had fled from the Township. They'd called on the police for protection, but the police had left. The more defiant among them gathered in the madrasa, where they waited and prayed.

Ko Win watched as the first of the open-back trucks approached the madrasa. Crowds of mostly young men spilled onto the street. Most wore traditional Burmese longyis. Some were bare-chested; others wore T-shirts with baseball caps. They made no attempt to disguise themselves.

They carried rocks and sticks. He saw the flash of a knife. He estimated the mob was at least two hundred strong. He stepped out of the doorway and began to take photographs. Then a bit of video. Alternating between the two. He knew from experience that a mob could be unpredictable. He felt their nervous tension as they closed in on the religious school. As individuals they were cowards; as a mob they were deadly. It usually took a trigger, a spark to start them off, and it was always hard to predict where that would come from.

Then a group of monks came to the front of the mob and started shouting at the madrasa through a megaphone. The sound was distorted and it was hard to hear clearly. The monks were carrying sticks. Except the one with the megaphone; he held a long machete-like knife, partially concealed under his flowing robe.

A man appeared from the madrasa. A Muslim religious leader, an imam. He appealed for calm, inviting the monks inside to talk. Ko Win videoed him. The imam took a step closer to the monk with the megaphone, holding out his hand. But the monk pulled out the machete and swung wildly. It sliced into the imam's shoulder, a sharp crack as it shattered the bone, the imam screaming as he fell to the floor, clasping at his gaping wound. Two men ran from the madrasa to help the imam, one of then lunging at the monk, who lost his footing and fell, hitting his head on his megaphone. Then the mob exploded, surging forwards, falling on the two men in a frenzy of sticks and knives, while rocks rained down on the madrasa.

The air was filled with angry chants. The mob parted for a group carrying tins of kerosene, which they splashed on the walls of the building and then poured through the smashed windows. Then came the flames; bottles of kerosene, rags stuffed roughly in their tops, lit and flung inside the building. The fire rapidly took hold. The horrible screams from inside only seemed to encourage the mob, the monks at the forefront, acting like deranged cheerleaders, egging them on.

Ko Win moved quickly amid the mob, cell phone in his hand. He lingered at the monk who had fallen on his megaphone. He had a small cut above his eye and Ko Win worked his camera. Stills and video. Plenty of both. Milking the moment, as the monk displayed suitable agony for the camera.

* * * * *

Police and soldiers arrived with firefighters only after the madrasa and several adjoining buildings were smouldering shells. They escorted the mob back to their trucks, showing due reverence to the monks. Then they gathered up survivors from the fire, the terrified dozen or so who had escaped the flames and then outrun the gauntlet of rocks, sticks and knives. They had taken refuge on the banks of a nearby river. They were told they would be escorted to a refugee camp on the border, for their own safety, and that there would be no time to collect their possessions from their homes, since that would be a provocation.

It took Ko Win half an hour to reach the centre of Yangon and to a newly renovated building on 50th Street, in the heart of the old part of the city. A sign on a balcony two floors up read 'Digital Futures'. At a door down a side alley, he entered a PIN code and then placed the index finger of his right hand on a fingerprint scanner. The door clicked open. He sat in front of a computer in a ground floor office and transferred the images from his phone. He had uploaded some of the more dramatic images during the journey back, but could now work faster, posting to scores of Facebook and Twitter accounts, together with the story of the Buddhist faithful defending themselves and their religion against an unprovoked attack by Muslim extremists. The Muslim dead and injured, shown in gory detail, became Buddhist dead; the burned-out madrasa became the home of a defenceless Buddhist charity. Then there was the injured monk, lying on the ground where he'd fallen on his megaphone. There were plenty of shots of his bloodied face, the victim of an unprovoked attack, though it took careful editing to remove the machete from his hand. The images went viral almost as soon as he posted them.

Ko Win then transferred onto a memory stick the video of the imam appealing to the monks for calm. That would need more expert work. The foreigners mostly worked on the floor above. A strange group, he thought, who went by unusual nicknames. He found the one who called himself Grom and handed him the memory stick, explaining what was on it.

'Thanks,' Grom said. We can have fun with that.'

* * * * *

The fire in Thaketa Township was still burning as the Thai Airways flight descended towards Yangon Airport through a blanket of grey clouds, rain lashing against its windows. It shuddered and bounced as it made its final approach just to the north of the township, where rain had doused the flames but intensified the smoke. The captain radioed ahead to report it.

A woman sitting in the second row of business class was too busy to notice. She was shredding documents by hand, tearing them into tiny pieces and stuffing them into an airline sick-bag. The documents carried the logo of the United Nations.

'Some things in Burma haven't changed,' she said to the man beside her, by way of an explanation, seeing him watching her. 'I don't want them sniffing through these as we enter the country.'

'Sorry,' said Chuck Drayton 'I didn't mean to pry. It's just a slightly unusual way to use a sick-bag. Why would they go through your stuff?'

They'd sat in silence for most of the hour and a half flight from Bangkok, and now the woman tried to squeeze a lengthy explanation into the final minutes before touch down. She told him her name was Margarethe Van Der Beek, and she was a special representative of the UN, monitoring the persecution of Burma's Muslim minority, the Rohingyas. She used the old name for Myanmar. She said she was based out of a UN regional office in Bangkok, where they'd reverted to paper documents after their computer systems were hacked.

'They broke into our main server in Bangkok and stole and destroyed files. Brought down our website too. We brought in experts who found spyware on our laptops. Then there's all the fake news and online hatred. Flooding Facebook and Twitter with the stuff. Scores of fake accounts. Stirring up Buddhist nationalism.'

She said the internet was relatively new to Burma, but was spreading fast, and that to most Burmese Facebook *is* the internet.

'What is it they used to say? That social media connects people, is somehow liberating. Not here. It's spreading hatred like the plague.'

The aircraft hit the runway with a heavy thud, the engines sounding like a badly tuned lawnmower as they went into reverse thrust.

'They even posted an interview online. Me in a village after an attack, saying Muslims had burned their own homes, *burned their own homes*, and defending the heroic work of the army. It was shocking.'

'You never said that?'

'I never even gave the interview. I was never in the village. How can they even do that?'

'But you've given other interviews. There are publicly available images and recordings of you?'

'Of course.'

'It's called a deep fake. They feed what they have of you into a computer, teaching it to imitate your voice and expressions and then generate the speech. They literally put words in your mouth and put you just about any place they want. The more data they have, the better the fake. It takes a lot of computer power and know-how. I'm surprised that's available, I mean here in Myanmar.'

'Oh, they're good. They *are* good.'

'Who are *they*?'

Van Der Beek shrugged. 'I'm guessing the government. The army. Or somebody working closely with them. Our experts couldn't say for sure.'

The aircraft came to a standstill. An airbridge edged to the door. Thunder rumbled beyond the windows. The UN woman looked out at several huddled figures, airport workers, the rain pounding off their shiny raincoats and hoods and jumping off the tarmac around their feet. '*Jesus*,' she said. 'Never fly in the late afternoon in the rainy season. It's a golden rule to avoid shredded nerves in the tropics, but one I always break.'

Drayton gave her a business card and asked her to keep in touch.

'Thank you Andreas,' she said. You don't sound German.' The name on the card was Andreas Fischer, Technical Director of AF Global Digital Solutions. It gave a German cell phone number beside an email address and website.

'I was raised in America,' Drayton replied.

He left the aircraft. A nonchalant immigration officer flicked though and then stamped his passport, which was German and also in the name of Fischer. It was the best that Schoenberg could come up with at short notice, though not ideal.

'We have to get you there as soon as possible,' Schoenberg had said.

Drayton's German was passable, he was reasonably fluent in small talk, but was far from being native. Norgaard had created a plausible website for the company and a LinkedIn profile for Fischer.

Walking out of the airport was like opening the door of an oven. Heavy damp heat and then a wall of faces. Men wearing skirt-like wraparounds they called longyis, some smoking long and pungent cigar-like cheroots. Hotel reps with spray-on smiles, always good to see you. Kids working their cell phones. A pair of monks. Anxious, expectant, excited. The faces of the new Myanmar. Several soldiers stood to one side, carrying ancient rifles and timeless scowls.

His taxi was an old and rattling Toyota, a steering wheel on the wrong side, which he shared with a single buzzing and diving mosquito with a voracious appetite and the disappearing skills of a blood-sucking Houdini. Spindly wipers struggled to cope with the rain, which was drumming heavily on the roof of the car. The road was dark and lined with the fuzzy outlines of old colonial-era mansions just visible beyond tall stained walls. Figures huddling under umbrellas. Billboards advertised cell phones. A bank. Beer. All in strange squiggly letters, barely visible through the downpour.

The traffic was quickly snarled up, reduced to a crawl.

Drayton checked his phone for messages from Anna. He'd tried calling her before leaving Berlin. Texting her that he was travelling to the Far East, apologising for what seemed like the millionth time, pleading for her to meet, if only briefly, or at least to respond. He knew he sounded pathetic, desperate even. And guessed she thought that way too, since there was no reply.

His hotel was in one of the old mansions set back from the road. Its driveway had become a lake. A concierge holding an oversized umbrella guided him to a lobby lined with black and white pictures of old Rangoon. The umbrella mostly did its job, but his shoes were soaked by the time he reached the check-in desk, and they squelched as a porter escorted him up a creaking stairway to a second floor room, sparsely furnished and overlooking a garden.

A storm was now raging outside, and the trees below his window swayed violently as they were lashed by the wind and torrential rain. They looked as if they might be ripped from the ground at any moment. The lightning was almost constant, like a flickering light bulb. The thunder came in waves. A deafening boom that shook the windows, as if somebody was firing a cannon from the balcony next door, followed by a deep rumble that seemed to go on for ever.

It was mid-evening. He'd been travelling for twenty-four hours, but he was wide awake, jet-lagged. The hotel bar was decked out in a nautical theme. Ship's wheels, dive helmets and all manner of brass gauges and levers. There was a piano in the corner and a television tuned to CNN. A familiar headline screamed of more cyber-attacks. This time on airlines, credit card data plundered. ATMs emptied in Asia. A nuclear power station in Japan closed down by ransomware, the same snarling three-headed dog.

He ordered a beer and picked up a local newspaper. A front page report described how Muslims were burning and looting their own homes. It said the army, in spite of its best efforts, found it difficult to stop these acts of self-harm. Elsewhere, watermelon prices were rising, MoMo, an elephant at Mandalay Zoo was celebrating its sixty-fourth birthday, and there'd been a crackdown on drivers, 'reckless ruffians' in search of cheap thrills.

He drank a silent toast to reckless ruffians, cradling his drink, replaying in his mind his last conversation with Wolfgang Schoenberg. 'The police believe Neo took his own life. That nobody else was involved. We have to assume otherwise.'

It was a chilling assumption. It meant Neo was working with Cerberus and had been eliminated before he could talk, that somebody had tipped off the three-headed dog. And the only people who knew they were onto Neo, apart from Drayton and his small team, were the Cardinals – Ric Cullen, Igor Strykov and Wang Yang.

Drayton opened his laptop, logged in to an email account and wrote a brief note saying he had arrived, which he saved to drafts. Schoenberg, Milo and Norgaard shared the password and login to the account and would pick up the message from the draft folder. '*Never* send the message. If it's not transmitted it can't be intercepted,' Schoenberg had said. He was adamant, 'This *must* be the *only* way we communicate.'

The Berlin Group's digital dead letter box.

Voice calls were emergency only, their identifying ringtone being *The Pink Panther* theme tune. Perhaps Schoenberg did have a sense of humour after all. Though it was more likely Norgaard who'd come up with that one.

A message from Milo contained rambling lists of names. Razor, Dim sum, Bubblegum, Tox, Phreak, Fisheye, Ghoul, Grom, Punch. Then there was a Batman and a Robin, an Archduke, Troy, Truck and a Dread. Next came Slimeball, Shark Toad and Stonefish. They were nicknames, the online handles of hackers. Milo had trawled through the logs of the dark web forums and chatrooms used most often by Neo, and these were the names that kept recurring during his eighteen-month journey from a terraced house in North London to East Europe, the Far East and his grisly death in Berlin. 'Could be that several are used by the same hacker,' Milo wrote. 'Can't say for sure. Lots of them. Neo was busy. Trying to narrow it down.'

Then Drayton opened a message from Schoenberg. It was short, just the address of the Yangon International Business Association and a local cell phone number.

Drayton called the number.

The first thing he heard was the noisy background hum of a bar or restaurant. Then a familiar voice said, 'This is Morgan.'

'Tony,' said Drayton. 'This is Chuck Drayton, how you doing?'

There was silence for a few moments before Morgan said, 'Chuck Drayton. What a surprise. What have I done to deserve a call from you? Or possibly not done?'

'It's a long story.'

'It usually is.'

'I'm visiting. Thought we might get together. For old time's sake.'

'Old time's sake? I doubt that. And in any case I've been doing my best to forget about our old times. What do you want?'

'Can I tell you when we meet?'

There was another long silence. Then laughter.

'Well, why not? Let's do lunch tomorrow. At my club.'

* * * * *

Shortly before noon the following day, Drayton's taxi pulled up outside an elegantly restored three-storey mansion, set back from the road, opposite Rangoon's main port. Morgan was waiting for him, smiling. Looking a good deal happier than Drayton expected, considering what had happened the last time the two of them had met, in China.

Morgan greeted him wearing a white linen shirt and long dark trousers, carefully pressed. He was tall and tanned, with closely cropped grey hair and designer-stubble. The familiar tortoiseshell frame glasses, eyeing the mess that was Drayton climbing from the taxi in a blue short-sleeved shirt and khaki shorts.

'Is there a dress code?' said Drayton.

'There is,' said Morgan. 'And you're breaking it. Only, as president of the Yangon International Business Association, and this being my club, I am prepared to give a waiver on this occasion. What brings you to Rangoon and how did you find me?' Morgan used the old name for Yangon.

Drayton ignored the questions, and they climbed together up broad steps into the club's main reception area, all marble and teak, chandeliers and fans hanging from a high ceiling. Tall pillars. A concierge in a smart white suit and gloves greeted them with a tray on which sat two chilled face towels.

Morgan had ripened his accent, a more cultured air of upper class English pomposity than Drayton remembered from China. Maybe that played better in a former colony.

'You're looking well, by the way,' Drayton said. 'Lost some weight?'

'That's what happens, Chuck, when you stop feasting on Chinese banquets.'

He didn't return the compliment.

'So how did you end up here?' Drayton asked.

The last time they'd met, Morgan was hiding out in a twenty-four-hour massage parlour in Macao, running from the triads, while the Chinese secret police had kidnapped his son and were blackmailing his wife, all on account of work he'd done for Drayton, gathering information on suspected hackers.

'I got out of China, though it was expensive,' Morgan said. 'The Caymans at first, since I had a place there. Found it a little boring, frankly. Banks are extremely accommodating, of course, but not too much else to offer, especially after Andrew went back to boarding school in England and my wife returned to China to care for her sick mother. Going back there wasn't an option for me, even if I'd wanted to. Which I didn't. And in business terms, this place is the new frontier.'

'How's that?' said Drayton.

'After decades under military misrule, it's opening up. This should be a rich country, Chuck. Oil, gas, precious stones, metals. It's got the lot. There's huge natural wealth here. It's the place to be.'

'And what's your role?'

'I'm a facilitator, Chuck.'

'Which means what?'

'Which means everything, but nothing. And how about you. Still working for the American government?'

Drayton gave him a business card.

100

'Well, nice to meet you Andreas,' Morgan said, reading the card and not looking the least bit surprised. 'Global solutions, what are they?'

'Everything, but nothing.'

They climbed a long spiral staircase to a lounge and dining area, where a server led them to an enclosed balcony, air conditioned and overlooking the port, where they sat in two big leather seats, a table between them, silver cutlery carefully laid out. Morgan ordered a large gin and tonic. Drayton said he'd have the same.

'So things are changing here?' Drayton said.

'Yes,' said Morgan. 'But not as quickly as we'd want. If I'm honest, there's a lot of disappointment at the pace of change. And the generals are still pulling a lot of strings, still controlling a lot of businesses. Having the son or daughter of a top general as your business partner still goes a long way.'

The server delivered their drinks, and Morgan waited for him to go before saying, 'Then there's the Rohingya situation, the army driving Muslims out to Bangladesh. They're getting away with murder. Literally. Like in the past. But everybody shrugs. The so-called democrats, because they've turned out to be Buddhist chauvinists first and democrats second. The West because they are terrified of driving this country into the arms of China.'

'Sounds like a mess,' Drayton said.

'A mess requires patience and a mess can give rise to great opportunity,' said Morgan. 'And investors are still arriving – at least the more intrepid ones.'

'And naturally you sell them on the opportunities?'

'Naturally,' said Morgan, smiling. That confident, anything's possible smile that Drayton remembered from China, relishing the atmosphere of the new Burma. Where others saw trials and trouble, Morgan saw challenges and opportunities. Though mostly he saw money.

Morgan pointed out two government ministers, a pair of journalists, and group of diplomats. 'This club is where deals are done, Drayton, doors opened, the wheels of commerce greased, all with a good dose of gossip.'

Morgan stood as four men passed the table, champagne in hand, wearing the uniform for business in Myanmar – linen jackets, open neck shirts and a breezy air of entitlement. They greeted Morgan with firm handshakes and bland words, spoken in a range of English accents, about the incessant rain, the traffic, and the country's poorly misunderstood leader. How she was being judged too harshly – 'She's a political leader now, not a human rights icon, for God's sake,' said an Australian. A sing-song Singaporean agreed – 'And as for these Rohingyas, they're not *proper* Burmese.' Nods all round. Moving seamlessly to bribes, or 'gift inflation', as it was called by an American. 'Gave the minister a car and I *still* didn't get the contract. There's dishonesty for you.' Heads shaking. That got them to the shifty Burmese – 'Don't get me wrong, I'm not against all this human rights stuff, but there's no respect any more. I'm not defending the military, you understand, but in the past you had discipline,' said another in what sounded like a Thai accent.

'Businessmen?' asked Drayton, after they had moved on.

'In a sense.'

'What sense is that?'

'Your fellow American, he was a banker to the generals. Speciality was money laundering. Used to take cases of cash down to Bangkok. But now that sanctions are over, that's no longer necessary. Our generals and their families are perfectly capable of laundering their own cash through their own banks.'

'Too bad,' said Drayton. 'What does he do now?'

'He still smuggles. Works with the Singaporean. Mostly precious stones. Jade usually, which the military still controls. To the markets in Hong Kong and Singapore. The man on his left, the Thai. He's in business with the son of one the top generals. Used to smuggle drugs. Speed. What they call *yaba*. It means crazy. They had factories near the Thai border, which made the stuff. The Golden Triangle. Everybody knew, but they were untouchable. Still are.'

'And what does he do now? Business must be good, judging by the champagne.'

'These days? Wildlife mainly. And logs. This country has a very rich natural habitat. Though probably not for much longer.'

'Tigers?' said Drayton.

'No, the tiger trade's mainly controlled by the Chinese. This gentleman is mostly into teak and rosewood. And elephants. Smuggling baby elephants into Thailand, where they are prized by the tourist industry. Very lucrative, but incredibly cruel.'

Drayton was no longer listening. He was watching a man standing at the bar on the far side of the dining room. Throughout his journey from Berlin, Drayton had tried to imagine how this moment would feel, seeing that face for the first time in more than a decade. Whether he'd even recognise it. He'd expected to feel hatred, fear, disgust. Instead, he felt nothing. The man wasn't tall, perhaps five-eight or five-nine and had filled out a little, a pressed white linen shirt hanging over blue cotton trousers. Tanned. His hair still a dark brown. His manner was the same, he could see that from a distance. The slightly agitated, fidgety way he stood, his face giving little away. Lean and set in stone, small eyes scanning the room, then glancing at a cell phone held in his left hand, while his right flicked mechanically at his hair each time it flopped down in front of his eyes, a barman asking Mr Dmitry whether he would like his usual champagne.

'We certainly have some of our more colourful members in today,' Morgan said, ordering lunch, some sort of baked fish he said was a speciality. Washed down with a bottle of New Zealand sauvignon blanc. Another speciality.

'Tell me about the man at the bar, right side. The one in the white shirt with the floppy hair.'

'That would be Dmitry Gerasimov. Russian, and one of our newer members.'

'And what does he steal, smuggle or launder?'

'Do I detect a little cynicism, Chuck?'

'Only a little. What business is he in?'

'He's helping to connect Burma. Internet. Telecoms. That kind of thing.'

'I'd like to meet him.'

They finished the last of the fish and wine and crossed to the bar, which was filling, and where Morgan was greeted with more smiles and outstretched hands. The American jade smuggler ordered another bottle of champagne and two more glasses, complaining about the tax on the bubbly – 'You're not paying off the right people, Tony.'

A French woman, a jewellery exporter, complained about the quality of the precious stones at the latest auction – 'And believe me darling, I know.' Dmitry was in the group, but not really part of it, not really joining in. Looking around the room again. Looking bored. Checking his phone. A few whispered words with a Chinese-looking man beside him.

Morgan introduced Drayton as Andreas Fischer, looking for opportunities in the computer business. More outstretched hands. Dmitry registered him for the first time, but blankly.

Not speaking. Those small sunken eyes impossible to read. Flicking his hair from his eyes. There were grunts of approval from the others. General agreement that more computer skills were needed. Grumbles about importing high-tech gear being an issue. Morgan said the association had raised it with the minister in charge.

'Dmitry here is helping build a digital Myanmar. And God do we need it,' said Morgan, placing a friendly hand on the Russian's shoulder. 'There's been an absolute explosion in cell phone ownership and internet use. Isn't that so, Dmitry?'

Dmitry just shrugged, barely acknowledging the question.

'Perhaps you have a few tips for a novice in business here,' Drayton said, smiling.

'It's all about having the right product,' the Russian replied blandly.

'Any advice on partners? Good to keep the military sweet, I guess. Avoid any issues.'

'We don't have any issues. We get what we need.'

Then the Chinese man stepped in. He introduced himself as Ken Tsang, from Hong Kong. 'I think the authorities here recognise the importance of what we're doing.'

There were more grunts of approval from around the bar, all agreeing that internet speeds had improved dramatically, especially in Yangon. Then Dmitry said, 'If you'll excuse me,' and left the bar with Ken Tsang close behind him.

Morgan ordered two more drinks, large gin and tonics for him and Drayton, and together they walked towards an open balcony, from which the bustling port of Yangon spread out in front of them. Morgan told Drayton that the club used to be a customs building. That it had been in a terrible state. Literally crumbling, like much of old Yangon, before his business association had bought the place and refurbished it.

'A man of few words your Dmitry Gerasimov,' Drayton said.

'He is a rather inscrutable character.'

They watched cranes unloading a row of cargo ships. A ship's horn reverberated along the quayside, though it was hard to tell whether it signalled an arrival or departure. Ships were lined up, sitting low in the water and waiting for a berth.

'Chinese, mostly,' said Morgan. 'They're pouring money into this place. I thought I'd escaped China, but it turned out to be wishful thinking.'

'The new Great Game. The battle for the wild east. America in retreat,' Drayton said.

Morgan sipped thoughtfully on his gin and tonic. 'I'd say no more than twenty to thirty per cent of the economy is what we might call visible.'

'Legal, you mean?'

Morgan ignored the question and said, 'I take it Chuck that you didn't come all the way here to lecture me about business ethics. What do you want?'

'What more can you tell me about the inscrutable Mr Dmitry Gerasimov?'

'Not a lot, frankly. He's a very private individual and like most of our members, he values discretion. Which of course our association respects.'

'I'm sure you do. All the same I would value a little insight into what makes Mr Gerasimov tick.'

'And how much would you value that insight?'

'It depends, Tony. On the quality of the insight.'

They walked back downstairs and into Morgan's large office, which resembled a craft emporium. Carved wooden elephants and Buddha heads. Traditional musical instruments. Puppets hanging in glass display cabinets. Colourful paper umbrellas. One wall was lined with photos of temples; another was hung with a series of paintings of buffalos wallowing in a river, cleverly drawn so the heads of the animals emerged from the canvas as if they were peeping out of the water.

Morgan locked the door and from from a filing cabinet behind his desk he pulled a small brown file containing Dmitry's membership application from six months earlier. It gave his place and date of birth as Yaroslavl, Russia, the 23rd of August 1980. A space for listing previous business experience and places of residence was blank. He gave as his last residence an address in Kiev, Ukraine. The name of his Myanmar company was given as Digital Futures, with an office address as 50th Street, Yangon. No building number.

Drayton pulled out his cell phone and photographed the page. 'Pretty thin,' he said.

'He pays his dues,' Morgan replied.

'What does 'Digital Futures' do exactly, and with whom?'

Morgan sat behind his desk. 'Exactly, I'm not sure. Broadly, as I said, internet, cell phones.'

'I'd appreciate a bit more digging.'

'Give me a few days, and I'll see what I can do.'

'I don't have a few days. How about twenty-four hours?'

'Leave it with me,' said Morgan, locking the file away. 'And 50th Street is ten minutes' walk from here, if that's what you're thinking.'

* * * * *

The road beside the port was lined with decaying old colonial buildings, some with balconies looking as if they may fall at any moment. Many already had, leaving dark scars in the wall. Some buildings were still in use; others were abandoned, with vegetation growing from open and crumbling windows, colonised by flocks of pigeons.

Away from the port, in old Rangoon, crowded narrow streets were lined with tall tenement blocks, their walls dotted with blue satellite dishes. Washing hanging from windows. Drayton heard singing, possibly from a school and then the muffled chants from a small temple. At street level, there was a mess of food stalls and small shops. The smell of spices.

A group of children followed him down the road, trying to sell him postcards and fading pirated guide books.

Some of the old buildings had been renovated. Others were being demolished. One corner was a construction site, where a soulless new apartment block was taking shape. But he could see nothing that looked like it might house Digital Futures.

Then he spotted a bar next to an e-sports centre at the foot of a newly renovated building. The renovation looked like it had been carried out in a hurry. It seemed to stop just below the top floor, as if they'd run out of paint. Up there, small trees were still growing out of disintegrating windows. There was a sign on a balcony, two storeys up. 'Digital Futures.' Another sign, a fading red billboard right at the top, amid the greenery, said, 'The army and the people cooperate and crush all those harming the union'.

He ordered a beer in the bar below. The place was quiet and bigger than it looked from the street. A tall ceiling with whirling fans. Just five customers. Twenty-somethings he reckoned. Geeky-looking foreigners. Two were playing table football to one side of a long bar that ran down the centre of the place, surrounded by stools. Another sat at one of several tall tables around the edge of the room, working on his laptop. One was in a poorly lit annex, the e-sports section, sitting and staring at one of a line of six gaming computers, wearing headphones. He looked intense. Grimacing. It was hard to tell what he was playing, what evil empire he was trying to destroy or conquer, but it didn't seem to be going well.

The fifth was on his own at a pool table, practising his break. Drayton asked if he wanted a game. He said yes, though with no great enthusiasm and in an accent that Drayton couldn't immediately place. He tidied up the balls in the rack and offered Drayton the first shot.

Drayton only managed to pocket the white cue ball. His opponent then sank five balls, one after the other, knowing his way around a pool table.

Drayton introduced himself as Andreas, a visiting businessman from the US, in the computer business. The guy just said, 'your shot,' and Drayton lined up his cue for another effort. He did hit a ball this time, but well wide of a pocket. The white stayed on the table.

'Where you from?' Drayton asked, trying to sound upbeat and friendly. But his opponent ignored him again, sinking more balls, which left him on the black. It was a tight shot, since the black was surrounded by Drayton's sea of balls. He nominated a pocket at the far end of the table, narrowly missing.

Drayton then sank one ball. A sitter. It would have taken great skill to miss. He stood back from the table, trying to slow things down, saying, 'You must be working for Digital Futures. Doing some good work, I hear.'

'It's still your shot.'

Drayton missed, and his opponent quickly pocketed the black, put his cue back in the rack and left the bar without looking at Drayton or saying another word.

'Great pool player, that guy,' Drayton said to the barman. 'And you know what, I've completely forgotten his name already.'

'Easy to do. That's Grom, he's from Brazil,' said the barman, a young Australian.

'Grom?'

'Yeah. Like the character in *World of Warcraft*. The game. You know, the chieftain. The one who's a really good blademaster.' The barman said all the kids from upstairs have nicknames. 'Some pretty weird ones.'

'Tell me,' Drayton said

'Well, we've got a Phreak, a Bubblegum. Even a Tox. There was a Razor when I first got here.'

All names from Milo's list.

'Ever had a Neo?' Drayton asked.

The barman yelled across at the kid on the laptop, 'Hey Ghoul, you remember some guy called Neo working upstairs?'

Ghoul looked over, not replying. Then he quickly closed his laptop, jumped from his stool and left the bar.

'Whoa. What's bugging him?' the barman said.

'Ghoul. Nice name,' said Drayton. 'Where're they all from?'

'All over. I lose track. Ghoul's Israeli, I think. I've only been here a couple of months, so still getting to know them, which isn't easy.'

'How's that?' Drayton said.

'I guess it's a thing about computer nerds. Not great with the talking.'

'How long's Digital Futures been here? It's just that I never noticed the place or the bar before,' Drayton said.

'Six months or so, as far as I know,' the barman said.

Drayton said thanks. Great bar. That he had to go, but would maybe come back, try his hand at some games, and the barman said he should come Wednesday, the day after tomorrow, which was always a big day for e-games. He said the bar would be busy since they had the new release of *World of Warcraft*, the new extension.

'Hey Ko Win,' he shouted at the kid at the gaming computer in the annex. 'What time are the games Wednesday?' Ko Win ignored the question, never taking his eyes off the screen.

The barman turned back to Drayton. 'It will be around lunchtime, it always is.'

It was dusk when Drayton left the bar.

He looked for a door that might lead to the offices above, but there didn't seem to be one, at least not out front. He followed the dark alley running down one side of the building until it reached an unmarked entrance with a keypad and fingerprint scanner, but then took a sudden step back, startled and for a moment blinded by a spotlight above the door, a motion sensor and surveillance camera alongside it.

He turned his back to face the wall opposite, unzipping his fly. Trying to give an impression of a drunk from the bar who'd come down there to relieve himself.

He heard the door open behind him. He waited, and then turned, making a big show of zipping up his fly, trying to make like he didn't have a care in the world. Drunk happy. The door only opened a few centimetres and Drayton tried not to look at it. Pretended not to notice. But it was impossible not to see the face. The face in the gap, hard and cold, a long scar down one side, and with closely cropped blonde hair. The man was holding the door with one hand, the other on the frame. Big hands. Thick arms. On his right arm, a tattoo, a spider, its legs wrapping around the man's elbow and wrist.

'Needed the bathroom,' said Drayton, waving, and moving back towards the road, trying to sound casual.

The man said nothing. Just stared.

Then he closed the door.

Drayton walked back to the main road, as quickly as he could without breaking into a run. Back to 50th Street. Only when he was well clear did he stop, pausing for breath, sweating heavily in the hot and humid evening air. His shirt was soaked.

He bought a bottle of water from a roadside stall, steadying himself against the wall.

That's when he saw the car. An old Toyota, black with tinted windows, an up-market version, a Crown. It was moving slowly a hundred metres or so behind him.

He turned left into a wider road. The Crown turned left too. And when he entered a side street, the Crown turned in there too. He ducked into a market that lined the road, a maze of narrow alleyways packed with stalls. He squeezed past tables straining under piles of clothes, shoes and bags. Then, deeper inside, bowls of spices, fruit and teas. He passed food stalls selling steaming noodles and tables weighed down with pirated DVDs. It was dark, crowded and loud.

He found another exit. There was no sign of the Crown, so he hailed a taxi and told the driver to take him back to his hotel, turning and scanning the road behind as they drove. The Crown might have been nothing. Probably was. But the face in the door of Digital Futures had shaken him, and his heart was still beating heavily. That might mean nothing too. Most companies employed security, usually pretty thuggish-looking. He felt stupid and angry with himself.

There was an entire colony of mosquitoes in the back of this taxi. A few more joined the feast each time the driver opened the door to spit. Drayton took out his frustration on the insects, and by the time he got back to the hotel, his hands were covered in the speckled remains of squished mosquitoes.

* * * * *

When Morgan arrived at Drayton's hotel early the following afternoon, the American was still in bed asleep. He'd slept solidly for fourteen hours, and when his phone rang, it took him a while to remember where he was.

He found Morgan sitting on a stool at the bar fiddling with a ship's telegraph and drinking a gin and tonic. 'Always loved this stuff,' the Englishman said, pushing the handle of the telegraph forward like he was on the bridge of a ship, sending instructions down to the engine room. Full ahead!

Drayton said the bar had a nautical theme.

'And very good gin,' said Morgan, taking a large sip. 'I charged it to your room. Hope you don't mind. A down payment on the work.'

'What did you find out?'

Morgan didn't answer immediately, telling Drayton that his car almost collided with a bus. 'It's an occupational hazard. You see they all drive on the right here *and* they have steering wheels on the right, so you can't always see what's ahead.'

'I've noticed,' Drayton said.

'They used to drive on the left until a military dictator ordered everybody overnight to switch sides.'

'Why would he do that?'

'Astrologers told him it was luckier. Changed the numbers on banknotes too, so they were all divisible by nine. There was a rumour that he bathed in the blood of dolphins because he thought that would keep him young, and whenever he travelled he had all the stray dogs slaughtered in advance.'

'Were they unlucky too?'

'Especially the ones with crooked tails.'

Morgan paused, pushing again at the ship's telegraph. Then he said, 'Your research is never straightforward Chuck.'

'If it was straightforward, I wouldn't have asked you,' said Drayton. 'Tell me.'

'The building where Digital Futures is based, and a lot of the other property on 50th Street, is owned by the army. Specifically, by the MI, Military Intelligence, which in its day was the most feared part of the junta. Nominally at least, Digital Futures is owned by a son of the MI's second in command, who also owns one of the county's largest cell phone networks and internet service provider.'

'You say, "nominally". What does that mean?'

'It was common during military rule, when the country was under sanctions, for outside investors to hide behind nominees.'

'But sanctions are over. Why do it now?'

'Old habits. Many still like to do business that way. You never quite know what might be around the corner. Keeps things discreet. Especially if your money is not entirely clean, your business slightly dubious, or your partner a little tainted. It also means that Dmitry has a powerful military protection.'

'What precisely do they do in that building that might not be clean?'

'Precisely, I'm not sure. "Systems development", is how Ken Tsang described it when I bumped into him and pressed him a little harder at the club later yesterday. He and Dmitry like to use our facilities for private meetings.'

'And where does Ken Tsang fit in?'

'The money man is my best guess. Talks the talk on cryptocurrencies after a glass or two of champagne. Wanted me to accept it in the club. Fool's game that, if you ask me.'

'Anything else?'

'Yes. It's sensitive.'

'How sensitive?'

'Very sensitive. I approached a good military contact. He was helpful at first. Then stopped returning my calls. When I eventually reached him, he sounded scared. Didn't want to go there.'

Morgan said there were others he was still waiting to hear from, that he'd be in touch if he learned more, though he was going upcountry to a place called Bagan.

'What's happening there?' asked Drayton.

'My association is sponsoring some temple restoration work. There was a lot of damage up country, from the earthquake. Only the chap evaluating the damage dropped dead. Complete bureaucratic pain in the arse. His body and personal effects are still in Bagan. It's been three months now. He wasn't an easy character, to be honest. In fact he was a difficult bugger. String of academic posts, from Oxford to Princetown via all points in between. More respected than liked. There is family, but mostly they don't want to admit to it, especially if it means coming out to Myanmar to sort out the old boy's body. There's a bitter ex-wife. American. She's asked me to deal with it, as his sponsor. Which doesn't exactly thrill me. It's hard to get a straight answer from the authorities up there. That's why I'm having to deal with it in person.'

'Yeah, well, good luck with that,' said Drayton.

After Morgan left the hotel, Drayton went back to his room and logged in to a *World of Warcraft* account that he hadn't used for a while. He'd been a good player in his day, but that was a while back. He needed to get up to speed on the new expansion, if he was going to come close to holding his own at tomorrow's games at the bar beneath Digital Futures. Going back was a risk. He'd drawn attention to himself, asking about Neo. But he figured that his best move now was to win a bit of respect in the gaming chair. Maybe that would get them talking.

It was as addictive as ever. That's the one thing that hadn't changed, and after several hours playing, Drayton couldn't sleep. He dozed on and off until nearly dawn, before falling into a deep sleep. When an eleven o'clock wake-up call came through he ignored it. It repeated five minutes later, and this time he got up.

He'd expected the bar to be busy, but when he arrived the door was locked, and further secured with a heavy chain and padlock. It was dark inside, no sign of life. Chairs stacked up. He knocked on the door and then on the window, but there was no response. He took a few steps back, and saw the Digital Futures sign had been removed.

The keypad and fingerprint scanner were gone from the entrance in the alley, as were the surveillance camera and motion-activated light. The door was slightly ajar. He pushed it open and went inside. He entered a dark corridor leading to a staircase, which he climbed, guided by the torch on his smartphone. A landing led to a large room with big windows overlooking the street. There were a handful of empty tables and some chairs, but everything else had been removed. Cables hung from wall sockets like a snake infestation. A single photograph of a golden temple at night hung at an angle from a whitewashed wall.

Back on the landing, two heavy filing cabinets stood empty. He climbed to a higher floor where a series of smaller offices has also been cleared of everything but bare furniture. Several plastic cups were scattered on the floor, stained with coffee dregs. He checked the desk drawers, all of them empty, the bookshelves too. More redundant computer cables.

Digital Futures had closed down, and it had closed quickly.

He turned to leave, but then stopped, crouching beneath a desk, pulling at something dark buried beneath a pile of plain printer paper. It was a brochure from a tour company with a scooter on the front, driving along one of the remnants of the Berlin Wall. 'Cold War Tours. Cold War Berlin by Scooter'. He folded it and put it in his pocket.

He heard the scrape of a chair behind him and the crunch of a plastic cup underfoot. Then felt something cold around his neck. A power cable, tightening around his throat, dragging him backwards. He could feel hot breath on his neck. He tried to force his fingers under the cable, struggling to breathe. He moved his head just enough to see the spider, the tattoo wrapped around a thick forearm. The cable cut into his fingers. He let go and with all the force he could muster, he thrust his elbows back hard.

The cable grip loosened just enough for Drayton to pull it away from his throat. He stumbled out of the room and down the stairs, pushing over empty filing cabinets behind him. He was in such a blind panic, dazed and still gasping, that he turned the wrong way into the alley, a dead end, a wall blocking his way. The wall was three metres high, and he began to climb a waste pipe that snaked up the side of the building close by. The pipe groaned under his weight, and began to peel away from the decaying bricks. Drayton fell onto a pile of bin bags, which pulsated and split, and he kicked and swiped as rats spilled over his feet, his legs, his stomach.

Then he saw him, the man with the tattoos approaching, silhouetted against the light at the far end of the alley. The pipe falling from the wall had wedged across the narrow alley, making it easier to climb. He scrambled up to the top of the wall and began to pull himself over. Then he felt a vice-like grip around his ankle. He kicked hard with his free foot into the man's face. The grip loosened and he tumbled over the wall and into a pile of bushes on the other side.

He was in the courtyard of an old house; a woman was cooking. She glanced up, then looked back down at her sizzling wok, ignoring him as he limped past. He had no idea where he was, following a series of narrow lanes, sticking to the shadows of the dark crumbling tenements, just wanting to get as far away as possible.

He paused to rest when he reached a broader, busier road. He was exhausted. He leaned against a tree beside the road, not noticing the car until it had stopped beside him. It was the black Toyota Crown. Its rear door swung open, and a voice from inside said, 'Drayton, get in.'

* * * * *

Drayton couldn't have run, even if he'd wanted to. He could barely put one painful foot in front of the other. And the voice was addressing him by name. It was American, it was familiar, and the tone didn't leave much room for discussion.

'So you come all the way to Burma and not a word to your fellow Americans,' said Ric Cullen. 'Bit fucking remiss don't you think, Drayton. Like maybe you've forgotten who you're working for. Forgotten our conversation in Berlin.'

'I'm on holiday,' Drayton said. 'Taking in some temples. Getting a bit of spirituality. You ought to try it some time.'

Cullen pushed Drayton hard against the Crown's window, grabbing a fist-full of shirt, which tightened around Drayton's bruised neck. With the other hand, he poked at dried blood above Drayton's ear.

Drayton could see his battered face reflected in Cullen's wrap-around sunglasses. Below the glasses, Cullen's teeth were clenched, his goatee beard tinged with sweat.

'Let me tell you something Drayton. You've just fucked up again. Good at that aren't you? This time you've fucked up an operation. A big operation. An important operation. You hear what I'm saying?'

Drayton ignored the question. Cullen's grip was so tight he couldn't speak. Then Cullen eased back. He pulled out an envelope from one of the multiple pockets of his short-sleeved khaki jacket and handed it to Drayton. 'It's an airline ticket. The next available flight out. To Bangkok.'

He looked at his watch. 'There's just enough time to call at your hotel, to clean yourself up and collect your stuff. Then we'll take you to the airport.'

Drayton struggled for breath. 'I can take a cab.'

'Burmese roads are dangerous Drayton. We wouldn't want you to get hurt – or miss your flight.'

* * * * *

Cullen watched Drayton check in for the Bangkok flight, and then walked with him to the security check.

'Thanks for the ride,' Drayton said, holding out a hand.

Cullen ignored the hand, drawing in close to Drayton, their heads inches apart. 'You're finished Drayton. You're a serial fuck-up hanging by a thread over a nasty fucking precipice, and I can cut that thread any time I like. If you want to salvage something, then you listen to me, and you listen to me good. You get the fuck out of Asia. Tell Schoenberg any shit you want. And next time I call, I wanna know what that old man's thinking, what he's hearing, what he's seeing and what he's doing. I wanna know it before even he does. From here on, I'm the one telling you how it is.'

As the border guard stamped his passport, Drayton turned to see Cullen still standing, waiting. Drayton waved. Cullen ignored him, only turning and leaving the building once Drayton was through all the formalities.

Drayton sat next to the gate, where he opened his laptop and checked the Berlin Group email account. There were fresh messages in the drafts folder, one from Milo and one from Schoenberg.

As usual, Milo's message took a couple of read-throughs to get what he was saying. It was more from his dark web burrowing. He'd refined his list of hackers, the ones he'd associated with Neo, the ones Neo had parried, bragged and worked with. It now consisted of nine names: Punch, Razor, Grom, Ghoul, Bubblegum, Tox, Phreak, Fisheye and Dim sum. Milo said that six months ago they'd drastically reduced their time in the chatrooms. 'Fisheye and Dim sum are more difficult to read. A bit separate from the main group, but still in touch with Punch. Maybe they went their own way. Loyalties shift all the time in that world. Love and affection one day, hate and abuse the next. And these aren't just regular hackers, they're good, the best.'

He signed off with an apology. 'Sorry, still been unable to match any real names to the handles.'

But Schoenberg had. At least one of them.

His message contained a photograph. Drayton looked at it, long and hard. It was somehow familiar. A young woman with a cold and impatient stare. Her eyes deep blue, her hair shaved on one side and long on the other, coloured a kind of purple. And piercings through her ears, but also her eyebrow, nose and lip. It was the same photograph Schoenberg had showed him during their first meeting in Berlin.

'What does the photograph tell you?' Schoenberg had asked him back then, and Drayton had said she looked confident with plenty of attitude. A rebel. Now the German gave her a name.

'Her hacker handle is Punch, though sometimes she goes by the name Phreak.' He said her real name was Viktorya Shevchenko, though she also used the name Elena Churikova and Vera Solovey. Mostly she was known as Vika, and she was twenty-four years old and Ukrainian. 'Last known location was Kiev, six months ago. Now believed to be in the Far East. Could be key. Find her.'

Six months ago.

That was the common thread.

When a group of elite hackers went off the grid. When Dmitry arrived in Yangon, giving a Kiev address on his application for Morgan's business club. When Digital Futures opened its doors.

And soon after that the Cerberus attacks began.

But it was now irrelevant. Digital Futures had shut down at the first hint of trouble. If Cerberus was Digital Futures and Digital Futures was Dmitry and his merry band of hackers, then they'd now fled. Cullen had a right to be pissed if the CIA was also watching the place.

There was a tinny announcement of a one hour delay to the flight. He fetched a beer and began to compose a message to Schoenberg. 'Dear Wolfgang,' he wrote, but then sat looking at the screen, unsure how to break the news that he'd fucked up the investigation almost as soon as it started. He deleted the draft and closed the laptop.

His phone rang.

It was Anthony Morgan saying he had a question and that he needed a favour.

'Let's start with the question,' Drayton said.

'Can a pacemaker be hacked?'

Drayton didn't reply at first.

'I know it sounds crazy,' Morgan continued. 'I mean, who would hack a medical device? Even if it's possible, which I doubt. They must be the most secure things in the world.'

He paused, and then said, 'Drayton, you still there?'

Drayton stood slowly and looked out of the airport's tall windows. He wiped sweat from his brow, and then said, 'Well, if it's connected. If it's a computer, then of course it can be hacked.'

Morgan said the professor, the archaeologist who'd died in Bagan, had a pacemaker, a new one with lots of bells and whistles enabling his doctors to monitor and tweak it remotely. His ex-wife now wanted to sue the company that made it.

'I thought the ex-wife didn't give a shit about him,' Drayton said.

'She'd doesn't. But she does give a shit about money. She smells cash. Damages. Or at least her lawyers do. The company says there's no evidence of any issue from the data sent by the pacemaker.'

'Nothing's unhackable,' Drayton said. 'But you'll need to get hold of the device itself.' He paused for a moment, and then said, 'What's the favour?'

'Chuck, would you mind going up to Bagan on my behalf?'

Morgan told the American that he had to return urgently to the UK because his son had been involved in an accident while on a school climbing trip. 'He's broken a leg in a couple of places and is badly shaken up.'

When Drayton hesitated, Morgan said, 'I figure you owe me one Chuck. For here. For China too. And you understand computers.'

Drayton said to give him five minutes. He sat thinking, thinking about the faces of the dead in the Mountville Memorial Hospital in Washington DC.

Of course medical devices could be hacked. They had been hacked.

He thought about Cullen, Cullen at the hospital back then, in Berlin and now in Yangon. Cullen threatening him. *You're a serial fuck-up hanging by a thread over a nasty fucking precipice, and I can cut that thread any time I want. If you want to salvage something, then you listen to me, and listen to me good. You get the fuck out of Asia.*

Then he phoned Morgan back and said, 'Sure, Tony. I'll go.'

CHAPTER FOUR

Vika (Punch)

Bagan and Mandalay, Myanmar

Morgan said Bagan was a special place. 'Temples the likes of which you've never seen.' Adding that he'd never actually been there himself. 'Heard about it though. Heard a lot.' Mostly in the air-conditioned comfort of his club. 'Quite a sight.'

But it was dusk by the time Drayton's small aircraft descended through a blanket of cloud, weaving to avoid the worst of the weather. All he could see below was water, the vast muddy greyness of the Irrawaddy River, streaked with sandbanks that resembled the scars on the hide of a battle-hardened rhino. The aircraft bounced and swerved as it touched down, before steadying itself and eventually coming to a standstill on the cracked and pot-holed tarmac.

Drayton's hotel sat on the river bank, a sprawling maze of tired single-storey buildings, each with around a dozen spartan rooms. An envelope was waiting for him on his bed, faxes from Morgan, which he took to a restaurant beside the river, ordered a beer and a local curry, and began to read.

Morgan was nothing if not thorough. There was a sort of power of attorney in English and Burmese, saying that Drayton represented the Yangon International Business Association, and through it the family of Professor Richard Pendleton. Then more biographical detail. He was certainly a big name in the archaeological world. His marriage had broken down a decade ago; the professor had gone on an archaeological dig and never returned.

There were details of the project to catalogue the earthquake damage to the Bagan temples and to support their restoration. Then technical information about the professor's pacemaker, which Drayton skimmed. Pendleton had a heart condition, and had come to Myanmar against the advice of his doctors, who insisted he be fitted with what was described as one of world's most advanced devices. It consisted of two parts; the pacemaker itself and a separate transmitter/receiver to which it was paired. Lawyers for Pendleton's ex-wife wanted to examine both.

Another fax contained the name of the hospital where the body was being kept, and where an autopsy was supposed to have taken place, but had not yet been made available. Then there was a number for the professor's Burmese assistant, a man called Tun Zaw, who'd be expecting to hear from Drayton.

He ordered another Mandalay Beer, a picture of a temple on the label. There was nobody else in the restaurant. He appeared to be the only person staying in the hotel. He texted Tun Zaw, who replied moments later. 'Welcome to Bagan, Mr Chuck. See you in the morning. Nine o'clock outside your hotel.'

Drayton overslept and it was nine-thirty by the time he left the hotel. There didn't appear to be a vehicle waiting. Just some rusting bikes for hire beside a temple of white walls streaked with black stains. Terraces sprouting weeds. There was a horse and cart beside the bike shack. Drayton was about to call Tun Zaw when the driver of the cart started waving his arms and called out for Mr Chuck.

The cart was for him.

He climbed onto a platform behind the driver. The platform had a simple canopy, the floor was covered with a worn layer of cushion, which did little to soften the bumps as it made its way down a rutted and pot-holed path lined with temples, mostly red brick and in various stages of disrepair. Some little more than crumbling walls or piles of brick. White stupas, stained and distorted like rotting pears. He could see why it was such a playground for archaeologists.

A crowd had gathered around a bigger temple, the atmosphere party-like, with stalls selling food and drink. Children chasing each other along the road. Men were breaking stones, swinging heavy hammers, the stones then loaded onto a crude pulley, which took them to the top terrace of the temple to be cemented around a tower.

'They're rebuilding the temple,' said a young man beside the cart. It was Tun Zaw, and that came as a surprise to Drayton. He'd expected someone older. But the person facing him, wearing a traditional blue-checked longyi and white T-shirt, seemed little more than a boy.

'Call me Tom,' said the boy, telling Drayton that the professor was hard of hearing, thought 'Tun' was 'Tom', and the name stuck.

'So this is what the professor was working on? Drayton said.

'Not *this*. Not what these people are doing. The professor hated this. He'd call it monstrous. The destruction of antiquity.'

'How's that?'

'When the professor talked about restoration he believed in returning the temples to their original form, using traditional materials and building techniques. That takes a lot of time and expertise. To the villagers they are living temples, places of worship; they just want to get them functioning again as quickly as possible. The professor never understood that. To him they were all museum pieces.'

Tun Zaw showed Drayton a shrine with a large Buddha statue. The walls were cracked, plaster falling away. He shone the torch from his cell phone at the ceiling to highlight fading Buddha images, intricately painted. Then he moved the beam slightly to show areas of bare red stone, where images had been peeled away, like the skin of an orange. There were several small crevices in the walls, which had once contained carved stone figures of the Buddha. The figures had gone.

'Earthquake damage?' Drayton said.

'Cut away. Stolen. It's a big problem.'

Drayton felt the wall. 'I guess they're worth a lot on international markets.'

'I guess.'

At another temple, this one a large and solid pyramid of red brick, Tun Zaw pointed to the intricately arranged brickwork, which had survived a thousand years of earthquakes, all without the use of mortar. He was enjoying playing the guide. 'It was built during the reign of King Narathu. According to legend, he ordered that bricks should be so tight that not even a pin could be passed between them. Any worker who failed the test had his arms chopped off.'

'And what are they?' asked Drayton, pointing at engravings above a temple entrance.

'Demons. They often used them to guard the entrance of a temple.'

To Drayton, they looked like the heads of dogs. Snarling dogs. And they looked familiar.

'Tell me about the professor,' he said. 'He can't have been an easy person to work with.'

'He lived in his own little world, that's for sure. Didn't have much patience. But he was a good man. And he taught me a lot.'

'Did you notice any change in his behaviour? Towards the end.'

'He was a bit more distracted. A bit more distant.'

'And did he seem unwell to you?'

'Not that I noticed. Nothing that he spoke about. I was surprised when I heard about his heart condition. And very sad.'

Nearby, a tall cell phone tower dwarfed another group of temples. There was a billboard at the foot of the tower advertising the 'super-fast' cellular network, which was also sponsoring sunset balloon rides over the temples.

'You been up in one of those?' Drayton asked.

'Now that would have lost me my job,' Tun Zaw said. 'It was everything the professor hated. The tourism. The commercialisation of Bagan.'

'He thought it was monstrous?'

'Extremely monstrous.'

As if from nowhere, there was an intense downpour so sudden it was as if a switch had been flicked, and they were both soaked by the time they clambered onto the platform beneath the cart's rickety canopy. Steam was rising from the horse's back.

'This is where the professor did most of his work,' Tun Zaw said, when they reached the workshop at the top of the archaeological museum. He unlocked one of the large cupboards, its shelves lined with Buddha heads mounted on smooth four-sided pieces of stone. 'This is where we keep the more valuable pieces or those not currently on display. There are no proper records, especially after the quake. That's what the professor was trying to do.'

Tun Zaw removed one from the cupboard and placed it on a table. There was writing on each of the four faces of the stone. 'They're inscription stones and in this style they can only be found in Bagan. These are around one thousand years old. They were usually placed beside a temple and describe who paid for the building, as well as why they'd done it, and the number of slaves they'd donated for construction. Things like that.'

'And these are valuable?' Drayton said.

'Very valuable, and very rare. Especially the four-sided ones. It's quadrilingual. That means it has four different languages. Mon, Burmese, Pyu and Pali. One on each face. Some of the earliest Burmese language documents that exist.'

To Drayton, they looked like random squiggles. 'The professor could read this?'

'He knew all the languages of ancient Burma.'

'And you?'

'Given enough time. As I said, the professor was a good teacher.'

'He certainly loved his artefacts.'

'Mostly he loved languages. Old languages.'

'Languages? You mean how they're made up? How they emerged? That kind of thing'

'Yes,' Tun Zaw said. 'But especially their power.'

'Power?'

'Yes. Power. In building a temple, a person was not only showing loyalty to the King and to the Buddha, but also his knowledge of not one, but four written languages. It's a statement of power. That's what Professor Pendleton said, that at a time of widespread illiteracy, language is power.'

When Drayton began to fiddle with his cell phone, Tun Zaw told him the strongest Wi-Fi was at the side of the museum, close to a monastery. Or else beside a small military base down the road. 'They have great speeds. Nice café by the base, too, if you've got a lot to download.'

Drayton said the speed at the museum seemed fine to him, and when he asked Tun Zaw how come the monks and the soldiers were so generous in sharing their Wi-Fi, the Burmese boy just shrugged.

'I've got logins and passwords for both if you need them,' he said, as if hacking their routers was the most natural thing in the world.

Mon, Burmese, Pyu and Pali weren't the only languages Tun Zaw had studied. He had learned to find his way around computers and taught himself how to code. He told Drayton he ran a business repairing computers around Bagan. He also sold the credentials for routers to a small but thriving community of young gamers hungry for bandwidth, 'And a few more bits of software to help them win.'

'That's maybe not the best way of using your skills, Tom.' Drayton said.

But Tun Zaw couldn't really see what other way there was. Not in Bagan. He said he was planning to take a proper course, and the professor was supporting him.

'I take it you didn't give him details of your business.'

'The professor didn't understand computers. Hated them. Even his phone. He used to joke that he could master the rituals of old civilisations, but not the digital world. I think he was afraid of it.'

'Pretty good of him to help you with the course. How much did it cost?'

'A thousand dollars. Only he died before he paid. It's a terrible tragedy.'

Drayton said that maybe he could help, contribute something, if Tun Zaw could translate for him at the hospital where the professor's body was being kept. Tun Zaw agreed, and they travelled there together on his spluttering motorbike. It was quicker than the horse and cart, though not by much, and was no more comfortable.

The hospital was a sprawling rundown building. Drayton hesitated as they reached the main entrance.

'You OK, Mr Chuck? It's only a hospital.'

A small reception area was packed with people waiting to see a doctor. Most were women with young sickly looking children. 'Malaria and dengue, mostly,' said Tun Zaw. 'Bad this year because the rains have been longer.'

They were led to a spartan office, where Drayton's documents were studied by an elderly, slightly stooped man in a blue shirt and red-striped longyi. He spoke a few words in Burmese, never looking directly at Drayton or Tun Zaw, before quickly leaving.

'He's the hospital director and he says they don't have any foreigners here, dead or alive,' Tun Zaw said.

They checked Morgan's fax. It was definitely the right hospital, and it named a Doctor Ko Shwe of the pathology department as the contact man for the body and the autopsy.

'Let's find pathology,' Drayton said.

They crossed an internal courtyard, overgrown and scattered with discarded medical equipment. It was surrounded by shabby low-rise buildings, a heavy flow of people between them, most of them looking at Drayton. At least that's how it seemed to him. A piercing scream and then shouting came from an open window above them.

Tun Zaw asked a nurse for Doctor Shwe, and she pointed to a door at the top of a cracked staircase. The door opened before they reached it and a middle-aged man stepped out.

'Doctor Shwe?' said Tun Zaw.

The man looked over, slightly startled.

Tun Zaw handed him the letter, which the doctor read. Taking his time. He glanced at Drayton, but quickly looked away. He began talking in Burmese, which Tun Zaw translated.

'He says Doctor Shwe isn't here.'

'So when will he be back?'

'He says he doesn't know. Maybe he won't be coming back.'

Then Drayton pointed to the name tag on the doctor's coat. It said 'Doctor Ko Shwe,' and it was in English. The doctor spoke a few more words in Burmese. Rapid, nervous words. Then he went back into the office, Doctor Shwe's name on the door, which he locked behind him.

'He says if we don't leave he'll call hospital security.'

Tun Zaw suggested a change of strategy. One that didn't include Drayton. He asked the American to leave, to let him make some enquiries on his own, saying he'd meet him at a coffee shop across the road, by the market.

Tun Zaw joined him there after half an hour. 'You shouldn't think badly of the doctors. They're frightened.'

'Of what?'

'The military ran Burma for a long time. It's hard to shake off the fear, especially for older people. Answering the wrong question. Having opinions. That could get you into trouble. And talking to foreigners. That could be dangerous too. Many worry that the recent changes are not so real.'

'So what did you learn?'

'He says he knows nothing about the autopsy.'

131

'And the body?'

'The body was sent to a temple. I have the name. It's close by.'

'Why did they send it to the temple?'

'It was what his family wanted.'

'But I am his family, for fuck's sake. I mean, I represent his family.'

Tun Zaw just shrugged. 'We can talk to the monks.'

This temple was more modern, a compound containing a small, scruffy office block and several pavilion-like buildings. The compound was empty, the monks escaping the early afternoon heat. A few dogs lay around. One of them stood, though it seemed a struggle. It looked at Drayton, growled and then barked half-heartedly before slumping back down, scratching itself and going back to sleep.

'This monk remembers the professor,' said Tun Zaw, emerging from the office block accompanied by a tall monk wearing a flowing and slightly soiled saffron robe. 'He dealt with the body.'

'That's great. Fantastic,' said Drayton, feeling a surge of relief. Progress at last. 'Where's the body?'

They followed the monk to a raised pavilion, where they climbed to a platform surrounded by a small fence, with a solid-looking cylindrical structure in the centre of it. The structure had a metal table in front, hard up against a big metal hatch.

It looked like a pizza oven.

'That's where they cremated him,' said Tun Zaw.

'They cremated him?' said Drayton. 'Why?'

'Because he was dead,' said Tun Zaw. As if it was obvious.

Drayton took a deep breath and ran a hand through his thick hair, his face reddening with anger and frustration, which he was struggling to contain. He kicked at a dog that had followed them to the platform. It yelped and retreated back down the steps.

The monk spoke some more, Tun Zaw translating, saying the ashes had been scattered in the Irrawaddy River. All as the family wanted. He turned back towards the steps.

'Wait, wait,' said Drayton. 'I am the family. I *am* the fucking family. Or as close as you're gonna get. Ask him about the professor's belongings. What happened to them?'

The monk spoke some more in Burmese.

'He says there was a case and a backpack.'

'And?'

The monk nodded towards the furnace that looked like a pizza oven, then went back down the steps.

'But there must be paperwork,' Drayton shouted after him.

The monk just kept walking, back to his office block, not looking behind him.

Drayton slumped against the small fence. Then he saw the monk again, standing in the shadows close to the entrance to the compound. He was waving some papers.

Drayton and Tun Zaw ran across the yard, and the monk gave the papers to Tun Zaw. They were in Burmese. Tun Zaw talked some more with the monk, and then said to Drayton that it had been a simple Buddhist ceremony. As the family wanted. That ten monks had been involved and it took them twenty minutes.

'And?' said Drayton, getting impatient again. 'Who authorised it? What does the paper say? What is it?'

'It's the bill. Four hundred dollars. For the coffin and the cremation. The family never paid.'

* * * * *

Drayton just wanted to crawl away into some dark corner. Or else find a wall to bang his head against. Tun Zaw suggested lunch, and they bumped back along the pot-holed road into old Bagan. Racing against the rain as dense black clouds advanced from beyond the temples.

Tun Zaw chose a small restaurant in the shadow of another big red-brick temple opposite a small guest house, set slightly back from the street. It was dark and damp, around a dozen wooden tables under a thatched roof, from which hung red decorative umbrellas. The walls were of bamboo, and two big, industrial fans creaked and hummed near a bar.

The place seemed popular with travellers, since most tables were taken by young westerners. Tun Zaw ordered soups and vegetables. Local specialities, he said. Drayton said he needed the bathroom, but stopped before reaching it. Stopped dead in his tracks, staring at a noticeboard covered in photographs.

'It was a great night,' said a young Australian, who introduced himself as the new owner. He said the pictures were from their opening party, a couple of months ago, and he began pointing things out for Drayton. A band that was *awesome*. Dancers that were *phenomenal*. And the booze. *Man*, what a night.

But Drayton was focussed on just one picture. In the foreground was a young traveller, standing and downing an enormous jug of beer, but behind him, almost out of frame, was somebody else. She was sitting alone at a laptop, and the photo caught her looking up ever so slightly, the flash lighting up her blue eyes. But most striking of all was her hair, shaved on one side, long on the other. And purple.

As Drayton bent closer to the photo, the Australian followed his gaze. 'Someone you know?'

'Is she a regular?' said Drayton.

'She used to come from time to time. Striking looking chick, yeah? Just sat there in the corner working mostly, on her computer. But not for a while now. Why?'

'Well, you see, she's my daughter,' said Drayton. 'We were travelling together, but had a bit of an argument. Big falling out actually. You know how these things can be?'

The Australian nodded, like he knew where Drayton was coming from.

'I've been trying to find her. You know, patch things up.'

Tun Zaw had now joined them. 'Your daughter? You never told me. She doesn't look like you.'

'She's got her mother's looks.'

The Australian said he'd ask around, and would get his Burmese staff to do the same. It was a small town. Somebody might know where she'd gone. Drayton said he really appreciated that, and gave his number, Tun Zaw's as well. If anybody knew anything about the girl, they might feel more comfortable telling him. That was one thing he'd learned from the morning.

Tun Zaw dropped Drayton back at his hotel, where he called room service and ordered a beer, the Mandalay brew with the temple on the label – 'The coldest in your fridge, please.' A server brought a lukewarm bottle with a glass of ice. But it was still the most welcome temple he'd seen since he arrived in Bagan. He fell asleep before he finished, a deep sleep. He wasn't sure for how long, but was woken by the ringing of the hotel phone, reception telling him there was somebody waiting to see him, and that it was urgent.

It was Tun Zaw, looking excited, telling Drayton he'd found somebody who might be able to help him find his daughter. Across the muddy road in front of the hotel stood a cart tethered to two large white bullocks with enormous humps. An elderly man wearing a big straw hat was crouched behind them. He glanced at Drayton and then tapped the bullocks with a whip-like stick, urging them forward. The cart began to move.

Tun Zaw fetched his motorbike.

'Get on,' he said. 'The old man wants us to follow him.'

* * * * *

The old man didn't make a lot of sense, at least not at first. He didn't get down from his cart. Just sat there buried under his big hat. He spoke in short mumbled bursts, punctuated by the grunts and snorts of his bullocks. Even Tun Zaw struggled to understand him.

Drayton and Tun Zaw had followed him out of town and down a narrow path to the bank of the Irrawaddy River, where they stopped next to the remains of three small temples and two white bell-shaped stupas, which sat on a raised piece of ground beside the path. The temples had been badly damaged by the earthquake, and a pack of dogs scrapped amid scattered heaps of red bricks.

'The old man says it happened a couple of months ago,' said Tun Zaw, translating. 'He was on his way back from his field, when he passed two people standing at the edge of the path. It was dark, and he didn't see them clearly. As he passed, there was a scream and somebody fell in front of his cart. There was a loud bang. Really loud. His bullocks went crazy and bolted down the riverbank.'

The old man pointed into the distance.

'He was way, way down there before he could bring them under control,' Tun Zaw said.

Drayton slapped at a mosquito that had landed on his neck and kicked at a dog that had come sniffing around his boots. His attention was starting to drift. The old man's story didn't seem to be going anywhere.

Then Tun Zaw said, 'It was only when he came back that he found your daughter. She was in a bad way, losing a lot of blood.'

Drayton took a couple of steps closer. 'Go on,' he said, now a good deal more interested.

'He says that after he calmed his animals he came back to look for some bags that had fallen off his cart. Tools and things like that. That's when he found the girl, lying by the edge of the path, semi-conscious and covered in mud and blood. It was a struggle, but he managed to lift her onto his cart and took her back to his village. His neighbour, the village doctor, treated her. She refused to be taken to hospital.'

Drayton asked about her wounds, and the old man said they were mostly superficial. She'd been lucky. She had some nasty cuts. An arm and thigh had been grazed by bullets. It was messy, but not serious.

'After two weeks she was able to leave,' said Tun Zaw, still translating.

'Who else knows about the girl?' Drayton asked.

'Just a handful of people in the village. She never said much, and they never asked her what happened. It was better that way. They decided to tell nobody.'

Drayton felt the old man's caution and fear. The paranoia that still existed in a country only beginning to emerge from a dark past. Only this time he was grateful for it.

'He says the girl appeared to be worried, agitated at times.'

'Why's that?'

There was a lot of back and forth between the old man and Tun Zaw, as if he was struggling to find the words. Then he raised his hands and made like he was playing a piano. Or maybe at a keyboard.

'Something about a computer?' Drayton said.

And Tun Zaw, said, 'Yes, yes. That's what he's trying to say. Your daughter was upset because she'd lost her computer.'

'Where did she go?' said Drayton.

The old man spoke a few more words, waving his arm towards the river this time.

'Mandalay,' said Tun Zaw. 'She took a boat to Mandalay.'

Then the old man turned to Drayton, the first time he'd addressed him directly.

'He says he hopes you find your daughter. That she was a nice person. He says she has a good heart,' said Tun Zaw.

Then he tapped his bullocks with a long stick and the cart's wooden wheels creaked and began to roll, the cart lurching forward and back along the path, the humps of the bullocks swaying in unison.

Drayton began to descend the steep, muddy bank. It was a long shot. She most likely lost her computer here, running. Trying to stay alive. Maybe it was swept away by the river. Or taken by those trying to kill her.

It was dusk, and the light was fading fast. He used the torch on his smartphone to guide him towards the river, but kept slipping, grabbing at scraggy bushes. The river grew louder, rushing below him. The mud became deeper and he fell, sliding towards the water's edge. He managed to hook his arm around the trunk of what used to be a tree, but had mostly been swept away. It protruded from the mud like the thick arm of a man being sucked under. He hauled himself back up, then began to pick his way slowly back towards the path above.

He slumped to his knees at the top, covered in mud and breathing heavily. Exhausted. Relieved to be away from the river, but angry with himself for being so stupid as to go down there.

Tun Zaw sat beside him. 'Is this what you're looking for?' he asked. He was holding a dark and muddy plastic-like case. It was about the size of a laptop. He said he'd found the case near the top of the bank, trapped under a bush and half buried by mud.

Drayton was too exhausted to speak. He wiped the mud from his hands, and opened the case, which was secured by two clips. It was one of those cases designed to take knocks and a bit of water. But after several weeks? Mud and water had seeped inside, but not as much as he'd feared. When he tried to turn it on, it didn't respond. He closed the case and pulled himself painfully to his feet.

'And Mr Chuck,' said Tun Zaw. 'I've checked the boats. There's one leaving tonight. For Mandalay.'

* * * * *

What Tun Zaw didn't tell Drayton was that the boat to Mandalay had been waiting for two days, sheltering nearby in a bend of the river, the water too high and the current too strong for it to attempt to moor at the small port that served Bagan. That afternoon, the water level eased slightly, and the captain managed to tether his boat to Bagan's rickety wooden pier. He was desperate to leave before the river surged again, ripping him from his mooring.

Drayton had just enough time to write a message for the Berlin Group email account, keeping it brief, sparing the detail. He said he'd located Dmitry and found the office of Digital Futures, but the place had shut down. 'Met a Grom and a

Ghoul in a bar beneath, and I think a Phreak, Bubblegum and a Tox had been there too. Neo even, though I can't be sure. Now up-country, heading to Mandalay on a tip-off, to try and locate the hacker called Punch. Will tell you more when I can.' He saved it to the drafts folder along with a copy of Dmitry's application form from the Yangon International Business Club.

He never mentioned Cullen.

It took a while for Drayton to spot the boat, since it sat so low in the water, a dark brooding shadow, straining at its ropes. Tun Zaw helped him across the muddy quagmire of a path to the pier, over a narrow wooden gangplank, and onto the slippery deck.

'I hope you find your daughter,' Tun Zaw said. 'Family's important.'

Drayton offered a hundred dollars towards the computer course. The Burmese boy refused the money, saying it was the least he could do, to help Drayton, to help the professor, who was a good man. And anyway, five hundred would be better. Drayton gave him three.

'Keep in touch,' Drayton said. 'Tell me if you learn more, then maybe I can help some more.'

The boat described itself as the Irrawaddy Super-Deluxe Express. It spluttered to life, then struggled to get up to speed, straining as it fought against the current. The sky was low and dark, without moon or stars. The water was pitch-black, just one vast empty expanse. Drayton could see no other traffic. The only light came from beyond the distant bank, where thick storm clouds flickered with lightning, the thunder drowned out by the boat's thumping, straining engine.

He was one of only three passengers, the others a pair of young European backpackers who'd gone ethnic, with plaited

140

hair and local dress. They sat on the fading canvas seats of an airless passenger compartment that reeked of oil and stale tobacco, holding each other close.

Drayton remained on deck, where a young Burmese boy stood beside him, looking up from a game he was playing on his cell phone. He name was Zeya and he told Drayton the boat was taking the safest course, hugging the shore, where there was less current. He said the shifting sand banks made the Irrawaddy especially treacherous at this time of year. That, and the wrecks. There were a lot of wrecks. But he said his father, the captain, knew the river well.

Drayton glanced at the captain. He was on his smartphone, scrolling with his left hand, while resting his right on top of the wheel, looking up from time to time, making small adjustments to the wheel and then returning to the phone. The boat was a family business. Zeya's mother was sitting on a tall stool beside her husband. She was playing on her phone too, some game that made lots of pinging sounds. A sister was sleeping, her phone still in her hand.

'We're the only boat making the journey at this time of year, and we don't get too many passengers,' Zeya said, which came as no great surprise to Drayton. Drayton asked about Punch, showing Zeya the photograph on his cell phone, but thinking it was still a bit of a long shot.

The boy smiled. 'Sure. Hard to forget. Looking like that.'

He said she looked like a character out of one of his video games. 'She borrowed my phone. To play some games, since she'd lost her own. The scores she got. She was incredible.'

'I can believe that,' said Drayton. 'She's always been good on computers.'

They passed beneath a metal bridge, so wide that Drayton couldn't see where it ended on the far shore. The near side was dotted with the silhouettes of yet more temples. Temples and cell phone towers. Both reaching to the heavens. Drayton pointed to a particularly tall bell-shaped pagoda, towering over their boat. 'I guess they bring a bit of spiritual comfort during these rainy months.'

'Mostly they bring Facebook,' replied Zeya, thinking Drayton was talking about the cell phone towers. He said there was now connectivity right along the Irrawaddy. 'It's changed our lives here.'

Then he looked again at the photograph on Drayton's phone. 'She cheats, though. When she plays video games. Knows how to break the rules.'

'I can believe that too, Zeya. She's not a big one for rules.'

Drayton found a power socket in the passenger compartment for Punch's muddy computer, to see if he could get any life out of it. Then he lay along a row of empty seats. The boat engine had settled into a smoother rhythm. It no longer felt like it was gasping for life and might pack up at any moment. He immediately fell asleep.

He wasn't sure how long he slept, but he was woken some hours later by yelps, moans and whimpering, and they definitely weren't coming from the engine. The backpackers were making out a few rows ahead of him. They were whimpering in English, and within a few sleepless minutes he felt he knew them intimately. That the one called Andrew was so, so good. So good. And Lisa baby was a special baby. So special.

On the deck, the wife of the captain was making breakfast, popping bread in and out of a rusting toaster. Sugary marmalade on the side. And for Drayton in that place at that moment, that was special. So special.

To his surprise, Punch's laptop powered up, showing him a log-in screen demanding a user name and password. He closed it down again. It was almost certainly encrypted and set to erase all data after a set number of failed attempts. She was a hacker, after all. He'd need more time to get into it.

The horizon began to glow, the rising sun breaking through the thick grey cloud. The water glistening. There was more traffic on the river now, barges mainly, laden with logs, and sitting so low that they looked like they might disappear beneath the surface at any time. Small chugging fishing boats clung precariously to the shore. The river looked deceptively calm, though there was a lot of debris.

A hill beside the river came alive as it was hit by the first rays of sunlight. It was dotted with golden temples, a towering bell-shaped pagoda at its peak. There were so many that the whole hillside seemed to glow. It was so bright that for a moment Drayton had to shield his eyes.

'What is that place?' Drayton asked Zeya.

'Sagaing, south of Mandalay. 'It's a special place.'

'Why's that?'

'There are many monasteries and places to meditate at that place. A Buddhist university too. Many foreigners go to study there.'

Then he turned to Drayton and said, 'Funny. The girl asked about that place too. What it was. And how she could get there.'

* * * * *

The road to Mandalay. To Drayton, it had an exotic ring to it. But not the highway that led from the port, which had a drab, temporary feel to it. All egg-box buildings, tied together by a jumble of power lines and neon signs.

His taxi driver was an uncle of Zeya, the boat boy. It was the same car Zeya had arranged for the girl. Another old Toyota with worn, sagging seats and a steering wheel on the wrong side. Air fresheners hung from every available crack, delivering a sickly lemony stench, but one that kept the mosquitoes at bay. Drayton asked the driver to take him to the same place he'd taken the girl.

The taxi followed the Irrawaddy River, though it was impossible to tell where the river ended and the land began, since the adjoining fields and villages were all flooded. The road ran along the top of a flood bank, lined with makeshift shelters of wood and tarpaulin, temporary places for those driven from their homes by the flood waters.

They crossed the Irrawaddy on a long, low metal bridge that seemed to creak and groan under the weight of traffic, and into Sagaing, the driver mumbling some kind of Buddhist incantations, taking his cue from a programme on the crackling car radio.

The temples looked even more impressive close-up, white stupas, golden pavilions and pagodas dotting the thickly wooded hillside above. Saffron-robed monks and nuns in long pink gowns shuffled along the cracked sidewalk near a monastery at the foot of the hill.

'Here,' the driver said. 'She got out here.'

A series of low white-walled buildings surrounding a courtyard, where groups of mostly young women with shaved heads and dressed in pink, moved between classrooms, huddling in groups under wide umbrellas, sheltering from heavy drizzle. Beyond the courtyard, squat pavilions and dormitories, freshly washed saffron robes hanging over balconies, the steady chanting of monks from some distant corner of the complex. But nobody had heard or seen anything of the young woman described by Drayton.

It was the same at three other monasteries. He found foreigners, devoutly meditating or blissfully stoned, it was usually hard to tell, but no Punch.

His frustration was intensified by hunger and thirst. The driver said he knew a place, further up the hill, a clutter of roadside food stalls, where they could take a break.

And that's where he almost bumped into her. A nun dressed in pink, her head shaven, leaving one of the stalls. There was something in the way she moved, without too much grace, and with plenty of attitude, carrying a plastic bag containing a coconut with a straw. When she looked at him, he was in no doubt. The piercing blue eyes, the holes in her ears and nose, where studs and rings used to be. They stood for a moment face to face. Then she looked away, quickening her pace to a motorbike, and drove away, further uphill.

Drayton raced back to his taxi, yelling to follow the motorbike. The driver kept on scooping noodles from a plastic box, not liking the interruption.

'The bike. That bike. The nun. Follow. Follow. Go. Go. Up there.'

The road climbed steeply before petering out where a footpath began, steep steps towards the peak. He'd lost her, she must have turned off the road. She'd been right there in front of him, but he'd let her slip away. Then he saw the bikes, several of them parked at the foot of the steps. They all looked the same, apart from one. A bag with a coconut was hanging from the handle bar. In her rush to get away she'd left her drink.

Drayton put the bag with the girl's computer around his neck and began to climb the steps. A monk ordered him to remove his socks and shoes, which made for hard going, since the tiles were wet and slippery from the drizzle, the brick cutting into his bare feet. Overgrown pavilions and prayer rooms dominated by big Buddha statues stood near the peak. The higher he climbed, the more deserted they became, a private rendezvous for kids looking for time alone. A couple

145

making out under the watchful eye of a dozen Buddha statues hastily tidied their dishevelled clothes as he passed.

He'd reached the top.

Another path, rough and muddy, led back down the other side of the hill. The rain was heavier now, but he could still hear distant chanting below. He put his shoes back on and followed the path until it reached another, smaller, pavilion to one side of the path, where he paused for breath, angry with himself for not bringing drinking water. But mostly for letting her get away.

A dog eyed him warily and then got to its feet, the three that were functioning, dragging along the fourth, which was more like a paddle. Crushed, maybe by a car. It was in a hurry to leave, seeing what was coming well before Drayton. The flash of pink, the swift and violent swinging of a leg, and a high-pitched scream that echoed around the pavilion. Then the intense pain to his ribs, the blow throwing him to the ground beside the pavilion's low wall. Then another scream and another blow, this time to his head.

He lay, stunned and winded, his vision blurry, the fuzzy pink blob coming slowly into focus. Her arms were raised, boxer style, readying for another blow. Wild eyes, like a cornered animal, only it was he who was at her mercy.

He raised himself to his knees, fumbling as he took the computer bag from around his neck, holding it out, like an offering. As if it were a piece of red meat to distract an angry and hungry predator.

'It's yours. Take it. Take it,' he said, pleading. 'I'm not here to hurt you. The old man. The bullock cart. The man who saved you. He told me you were here. Do you think I'd have brought this to you if I meant you harm?'

She watched him with those piercing blue eyes. Her fists moving rhythmically. She was swaying. Shifting her weight from foot to foot, readying those deadly weapons. She moved forward abruptly, snatching the computer. Drayton fell backwards and over the wall, rolling down the steep embankment. A tree broke his fall, and he forced himself to his feet and began to run. The mud and loose stones of the hillside gave way beneath him, and it was like he was surfing, sliding down the slope, gripping trees and bushes in a frantic effort to slow his descent until he reached the road below. He slumped painfully against the wall of a small roadside shrine.

The dog with the paddle for a leg sauntered into the shrine beside him, rolled itself into a ball and went back to sleep.

* *.* * *

Drayton woke several hours later in a flea-pit of a hotel. His ribs and his head ached, and his face, arms and legs were covered in scratches. The hotel was owned by another uncle of Zeya, the boat boy, and Drayton only vaguely remembered being helped there by uncle number one, the taxi driver.

It was painful to open his eyes at first. They were encrusted with dirt and dried blood. And then the sudden light. The room's flimsy, ripped curtains were worse than useless at keeping it out. His eyes came into focus on the mosquito net above him, over the bed, and then on a bloated blob of a mosquito. It was *inside* the net. And it was so fat it couldn't move. When Drayton flicked it, the thing exploded, leaving a dark red splodge on the net. His blood.

Then he noticed the smell. The pungent smell of a cheroot, which he assumed was coming from outside. The window must be open. He pulled back the net, steeling himself to get up, but froze because he had another visitor, this one the other side of the net. The hacker called Punch was sitting in her nun's pink robe at the end of his bed, smoking, a cheroot between her fingers, watching him.

The first thing she said was, 'What the fuck are you? Spy, cop, hacker, or something else?'

'Well you tell me,' said Drayton, since she had his passports in her hand, his original American one, and the German one in the name of Andreas Fischer. His laptop was open on the desk beside her.

'You know the most common and stupid passwords are names of partners or pets. Frequently with their year of birth. "Anna1984" is really not smart. You were pictured in the art pages of the *Berliner Morganpost*. Gallery owner Anna Schultz and her partner Chuck Drayton at the opening of an exhibition, "Data as Art". And this Anna Schultz is very active on social media, and makes no effort to mask her date of birth. You're an ex-diplomat, without a particularly distinguished career. A cybercrime specialist – though I find *that* so fucking hard to get my brain round. And do you know how long it took me to find this out? About *two* minutes. Your life's online, Drayton. Never forget that.'

She paused for a drag on the cheroot. He was surprised by her accent. Good, confident mid-Atlantic English, with only a hint of East Europe. But plenty of sarcasm, enjoying putting Drayton in his place.

'You communicate by using a shared email account as a digital dead letter box, saving everything to drafts, never sending. Smart, if a little retro. But you have allowed your computer to auto-save your login and password. Very stupid.'

She scratched her shaven head. Drayton watching her through the gap in his mosquito net. This woman. This hacker, who'd broken into his computer and read it as if was a public noticeboard.

'Your IP address is exposed. Which means that so is your location. I've installed a VPN to mask your address, and a different browser. Tor, the onion browser. Nobody with even a passing concern with privacy should be using Google, for fuck's sake.'

Dayton took a swing at a passing mosquito, trying to sneak in under his net.

'These are the basics, Drayton. Call yourself a cyber guy? The way I accessed your computer, that wasn't even hacking. It was walking in through an open door.'

'Well, that's me covered,' Drayton said, trying to make light of it. 'Why don't we talk about Viktorya Shevchenko? Or is it Elena Churikova? Or Vera Solovey? Maybe even Punch?

When she didn't answer immediately, he said, 'I like Punch. That kinda works for me. Who and what is she, and what brings her to Myanmar?'

'Vika will do. And maybe I'm on holiday, taking in the temples. Meditating. Looking for enlightenment.'

'And boxing. Thai-style. Where did you learn that?'

'It helps me relax.'

She picked up one of his shoes and threw it hard across the room towards the bathroom door, where a rat was watching them from a hole in the wall. She missed, and the rat glanced across the room before nonchalantly backing away.

'Shit, she said. 'I was a pretty good shot at the monastery.'

'Who were you hiding from, Vika? Who tried to kill you?'

She ignored the question, opening the window to clear the smoke from the cheroot, which hung like a thick fog. The room filled with the sound of car horns and shouting from the road below.

'Where's Dmitry?' Drayton asked.

'If I knew that, do you think I'd be here, sitting in your room, at the end of your bed, chasing away your fucking rats? Get your arse out of bed, Drayton. Clean yourself up. We have work to do.'

'*We?*' said Drayton, almost falling off the bed, and giving up his pursuit of another mosquito.

'Yes. *We* Drayton. Because you know what? On your own you're never going to find Dmitry.'

She paused, crushing the remains of her cheroot on the floor.

'And another thing. As far as Dmitry's concerned, I'm dead. That's a very useful asset.'

* * * * *

Vika was giving very little away. She was cautious, cryptic even, weighing her words. She had the paranoia of a hacker, for whom trust never comes easily. She'd made a fool of him over the security of his computer. Rightly so. They were idiotic lapses. She'd hacked his computer and read his messages. She had the upper hand and she knew it, so did he.

'Don't flatter yourself, Drayton. Your poking around in Yangon might have made Dmitry shut down quicker, but that was always his plan, to get out just as soon as he had what he needed.'

'And what did he need, Vika? What's he now got?'

She ignored the question, watching as he got dressed, pulling on a clean pair of cargo shorts and a blue T-shirt.

'There was a new message in the drafts folder of the shared email account, from Wolfgang Schoenberg,' she said, taping his laptop. 'It was short. He says, "Find the girl." So well done on that one. Top marks.'

'Can I see?'

She closed the laptop.

A chorus of tapping, rapid and discordant, drifted in through the open window, together with a loud-pitched screeching noise that came and went. Drayton thought it must be a motor workshop, knocking cars back into shape, but it seemed too intense for that, unless the garage had been highjacked by a million woodpeckers. And in any case, Burmese drivers wore their dents with pride.

The woodpeckers turned out to be carvers, their workshops lining the narrow roads around the hotel, working on slabs of stone, chiselling and then sanding them until they took the shape of the Buddha. Through the thick dust, Drayton could see dozens of completed figures at the back of each workshop. Some were just a few centimetres tall, others towered several metres. He picked up a small jade carving, close to where a woman sat cross-legged sanding a statue that lay across her waist, a mottled brown dog asleep beside her.

Vika told him to wait while she entered a monastery behind the workshops. A crowd had gathered close to the monastery entrance, where the wall was plastered with pictures printed from the internet, images of dismembered and burned bodies, burning villages, a monk with a bloodied face lying on the ground. Another showed the head of a pig superimposed on the body of a Muslim cleric. The captions below were in Burmese, but Drayton didn't need a translation to feel the hatred. It was written in the faces of the crowd. He backed away, and then Vika was at his side again, a rucksack over her shoulder.

'You'll find this kind of stuff everywhere,' she said. 'Most are fake, claiming to show Muslim violence against Buddhists. Usually it's the other way round.'

'How do you know that?'

151

'Because this is one of the services provided by Digital Futures. It's how Dmitry paid the rent. How do you think he got army protection?'

'So he ran a troll farm?'

'Sure, a zillion fake social media accounts spewing digital poison, spreading like wildfire. But much more than that. Hacking, spying on demand for the military. Human rights groups, journalists, even the UN.'

'Deep fakes. Fabricating interviews using face and voice recognition?' Drayton asked, remembering the UN woman on his flight to Yangon. 'Was that a speciality too?'

Vika shrugged. 'You know what? The monks are pretty good at spreading hate all by themselves. The head monk at my monastery said that to be a better Buddhist, we should have compassion for mosquitoes, put ourselves in their place. But not Muslims.'

She led Drayton away from the monastery. 'We need Wi-Fi,' she said.

They sat in the quiet corner of a coffee shop popular with travellers. It had the kind of overcool vibe that Drayton usually tried to avoid, but the coffee was good.

'And what else did you do at Digital Futures?' Drayton asked, talking to the top of her head as she worked the keyboard of her resurrected laptop.

'What didn't we do,' Vika replied, not looking up.

'Razor, Grom, Ghoul, Tox, Fisheye, Bubblegum, Dim sum.' Drayton slowly recited the hacker names, at least those he could remember, from Milo's list. 'Hackers. Among the best. Friends of yours?'

When she didn't reply, he slowly pushed shut her laptop, emphatic enough to get her attention, but not hard enough to provoke her. He knew where that could lead.

'And Neo. The hacker handle of one James Timothy Edwards, from London. He didn't have your luck, Vika. Or the weapons you call legs. He was in Berlin. Looking to invest his Bitcoins. To cash out. We were watching him. And maybe Dmitry was too. Because you know what? He took a dive from the sixth floor of a Kreuzberg squat. Made a real mess of the sidewalk.'

She looked up slowly. If she recognised the name, she didn't show it. Just sat, sipping her coffee, saying nothing. She looked beyond Drayton, towards the road, and began to squeeze one of her ears between a finger and thumb, pulling at the pierced lobe. With her other hand she put the coffee cup back on the table. Was her hand shaking, ever so slightly? It was hard for Drayton to tell. But the news about Neo seemed to have pierced that cold veneer.

'What were you doing in Bagan, Vika?'

Then, when she didn't answer, Drayton said, 'Let me tell you what I think. You hacked Richard Pendleton's pacemaker. You were controlling him, holding him hostage. But why? Why would you do that?'

She leaned forward, slowly bringing her face close to his. 'Maybe Dmitry likes Buddhas.'

'Enough to kill for?'

She snapped the laptop shut and rose angrily to her feet. 'Do you think I had a choice, Drayton? You think I had a fucking choice?'

'You don't look like the sort of person who likes to do as she's told, Vika.'

'Well, maybe that's why Dmitry tried to terminate my contract.'

She moved towards the door, and then turned back to Drayton. 'I tried to save him. I tried to fucking save him.' Then she stormed out to the street.

Drayton followed her, but by the time he was out front, she was gone. He followed one narrow street until it reached another, and then another, all looking the same. It took him an hour to reach his hotel, even then he nearly missed it, the place looking a little different from the other buildings lining the street.

'Mr Day-toon. Mr Day-toon,' came the calls from the two uncles, shouting and badly mangling his name, when they spotted him passing.

The first thing he noticed when he entered his room was the smell. A kind of incense this time. Then he saw something glowing like blue touch paper beside his bed. A mosquito coil.

'You've got a serious mosquito problem, Drayton. What kept you?' Vika was sitting on his bed, under his mosquito net. She had her computer open in her lap. 'Razor,' she said. 'Razor could lead us to Dmitry.'

Drayton pulled back the net. 'And how's Razor gonna do that?'

She said Dmitry had sold a package of surveillance tools to the Thai military government, so they could keep tabs on their opponents. It was a standard off-the-shelf package he'd sold to several clients, some government, some corporate, to take control of opposition computers and smartphones, to track and listen to them, read all their stuff.

'It all went fine at first, but the Thais wanted more, including voice and face recognition tools. So that the surveillance could be far better targeted. They claimed Dmitry had given them second-rate kit. So he sent Razor to Bangkok to give them an upgrade.'

'So who exactly is this Razor who does spyware upgrades?' Drayton asked.

'Razor's the handle of a British hacker called Matt Dobberman. Brilliant. An obsessive and a creep, but one of Dmitry's favourites. The Thais kidnapped him, put him under house arrest and refused to let him leave until he upgraded the tools to the spec they wanted.'

'Why a creep?' Drayton asked.

'I didn't like his browsing habits.'

'Which are?'

'Use your imagination, Drayton,' she said, a look of revulsion on her face. 'And he was sloppy, very sloppy.'

She took a sip of water from a plastic bottle beside the bed.

'Dmitry told everybody to keep a low digital profile, to take care even with dark web forums. And no social media. But Razor didn't seem to care. He was good, one of the best, and Dmitry needed him. They were close. And he may still be in Bangkok. The Thais aren't going to let him go anywhere until they've got their upgrade, and my guess is that he's still in touch with Dmitry. He'll know how to find him.'

An Instagram account in the name of MadDog, an ugly mutt for a profile picture, a play on Dobberman's name, was open on her screen.

Drayton climbed onto the bed beside her, so they were both looking at the screen.

'It's a long shot,' she said.

Most of the posts were old. Well before Razor had come to Asia.

Then Drayton said, 'Hey, hang on. What's that?'

He was pointing at a photograph with a backdrop of a wild sky, a big storm. In the foreground, wind and rain lashed a small food stall in which two women sat using upside down woks for rain hats. It was a good photo, simply captioned 'Downpour in Asia'. But Drayton and Vika weren't looking at the photo, but at the date it was taken. Just one week ago.

'He's still there,' she said, raising her hands in triumph. 'Yes! The creep's still in Thailand.'

She clicked on a line of squiggly Thai words above the picture and just below the account name MadDog and the profile picture of the dog. A map opened with a locator in a narrow street in downtown Bangkok.

'I don't believe it,' Drayton said. 'He hasn't switched off his location data.'

'I told you he was sloppy,' Vika said.

* * * * *

Vika left for Bangkok ahead of Drayton, saying they should travel separately. When he asked where they should meet and how they'd keep in touch, she just said, 'Don't worry, Day-toon,' parodying the way the uncles mangled his name. 'I'll find you.'

Drayton spent much of the next day and a half clinging to the toilet. Praying to that porcelain god. The sickness hadn't crept up on him, it had hit him with the force of Vika's formidable legs. At least that's how it felt. When he wasn't sitting on the toilet, he had his head down it. The pain in his guts came in agonising convulsions. He was dizzy, his head ached, and he was soaked with so much sweat that he felt like he was melting.

Most likely it was something he'd eaten. Or maybe something spread by that gluttonous mosquito he'd found inside his net. Now he didn't even have that shelter. He was curled up on the toilet floor, terrified that if he left the room, he'd never make it back in time. He pawed pathetically at passing mosquitoes.

When he saw the rat poking its head out of the hole near the door, looking at him, he was sure it was smirking. He tried to yell, not having any ammunition at hand, but the yell came out as more of a muted moan. The rat didn't look impressed, but left anyway. Maybe the stench and mess of the toilet was too bad even for rats.

Drayton stuffed the rat hole with wet toilet paper.

Uncle number two was sympathetic in an amused sort of way, and brought Mr Day-toon some water with a noxious potion that he drank, but then immediately threw back up. He found some antibiotics in his medical kit, and some other anti-diarrhoea tablets. He took both. Then when the convulsions began to lessen, he crawled back to his bed, secured the mosquito net and slept. He was out for fourteen hours solid. Maybe more. And when he woke he felt better, but drained.

He powered up his laptop and was surprised to find a message from Anna. She said she was sorry they hadn't been able to meet at the Berlin coffee shop that night. That it would have been good to talk, to explain why she felt she needed to move out. She said she hoped they could meet when he got back from his trip. That in the meantime things were going really well for her. That Efren Bell had asked her to help with some projects. And wasn't that simply amazing? There were then a whole bunch of exclamation marks and smiley faces.

He deleted the message. He'd been enjoying it up to the bit about Efren Bell.

Then he went to log in to the Berlin Group's shared email account. It rejected his credentials. He tried again, and was rejected again. A third time too. The password had been changed. Vika had locked him out.

CHAPTER FIVE

Razor (the Creep)

Bangkok, Thailand

Drayton was four days behind Vika by the time he left Mandalay for Bangkok, without a clue how to find her.

But she knew how to find him.

As he exited the aircraft in the Thai capital, he was greeted by a woman in a tight purple skirt and jacket, a big orchid in her carefully set hair, standing with a board in her hand with the words, 'Siam Pro-Golf International' and the name Chuck Day-toon.

'Mr Day-toon?' she said. 'This way please.' She led him to a little electric buggy. 'We can use the VIP channel.'

The buggy zig-zagged down long airport corridors, around groups of languid holidaymakers on their long trek to immigration. The orchid woman took Drayton's passport to be stamped. He gave her his American one, in his own name.

A big BMW was waiting for him outside. She held open the rear door for him and wished him well with the tournament. 'I bet you've got quite a handicap,' she said, smiling.

'Yeah,' he said. 'Tell me about it.'

She handed him a brown envelope as he climbed into the car. 'This is from your agent.' she said.

The envelope contained an old Nokia phone, which was clean, with no record of calls or messages and no contacts. He'd have to wait for Vika to call him. The limo dropped him outside a tower of glass and steel, a concierge welcoming him with another smile, 'Please sir. This way to reception.' A bell-hop took his bag, 'If you'll allow me, sir.' A cold face towel was dangled in front of him. The lobby was all wood? and marble, with fierce air conditioning. Modern art on the walls, but mostly stylised elephants and Buddhas. Big mirrors alongside them. A cold drink waiting at check-in. 'How are you? And how was the journey?'

Only they could find no reservation for a Day-toon, or even a Drayton.

'I'm afraid we don't seem to have any record of you,' the check-in girl said.

Then the old Nokia rang.

'So you made it,' said Vika, giving him instructions about how to get to another hotel. The one where she was staying. And where Drayton would be too.

'Get real,' she said. 'You think I'd book a place like that.'

'I kinda got my hopes up.'

He followed her instructions, taking a series of back streets. He arrived at a group of food stalls with yellow plastic stools and tables, food sizzling in big spitting woks. It looked familiar, except the big women at the stall were cooking in the woks and not wearing them, as they had been in Dobberman's Instagram photograph.

The smell of spice was so powerful it stung his nose.

A narrow alleyway led to something called 'The Best Guest House', a four-storey place painted in garish red, a boutique experience according to a plaque beside the door. He crossed a small carpeted lobby. There was no elevator, so he climbed the stairs to the top floor.

Vika had taken a corner room, windows on two sides. Two queen-sized beds. It wasn't like the place around the corner. No way. But a good deal better than Mandalay.

'Nice to see you,' she said, opening the door, no longer a nun.

She was wearing blue jeans with designer rips and a white T-shirt. The rings and studs were back in in her ears, eyebrow, nose and lip. The shaved nun's head giving way to a carpet of blonde stubble. 'What took you so long?' she asked.

He tapped his stomach. 'I was hugging the toilet.'

Vika wrinkled her nose in disgust.

'Thanks for organising the ride,' Drayton said. 'I was kinda looking forward to the golf. How did you arrange that?'

'Trade secrets. But it's not difficult to access airline passenger lists. And there is a big golf tournament coming up. The organisers have lousy security on their website. Even worse on their database. So I entered you for the competition. I had great fun with your bio. Day-toon is now one of the world's greatest golf players. And they had VIP transfer from the airport.'

He said he'd never been so sick as in those last days in Mandalay, that on the very last day he'd woke up with two large cockroaches in his bed.

'Well, we all make mistakes Drayton,' she replied, having a laugh at his expense. Drayton laughed too. It was pretty funny. She was loosening up, and that was good. But then he remembered the email account.

'So you locked me out,' he said, no longer smiling.

'I changed the shared password. Basic security, Drayton. And don't worry, there's been nothing urgent. I sent a short note to Schoenberg saying you'd found me, together with the new password. Or rather you sent it.'

Drayton threw his bag hard onto one of the beds. 'We have to trust each other,' he said, but realised immediately how stupid that must sound. In cyberspace, trust died a long time ago. 'What else have I told him?'

'That's about it. He replied pretty quickly. Just a short note. A man of few words, Herr Schoenberg.'

'Saying what?'

'Saying, "Stick with the girl." So top marks again Drayton.'

She handed him a pair of binoculars and pointed down the street to a compound surrounded by high walls topped with embedded glass, the wall broken only by a security post beside a big metal gate. In the middle of the compound, two squat wooden houses were surrounded by tall trees, a pair of satellite dishes to one side.

'That's where the creep's under house arrest,' she said.

'We need to access his laptop,' Drayton said. 'Something that seems to come naturally to you.'

'Forget it,' she replied, ignoring the sarcasm. 'He always leaves it in the compound, and getting into that place would be tough. Security is tight. And even if we did get in, we'd need to get to the laptop while it's awake. That's maybe a one minute window, depending on his settings. As soon as it goes back to sleep, it's locked. Enter a password incorrectly three times and all data is deleted. And in any case, his files will be encrypted. It's basic stuff. Standard security.'

'How do we know that? Look at his Instagram account. The location settings. That was stupid security. Suppose he's just as sloppy on his laptop.'

'I doubt that. And anyway, it's not worth the risk. Believe me, Drayton. Accessing his laptop will be a whole lot tougher.'

She paused, taking the field glasses back from Drayton.

Then she said, 'We need to go after his phone.'

She had a plan, which she began to outline as Drayton angrily paced the room. She'd thought it all through. What she was suggesting was risky, but he had to admit that it made a lot of sense.

The plan was good. Very good.

* * * * *

It was well after dark when Vika's laptop made a loud claxon sound, like a submarine about to dive. The screen came alive to show two large video windows, each displaying a black and white image. One of a yard, the other a road.

'The creep's on the move,' she said, throwing a pillow at Drayton, who was sleeping on one of the room's two queen-sized beds.

Drayton joined her in front of the computer, still sleepy. It took him a while to realise what he was looking at. The images were from two surveillance cameras above the gate of the house where Dobberman was being kept. One was pointing at the compound; the other gave an outside view. Both had been hacked by Vika. As had a motion detector, which triggered lights on the gate – and also the alarm on the laptop.

Two figures crossed the compound.

'That's him,' Vika said, pointing to the shorter of the two men. Short and dumpy. Though it was hard to see too much detail in the grainy video image. The other man was taller and leaner. Vika said he was a cop. The creep's minder, who'd usually stay with him for part of the evening.

'He also wears an electronic tag on his right ankle,' she said. 'So they can keep tabs on him when he's out on his own.' It was a simple GPS tracker. And she'd hacked that too.

Dobberman and the cop left the first screen, and then appeared on the second, beyond the sliding electric gate, the image showing their backs this time, as they walked up the road, away from the compound.

'Get yourself ready, Drayton,' Vika said. 'You're going to work.'

They left the hotel five minutes later, Vika saying the creep had followed the same routine for three of the last four evenings.

'He hangs out in a go-go-bar,' she said. 'He stays there for two or three hours before taking a girl, maybe two, to a short-time place around the corner, where rooms are hired by the hour. The cop usually leaves the bar early. But the creep always comes back to the house on his own before midnight, as if that's his curfew time.'

They reached a narrow road, crowded and brightly lit. All neon and thumping music. Bar girls stood around in groups, wearing skimpy bikinis, shouting and grabbing at passing men, trying to entice them inside the bars.

'Let's go through this one more time,' Vika said. 'The girls names?'

'Lek and Noi,' said Drayton.

'And the mamasan?'

'Meow. Khun Meow. What sort of name is that, anyway?'

'It's a nickname Drayton. The Thais like nicknames and some are pretty stupid. That's not important. But she is. Very. The mamasan controls the girls. She manages the place. She was worried about the plan, at least at first, but I've reassured her that it won't come back to hurt them.'

Vika said it was Lek whom the creep mostly took to the short-time hotel, but sometimes he took along her friend Noi too. She said that both were scared of him. That often he didn't pay them, and he was rough. He'd push them around. Hit them sometimes, when he was drunk.

'So why do they go with him?

'They wouldn't if they had a choice. They know he has some sort of connection with the police. They're not sure precisely what. But they see the guy he comes in with, and they can tell a cop when they see one. And the cops control the bars here. Everyone pays protection. Sometimes the cops own the bars. You don't cross them. At least not openly.'

Vika reached into her pocket and pulled out a small piece of foil, folded several times, and handed it to Drayton.

'Don't lose it. And Drayton, try not to talk to him about algorithms.'

'Algorithms?'

'Yes, mathematical recipes. Avoid them. Now go do your stuff.'

She watched the American walk down the street with its jostling mass of semi-clad bodies.

Dobberman's bar wasn't hard to find, a big prancing neon horse above the entrance, and as soon as Drayton paused outside, a girl grabbed him by the hand, leading him beyond the curtain.

It was busy, with three tiers of seating on either side of a central stage, a bar at the far end. Stools right beside the stage too, for the full-on voyeurs to get a better view. Though right now that didn't look to Drayton like a smart place to be, since girls dressed in nothing but cowboy hats and boots were climbing and swinging around poles before crashing their boots to the ground. All to the beat of heavy metal music. AC/DC, 'Highway to Hell'.

He sat close to where the mamasan called Meow was conducting the whole thing, like an orchestra, mic in hand. The noise she made was more Rottweiler than cat. Barking orders at the girls. Directing the next shift to the stage; ordering others to go schmooze the customers. She had a whiteboard behind her, a record of which girls had left with customers to the short-time place around the corner and how long they'd been away.

Drayton ordered a beer.

Then he introduced himself to Meow, who came and sat beside him.

The first thing she said was that the girls were lazy. That this was easy money for them, and that the customers were stupid. Really stupid. She never looked directly at Drayton, always watching the bar. Eagle-eyed. Ready to pounce.

She was middle aged and struck Drayton as a veteran of the bar business, who'd likely come up through its ranks. Hard-nosed, yes, but protective of the girls. Her girls, as she called them. She was quick to step in if her leering, groping customers overstepped the line. Though it was never clear where that line was, and it tended to move depending on how much money they were spending.

She detested Dobberman, who hadn't just crossed the line, but had taken one great leap in his abuse of the girls. Calling him *ding-dong, ai wen,* and a *yet pet.* Drayton didn't have a clue what that meant, but she kept repeating the words, spitting them out with such anger that whatever it was, it wasn't good. Then she said Dobberman was a creep. Mr Creep. Which she said she'd learned from her friend Vika, which she pronounced more as a Veeeka.

She said she liked Veeeka. That the girl spoke good Thai and had big balls.

Drayton said he couldn't argue with that.

Meow had eagerly agreed to Vika's plan. Anything to punish Mr Creep. But she warned Drayton that it mustn't hurt the girls.

He said he was sure it wouldn't and handed her the small piece of folded tinfoil, which she placed in a top pocket of her shirt.

'The creep's friend. The cop. He's leaving,' she said, pointing across the bar, where the tall Thai from the surveillance video was heading towards the door.

'This way please,' she said to Drayton. 'Let's find you a seat with a better view.'

She led him around the stage, and gave him the place vacated by the cop, right beside Dobberman.

The stage was now filled with girls dressed as angels with big wings on their backs, prancing around to a song called 'Zombie', and quickly stripping off the angel gear as the song droned on, until they were naked, apart from stockings, which were stuffed with money by the rubbernecked voyeurs with the ringside seats.

Close-up, Dobberman was a mess. Vika had said he was mid-twenties, but he looked older. He had a fat, pale, unshaven face. Bloated-looking. A double chin and no neck. Drayton thinking that house arrest can't be all that bad, and whatever conditions they were keeping him in, he wasn't short of food.

He was unshaven, messy unshaven, not the geeky designer stubble look. His hair, short, curly and greasy, looked like it hadn't been washed or combed in a while. He was wearing a pair of square-rimmed glasses that sat awkwardly on his nose, as if they'd been sat on and bent out of shape. He wore a stained grey T-shirt and blue jeans. There was a topless girl sitting to his left, whom he mostly ignored, working his phone, on which he seemed to be playing a game. Looking occasionally at the stage. Guzzling beer like it was water.

The lights went down and next up on stage was a paint show. A man with a big brush splashing fluorescent paint on naked bodies, which gave Drayton his cue.

'Man, gives a whole new meaning to modern art. Imagine hanging one of those on your wall.'

Dobberman looked up from his phone. 'Yeah. But this guy's not so good. They had a better one before.'

'You're from the UK?' said Drayton, holding out his hand. 'I'm Chuck. Good to meet you.'

Dobberman shook the outstretched hand and said his name was Matt and that he was from London. Drayton said he was a New Yorker and asked what brought Matt to Bangkok.

'Oh, consultancy shit. And you?'

'Holiday,' said Drayton.

'What do you do back in the States?'

Drayton said he taught Computer Science, but then immediately regretted it, since Dobberman put his phone away and turned more fully towards Drayton. Intense, but looking beyond Drayton, never looking at him directly in the eye.

'Do you like recipes, Chuck?'

'Recipes? Food, you mean?'

'Maths. Mathematical recipes. Algorithms. I love algorithms.' He spoke with a posh English accent, which surprised Drayton, expecting something coarser. Vika had warned him, but it still seemed a pretty weird place to have a conversation about algorithms. A dozen more girls, this time dressed as maids, getting their kit off on stage, and the guy talking maths.

'I don't mean the algorithms that Amazon or Netflix use to give you recommendations. Or Facebook to give you updates based on your behaviour. I mean algorithms that can make sense of everything. *Everything*, Chuck.'

The maids had now got rid of everything they were wearing, except the stockings for the cash, and were sliding up and down and around the poles. Guns N' Roses pounding out this time. 'Sweet Child O' Mine'. They started spanking each other with their maids dusters, lengths of floppy rubber tubing with feathers on top. Giving some customers punishment too. One of the naked maids threw a duster, which landed just in front of Dobberman, almost taking out his drink. But he hardly noticed. He was still talking maths.

'Do you believe in the perfect algorithm? I mean the ultimate algorithm, an algorithm that can make sense of everything, Chuck?'

He didn't wait for Drayton to answer. He was getting up to speed, talking real fast. Gabbling almost. In quick-fire bursts. Getting excited.

'The way I look at it, algorithms are like your best friend. Your child. Or maybe your pet. That's how we should see them. You need to nurture them. Feed them. Give them nutrition and help them mature and grow. And you know what they feed on, Chuck? Data. The bigger and the better the data, the better they grow and learn.'

'With computers, I've always thought, garbage in, garbage out,' Drayton said. 'And as for big data. Big garbage in. Big garbage out. They can amplify mistakes and prejudices. It can be dangerous to put too much faith in them.'

But Dobberman wasn't listening. He paused to knock back his beer, ordering another, a hand on the breast of the girl beside him, twiddling her nipple like it was a knob on an old radio, searching for a channel.

'It's beautiful,' he said.

But he wasn't talking about the girl.

'Once it's fully trained, you have the perfect algorithm. The ultimate algorithm at your service. A master recipe that can solve anything and everything. Make anything,' he said, still trying to tune the radio.

'Or possibly break everything. All on its own,' said Drayton.

Dobberman laughed. Not so much at the answer, but at Drayton, who'd ducked and was taking cover behind the chair in front of him. The girls now using little blow pipes to shoot arrows at balloons hanging around the bar.

Except they weren't using their mouths.

Drayton said he wasn't sure what he'd tell his insurance company if one caught him in the eye.

By the time he resurfaced, Dobberman was still crunching numbers, this time trying to decide between girl number thirteen and twenty-seven. Lek or Noi. All the bar girls wore numbers, usually on boots or stockings. To make life easier for the customers. Though it still seemed to be posing a mathematical challenge to Mr Creep. Drayton thinking that maybe there should be an algorithm for it.

Dobberman decided on Lek. 'I need to slip out for a while. Get laid. You should take Noi here. She's pretty attentive.'

'Thanks for the tip. I'll do that,' Drayton said, ordering two more beers as the girls went to get changed. Sling on a few clothes for the walk around the corner. Meow the mamasan brought the beers over, looking at Drayton and tapping on the beer that was for Dobberman. So there would be no mistake.

It was a five minute walk to the short-time hotel, where basic rooms were rented for up to three hours, and where Drayton and Noi were given a room just along the corridor from that of Dobberman and Lek.

Noi put on the television while they waited. Some Thai soap with lots of shouting. Drayton pacing the room.

Noi got bored with the soap, and said she could take good care of Drayton while they waited. He said he'd pass, not that it wasn't tempting, but because he felt the ghost of Vika in the room, as if her face might appear at any moment, peering in the window. Or out of the screen of his cell phone.

Then Noi started to talk about sex with Mr Creep, that *yet pet*. She made his approach to sex sound like coding. Cold, calculating and impersonal. And she showed Drayton the bruises on her arm where he had grabbed her in a drunken rage, blaming the girls when he couldn't perform.

'He likes to do videos. Weird stuff,' Noi said, wrinkling her nose in disgust.

After forty-five minutes, Drayton was getting worried.

Maybe Vika had got the dose wrong. She'd insisted on obtaining the sedative herself, not trusting the pills that could be sourced by Meow or the girls, which were sledgehammer-strong, knocking you out for hours or even days. She wanted something more finely calibrated, so Dobberman could be up and around fairly quickly and without suspicion.

Maybe it wasn't working at all.

Then Noi's phone buzzed.

'He's asleep,' she said.

They walked down the corridor to Dobberman's room, where Lek let them in, a towel wrapped around her. Dobberman was asleep on the bed, on his back and naked. It wasn't a pretty sight.

Drayton picked up Dobberman's smartphone from a side table, sitting on the bed beside him, lifting his hand and trying each of his fingers on the phone's fingerprint ID sensor. The index finger on his right hand brought the phone's home screen to life.

Then Dobberman grunted and coughed. Drayton backed away towards the bathroom door. Lek yelped in shock. Dobberman seemed to be trying to pull himself up. Coughing again. But then slumped back into the flaccid pillow.

'Quick. Quick,' said Lek.

Drayton opened the browser on Dobberman's phone and entered the address of a website created by Vika. From that website he downloaded an app. He then opened and updated the app, activating the spyware inside, which would give them remote control of the phone.

Then Drayton hid the app. As they'd expected, Dobberman's phone was clogged with apps, several screens full of them, so many that he probably wouldn't notice the new one. But to be sure, Dayton created a folder for the spyware app and then scrolled through to the last of the screens and buried that folder inside another that had been marked as 'Miscellaneous'. He placed the smartphone back on the side table.

He picked up a small wallet from the table. There was not much in it. Just a couple of hundred dollars in local currency, and a debit card. The card wasn't one he recognised. It was plain grey with the logo PEARL DELTA CARD across the top. Below was the word PREPAID in small letters. It didn't carry Dobberman's name. Just a number.

Drayton put it back in the wallet, and put the wallet back on the table, Noi pulling his arm now.

'Mister. Please. We go now.'

The creep groaned and then farted.

As they left the room, he began to murmur. Drayton couldn't make out for sure what he was mumbling about, but it sounded a lot like algorithms.

* * * * *

Vika was waiting in a pub at the end of the go-go bar road. She was sitting in a quiet corner, back to the wall, and with her laptop open in front of her. So that nobody else could see the screen. It was connected to the pub's Wi-Fi.

'What's a *ding-dong*, an *ai wen* and a *yet pet?*' was the first thing Drayton asked when he joined her from the short-time hotel. 'The mamasan. The girls. That's what they called Dobberman.'

'Well, roughly speaking, that would be a crazy bastard duck-fucker,' Vika said. 'And they're right.'

'Where'd you learn that stuff? Can't imagine it's in your average language book. Lesson one. How to win friends and influence people in Bangkok. "Good morning Mr Duck-Fucker." I don't think so. Or was it something you picked up around the boxing rings?'

'I've spent a lot of time here, on and off,' she said. 'The Thais have a lot of colourful language for creeps. And a lot of creeps visit Thailand. Mostly middle-aged western men like you Drayton. Hanging out in places like that.'

'Well thanks,' said Drayton, ordering a beer. 'I was working, you'll recall. And since you asked, the job's done.'

'I know,' she said. 'I can see.'

Drayton sat beside Vika, both of them looking at the screen of her laptop, which displayed a control console for the spyware. She had a map open, a little blue circle in the middle of it, which began moving down one of the roads.

'He's leaving the hotel,' she said.

The little blob stopped outside the go-go bar, as if it was thinking of going in there again, or maybe dropping the girl back. Then it was on the move again, into a bigger street, where it made another stop.

'McDonald's,' Vika said. 'He'll be ordering a Big Mac meal. Always does at this time.'

'You sure?'

'Let's check.'

She activated the phone's cameras, back and then front, and its microphone, but the picture was black, the sound muffled, most likely because it was in his pocket. Then the creep pulled it out, looking at something on the screen. His fat face filled a video window on Vika's console, stuffing the last of the Big Mac into his mouth. Vika handed Drayton an ear bud, so he could hear the action, the background buzz of the place, but mostly Dobberman chomping away then sucking the straw from a big Coke.

'Fuck, that's not nice,' Drayton said.

Then Dobberman put his phone back in his pocket, the picture on Vika's screen going to black.

Vika seemed proud of her bug. 'It can do pretty much everything, just as long as the phone's powered up and online. It can take pictures and video with his camera, listen to his conversations, collect all location data, call history, emails, messages, contacts. The lot.' There was only one drawback. They'd need to wait until Dobberman was on Wi-Fi back at his house before they could download all his existing data.

As the blue blob left McDonalds, it began to move faster, like he was running. Which seemed weird, Vika looking at Drayton, puzzled by the blob's sudden urgency.

Then there was a huge crash of thunder, echoing around the nearby office towers. Then intense, pounding rain that seemed to come from nowhere. The blob was trying to beat the downpour, and Drayton watched it move, willing it on, afraid their evening's work was about to be washed away along with Dobberman's smartphone.

The blob made it back to his house. But Drayton and Vika were stuck, watching the sound and light show from the bar.

Drayton asked about the deal with the girls. Vika said it was done. All sorted. That she'd paid them, and paid them well.

The rain stopped almost as abruptly as it had started, and they left onto flooded streets. It would have been easier to wait for the water to recede, as it usually did, pretty quickly. But they needed to get back, which meant wading through flood water that in places was almost knee-deep.

Vika stopped at a food stall, water lapping halfway up its wheels, an umbrella sheltering trays of little snacks. Drayton said they looked like insects, and Vika said that was because they were. That bugs, the crawly ones, were a delicacy in the north-east of Thailand. Full of protein. She bought what looked like fat maggots, together with a handful of fried grasshoppers. She said she'd eaten scorpions once. And dung beetles. But they gave her a bad stomach.

'Funny that,' said Drayton. 'Who'd have thought?'

'You want one?'

Drayton said he'd pass. 'I just sleep with insects. Cockroaches, you'll recall.'

'Watch where you put your feet. The sidewalks are riddled with holes, and legend is that each year during the rainy season, scores of people simply disappear into the subterranean depths of the city.'

'Well, great,' said Drayton. 'Maybe that's what's happened to Dobberman, and as we speak, the duck-fucker is being swept into some distant sewer.'

Vika said she kinda liked that idea. That it was where he belonged. But only after he'd led them to Dmitry.

Though it had stopped raining, the sky was still flickering with lightening. Another malfunctioning light bulb. The air filled with the sound of wailing dogs and croaking frogs, their discordant duet peaking with each distant rumble of thunder.

Vika opened her laptop as soon as they got to their room. The blue blob was still on the map, stationary in his house. She couldn't get any other response from Dobberman's phone. She rebooted her laptop, but still nothing.

Drayton flopped onto the bed closest to the window. 'Maybe it was damaged by the water. Caught in the downpour. Or he's found the bug.'

'The battery could be drained. Could be as simple as that. The bug's pretty hungry on power. Or else he's switched it off,' Vika said, trying to sound upbeat, but looking worried, the bug no longer talking to her. She set an alarm on the console for when the phone came back online. If it came back. That's all they could do for now. Wait and watch.

Drayton looked away from her, feeling awkward.

She was getting undressed. Right there, in the room. As if Drayton didn't exist.

He picked up the television remote and started flicking through the channels. Then started playing awkwardly with his phone. Looking to the window. Trying not to pay attention to her, but not doing a very good job of it. She was skinny, but athletic. Pale and well-toned, he assumed from the boxing.

But it wasn't just her nakedness that drew his eyes, it was her tattoos.

A snarling tiger covered her entire back, wrapped around her spine. Its head was just below the nape of her neck, its tail ending in the small of her back. Big claws reached for her shoulders, which were decorated with slithering snakes. A tarantula sat above her left breast, one of its legs reaching down towards a pierced nipple. Something that looked like an owl peered from her left buttock. A flock of birds around her ankle. An enormous dragon curled up around the inside of her left thigh, its head just below her navel, breathing jagged fire towards her shaved pubis.

She wrapped a towel around herself and then looked at Drayton.

'What's up?' she said. 'You never see a naked woman before? Were you wearing a blindfold in those bars tonight?'

'Not with tattoos quite like that. What do they mean?'

'Whatever you want them to mean. The Thais call them Yantra. They're spiritual. Popular with boxers. Power, protection, fortune. That kinda shit.'

'And you believe that?'

'Not really. But I like tattoos.'

Then she went to take a shower.

While she showered, Drayton undressed and climbed into bed. He switched off all the lights apart from the one beside Vika's bed. He'd never particularly liked tattoos on women, and she was covered in them, yet he found Vika's rawness attractive. He was aroused by her in a way he would never have expected or couldn't explain. But now he felt cautious, nervous even. And not just on account of the way she wielded those legs. It was the way she looked at him. The attitude.

He was wide awake when she came out of the bathroom, but kept his back to her, embarrassed by his squeamishness. He could hear her moving. Switching the light off. And then he felt the warmth of her body beside him, the cold of the nipple ring pressing into his back. She curled a leg over him, then pulled him towards her. He needed no encouragement, his caution evaporating as her pierced tongue darted towards his. In the near darkness, it looked like the snake on her shoulder, the stud on its tip catching the light from the window. It was as if they were battling for a boiled sweet that bobbed and slithered around their mouths.

She never spoke, not a word, neither of them did, the tattooed animals demanding his attention. The snake, the birds. Then the tarantula. After that, the glaring owl. Then he was face to face with the dragon as it curled up her thigh and he followed the trail of its fiery breath. She dug her nails into his back, her cry transporting him back to the pavilion where she'd ambushed him. Only now her swinging legs were wrapped tight around him.

She left his bed as suddenly and wordlessly as she'd arrived, back to her own. He began to follow her, wanting to chase the animals one more time, maybe a more leisurely safari, taken at his pace this time. But when he drew close he saw she had her back to him, and all he could see was the snarling head of the tiger poking out above her sheet, it's wild eyes fixed on him. Don't even think about it.

* * * * *

Drayton was in a deep sleep when Vika's computer started quacking like a duck, the alarm she'd set to tell them when Dobberman the duck-fucker's cell phone was powered up and back online. It took a while for Drayton's brain to boot up, to fully remember where he was. A shoe bounced off the headboard of his bed, then a pillow hit him. Which is about when he heard Vika's voice ordering him to get his arse over to the laptop.

'It's show time,' she said.

She activated Dobberman's microphone, and then his cameras, switching between front and back as they tried to make sense of what was going on.

The first thing they saw was a grainy image of the creep's chubby, unshaven face, half asleep and staring at the phone. Staring at them. His face illuminated by the light from the screen. Maybe checking the time.

The microphone picked up his heavy breathing.

Vika adjusted some of the settings on her laptop, trying to increase the brightness. Preparing to download the creep's data. Plunder the phone. She was smiling now. Enjoying herself.

Dobberman was muttering to himself, the sound not good. Fucking something-or-other. Stretching the arm with the phone and hitting a bedside light switch that didn't respond. A fat finger filling the screen. Click. Click. Click.

The power seemed to be out.

Vika switched to the phone's back camera for a better view of the room.

Dobberman switched on the phone's torch, and got out of bed. As he moved, the image on the laptop screen moved with him, swaying along with his arm. The camera caught the fuzzy outlines of a desk, a chair, a fan.

It looked pretty surreal. Drayton now smiling too.

The microphone picked up the whirring of the fan, then the distant hum of cicadas. The clicks of a gecko. Dobberman turned into another room, or maybe a corridor. Either way, it was much narrower, the image fuzzier. He said something, but it wasn't clear at first, the mic not properly picking it up. Then he said it again. More distinct this time.

'Hey, is someone there? Hey, who is that?'

Vika and Drayton leaned towards the laptop.

Both stopped smiling, as the image on the screen moved sharply, a sudden and rapid jolt. The mic picked up a heavy thud. The image froze. Then it was moving again. Moving randomly. Jumping and falling. As if the phone was being waved around. The laptop showed a jumble of fast-moving and blurry images. Blacks. Whites. Jittery lines at all kinds of angles, coming in and out of focus. Washed out as the light from the torch was reflected back from a mirror.

Then the phone seemed to fall again before making a hard landing. But it was still in Dobberman's hand, the camera pointing towards him, his fat face in profile, filling the screen. He was on his back, on the bed, a hand hard over his mouth.

He was trying to shout. Trying to scream.

Then the hand was replaced by a pillow, a pair of thick arms pushing hard on the pillow, squeezing the breath out of him. Dobberman writhing beneath it. The mic picked up his desperate, muffled cries. The image started to move again. A series of sharp and violent downward movements, the mic picking up dull smacks at the end of each. He was fighting back, smashing his phone into the back of the person on top of him.

The movements became slower. The rasping fainter. Until they both stopped. The arms kept the pillow in place for a while longer. Just to be sure. Then the arms slowly eased their grip. The camera was still pointing at the pillow. And at the arms holding it in place.

Vika and Drayton both saw it. The tattoo on the nearest of the thick arms. It was a spider. Thick spider legs reaching down towards the wrist and wrapping around the forearm.

The arm reached for the phone, picking it up. For a moment a face filled the lens of the camera, and in turn the window of Vika's laptop. It was the cold, chiselled face of a man with cropped blonde hair. A deep scar on the right side of his face running from his forehead to his eyebrow, then starting again below his eye. A deep crevice down his right cheek that seemed deeper and darker in the light from the phone's torch. Then he turned off the phone and the window on Vika's laptop went to black.

She continued to stare at the screen, a clenched hand over her mouth. Drayton put a hand on her arm. Then she slowly closed the laptop.

'Yuri. It was Yuri,' she said.

'I think I've met him,' Drayton replied

'We need to go,' Vika said. Quiet, but urgent. 'And we need to go now.'

They left the hotel through a back entrance, to a narrow alleyway, to avoid the road that led to Dobberman's house. Vika said they should get clear of the area just as soon as they could. That she knew a place. Somewhere outside the city that would be safe while they figured out what to do next.

The dingy tourist hotel seemed safe enough to Drayton. But there was an urgency about Vika that he hadn't seen before and which he wasn't about to question. She knew those people. Knew what they were capable of. And she knew what was at stake.

The alleyway led to a wider and busier road, but as they turned onto that road they froze. A man was standing in the shadow of a storefront a few metres ahead of them. A tall man with a shaved head. There was no mistaking it, even in the early morning gloom. The man raised his arm, reaching out, something shiny in its hand, raising it towards them.

The man moved out of the shadows. Approaching them. They began to back up, but then stopped because he was wearing a saffron coloured robe and was holding out a bowl. A monk, a shaven-headed monk, collecting alms. He was joined by two more, doing their dawn rounds. Drayton emptied his change into the bowl. Rarely had he felt so relieved to be parting with a fist full of coins.

Vika hailed two motorbike taxis, their drivers wearing numbered orange vests.

'Where are we going?' said Drayton.

'A place. Like I said.'

Vika took the motorbike in front, riding side-saddle, as if she'd done it many times before, rucksack flung casually over one shoulder. Drayton almost fell off as soon as he'd got on his. Holding his bag on his knee with one hand, gripping a bar behind his seat as tightly as he could with the other.

Hating every second of the ride.

The sun was coming up. A hazy, muggy morning. Traffic was light, but that didn't make the journey any less nerve-wracking for Drayton, terrified at each turn, convinced he'd end up under a bus, or else be asphyxiated by the noxious fumes.

The motorbikes dropped them under a bridge near a wide river, and they walked the last few metres to a waterside platform, alongside which, moments later, swept a long torpedo-shaped boat. The Chao Phraya River taxi. It hovered by the platform, just long enough for passengers to clamber on and off before a conductor shouted and blew his whistle. The engines crackled and then roared, and the boat bounced and then swept back into the churning waters of Bangkok's main waterway.

Even at this hour, the river was busy with dodging, jostling boats of every shape and size. The river taxi quickly became packed. A heaving mass of school kids, monks, office workers and a handful of intrepid tourists clinging to seats and overhead bars. There were red plastic seats in pairs on both sides of the boat, and Drayton sat beside Vika, watching the river traffic playing what seemed to him to be an enormous game of chicken. To see who'd move out of the way first. After a while he stopped watching, thinking that was better for his shredded nerves. And as the hot sun hit the boat, he was grateful for the clouds of spray that showered them each time they thudded against turbulent water.

At first the river was lined with high rises. This was the modern Bangkok of tall hotels, shopping malls and towering office blocks. There were temples. A gilded palace. But they soon gave way to the older Bangkok; a more ramshackled collection of wooden buildings and homes on stilts. Some derelict. Piles of rubbish. Then, as they left the city behind them, flooded fields of tall grass.

'This is us,' said Vika, as they approached a small covered platform, where the boat thrust its powerful motors into reverse, hovering just long enough for them to step ashore.

They followed a raised walkway across a flooded field, which led to a cracked deserted road, a handful of wooden homes and a general store on one side. Kids playing in a yard. The road crossed a swollen canal and then passed a pair of towering electricity pylons, beyond which sat a large low building of wooden walls and corrugated metal roof.

Drayton heard a rhythmic thud, thud, thud from within.

Grunts and shouts.

The building was open on one side, facing a yard, lines of punch bags hanging from the ceiling, boxers pounding them with their fists and legs. A raised boxing ring beyond. Others were sparring. Boxers kicking at trainers wearing flat gloves to absorb the blows. Several boxers were doing push-ups in the foreground; others were preparing for a run.

'We're here,' said Vika, jogging ahead of Drayton, dropping her rucksack, and landing a series of blows to the nearest punch bag. Then she sent her shin crashing into the gloves of a trainer standing nearby.

'Well hello Punch,' said the trainer with a strong American accent. 'Always good to see you back. In trouble again?'

CHAPTER SIX

Bret (Fisheye)

Near Bangkok, Thailand

'Good to see you Fisheye,' said Vika, smashing her shin into his gloves again. 'We could do with somewhere to hang for a few days.' She reached for a pair of boxing gloves, quickly and effortlessly slipping her hands inside.

'This is Drayton,' she said. 'He's working with me. Drayton, this is Bret. An old friend.'

Bret nodded towards Drayton, raising a glove, eyeing Drayton warily.

Drayton raised a hand and attempted a smile. So this was Fisheye, *an old friend*, and another one of the hacker handles on Milo's list.

Drayton reckoned Bret was around his age, or pretty close to it, and in good shape. There were streaks of grey in his short beard. Long fair hair held up in a bun and bleached by the sun. Tattoos on bronzed muscular arms. A tiger's head and a dragon. He was wearing a pair of dark red shorts and a white T-shirt with the words 'Fuck Google. Ask Me' below the search engine's logo.

'There are spare rooms out the back,' he said. 'Help yourself. You know where they are.'

'Bret runs the school with his Thai partner,' Vika told Drayton. 'They have kids coming from all over the world to train here.'

'So this is where you learned to box?'

'On and off,' Vika replied, sounding vague. Non-committal, as always.

There was an intimacy between Bret and Vika, which wasn't hard to see. But not one of lovers. Watching them together, it struck Drayton as being deeper than that. An intimacy of old friends and confidants. It quickly became clear to him that Vika had told Bret everything that had happened in Bangkok, and on their second morning at the boxing school, he found them together in Bret's bright, air-conditioned office on the ground floor of a newer two-storey block to one side of the yard. They were reviewing Vika's recordings from the hack of the surveillance cameras at the house where Dobberman was being held. The camera was cut off around half an hour before Dobberman was killed.

'That's why they cut the power. To take the cameras out,' Bret said. 'Probably from a junction box in the road.'

They didn't immediately see Drayton. Too pre-occupied with each other. He was about to knock, get their attention. Walk over and join them. But then he stopped and backed up slightly because they started to talk about Vika's brother.

'Have you heard from Thomas?' Bret said.

Vika didn't immediately answer, looking down.

Then she said, 'Nothing. He's dead. I feel it.'

'Hey,' said Bret. 'Look at me. You can't give up hope, you hear me? You can't give up hope. It's Thomas. He'll find a way ...'

Bret stopped mid-sentence, and both of them looked towards the door. Towards Drayton. Because a toddler had come crashing past his feet, riding a toy car, pursued by a young Thai woman.

Vika left the room.

Bret picked up the toddler, a boy, maybe two years old. He held him high, making cooing noises that made the toddler giggle. He kissed the child, then kissed the woman before handing her the child.

'I'll be up soon, honey,' he said, before turning back towards a bank of three computer screens on his desk.

'Nice looking kid,' said Drayton.

Bret didn't reply. Just kept looking at the screens.

'Tell me about Thomas,' said Drayton. 'What's happened to Vika's brother?'

Bret looked at Drayton now, but all he said was, 'Didn't she tell you?'

Then he stood and followed the woman and the child out of the room.

Several stray dogs watched Drayton as he crossed to where the boxers trained. The same wary look he'd got from Bret. Maybe that's where the dogs learned it from.

There were two training sessions a day. One at dawn and the other late afternoon. The place was now empty except for one boxer, pounding a punch bag. Relentlessly. Intensely. It was Vika, landing blow after blow. Drayton watched for a while, wondering what she was thinking. Who she was thinking about as she pummelled the heavy bag with her shins, knees and fists.

He bought a couple of cold beers from the general store beyond the canal, then sat watching kids play soccer in the street. They asked him to join, dragging him into their game, and soon he was playing the pied piper, dribbling a football, a dozen kids snapping at his feet. Then several older boys joined the game, which was like no other soccer match Drayton had played before. A no holds barred and chaotic scramble for the ball. He retired towards the general store to buy another beer, exhausted.

It was dusk by the time he got back to the boxing school, the late afternoon training session coming to an end. He found Vika and Bret in the office, at a coffee table in front of an ice bucket and a couple of bottles of Mekong whisky. They were well into the first bottle.

'Pull up a chair, Drayton,' said Bret, offering a glass of the whisky. 'It's one of Thailand's finer exports. This and kick-boxing.'

Bret seemed more relaxed. Vika too. The whisky starting to do the talking.

Drayton asked them how long they'd known each other, and Bret just said that it had been a while. Then he left the room because his toddler was having a meltdown outside.

Vika poured herself another whisky. 'He was one of the best fucking software engineers in Silicon Valley. Amazon, Google, Facebook, Apple. A bunch of start-ups. Even Efren Bell. He's worked for them all.'

'And now he boxes. Interesting career move,' Drayton said, and then when she didn't immediately respond, he asked, 'How did you guys meet?'

'I had a company. In Kiev. We looked for flaws in software. In systems.'

'Zero days?'

'They were always the most valuable. The big tech companies were among our best customers in the early days, paying us for finding bugs they didn't know about. Paid us a lot. For a while, Bret was the guy we dealt with.'

'Bug bounties?' said Drayton.

She nodded. 'Then when he left the Valley, we still worked together from time to time. And boxed. We boxed a lot.'

Bret returned to the room bringing a tray of snacks – dried banana and mango, prawn crackers, long chewy strands of dried fish – which he laid on the table beside the whisky.

'So why did you leave Silicon Valley, Bret? That must have been a great gig.'

Bret lit a cigarette, handing one to Vika.

'It was, for a while. The stuff I was working on, it was cutting fucking edge. Artificial Intelligence. I was living the life, driving a Porsche, earning so much fucking money, man. And it wasn't just the money, I thought we were building the future, empowering people. Google's motto, 'Do no evil'. Remember that? At first I actually believed that shit, but the only people we were empowering were ourselves. We thought we were gods, a new priesthood, and in a way we were. But I began to see Silicon Valley's dream for what it was, a fucking nightmare.'

'That's a big call.'

Brett poured another whisky, adding ice. Well into the second bottle now.

'You remember Steve Jobs once boasted about knowing what people want before they even know it themselves?'

Drayton said he remembered something like that from the Apple founder.

'Well, that's what I was doing my friend. That's what I was doing for those companies, but especially at the end for Efren Bell. We called it behavioural algorithms, algorithms that tell what you want before you even know it yourself. Give you stuff before you've even thought about it. Enhancing your experience, they call it.'

He laughed. A contemptuous laugh.

'Those algorithms are hungry, man. They need data, shit-loads of data. Goodbye privacy. Big Tech is one big spying empire, tracking everything you do, and you know what they say? "Your data's safe with us." Sure, it's safe, just until the moment it isn't. Until it's stolen or sold. Used to manipulate you. Advertisers, politicians, any creep who can get his hands on it. To serve you better, they say. "Our intentions are good. We're good guys." Sure, just until the day they aren't, and then it's too late. It's the behaviour of dictators, cults. You know what I'm saying, Drayton? And you ask me why I wanted out.'

He was ranting, slurring his words.

'Remember the early days of the internet? All the promise? Now it's one big fucking sewer, destroyed by fake news, trolls, spammers and big corporations. Especially big corporations. Code is power, man.'

Bret's toddler was screaming again, the noise cutting through the building's flimsy walls as if they weren't there. Its mother was screaming too, at the child and also for Bret to get his arse upstairs and help her out. But Bret hadn't finished yet. He was on a roll, talking about creepy men in white coats.

'Imagine you're in a mall and you're followed everywhere by a man in a white coat with a clipboard, recording everywhere you go. Everything you do. I mean *everything*. He's right on your shoulder, noting down how long you stop, what you pick up. You grab a coffee, he's noting the brand, counting the sugar. Blow your nose, he's got that too. Creepy yeah. Well that's what trackers do when you're online. Fucking cookies. To improve your experience. Fuck that.'

Bret said that after he escaped Silicon Valley, he went off the grid. 'One big fucking computer detox, man. Came to Thailand, didn't look at a screen for months and felt a whole lot better for it. Met my girlfriend and started the boxing school, investing some of the cash from the Valley. Tip-toed back online, doing stuff with Vika.'

'What sort of stuff?'

'Stuff,' said Bret, sitting back down because the toddler had stopped crying. And Vika was giving him a look. The kind of look that said, 'shut the fuck up.'

* * * * *

Drayton woke the following morning fully dressed, on top of his narrow bed, with a brutal hangover. His head throbbed and creaked each time he moved it. Like there was something in there hammering away, straining to get out, and it might burst at any moment. A Mekong whisky hangover.

So he lay as still as he could, watching the fan on the ceiling above and surveying the inside of his mosquito net for signs of life. He seemed to have done a good job closing the net before he passed out and could see no sign of any sneaky bloodsucker staring down at him. Maybe they just didn't like blood laced with Mekong whisky.

He hadn't done so well with the door of the room. It was slightly ajar and one of the dogs from the yard had crept in and was curled up asleep at the foot of his bed. He reached out of bed to find something to throw at it, but the movement was too painful. He'd have to put up with the dog, at least for now.

Bret knocked and entered the room looking much healthier than he deserved to. He was carrying a tray with a mug of coffee for Drayton, milk, sugar and painkillers on the side. 'Man, you look so fucking bad,' he said.

'Yeah, sure. Thanks man,' was the best Drayton could do by way of a reply.

He sat with his laptop on his room's small terrace, intending to check the Berlin Group account, but then slammed the lid shut and hit it hard with the flat of his hand. 'What the *fuck*?' Remembering that Vika had changed the password. He hammered on the door of her room. 'Vika, Vika, we need to talk.' There was no response. Then he spotted her across the yard, a solitary figure in the main building of the boxing school, pounding another punch bag. He tried to attract her attention, shouted again, but the words came out as a painful rasp, and anyway, she was too absorbed with herself, with her swinging fists and legs, to notice.

He almost fell over one of the sleeping stray dogs, kicking at it as he returned to his terrace, and to his computer.

At first he didn't see the message from Tun Zaw, buried amid the clutter of his private email account. It caught him by surprise. He'd asked the Burmese boy to be in touch if he heard more, hinting at further cash for his computer course, but hadn't really expected to hear anything, at least not so quickly. The message was titled 'Professor Pendleton', Tun Zaw saying he'd hacked the hospital's computers and accessed Dr Shwe's notes, sounding matter-of-fact about it, as if breaking into the hospital's system was the most natural thing in the world.

'The notes were a bit of a mess. The professor's body was found near a temple wall, been there all night, so the dogs had made a mess of him. He'd had a massive heart attack.'

No surprises there, thought Drayton, not even the dogs. It was what came next that really got his attention, Tun Zaw writing that soldiers had collected the body from the hospital and had also demanded all the old man's possessions and the autopsy report. They'd been particularly concerned about what the Burmese boy called 'all his pacemaker stuff'.

Tun Zaw ended by saying his computer studies were going well. 'Though still short of money for the course'.

Drayton wrote a brief note back. 'Thanks. Good job. Anything more, especially about the soldiers, would be useful.'

Then he looked again at the faxes Morgan had sent to him in Bagan, concentrating on the technical spec about the pacemaker. It described the device as a prototype, containing a new chip with military grade security. It said the pacemaker was unhackable.

*****

When he could no longer hear the pounding of the punch bag, Drayton crossed to Bret's office, expecting to find Vika there. But Bret was alone in front of his computer screens, wearing a big pair of headphones and drumming hard on the desk, following the beat of whatever was blasting into his ears.

'You seen Vika?' Drayton shouted, a hand on Bret's shoulder.

'Sit down,' Bret said, removing the headphones. 'I've got something to show you.'

Each computer screen was a mosaic of small video windows. Bret clicked between them, each click enlarging a window, bringing the video to full frame. First up was a wide shot of a windy beach in Alicante, Spain, where a man was walking his dog. The dog taking a crap and the man pretending not to notice.

'I hate it when they do that,' Bret said.

Then a mall in Berlin with shoppers laden down with bags. A woman accidentally knocking over a pile of clothes, but walking on because she thought nobody had seen. Next, a couple browsing in a Paris book shop. The fine arts section. Students perhaps, getting affectionate between pulling out books, stealing a kiss behind the shelves where they thought they couldn't be seen. Then a Boston coffee shop, where a young woman at the counter seemed like she was complaining about her drink, handing it back. The barista turning to make her another. Not looking happy.

'I think she was telling him the cappuccino was all froth,' Bret said. 'Sure looks like froth.'

He clicked another and up came a London launderette, with a couple of customers sitting and watching their clothes going round and round in the wash. Then a mass in a church in Rome, a priest giving a sermon, the congregation bopping up and down in their pews. Kneeling, sitting, standing, kneeling again.

It took Drayton a while to realise what he was looking at. 'Surveillance cameras, right?'

'Right,' said Bret, clicking again on the one in the laundry and taking control of the camera. Moving it side to side, up and down. Stopping on a guy pulling sheets out of a drier. Then putting them back in because they weren't dry. Feeding in more money, but then thumping the coin slot because his coin had got stuck.

'Do you know how many surveillance cameras are sold around the world each year Chuck? One hundred million. And do you know what most have in common? Zero security. Security cameras with zero fucking security.'

Bret clicked through to the home page of the website with all the videos. The site's logo was a cartoon image of a faceless spy in fedora hat, dark glasses and with a raised collar. Beside it were the words, 'WATCHING THEM WATCING YOU'

It was Bret's website, and he described it as his playpen. 'It's hosted in Moldova, one of those East European dives that don't give a shit, and I run it anonymously, through a network of proxy servers. I'm not even sure that what I'm doing is hacking. This isn't Jason Bourne, Drayton. Breaking into these things is child's play. These are mostly IP cameras. You know, the picture streamed via the internet. Very few are encrypted. So, once you've located them, sniffed them out, it's pretty easy to tap in.'

He said that controlling the cameras was straightforward too, since most had no password, or they used the login and password out of the box. 'Even when they change passwords, most are so stupid, they're easy to crack. I've got almost 100,000 online security cameras on the website.'

He showed Drayton how he'd indexed them by country, city and type. Shops, bars, clubs, traffic junctions, airports. Even animals. A camera watching horses. Offices. A few barbershops too. Everywhere. 'I draw the line at baby-cams and home security. I don't want to help perverts or get folk burgled.'

'Now I see why they call you Fisheye,' said Drayton. 'But why? What's the point?'

'To show how internet security sucks. And how they don't give a shit about privacy. People have a right to know they're being watched. And they can come to my website and search their neighbourhood. See who's monitoring them.'

'Pretty spooky,' said Drayton.

'That's my point,' said Bret. 'That's precisely my point.'

To Drayton, there was something compelling in their ordinariness. Addictively mundane. Regular people just doing regular stuff and with no idea they were being watched. Permanently monitored.

Bret crossed to a big fridge, collecting a couple of beers, saying it would help with the hangover.

'Did you work with Vika in Kiev?' Drayton asked.

'A little. Though mostly I did my work from here.'

'And what sort of work was that?'

When Bret didn't answer, Drayton said, 'Grom, Ghoul, Tox, Bubblegum, Dim sum, they were part of the Kiev team too? And Razor, and another hacker called Neo?'

Bret sat down with the beers. He didn't answer directly. 'Vika always had a good eye for talent. But organising hackers

193

is like herding cats. The Kiev company belonged to her and her brother Thomas. They were the best. Still are.'

'The best at finding zero days?'

Bret shrugged. 'That's where the money's at.'

Then Vika came into the office. She sat down at a coffee table, placing her open laptop in front of her, the online edition of the *Bangkok Post* on its screen. 'Shut the fuck up, the both of you, and come and sit down.'

She pointed at a headline, 'Police hunt hit and run driver'. It reported that a stolen pick-up truck hit a motorbike in Chiang Mai, a city in northern Thailand. Slammed it hard. Killing the driver and his passenger, who were thrown across the road. It identified them as two young tourists. There was a large photograph of a woman, who was British and had only been in the country for a few days.

The other tourist, a man, had been driving the motorbike and was described as her boyfriend, though it seemed they'd only hooked up in Chiang Mai. His photograph was smaller, taken by an immigration camera as he arrived from Myanmar. It named him as Eduardo Neves, twenty-seven years old and from Brazil.

'It's Grom,' Vika said. 'They've killed Grom.'

Drayton recognised him too. The dour pool player from the bar beneath the Digital Futures office in Yangon.

They sat in silence, staring at the newspaper.

'Perhaps it was just an accident,' Drayton said.

Bret was already at his computers.

'Is there a precise location?' he asked.

Vika gave him the name of an intersection, on the edge of the city, and within five minutes Bret had identified seven surveillance cameras in and around the area.

'Shit,' he said, finding that a police traffic camera monitoring the junction was out of action. It seemed to have been down for days. Another was focussed on the entrance of a bank. A third in a coffee shop. Two more in a mall and, anyway, too far from the junction. A sixth covered what looked like the yard of a factory.

The last was monitoring a petrol station forecourt.

'Yes,' said Bret, banging a hand on his desk.

Vika and Drayton joined him at his computers.

'It's a bunch of petrol pumps Bret,' Vika said.

'Look! Look! The petrol station is on the intersection. And the intersection is right there,' he said, pointing to the top of the screen, beyond the pumps.

It took him less than a minute to take control of the camera.

'What time did it happen?' he asked.

'Early afternoon is all the paper says,' replied Vika.

Bret accessed the camera's memory, and looked back at the previous day's video, starting from midday, scrolling quickly.

'There,' he said, as the camera's clock registered 13.42. He scrolled back and then zoomed in to the top of the image, where it showed the intersection, slowing it down. It was not the best-quality camera and by zooming in, an already grainy image became fuzzy and washed out.

But it was enough.

The motorbike came from the left, the pick-up truck from the right, the truck veered across the road, like it was targeting the bike, which flew into the air as it was hit, the two fuzzy blobs that were its passengers, thrown violently and in different directions.

The truck left the frame and the two bodies lay motionless a few metres apart. Moments later, a tall figure walked to one of the bodies, leaned down for a moment and picked something up. Perhaps a bag, it was hard to tell. The man's head was all black, as if he was wearing a ski-mask. He then left the frame, carrying whatever he'd taken. He ignored the other body.

'You want to see it again?' Bret asked.

'Not really,' said Drayton. 'I think we can safely say that wasn't an accident. What do you suppose the guy took?'

'Phone. Laptop. That would be my best guess,' said Vika, sitting back down at the coffee table.

'Hey Bret,' she said. 'You got another one of those beers?'

Bret crossed to his fridge, and as he returned with more beers. Drayton said, 'I think you guys gotta level with me.'

'Level with you Drayton?' said Vika, 'About what exactly.'

'Let's start with Bagan, Professor Richard Pendleton's pacemaker. It contained an advanced chip. Military grade. Unhackable, the company said.'

'Nothing's unhackable,' Vika said.

'But you didn't just hack the pacemaker, sending the professor a little jolt from time to time, to remind him who he worked for. Whatever you installed was smart. It disguised itself, it adapted, it hid. It kept sending bullshit to his doctors, telling them whatever they wanted to hear. Why go to all that trouble for a few Buddha heads?'

Bret looked at Vika, who sat staring coldly at Drayton, saying nothing.

'Tell him,' said Bret.

Vika looked out towards the yard where the steady pounding of gloves on punch bags had started up again.

'We were testing a zero day,' she said. 'It was a trial.'

'And this trial, it worked, didn't it Vika. Because Dmitry now has what he wants, that's what you told me. The professor was no longer needed. He was shut down. And so was Razor, and so was Grom. You too, almost. And maybe your brother, Thomas.'

Vika looked across the room at Bret's computers, the screens still showing the images from the surveillance camera at the intersection in Chiang Mai. Drayton's words had blown away the lingering fog of their hangovers a good deal more effectively than the beer.

'And it wasn't the first time the bug was used, was it Vika? Mountville Memorial Hospital, Washington DC. November the twenty-first last year. Tell me about that. Targeted a connected drug-infusion system hooked up to a Russian double-agent. Killed him, and fourteen others on life support. Innocent people.'

Vika stood abruptly, turning to leave. Drayton grabbed her arm.

'Defeated some of the best cyber defences. And you know how I know that? Because they were my defences. I was there. Now talk to me Vika.'

She pulled her arm away, raising her fists. Bret jumped to his feet, placing his hands over hers, and for a few moments nobody spoke.

The silence was broken by a sudden sharp noise, high-pitched and repetitive. Vika's laptop was quacking like a duck, the alarm that Dobberman's phone was back online. Somebody had powered it up, and it had an internet connection.

Vika dropped to her knees in front of the laptop and opened the spyware console, Bret and Drayton were quickly at her shoulder. It opened with the map of downtown Bangkok, a blue blob showing where it had last been online, in the house where the creep had been under house arrest, and where he was killed.

But then the map started moving, whipsawing around at first, trying to get a location for the GPS data coming from the phone. It zoomed out and then began to move rapidly, flying across Cambodia and Vietnam, before the blue blob stopped moving and the map zoomed in on an island off the coast of southern China.

Dobberman's smartphone was in Hong Kong.

CHAPTER SEVEN

Raymond (Dim sum)

Hong Kong, China

From a distance, the place looked like it had no right to be there. It clung precariously to the side of the mountain, defying gravity. Beyond its high walls Drayton could see the tops of buildings with large windows and balconies. It seemed more like a medieval fortress than a home.

'Are you sure we've got the right place?' he asked.

'There's nothing else up there. That's where the blue blob landed,' Vika said.

They were standing on a path, a viewing point on the Peak, Hong Kong Island, high above the harbour and lined with coin-operated binoculars trained down on the jungle of steel and glass on the waterfront below. Except for the binoculars in front of Vika and Drayton, which they'd swung round to focus on the slope above.

'The phone was only online very briefly,' Drayton said, sounding sceptical.

'It was long enough,' said Vika, impatient with the questions. 'It was up there. In that house. Believe me. There's nowhere else.'

They were swamped by a group of tourists, jostling for a place to pose for selfies, and Drayton winced as he was struck and prodded by out-of-control selfie-sticks. The noise was like standing in the middle of a chicken coup, and Vika and Drayton had to shout to hear each other.

'There's nothing else up there,' she repeated.

They'd travelled to Hong Kong on the same crack-of-dawn flight, though with separate bookings on a low-cost carrier out of Bangkok's smaller airport, because that seemed safer. Bret had dropped them at the airport, saying to take care and to be in touch if he could help.

Drayton told Bret he'd wave next time he was in a launderette.

They'd not had much chance to talk further, the tension still there from Grom's killing and the conversation in Bret's office. Some things were clearer, like the hack on the professor's pacemaker, Dmitry's grotesque field test of the zero day that had become Cerberus, the snarling three-headed dog.

But why had Vika gone along with it? Why abandon the business she'd run with her brother in Kiev to come to the Far East to work with Dmitry? She said she had no choice, but what did that mean? And where did the hospital attack fit in, an attack that came far earlier and was commissioned by Russia? Was Cerberus a Moscow front? For now, he put those questions to one side. They were back on Dmitry's trail, and Vika was as hungry to track him down as he was, maybe more so.

He looked again at the building perched high above. He told Vika that Hong Kong property followed one simple rule. The higher up the Peak, the more expensive and exclusive. Home to Hong Kong's richest and most powerful. And it didn't get much higher than the place marked on maps simply as Delta View.

'That must be a fifty million dollar house,' he said.

'Probably more,' said another voice, which wasn't Vika.

He turned to find a young Chinese man in a loosely fitting black T-shirt and jeans. Across the front of his T-shirt were the words, 'Born to code. Forced to work'. He had short, straight black hair and square rimless glasses, a small rucksack slung over one shoulder.

'Hey Dim sum', said Vika. 'Good to see you.'

Dim sum. The name immediately put Drayton on alert, another hacker handle from Milo's list of those associated with Neo.

Vika introduced him as Raymond. Another old friend.

They followed Raymond away from the viewing point and onto another path, a walking or jogging trail that passed below and behind Delta View.

Drayton reckoned Raymond was in his mid-twenties, though he found it hard to tell for sure. He was nervous-looking, and when he spoke, he had the habit of looking at his feet, or maybe the Peak or the harbour. Just about everywhere apart from at Drayton.

They left the path and climbed a few metres to a small clearing out of sight of any passing walkers, where Raymond removed a small white drone from his rucksack, a four-engine quadcopter with a high definition camera hanging below it, together with a control console. He attached his smartphone to the consul and then launched the drone.

The drone buzzed like an angry bee as it soared into the air, Raymond controlling it using two small joysticks. He said he wanted to get it as high as possible, so that it couldn't be seen or heard from Delta View. But not so high that he lost contact.

After a few minutes, the house appeared on the screen of the smartphone. It looked far bigger from above, and was more of a compound, a big compound. There were several buildings, a swimming pool and yard. A helipad too. There were delivery vans in the yard, people moving around, preparing for something. Two cars on the far side of the yard, one a sports car. Maybe a Ferrari, though hard to be sure, the other a Mercedes. A garden, a big lawn, nice flowers, part of the lawn covered by a marquee.

'Looks like they're getting ready to party,' Raymond said, talking to the console.

He then manoeuvred the drone out to one side of the compound to give more of a profile. Most of the buildings were two or three stories. Vika asked Raymond to zoom in as tight as he could on the surveillance cameras, to get the make. On the cars too, to try and get the registrations. And on a tennis court, where two players were warming up.

Then Raymond brought the drone back, not wanting to leave it hanging there too long, landing it perfectly at their feet and saying the footage was all recorded, so they could look at it all in more detail back at base camp.

* * * * *

The place Raymond called base camp was a houseboat moored in a marina on the south side of the island. It wasn't in the best of condition. Not the sort of boat you'd want to take out to sea. But Raymond said it had the essentials, by which he meant broadband internet.

He told Drayton and Vika they could find somewhere to crash at the front of the boat, since it might be tough to get a hotel right now, there being a big tech conference going on, with lots of people in town.

Two other people sat at laptops at a wooden table on the boat's covered deck, the table littered with empty Coke cans and half-finished packets of crisps. It had the feel of an internet café. They were both younger than Raymond. A girl wearing a back-to-front orange baseball cap and a large pair of earphones, and a guy, scruffy in a student sort of way, wearing a grey headband and dark glasses. They greeted Raymond with high-fives, telling him it had worked like a dream and the computer servers had been down for an hour.

Raymond smiled for the first time, looking at the laptop screen in front of the girl. The three then began talking fast, in Cantonese this time, laughing, slapping each other's backs, before going down below deck to a living area, where they had bigger, desktop computers set up, leaving Vika and Drayton up top.

'What are they celebrating?' Drayton asked.

'Seems like they've crashed somebody's system.'

'Anybody in particular?'

Vika shrugged. 'With Raymond, it depends on his mood. Could be political. He doesn't like the Chinese government. Could be that somebody just pissed him off. Maybe just because he can. Or else he took somebody down for a laugh. For the lulz.'

'Dim sum, that's his hacker handle?'

'Mostly.'

'As in Hong Kong's favourite brunch? Likes food does our Raymond?'

'He likes Hong Kong.'

'But he worked with you too – in Kiev?'

'We've worked together on and off,' she replied cautiously.

'So what does he do, bombard computers with soggy dumplings and steamed buns?'

'Not far wrong.'

'So, tell me.'

'Death by food. That's what some people call dim sum. All the small portions invading your table, dropped cleverly by cunning servers with metal carts, so you lose track of what and how much you've eaten until you're broke, bloated and then seize up. Hackers around here, they borrowed the term.'

'For a denial of service attack? Blitzing a target until it crashes? That works for me.'

'Raymond's a bot herder. He commands a massive botnet. His zombie army is one of the best and the biggest,' Vika said.

Which was more hacker talk, a botnet being a robot network, computers that have been secretly taken over and are under the control of a hacker known as the herder. The individual machines are called zombies, the idea being that they no longer have a mind of their own and can be ordered into action, all at once, when the herder wants to launch an attack, bombarding the target with messages or just electronic pings in order to cripple or crash it. Zombie armies can consist of thousands of hacked machines.

'That's an awful lot of steam buns,' Drayton said.

'Dim sum likes connected home devices,' Vika said. 'Especially TV set-top boxes. But fridges, kettles, thermostats and toasters too. The internet of things. Easy to hack, sitting ducks. Perfect conscripts into his zombie army.'

The thing Drayton always found spooky about botnets, is that you never really knew if your computer had been hacked and was part of one. Who your laptop or even your kettle might be working for. They were like an invisible army, and bot herders were the celebrities of the hacker underworld, hiring their botnets out through the dark web.

Only Raymond didn't really look like the commander-in-chief of anything. Offline he was almost timid, joining them on the covered deck, asking if they'd like a drink and a snack. Drayton asked for a beer, but Raymond said they didn't have beer. Just Coke. Diet Coke, Coke Zero or the regular stuff. And lots of crisps.

Looking at Drayton this time.

Drayton said he'd have a regular Coke. So did Vika.

Raymond said Hong Kong was under attack from Beijing, under siege. Then he looked out across the marina. Drayton followed his eyes, half-expecting to see Chinese landing crafts and attack helicopters surging over the horizon.

'We're talking cyber, Drayton. It's the cyber siege of Hong Kong. Beijing's attacking us with every possible cyber weapon. There's a war going on.'

Like Bret, Raymond was smart and angry and fighting what he saw as tyranny. Bret's tyrant was Big Tech; Raymond's was Beijing. Bret was a disillusioned escapee from Silicon Valley, but he had retained that brash, pushy libertarian attitude that was a mark of the Valley. Raymond was a fidgety introvert. Until he got excited. Then he wouldn't stop talking. He was wiry and earnest, his war powered by Coke, not Mekong whisky. He sat on a stool on one side of the deck, now a good deal less timid, shaking his foot nervously as he spoke in his machine gun-like bursts about Beijing's cyber aggression. Perhaps, Drayton thought, Raymond could do with one of Bret's punch bags to hammer from time to time. Maybe paint a picture of Mao on the front.

Drayton had visited Hong Kong while he was based in Beijing as a diplomat. Not often, but enough to see the way China was eroding the liberties it promised when the British left, none of which came as any great surprise to him. The Communist party wanted control, needed control. It was all the party understood. And when the people of Hong Kong demanded greater democracy, as they thought they'd been promised, hundreds of thousands taking to the streets, the party tightened the noose, not by sending in the tanks, but in just about every other way they could. And cyber was right up there among the weapons of choice.

Raymond was a veteran of those protests. Now he'd taken his fight online, part of a group of computer experts and hackers fighting back. 'Hacking for democracy', he called it. A fierce battle in the cyber shadows.

'The computer we hit today, it was the web server of the tech conference. The big one that's happening here this week. Blew it right off the net.' He made a big sweeping gesture with his arm. 'Do you know what they call the conference? Imagining the Future. Well, they'll have to imagine it without a website for the next few hours.'

He said one of the conference's main sponsors was a Chinese tech company developing voice and face recognition techniques for the police. That Western companies were working with them. 'Collaborating with repression,' he called it.

'They say it's cutting edge artificial intelligence. But you know what that means? It means spying. Mass spying. I don't care really what they do in China, but we don't want that in Hong Kong. China wants to lead the world in AI, and it probably will. You know why? Because it has no constraints. It can do what it wants, harvesting the data of one point four billion people, and lock up anybody with the courage to disagree. *Anybody* Drayton. The Communist Party doesn't give a shit about privacy or individual rights. And you know what? Neither does Western Big Tech. So they're perfect partners. And they're lining up to work with Beijing. Big data meets Big Brother.'

He began to describe how he had a few more surprises before the conference was over, but Vika interrupted him, saying, 'The drone footage, Raymond. That's all pretty fucking outrageous for sure. But we need to look at the drone footage.'

Raymond connected the smartphone with the video to one of the laptops and they all gathered around. The images filled the screen. Vika asked him to zoom in on the tennis court, on the smaller of the two players warming up. The picture lost resolution with the zoom, but the way he moved, the way he stood, the aggressive and not particularly effective slashing at the ball, and the headband keeping his floppy hair out of his eyes. It was Dmitry. No doubt. And his taller opponent was his business partner, Ken Tsang; the moneyman.

The drive and garden were much busier than they'd appeared on the smaller smartphone screen. Trays of fresh food carried inside, large trays, crates overflowing with seafood. Then boxes of wine and champagne. Tables were being set up in the garden. A handful of smaller tents they hadn't noticed earlier. Several large screens. A stage.

'Whatever's going on there, it's big. And it looks like it's happening soon. Maybe even tonight,' said Raymond.

'Well, whatever it is, we need an invitation,' Vika said.

* * * * *

Raymond would probably have relished the challenge anyway. To breach the digital defences of the mansion on the Peak. That was his kind of thing. But it got better with each additional piece of information uncovered by his little team of hackers. And by the time he discovered the owner of the place, he was virtually salivating over his keyboard.

Raymond had trawled through the records and found it had been built by a Hong Kong property billionaire, who'd sold it a year ago to a Chinese company called Pearl Digital. That company was fronted by a Chinese tech tycoon called Wu Hongwei, who liked to model himself on Apple's Steve Jobs, right down to the faded jeans and black turtle-neck at elaborately staged product launches.

'When he started out, most of his products were just bad rip-offs of those made by Apple,' Raymond said. 'Artificial intelligence and virtual reality are his big thing now. His company is beyond opaque. Pearl Digital is owned by something called Delta Digital Holdings, which is owned by another company and then another, shells within shells, which eventually lead to a company registered in the British Virgin Islands. A dead end.'

'Which means what?' asked Drayton.

'Which means the ultimate owner is very private. It's tough to say who that might be or where their money comes from. Though my best guess is the Chinese government. The Communist Party. Wu himself started life with the People's Liberation Army, though he's now scrubbed that from his résumé.'

Raymond was on a roll, but the thing that really excited him, the real icing on his hacking cake, was that Pearl Digital, Wu's company, was one of the sponsors of Imagining the Future. The big conference now taking place in Hong Kong was billed as the biggest of its type ever held in Asia. In his eyes that was like painting an enormous target on the mansion on the Peak.

It didn't take him long to discover that the preparations they'd filmed from the drone were also linked to the conference. A reception for what they called 'global technology leaders'. And it was taking place that evening. It was a kind of welcoming party for the tech elite.

Raymond's team again targeted the server of the conference organiser, not to shut it down this time, but to break in and sniff around. When they found the database with the guest list they added one Andreas Fischer, Technical Director of AF Global Digital Solutions. They gave Andreas a glowing résumé that made him sound like a cross between Steve Jobs and Albert Einstein, uploaded a head-and-shoulders photograph and printed out an official letter of invitation.

Raymond handed Drayton the letter. 'There you go, Andreas. Enjoy.'

Raymond then set about hacking the house itself. The defences were good.

Vika sent Bret details of the surveillance cameras, and although Bret had easily identified them and found the video feed, the pictures were encrypted and with a password that was tough to crack. He said it might take time.

Raymond probed the mansion's Wi-Fi, thinking that hacking connected gadgets would be the best way in. It usually was. Breach one and you could potentially control the lot. It meant a couple of trips up to the Peak, but by the end of the afternoon he was inside.

'Wu's a lazy cleaner,' Raymond said. 'He has a pair of smart vacuum cleaners. Little robot housekeepers. They map the house as they work, in that way they can navigate around without knocking over lamps and stuff, clean the place and then return to their charging station. They've even got little video cameras. But no password protection.'

He opened his laptop and showed Drayton the layout of the house, which he'd extracted from the cleaner. Then he remotely powered up the cleaner, a video image from its camera showing a wide shot of a large but sparsely furnished room.

'Nice,' Drayton said.

'Yeah,' said Raymond, enjoying himself now. 'I think we're gonna have fun.'

'I should go,' Drayton said.

'Sure. Yeah. We'll be watching your back.'

They joined Vika on deck.

She'd personally supervised Drayton's purchase of a new pair of black jeans, turtle-neck and light grey jacket. So that he would look the part.

'You're the real geek,' she said.

'You know where that came from? The word geek,' said Raymond, who was a mine of the sort of technical information almost guaranteed to send mere mortals into a coma.

Drayton said he had no idea.

'It dates back to the early 1900s and came from travelling circuses. Geeks were performers who bit the heads off chickens or performed other weird or disgusting acts. Only recently has it become more techie.'

'I prefer the circus version. Though they've got a lot in common,' Drayton said, thinking that he'd tell that one to Anna if he ever got to talk to her again. A new email from her was mildly encouraging. After asking whether he'd seen her earlier message, she said she *really* would like to clear the air, that things were really cool in Berlin, going *soooooo* well, followed by a bunch of smiley faces. Drayton smiled too, until she started on about Efren Bell, what a *wonderful* person he is, *amazing* project work, the chance to travel …

He started to compose a reply, then stopped, partly because he wasn't sure what to say, but mostly because he saw Vika, an intense look on her face, as she turned up the volume on a television in the corner, tuned to CNN, a report from Ukraine. A series of fast moving, disjointed images. Burning, smoke, a tattered Ukrainian flag above an entrance to a school, beyond it screaming and shouting, a wailing woman on her knees, another shaking, her face in her hands. A crater where the school yard used to be, a reporter holding a fragment of a rocket case, the writing in Cyrillic, the reporter saying that twenty children were dead, maybe more since they were still sifting through the body parts. Not us, says Russia, the Ukrainians must have done it themselves. A spokesman in Moscow, denying it with a straight face, the same straight face that denied invading Crimea, not our little green men without insignias. And denied shooting down a Malaysian passenger jet high above the battlefield, killing all 283 people onboard. The more overwhelming the evidence, the straighter the face.

Drayton tried to read Vika's face. Was it disgust? Shock perhaps? She certainly seemed to grow uneasy as the report described a flare-up of fighting along the front line between Ukraine and the Russian separatists in the east of the country, concentrating hard, and then turning to Raymond saying, 'I need to use a phone. A secure phone.'

Raymond gave her an old Nokia that had been lying amid the empty Coke cans, and she went outside to make a call. She returned ten minutes later, throwing the phone back on the table and saying to Drayton, 'You need to go.'

Raymond said he'd arranged a van, and they'd travel up together. He said he'd be working from the van.

Drayton looked at Vika. She seemed pre-occupied. Her mind elsewhere.

They left the boat, Vika and Raymond leading the way. As they stepped up onto the wooden walkway against which the boat was moored, Drayton said he'd forgotten something, and ducked back into the boat. He picked up the phone that Vika had just used, scrolling through to the log of the most recent calls. There were two listed. Both international. One was to Ukraine. The other to Germany.

* * * * *

Delta View sat at the top of a steep narrow road, beyond a heavy sliding security gate. It was a forbidding-looking gate, but it had been opened for the occasion and strung with fairy lights. Police directed the flow of expensive-looking limousines up and down and in and out of the compound beyond.

It was dusk when Raymond and Vika dropped Drayton at the bottom of the road and he walked the last stretch. He was greeted by a young woman wearing a body-hugging traditional Chinese dress, a cheongsam, and wielding a hand-held computer. She checked Drayton's letter of invitation and his passport against the guest list and then printed a tag with his photograph above the words, 'Andreas Fischer, Technical Director, AF Global Digital Solutions'.

She smiled and tapped the sticky tag into place on his lapel. 'What sort of solutions are they?' she asked.

'Global digital ones,' he said.

'That's so cool. Have a nice day.'

She also gave him a plan of the compound, which was big, and a schedule, which involved several presentations and a welcome from Wu Hongwei, whom it described as the creative genius behind Pearl Digital.

The next person Drayton met was an earnest young man who described himself as the Hong Kong Government Engagement Lead. He said that Hong Kong was committed to a tech policy that was agile, inclusive, focussed and sustainable.

Transformative too. And was Andreas aware that technologies were challenging existing regulatory and mitigative systems? Drayton said he wasn't aware, and good luck with that, handing him a business card.

Drayton hated receptions like this. The posturing, the posing. Where Bret and Raymond saw dark political forces and Big Tech conspiracies, he just saw bullshit by the bucketful. Self-important geeks spouting incomprehensible jargon. Artificial Intelligence with everything. AI-driven. AI-powered. The way Drayton saw it, most were heavy on the artificial and light on the intelligence.

When a robot server sidled past with a tray of champagne, he just wanted to kick it, but then had second thoughts because that would have been a waste of good champagne. He took a glass instead.

'Enjoy,' said the robot, programmed with a horrible French accent. It was around three feet tall, with a head that looked like a motorbike helmet, lights flashing beneath the visor when it spoke.

Drayton looked at the harbour below. As the last of the natural light drained from the sky, it was replaced by a wall of bright lights and neon signs from the tightly packed skyscrapers lining the waterfront on both sides.

Lights came on in the garden, where several tent-like shelters were hosting presentations. The main house, at the back of the garden was a sprawling three-storey building with large windows and wide balconies, fat turret-like structures at each corner. There were rows of small lights marking the contours of the house. Video screens showed simulations of the brave new world of robots, autonomous vehicles and space travel. Even the bathroom didn't provide a sanctuary from the brave new future. After he relieved himself, Drayton was confronted by an interactive mirror with a display on the glass offering him urine-test results derived from a sensor in the connected toilet.

It was the sort of place that gave him bad dreams.

In one tent, social media executives were talking about fake news, making the flood of digital excrement swamping their platforms sound like a minor irritation. Insisting on the purity of their mission to connect the world for the common good. There was only one thing that could solve the challenges facing social media, and that was more social media. Drayton left the tent.

The next contained a mock-up of an autonomous car. Drayton peered inside. Sat inside. A round-faced man wearing small rectangular glasses and regulation stubble, leaned in the car window. 'The problem is still consumer acceptability,' he said. He described himself as a developer. 'It's still a challenge to get people to accept the idea of being driven around by a computer. It's like elevators in the old days. The first elevators all had attendants pushing the buttons. When technology advanced and the attendants were removed, people at first were too afraid to take the elevator, because it no longer had a driver. You get me? But they learned to get used to it. The same thing will happen with autonomous cars.'

'People still get trapped in lifts,' Drayton said. 'And anyway, suppose I *like* driving?'

The developer didn't immediately answer, the idea of personal choice wasn't something he could immediately compute.

'Still, it's a nice car,' Drayton said, leaving the tent and stumbling into a group wearing giant ski-type goggles, bending and thrusting their arms, ducking and weaving.

'Augmented reality glasses,' said a woman standing nearby. 'Turbocharging creativity and innovation. Enhancing the real.'

'I quite like the real,' Drayton said. 'And anyway, they used to say that about acid. You know, mind-bending drugs?'

But the woman was no longer listening. She was putting on her own pair of ski-goggles, popping her own technical pill, and was soon swinging her arms, which made Drayton think of the mosquitoes in Myanmar. Maybe that's what gave her a thrill. Battling augmented mosquitoes.

In another tent, five middle-aged white men were sitting on a small stage discussing diversity in the tech industry. Nearby, a man in a red T-shirt with the words 'Embracing the Future' on the front invited Drayton to a session on what he called intelligent enterprises preparing for the digital transformation. Drayton said he wasn't entirely sure what that meant, and the man said it was pretty straightforward.

'We need to move on from the paradigms of conventional space and embrace the different paradigms of cyberspace.'

Another man in a grey turtle-neck and more stubble said that wasn't just right, it was *so* right. He described himself as a venture capitalist looking for the next big breakthrough. Billion dollar start-ups, which he called unicorns.

'And what makes a unicorn?' asked Drayton, struggling to sound interested. 'Apart from a big horn in the middle of its forehead.'

'They're disrupters, Andreas,' the turtle-neck said, looking at Drayton's name tag, and not really understanding the bit about the horn. 'They shoot for the moon. Boil the ocean. Embrace the future. You get what I'm saying?'

'Absolutely,' said Drayton, embracing another glass of champagne from a passing server robot. The robot said, '*Ciao*,' sounding Italian this time.

'We need to enrich the conversation and move it forward,' said a man in a black collarless shirt.

The way Drayton saw it, the main thing Big Tech was enriching was itself, at their most innovative avoiding taxes, but he kept that to himself. The black collarless shirt began to yell into his cell phone, 'We need to get more energy into that.' Maybe he was talking to his accountant.

In another tent, more stubbled chins, talking this time about data breaches, making them sound like something trivial. 'We have to keep moving forward.' Drayton moved forward and out of the tent, thinking, 'Who would *choose* to come to a conference like this? It felt to him like some kind of cult. A bunch of New Age wackos.

Drayton headed for the main house, where Wu Hongwei was due to begin his presentation on the stage in the large sparsely furnished room Drayton had seen in the video from the hacked robot vacuum cleaner.

But it wasn't Wu on the stage, but Efren Bell, in the same geeky uniform of black suit over a grey turtle-neck that he'd been wearing in Berlin. Greying hair slicked back into a ponytail. He was talking about data, calling it the new oil of the global economy. The fuel of the future. The thing that powers artificial intelligence. He was talking about rethinking privacy. About the need to see personal data as an *investment* for better, more personalised services that could *anticipate* your needs.

'To serve customers we need to get inside their heads,' he said to loud applause.

For a moment, Drayton was back in Bangkok. In the seedy go-go bar with Dobberman obsessing about perfect algorithms while naked women climbed poles in front of him. Dead Dobberman. Dobberman whose phone had led them to Hong Kong.

A map of the world behind Bell showed what he called the pipelines of the future, a network of fibre optic cables he was building for transferring hitherto unimaginable amounts of data around the world. Feeding the hungry algorithms of AI. Knowing what the customer wants before they know it themselves. A large caption above the map read, 'Building a shared future in a fractured world'.

'Look at China,' he said. 'There are so many exciting things happening. Such a *positive* attitude towards AI.'

Then Wu bounded up on stage wearing a similar uniform to Bell and they announced a new partnership. He talked about voice and face recognition. Picking one individual out of a crowd of thousands, and matching that image with countless other data sets in seconds. Not just recognising faces, but reading emotions. And by reading emotions, reading intent. The end of crime, since there'd truly be nowhere to hide. Monitoring not just identities, but bad intentions.

Efren Bell led the applause, and then said, 'That's what the Digital Pagoda Fund is for, backing the technologies of the future. *Secure* technologies. To make the world a safer place.'

The logo of his fund, the image of a golden bell-shaped Buddhist stupa, superimposed on the padlock that represented security, appeared on the screen behind him, and on several others around the edge of the room.

Then Wu said, 'It's a pleasure to be part of your initiative, Efren. Here's to the tech superstars of the future.'

The room was packed, and Wu welcomed his audience to his connected house – 'Possibly the *most* connected house in Hong Kong,' he bragged. 'Meet Mimi, my *indispensable* assistant.' He gestured towards a black, flask-shaped object sitting on a table beside him. 'She's a prototype. She controls everything in the house at my command. And I'm training her to *anticipate* my needs.' Mimi flashed her lights at mention of her name. 'Let's organise the toast, shall we Mimi.'

Mimi flashed some more lights and then several robot servers entered the room, each with a tray brimming with glasses full of champagne. But instead of stopping at outstretched hands, they picked up speed, manically weaving around and under the tables. Then two of them collided, trays of champagne crashing to the floor. Another ran straight into the wall. While two more dropped their trays and sped out of the room, onto the lawn, heading for the swimming pool.

There was nervous laughter, some thinking that it might just be a joke. Wu looked flustered, the look of an actor struggling with his lines and not a prompter in sight. He eventually decided it was better to say nothing, and just gestured to a server to bring more champagne and the food, but to forget about the robots. But the server seemed anxious, and Drayton overheard her telling one of Wu's assistants that something weird had happened. The fridge had become a freezer and most of the champagne and the sandwiches were now like slabs of ice.

Wu was perspiring heavily. Everybody was looking hot. And everybody was looking at him. So he turned to Mimi and asked the voice-controlled organiser to turn up the air con.

'Certainly Mr Wu. What temperature do you have in mind?'

Wu leaned towards Mimi and hissed, 'I don't give a fuck, just cool this place down.' Mimi told him there was no need to swear, and with an audible whoosh the air con that was embedded in the ceiling of the room, stepped up a few notches in speed.

Except the air it was pumping out became even hotter.

Wu stood and said it was time to relax. For music.

But he was interrupted by a robot server coming back to life, spinning round and round, and yelling. '*Ciao. Ciao. Ciao. Enjoy. Enjoy.*'

Wu ignored the robot and turned again to Mimi.

'Some classical music Mimi. Mozart. A string quartet. Medium volume.'

But Mimi wasn't in the mood for classical, and powerful speakers around the room began to thump out gangster rap. Full volume. The room shaking. Tha Dogg Pound rapping, 'That's right. Some of that shit you just can't fuck wit. Tha Dogg Pound flava. For the nine-fever. Know what I'm saying?'

Wu told Mimi to turn it off, but she ignored him.

There were gasps around the room. Some uncomfortable laughter, and a lot of confusion. Hands went to ears to shield against the noise; others made for the exits.

Wu grabbed Mimi, holding her close, shouting instructions. Yelling at his indispensable assistant to shut the fuck up. But Mimi had a mind of her own, and his words were drowned out by the ear-piercing rap. 'Give a fuck, what's your name, what you claim. Or why you came, motherfucker don't explain. Simply, don't tempt me, cause I'm simply layin' hoes life's empty, the invincible me.'

Wu flung Mimi at two security men, who grabbed her, wrapped her in a tablecloth and took her outside. From under the cloth, Drayton could hear Mimi squeaking, 'Leave me alone, you fuckers. Leave me alone.'

It sounded a lot like Raymond.

Drayton left the room towards an alcove to one side, but he was blocked by a robot vacuum cleaner. The cleaner was a chunky cylindrical thing. Reaching to just below Drayton's knees, and with the words 'Dust Dog' on top beside flashing lights. Drayton went to step around it, but the cleaner moved again, so that it still blocked his way. Then he remembered that Raymond was controlling the cleaner, which meant Dim sum was sending a message – 'Don't enter the room!'

Drayton looked ahead and saw why.

On the far side of the adjoining room stood Yuri, Dobberman's killer, the man who had tried to kill Vika and attacked Drayton in the Digital Futures office. He was wearing a suit, a badly fitting suit, but there was no mistaking him. He was standing with Dmitry and his moneyman, Ken Tsang. Yuri began to move towards the door. Drayton turned away and leaned down as if to tie his shoelaces, Yuri passing behind him and out into the garden.

Drayton entered the room.

There were perhaps twenty people milling around with drinks. He approached Dmitry and Tsang, his hand outstretched. 'Andreas Fischer. How you doing?'

They shook hands, though with no great enthusiasm. Neither was wearing a name tag, and neither volunteered a name.

Ken Tsang looked at Drayton's name tag. 'So what's AF Digital Solutions.'

'Oh, secure health systems mainly. Are you familiar with them?'

Dmitry flicked back his hair. He looked beyond Drayton at the window overlooking the lawn, where security officers were still chasing the robot servers, the ones that hadn't ended up in the swimming pool.

'Quite a party,' Drayton said. 'Neat cabaret from the robots.' Then, when neither man answered, he said, 'Dmitry, isn't it? And Ken. I think we met briefly at a business club in Yangon. I was there looking for business opportunities. Good to see you again. What brings you to Hong Kong?'

Dmitry looked at Drayton now, the small grey expressionless eyes drilling into him. The Russian flicked back his hair, and then with a heavy Russian he said, 'I think you must be mistaken, Mr Fischer. I think you have the wrong person.' He began to move away, but then stopped, looked towards the door and then back towards the man who'd just claimed to be Andreas Fischer.

Drayton heard the familiar voice before he saw her. It was coming from the doorway.

'Chuck! Chuck! I don't believe it. What are you doing here?'

The voice got louder as it closed in.

'Chuck. It's me. Anna.'

* * * * *

Drayton's first thought was to intercept Anna, take her gently by the arm, and guide her out of the room just as quickly as he could. To lead her back out to the garden. But she moved quickly, too quickly. And before he had time to act, she was at his side, full of bubbly enthusiasm, just like in the early days in Berlin.

At any other time, in any other place, that would have made him feel good.

Instead, a horrible feeling of dread welled up in his stomach.

'It's so good to see you Chuck. I'm here with Efren, helping at the conference. It's so exciting.'

Drayton tried to remain calm, smiling, but with a terrible sense of dread, thinking quickly. Chuck could be a nickname. His middle name maybe. He'd make some quip about everybody calling him Chuck. They weren't to know.

He began to speak, 'It is a small world ...'

But she interrupted him, shaking her head. 'Chuck, somebody's made a really stupid mistake.' She took his hand, gripping it warmly with both of hers. 'Your name tag, Chuck. They've given you the wrong name tag.'

Then she turned to Dmitry and Ken Tsang, smiling. 'We're old friends from Berlin.' Then to Drayton again. 'I can't believe you're here. I really can't believe it.' Squeezing his hand. Then another smile, a big playful smile. 'Still chasing bad guys breaking into computers, Chuck?'

Drayton turned and headed for the door. He glanced over his shoulder and saw Anna staring after him in confusion. Dmitry was already on his cell phone. As he reached the main door of the house, Drayton saw Yuri crossing the lawn towards him. He turned back inside and went up a staircase. The map that Raymond had hacked from the robot cleaner showed a back exit from the first floor, but the actual house seemed more complex than it appeared on the map and he quickly got lost, following one long corridor and then another shorter one.

He reached a room with a large curved window and a double door out to a long balcony, a panoramic view of the south side of the island in front, a sheer drop off below. At least two hundred metres to a rocky ridge and then forest.

He turned to return to the room, but collided with something hard, blunt and painful. The force of the blow threw him backwards and onto the floor of the balcony. His first thought was that he'd walked straight into the glass of the balcony door or an overhead beam. His head was throbbing, his vision blurred. He felt blood dripping from above his hairline.

He raised his throbbing head, his eyes coming slowly back into focus. The first thing he saw was the spider tattoo, then the tattoo of the cupola poking out of the top of a white short-sleeved shirt, the gold chain, the face with the deep scar, like a pink crevice down one side.

Yuri had taken off his badly fitting jacket, which he'd thrown over a chair. He stood over Drayton, in one hand he had the fire extinguisher he'd hit him with, a gun in the other, weighing up which to use next. Then he tossed the extinguisher on the chair beside his coat, pocketed the gun, and looked out from the balcony, as if he'd decided that throwing Drayton over the edge was a neater way of disposing of him. He leaned down and grabbed a fist full of Drayton's turtle-neck, lifting him to his feet and pushing him hard against the balcony rail.

Drayton began to struggle, but his arms were pinned behind him, and he was still groggy from the blow from the fire extinguisher. Yuri's hand grabbed his neck, squeezing and pushing him backwards, over the rail, lifting him off his feet. Then Yuri released his grip, turned and looked back in the room.

The sound was like a sharp but prolonged intake of breath. As if somebody was sucking air through pursed lips, and it was getting louder.

Like a vacuum cleaner.

A stubby cylindrical object had entered the room, and was accelerating towards the balcony, faster and faster. Was the look on Yuri's face one of contempt or confusion? It was hard for Drayton to tell, but the Russian seemed to freeze as Dust Dog raced towards him, crashing into his shins, whipping his feet out from under him, and throwing him into the air. Drayton watched the spider arm flailing around, grasping for the rail and then at nothingness, because he was already over the edge and falling, falling quickly.

Drayton heard a dull thud below.

He got painfully to his feet. Yuri's body was face down on a rocky ridge below, his limbs in horribly contorted positions, blood forming a dark shadow around his head and chest. Dust Dog was waiting near the door, and Drayton followed the machine down a corridor and then through an empty gym to a fire door that led to a path behind the house.

He kept to the path, a hiking trail that wound its way down the mountain, stopping at a public bathroom to clean the blood from his face. It was dark now, and in places it was hard to see the path. But he didn't want to go near the main roads. It was a long and circuitous route, mostly downhill, but still took almost three exhausting hours to reach the marina where Raymond's boat was moored.

At first he thought he'd boarded the wrong boat.

But it had to be Raymond's. It was the shabbiest in the marina.

Only nobody was there, and everything had been cleared. The computers. The clutter of Coke cans and crisp packets. It was all gone. All that was left were Drayton's bags.

He sat at the table that only hours earlier he had shared with Vika and Raymond. In the middle of the table was a memory stick, nothing else. He powered up his laptop, inserted the device, and opened a file marked 'Drayton,' which contained two items, a document and an audio file.

The document was a short typed note from Vika.

The creep's phone came back online again, but all I got this time was a brief audio recording. Now I have to leave. Sorry and good luck. Take care. V.

The recording was around thirty seconds long, a series of sounds. First a kind of clanging and screeching, getting louder and then fading. The ringing of a bell came next. Then something like faint bursts of static. That was followed by a deep rumbling and then jazz. Brubeck's 'Blue Rondo à la Turk'. Definitely Brubeck.

Then it ended.

To Drayton the sounds had a strange familiarity about them. But he couldn't place them. They definitely weren't sounds from the house on the Peak.

The phone had moved on. And so had Vika.

* * * * *

Drayton slept on the boat, on a long padded bench at the edge of the covered deck. Perhaps it wasn't the wisest thing to do, but his head hurt like hell. He was also exhausted by the trek down from the Peak, and he still hoped Vika might return.

He was woken early by the crackle of a boat's motor. There was shouting in a language he didn't understand. He crept to the back of Raymond's boat and looked out across water that was a leaden grey in the first light of morning. The spluttering engine and the shouting grew lounder as a beetle-shaped sampan passed close to the bow of Raymond's boat. The noise faded, and Drayton relaxed and returned to the bench. The sampans provided a taxi service for those living on the boats. And the language was Cantonese, the local dialect, which always sounded angry and loud to him, even when it wasn't.

He looked again at Vika's note: Now I have to leave. Sorry and good luck. Take care.

It had a finality about it, but also a tone of regret.

Why? What was so important to her that she'd abandoned their search, just as they seemed to be making progress? She'd seemed determined to hunt down Dmitry. She was the one who'd been taking the lead, driving them forward.

He thought about her mood. How distracted she'd been before he'd left for the party on the Peak. After she'd seen that report about fighting in Ukraine. And then her phone calls to Ukraine and Germany. What was it that could have shaken her so badly?

He opened a news app on his cell phone and searched for Ukraine. There was plenty about the school attack, almost certainly a stray Russian rocket, but that wasn't what had most shaken Vika. It was something else. There were several reports about renewed fighting on the front line in eastern Ukraine, but the details were confusing and contradictory. One in particular caught his attention. It described a raid by masked men to free a high profile hostage being held by Russian separatists in what it called a fortified and well-defended compound, possibly a prison, though one Ukrainian website claimed it was a cyber bunker, a Russian-run control centre for cyber-attacks.

He then started to write an email to Anna. 'I owe you an explanation,' he wrote. But then he stopped. How could he even begin to explain? Maybe it was better to wait until he was back in Berlin and talk to her there, if she would even speak to him again.

Among a clutter of unread emails he saw messages from Milo Müller and Wolfgang Schoenberg, both marked 'urgent'. Both sent to his personal email.

Milo's message contained a request and a warning. He asked for more information about the people Drayton had met. 'Everybody you have come across. However minor they may seem. Every detail will help me find patterns in the dark web'. Then came the warning. 'From what I have been able to piece together, Viktorya Shevchenko (also known as Vika or Punch) is still working for the GRU, the Russian military intelligence.'

Drayton closed the email without replying.

Wolfgang Schoenberg's message was brief. 'I am on my way to Hong Kong,' he wrote. 'Meet me at 1 p.m. at the old police station in Tai O. Tell nobody and come alone.'

* * * * *

Tai O's old police station was a grand relic of British colonial rule. It sat high on a hillside, on a remote headland jutting out into the mouth of the Pearl River. A plaque near its entrance said it had been built as a lookout post, to stop rampant smuggling and piracy in the waters below.

He was an hour early, and took a seat on a terrace beside the building's whitewashed arches. Below, to his left, he could see the sweep of Tai O's main village, with its packed, stilted houses lining the waterfront. To his right was the ocean, a parade of ships heading up the Pearl River to the factories of southern China.

A server brought Drayton a cold beer, telling him this was just about the most western spot of Hong Kong. What he called China proper started just out there, he said, pointing vaguely out to sea, towards an invisible line in the water. He said it with a distaste, not uncommon among natives of the former British colony.

The police station had been turned into a hotel, the old buildings spruced up. Right down to the old cannons, the watchtowers and the search light. The server said that in its day it had been a great spot for spies, which made Drayton smile. Maybe that's why Schoenberg had chosen this remote lookout as a place to meet.

He was looking forward to meeting Schoenberg. But at the same time, he was uneasy. What could be so important that the German felt the need to fly out personally to Hong Kong? And Schoenberg had been adamant about their encrypted messaging system. *This account must be the only way we communicate.* Yet he'd broken his own rule. Both he and Milo had sent messages to Drayton's regular email address. Perhaps they realised he'd lost access to it. Maybe it was the urgency. But it wasn't like Schoenberg at all. He wasn't a spur-of-the-moment kind of person. Milo, perhaps, but not Schoenberg. He wasn't impetuous. He was fastidious, calculating even.

As he drank his beer, Drayton tried to suppress those nagging doubts.

He ordered another beer and looked at his watch. Still forty minutes to go. He imagined what it might have been like in colonial times. He pictured police officers sipping their gin and tonics at this very spot while smugglers and pirates crept in and out of the village below.

Another five minutes passed. He was willing on the time.

Then his cell phone rang. The screen told him nothing, an unknown number. But the ringtone told differently. It was *The Pink Panther* theme tune. An emergency call from Schoenberg.

Drayton sat bolt upright in his chair, almost knocking over the beer.

He took the call, saying nothing at first. Then the silence was broken by the unmistakable voice of Wolfgang Schoenberg. 'Drayton. Where are you?'

'I'm here. In Tai O. At the meeting point as you asked. Waiting for you.'

Schoenberg's voice was clear, sharp and urgent.

'Get out of that place, and get out right now.'

* * * * *

Drayton rose slowly to his feet, his heart pounding from fear and anger. Fear, because they had him where they wanted him, in this remote corner of Hong Kong, and he knew the violence they were capable of. Anger at himself for being so stupid, for taking the email from Schoenberg at face value, when the German would never break his own rules. It had clearly been a fake.

He looked at his watch. Half an hour left before the meeting was due. Half an hour to get clear of there. For all he knew, they might already be watching him. He needed to appear calm.

He looked along the deserted terrace, then took a few paces to the edge, to a low wall from where he looked down on a path along the seafront. He raised his phone as if to take photographs. The sort of thing a visitor might do, somebody without a care in the world, zooming in on a small pier to his right, two fishermen sitting at the end of it. Nothing suspicious there. Then to his left, towards the village. The path was quiet, just an old man sleeping in a doorway.

There was no access to the old police station by vehicle. The only route in was on foot along the path, which began in the village. They'd have to come that way, or else by boat. And as far as he could tell, they were also the only routes out.

He entered the hotel lounge at the back of the terrace, past big leather chairs and bookshelves. On one shelf, beside a book about the migratory birds of Hong Kong, were two small pairs of binoculars. He placed one pair in his pocket. A rear door led to a store room, which opened onto a narrow alley behind the hotel. He turned left and followed the alley, which was sandwiched between the rear wall of the hotel and the steep hillside.

Then he heard footsteps behind him, getting closer. He began to walk faster, without turning. The footsteps got faster too, and closer, until he felt a hand on his elbow. He span round and was looking at the server, a piece of paper in his hand.

'The bill sir. You forgot the bill.' The server sounded business-like, as if guests slipping out the back of the hotel without paying was an everyday event. Drayton handed him a one hundred Hong Kong dollar note, saying to keep the change.

'I thought I'd take a different route to the village,' Drayton said.

'Not that way,' said the server, pointing to a sign beside the path, alongside some steps climbing the hill. The sign was in Chinese and English, in capital letters, saying, 'LAND USED FOR MILITARY PURPOSES. NO TRESPASSING.'

'The PLA,' said the server. 'The People's Liberation Army has a base above the hotel. They don't welcome visitors.' He pointed to another route down behind the village. 'Take that one.'

Drayton handed the server another note, one hundred US dollars this time. 'Look, I can't really explain, but if anybody should ask, I was never here.'

The server took the money, looking at Drayton. Thinking. Then he nodded and went back into the hotel.

The path was cracked and overgrown. It followed a ridge along a hill above and to the back of Tai O village. He reached a small shop made of sheets of metal with small wooden windows, an old woman wearing a knitted woollen hat and thick cardigan was sitting in the entrance. Drayton removed the binoculars from his pocket and flapped his arms, doing a poor imitation of a bird. The woman laughed, took his arm and led him past shelves straining with dried seafood, snacks and drinks, to a small veranda.

She'd had birdwatchers passing through before, and it was a perfect spot.

He trained the binoculars down onto the path out of the village, which was becoming busy, mostly with youngsters, day-trippers from the city coming out for a glimpse of Hong Kong's wild side. Together with elderly villagers. Twice the old woman came out of the shop and tapped him on the shoulder to offer more tea and to tell him that generally speaking sea birds could be found at sea.

The second time, he humoured her by pointing the binoculars towards the water, which is when he saw the black and white speedboat entering the bay, moving fast, but then slowing sharply. It swung around and then cruised slowly to the small pier below the old police station. Four men got off the boat and headed for the steps leading to the restored colonial-era building above.

Drayton recognised Dmitry and Ken Tsang. The other two were big, athletic-looking men. Military types. One European and one Chinese. They climbed the steps towards the old police station.

Drayton didn't have a clear view of the terrace on which he'd drunk his beer, so couldn't see if the men had met the server. He had no immediate way of knowing whether the server was denying his existence or betraying him. He'd had a good feeling about him, but as the minutes passed, he became anxious, and his confidence began to crumble. He stood and turned towards the entrance, preparing to leave.

He shouldn't have trusted the server. Shouldn't have stopped at the shop.

That was more stupidity.

But then the men emerged again, back below the old police station. They stood, Dmitry making a call, then returned to the speedboat, which swung around and accelerated rapidly out of the bay. Drayton let out a sharp breath, and punched the air. He lowered the binoculars and asked the old woman if she had a beer. She brought him a warm one, but it would do. He embraced her, for no other reason than huge relief.

She smiled and said, 'I told you you'd see more looking out to the water.'

When he left her shop a few minutes later, the old woman smiled, waved and flapped her arms like a bird. Drayton waved back, thinking that a pair of wings would not be a bad asset right now. He needed a get out of the village. To find a place to think.

After a while, the path seemed to peter away before entering a scrubby clearing behind the village. The clearing was littered with discarded equipment for fishing boats: rope, large plastic tubs and woven baskets. There was a waterway just beyond the clearing, one of several channels that stretched in from the bay like spindly fingers into the valley behind the village. It was lined with more houses on stilts above the water, fishing boats tied up beside them.

He found a narrow bridge over the waterway and then followed an alley that led to the main pathway through the village. It ended at a car park with the bus stop just beyond, where he waited, standing in the shadows between two stalls selling dried seafood. He watched as a woman, a baby asleep in a pouch on her back, methodically packed strips of dried fish into plastic bags. She then leaned down and rearranged a series of small china figures in a shrine near the shop entrance.

The air smelt of seafood, tinged with incense and spice.

Washing hung from windows above the shops.

A bus pulled up, and Drayton walked quickly towards it. When he hesitated at the door, the driver said, 'Where do you want to go?'

'Wherever you're going,' Drayton replied, climbing on board.

That turned out to be a concrete jungle of a town in the north-east of the island, close to Hong Kong airport. It was dominated by a series of giant apartment blocks, fifty storeys high and stretching like a wall along the waterfront. But with no shortage of coffee shops with good Wi-Fi connections.

Drayton chose a place at the foot of one of the monster blocks. He took a table at the back and ordered a large Americano and a muffin. Then he powered up his laptop and logged in to the coffee shop's Wi-Fi. He looked again at the fake emails from Schoenberg and Milo. He should have trusted his instincts. Schoenberg would never break his own rules. And the one from Milo should have been obvious. The way it was written was coherent and grammatically accurate. In made sense in one reading. Milo never made sense the first time round. He wrote emails the way he spoke and thought. Mostly a stream of consciousness, with only a passing resemblance to the English language.

He checked the addresses. The accounts were real. He'd received messages from them before, back in Berlin. Which meant they had been hacked. Somebody had broken in and taken over their email accounts in order to send the messages. Milo's to muddy the trail; Schoenberg's to trap him.

He sat back in his chair, took a sip of his coffee and scraped the last remnants of the muffin from its paper wrapper.

A television hung from the ceiling in the corner of the room. Familiar news headlines. American warships, the most advanced on the planet, playing bumper cars with rusting freighters in the South China Sea, a US admiral denying their guidance systems had been hacked. Production suspended at

Russia's biggest gas field because of a computer glitch. No more details. Shipping suspended at the port of Shanghai, the world's busiest, an army of cranes at a standstill after an unspecified computer software issue. Britain's smart motorway system suspended after the digital information screens started spouting gibberish; a twenty-three car pile-up after northbound cars were directed into oncoming traffic. Another unspecified system failure.

Was Cerberus upping the stakes?

Then Drayton stood and moved closer to the television screen, where he could hear it more clearly.

Breaking news. A reporter standing on the seafront on one of Hong Kong's outer islands. She said the body had been found that morning. Initial forensics suggested the woman had drowned and been dead for several hours. There was video of a black body bag being carried from the beach and placed in an ambulance. The reporter said the woman was last seen alive on board a junk, a traditional boat popular for late-night partying in and around Hong Kong.

It named her as Anna Schultz, a German national.

* * * * *

Drayton wasn't sure how long he sat there, staring blankly out of the coffee shop window, his hands gripping his empty mug as if it were a lifeline. The room suddenly dark and airless, the walls closing in. He focussed hard on a spot in the harbour, where an old ship was moored, taking long deep breaths, the way he'd once done as a child to overcome car sickness. The buzz of the coffee shop was just a distant hum.

He was startled by a hand on his shoulder, firm but comforting. It turned out to be a barista offering a refill, an ultimatum disguised as a question. The Hong Kong way of saying, 'Spend more money or leave'. So he spent more money, another Americano with a double shot, while he tried to make sense of what had happened, tried to focus. But the strong coffee only seemed to aggravate the knots in his stomach and the cold shivers as the images of the body bag replayed endlessly in his mind, each replay an accusation, that if it hadn't been for him Anna might still be alive.

Perhaps her death had been an accident, and she had fallen from the boat and drowned. But he doubted that. The story was spreading quickly on social media. It had that right mixture of tragedy and glamour with more than a hint of scandal, and quickly it became poisoned with rumour and assertions masquerading as facts. A harbour cruise became a wild orgy of depraved techies, fuelled by alcohol and drugs, Anna drinking heavily and last seen on the deck, stoned or drunk, and unsteady on her feet.

Absent was any mention of the man with whom she'd come to Hong Kong and for whom she'd been working: Efren Bell. And in all the time Drayton had known her, Anna had never touched a drop of alcohol. She hated the stuff. She used to joke that Drayton drank more than enough for the both of them. As for drugs, she'd hesitate even to take a painkiller.

He left the coffee shop and took a bus to the airport, a short ride, from where he boarded a fast ferry to Macau from the airport's pier. It was packed with gamblers heading to the casinos, silently doing the mental calculations they thought would make their fortunes at the Baccarat tables, as if it was anything more than pure luck. They looked like joyless commuters heading for another day at the office, but for Drayton the ferry provided a comforting anonymity.

The grief and the guilt came in waves. As did the anger and the fear. He'd come to the Far East on a mission to hunt the snarling three-headed dog; now it was hunting him. Anna had been caught up in something she never understood. Caught up because of him.

As the ferry cut through heavy smog hanging over the Pearl River Delta, he looked at the last messages from Anna, forever the breezy optimist, the hint of them getting back together.

He listened again to the recording from Dobberman's phone. The strange sequence of noises. The clanging and screeching, the bell, the bursts of static. A rumbling. Then Dave Brubeck. There was definitely a familiarity about it. A haunting familiarity.

From Macau he flew to Kuala Lumpur, changing aircraft in the Malaysian capital, then changing again in the Middle East. From there he took a flight to Frankfurt and then a train for the last part of the journey. It was a convoluted route, travelling on the passport of Andreas Fischer, but somehow it seemed safer that way.

It was part instinct that brought him back to Berlin, a feeling that Berlin was where he'd find answers, but mostly it was because he had no real choice.

CHAPTER EIGHT

Cold War Tours

Berlin, Germany

The Berlin traffic was light and it took just five minutes to reach Potsdamer Platz by taxi from the city's main railway station. It was a cold, crisp morning. Bright sunshine with faint strips of high cloud, the sort of morning that had made him feel so good about living in the city. Especially when he'd woken up beside Anna.

He went straight to the office of the Berlin Group, the lobby busy, fingers punching at buttons in a crowded lift, the buttons lighting up in response. Except the one marked with a 10, which merely flashed when he pressed it, before returning to its dull, dormant state. So he left the lift at the ninth floor and walked up the emergency stairs.

The Berlin Group was the only occupant of the tenth floor, which was now in near darkness, double glass office doors locked, the rooms beyond empty and deserted. Everything had been removed. Some post had been pushed under the door, two big envelopes propped up against it. He picked up the envelopes.

Then he heard movement behind him. Light from the beam of a torch reflected off the door in front of him. He turned and was blinded by the bright light, shining in his face. A voice demanded to know what he was doing.

'Please,' he said, 'The torch.'

The torch was lowered, and Drayton saw a uniformed security guard, who began to bark at him in a hybrid of German and English.

'This floor is verboten. Here ist forbidden.'

Drayton waved the envelopes he'd picked up from the floor.

'Delivery,' he said. 'I have an urgent letter for them.'

The guard looked at the envelopes, then back at Drayton. He turned and pointed the beam of his torch towards the stairs.

'Must go,' he said.

Drayton followed the beam of the light, and then retraced his footsteps back to the floor below, and back to the lift. He hailed a taxi outside the building. 'Lake Tegel,' he told the driver. As he drove, he tried ringing the cell phones of Schoenberg, Norgaard and Milo. *Voice calls only in an emergency*, Schoenberg had said. This was now an emergency, but they were all unobtainable.

Two police cars guarded the entrance to the narrow lane leading to Schoenberg's house. Behind them, a tape stretched across the road, tied to trees at either end. 'POLICE. NO ENTRY' printed multiple times. Drayton asked the taxi driver to keep going, past the road, stopping around half a mile away, close to the shore of the lake.

He asked the taxi to wait, then walked along the shore of the lake, cutting inland along a narrow path through the forest, which brought him to the back of Schoenberg's house. He climbed over a low fence. The garden was mostly overrun, scrappy plants and weeds, which surprised him given how fastidious the German was in so much else, but it provided ideal cover as he moved quickly to the rear windows. There was no sign of life in the gloomy living room with its heavy dark furniture and imposing pictures, where he'd first dined with the German. He moved around the house, and beyond each window was the same empty scene. He knocked gently on a rear door. Then on a window. Nothing.

He returned to where he'd left the taxi. 'Prenzlauer Berg,' he told the driver. He had the yellow Mercedes drop him a few blocks from his apartment. It was a risk. Possibly even stupid, since there was a good chance his apartment was being watched. But he needed to collect clothes, as well as cash he kept there. And there was a back way in, through a courtyard.

The apartment was in semi-darkness, the curtains closed, as he'd left it, which was reassuring. Plates still in the kitchen sink, a pair of coffee mugs still on the table, the sort of mess that Anna had hated. He took a beer from the fridge. Anna's electric toothbrush still stood to attention in its charging cradle in the bathroom, her favourite coffee mug nearby, the one with a big pair of painted lips on the side and the words, 'Don't shush me'. She must have overlooked them when she moved out, unless she'd been hedging her bets. He sat on the seat of the toilet, starring at the mug, burying his face in his hands, the image of the body bag carried from the beach repeating itself in slow, vivid detail.

His cell phone jolted him back to the present, vibrating in his back pocket, the ringtone becoming louder and clearer as he pulled it out. *The Pink Panther* theme tune. Schoenberg. But he stopped without answering it because he'd heard something else, something moving. The creak of a chair in the living room.

Then a voice said, 'You can tell a lot about a man by his ringtone.'

It was a familiar voice.

'Come in, Drayton. Take a seat. Make yourself at home,' said Ric Cullen, sitting in one of Drayton's old leather armchairs, sipping one of Drayton's beers.

The phone rang again. Still *The Pink Panther* tune. Drayton rejected the call, and powered the phone off, locking it. He sat at a desk a couple of metres from Cullen. 'My ex-wife. She can be very persistent.'

'You know, Drayton, I was in Pakistan, in the tribal areas, meeting a mullah who ran a religious school that trained the Taliban. Churning out fanatics. Fucking terrorist factory. I was trying to convince him of the error of his ways. I thought he was dangerous. Then his cell phone rang. And do you know what?'

'I have no idea.'

'It was 'Jingle Bells'. Fucking 'Jingle Bells' for a ringtone. I could never take him seriously as a jihadi after that.

'Another time I was negotiating with the Russians over some issues we were having in Syria. I was dealing with a real hardass. At least that's what he wanted me to think. I was preparing to give ground, make concessions, but then his phone rang. It was a barking dog. I knew straight away that he was an arsehole. All bark and no bite. That he was bluffing. Crying babies, quacking ducks, opera arias, rap. They're the worst. If ever I hear them, I know I've won before I even get started.'

'Impressive. You're clearly in the wrong job,' Drayton said. 'You should write a book. Ringtones for diplomats. Ringtone warfare. Might work well on the curriculum at West Point. You know, squeezed between nuclear deterrence and counter insurgency. Might even save the world. And what about *The Pink Panther* theme tune, what does that tell you?'

'That you're a loser Drayton, but then we know that already, don't we?'

'I'll change my ringtone. Maybe the spaghetti western, *The Good, the Bad and the Ugly*. Keep them guessing. Or maybe just the one that comes installed.'

'Default is boring. Cries out lazy and unimaginative.'

Cullen walked to the window, opening it slightly as a tram rattled past.

'Your ex. What's her name? Debbie, isn't it? Can't blame her for being angry. Her husband screwing the wife of a German government minster, then it all blowing up so publicly. Yeah, must have been tough on her. And not just any old minister, but Herr Wolfgang Schoenberg.' He paused to finish his beer. Then fetched another from Drayton's fridge. Making himself at home. 'Yes, dear old Wolfgang, now your boss. Ever thought he might be setting you up, Drayton, revenge for fucking his wife?'

Drayton struggled to remain calm. He had thought about that, thought a lot about Schoenberg's motives, but he didn't need to hear it from Cullen. He clenched his fists in his lap, the anger rising inside him. But he still said nothing. Showed nothing. He didn't want to give Captain America that satisfaction.

'You should have taken my advice in Burma, Drayton. Then all this unpleasantness could have been avoided.'

'What unpleasantness is that, Cullen?'

'I'm sure you've noticed that you no longer have an office to go to. The Berlin Group has been disbanded. The US government was obliged to share with our international colleagues some very disturbing information about Wolfgang Schoenberg, and it was decided that it was in all our best interests that his operation be quickly and quietly shut down. You've been used Drayton. Schoenberg betrayed you. He betrayed all of us.'

He paused, looking at Drayton, waiting for a response. But Drayton still said nothing, still trying to show no emotion.

Cullen took another sip of beer. 'You don't seriously think that a thug like Dmitry Gerasimov is running his little syndicate all by himself, do you? That he alone is responsible for Cerberus, the snarling three-headed dog, plotting his cyber terror all on his own account?'

'It did occur to me that somebody might be sponsoring and protecting him,' said Drayton.

Cullen began slowly to clap. 'Well done,' he said, leaning over Drayton and slapping him slowly and rhythmically on the cheek. 'Brilliant. No wonder you're a cybercrime investigator.'

Then he pushed Drayton hard against the back of the chair. 'And that *somebody* is Herr Wolfgang Schoenberg.'

* * * * *

They sat in silence for a while, Cullen throwing his empty beer can across the room towards a bin, which he missed, the can bouncing back to the middle of the room.

'Does it surprise you?' Cullen asked.

'I'd thought better of him.'

'So did we all. Seemed like such a decent man, don't you think?,' a note of sarcasm in Cullen's voice. 'A lot of clout with Interpol and the German government. That's how he was able to set up your little team. But it was all a front. Schoenberg's a disturbed character, Drayton. How much do you really know about him, about where he came from?'

When Drayton didn't respond, Cullen said, 'He was born in 1950 in the East. In Dresden, in communist East Germany. Studied at the Technical University in that city. It was about the best tech education the communists had to offer. He went on to work on their first personal computer and first computer network. Both pretty basic compared with the West at the time, much of the know-how stolen from us, but it was still cutting edge for the Soviet bloc. When the wall came down, he became a member of parliament in united Germany, chairing the Bundestag's committee on research and technology. Then he headed a string of ministries. Intelligence jobs. And most recently, of course, your cherished Berlin Group.'

'I don't see how that makes him a cybercriminal,' Drayton said.

'Well, here's the thing, Drayton. You couldn't succeed at top levels in science and technology in East Germany without being a member of the party and without cooperating closely with the secret police, the Stasi. The Soviet secret police, the KGB, took a strong interest too. And Herr Schoenberg served them all with enthusiasm. He never gave up those loyalties.'

'Loyalties to what? To a bankrupt ideology? To a country that no longer exists?'

'You should never underestimate the hatred that grows out of resentment and humiliation. The humiliation of seeing the country you've served dismantled and subsumed by the West, your work belittled. Laughed at. He has in the past provided services to the Russians; sometimes to the Chinese. Even North Korea. Mostly he's motivated by revenge and money.'

Cullen paused, waiting for a response from Drayton. There was none.

'He assembled a group of hackers. The best in the world. Based them in Kiev. They were a kind of cybercrime service centre. They searched for flaws in major global computer systems. Zero days. And a few months ago they came up trumps. They found a flaw in the world's most widely used computer chip. The ultimate zero day.

'He sold an early version to the Russians. That's what they used at Mountville Memorial Hospital. The one that defeated Chuck Drayton, but you don't need me to tell you about that, do you?'

He picked up his empty beer, crushed the can, and had another shot at the bin, getting it in this time. 'Now he's holding us all to ransom. 'We need that zero day, Drayton. We have to avoid it falling into the wrong hands.'

'And which hands are those?'

Cullen ignored the question.

Then he said, 'Schoenberg lost control of his hackers. He needed to find them and eliminate them. They had outlived their usefulness. He had what he wanted. That's where you came in. The useful idiot.'

'He seemed like an idealist,' Drayton said. 'He wanted to *stop* the trade in zero days.'

'Yes, a cyber Geneva Convention, isn't that what he talked about? All very worthy, but breathtakingly fucking naïve and another deception. To weaken us. Because who would benefit from cyber-arms control? It would be the Russians, the Chinese, the Iranians, the North Koreans. That's who. It's cyberspace, Drayton, everybody cheats and everything's deniable. And why would we give up our advantage, and agree to something that would leave us weaker? Do you think Ronald Reagan won the Cold War by signing treaties? He intensified it, and the Soviets couldn't keep up. We won through strength and resolve.'

There was another long silence, and then Cullen said, 'What you need to understand Drayton is that we are on the same side.' He banged his fist against the arm of the chair for emphasis. 'Schoenberg is on the run. His organisation is crumbling, but there is important information we need.'

'What sort of information?'

'Think back to Digital Futures in Yangon. What did you find there?'

'The place was empty.'

'Then think harder. Secondly, we need to know everywhere you went and everybody you met during your little holiday in the Far East. Most importantly, we want you to arrange a meeting with Schoenberg, which of course you will inform us about.'

'How do I contact you?'

Cullen stood and started walking to the door.

'Don't you worry yourself about that, Drayton. We'll know how to find you and will be in touch when we need to. You have forty-eight hours.'

'And then what?' Drayton said.

'If we don't have what we want, things could end badly for you, Drayton. Very badly.'

* * * * *

Drayton closed the window and then sat in the big leather armchair vacated by Cullen. He listened to Captain America's fading footsteps on the stairs and then the faint click of the door to the apartment block as Cullen let himself out to the street.

Drayton had to assume that Cullen's people were watching him closely, that everything he now did was being monitored. But at least Captain America had an interest in keeping him alive, at least for the next forty-eight hours. Cullen thought Drayton had important information; that he was the key to finding Schoenberg.

He replayed Cullen's words in his head. *You're a loser Drayton.* Now he needed to think like the investigator he was supposed to be. He owed that to himself, to prove Cullen wrong, but mostly he owed it to Anna.

He hailed a taxi outside the front of his apartment, and asked the driver to take him to the eastern part of the city, to Normanstrasse, to the former headquarters of the Stasi, the East German secret police. He quickly spotted a black Mercedes with darkened windows, trailing his taxi and making no great attempt to disguise the fact. Drayton smiled. With all the cyber tools at their disposal, it seemed almost quaint. But he assumed that was the point, that they wanted to tell him he was being watched, Cullen wanting it to be obvious. When the taxi dropped Drayton at the old Stasi HQ, the Mercedes pulled into the car park. Waiting.

He asked for Heinz, to whom he'd been introduced by Schoenberg just before leaving for the Far East. Schoenberg had called Heinz the man behind the museum, and they had seemed very close. Drayton waited beneath the watchful eyes of Karl Marx and Felix Dzerzhinsky before a woman appeared and told him Heinz was at the former Stasi Prison in Hohenschoenhausen, preparing for an exhibition. She gave him the directions.

Behind him a tour group was being given an introduction to the Stasi, their guide standing beside a box-like van, cream-coloured and with logos for a food delivery company on its side. She opened a van door to reveal five tiny, windowless cells, explaining that the Stasi operated a fleet of the vans, and used them to snatch people from the streets. She said the East German secret police had built a suffocating system of state surveillance of every citizen. 'Can you imagine living in a country where everything you do is watched?' the guide asked, as Drayton left the building and walked out of the former Stasi compound, trailed by the black Mercedes.

It took him forty-five minutes to reach the prison, walking along roads lined with drab Communist-era slab-like housing blocks. Back then, they came in three shades of grey, and to Drayton not even the bright new facades could disguise their intimidating monotony.

Under the communists, the Central Remand Prison of the Ministry for State Security had been a holding an interrogation centre for opponents of the regime, which meant just about anybody the party decided was suspect. It too had been preserved as a monument and museum, its solid brick walls still topped with wire, watchtowers at its corners.

The Mercedes disappeared for a while, maybe getting a little bored, but was waiting for Drayton when he arrived at the prison, parked just across the road. A man at the ticket office beside the prison's big sliding metal gate told Drayton he could find Heinz in the interrogation block.

Heinz was supervising the hanging of pictures and framed documents at the end of a long corridor lined with identical interrogation rooms. Each room had tables arranged in a T shape. The top of the T was in front of the window with a single chair behind it, facing into the room. There were two more chairs, one either side of the stem of the T. The only other furniture was a heavy metal filing cabinet. The floor was made of fading lino, the walls hung with stained wallpaper.

As Drayton approached him, Heinz was lifting a large frame into place on the wall. It contained the quote from Erich Mielke, the long-time head of the Stasi. It was in capitals in German and English and read, 'COMRADES, WE MUST KNOW EVERYTHING'.

'Sounds like they were busy,' Drayton said.

'Very,' said Heinz. 'By their own definition, the entire population was a potential enemy and needed to be watched.'

When Drayton introduced himself, Heinz said he remembered him and how was Herr Schoenberg? Drayton asked if they could speak in private and Heinz led him into one of the interrogation rooms.

Drayton went to take the seat at the top of the T, in front of the window, but Heinz stopped him, saying that's where the interrogator sat. 'Their interrogations were very sophisticated. The interrogator always sat in front of the window, in front of the light, the light that represented freedom, presenting himself as the friend. Your biggest friend. The key to your freedom. If only you would cooperate. If only you could denounce your other friends and family. It was psychological torture.'

'Well, I promise I am not here to interrogate you,' Drayton said, the two of them sitting either side of the stem of the T. 'It's just that I fear Herr Schoenberg may be in trouble. You see there are those questioning Herr Schoenberg's good name. His credibility.'

He was trying to pick his words carefully, not sure of the reaction.

'There are those who say Schoenberg cooperated closely with the Stasi when he was a scientist in the East, and that he has never given up those loyalties…'

Heinz raised a hand for Drayton to stop, and then began to laugh and kept laughing, so loud it echoed around the small room. It was a bierkeller kind of laugh, as if Heinz had just been told an outrageous joke over two large steins of beer.

'Please. Please. Mr Drayton. Wolfgang Schoenberg a Stasi spy?'

'But he did work on East German computer systems and the East Germany's first network. Would that have been possible without close connections with the party and secret police?'

'You are right that as a young man he worked on those systems, and you are right that the party took a close interest.

But Schoenberg refused to join the party and refused to cooperate with the Stasi. He argued for the purity of science. But for the party, science and technology were always a tool, to serve a political end.'

The humour had vanished now, and Heinz was staring hard across the table at Drayton.

'They accused Wolfgang of being unreliable, restricted him from travelling and threatened to cut his research funds. But still he refused to be compromised. In 1985 he finally quit rather than submit himself to them. He moved from Dresden to Berlin. He had little choice, since they took away his home and car. In Berlin he stayed with relatives, did a little informal teaching and wrote plays. He also became involved with the dissident movement here. While all the time they watched and harassed him, ensuring that he never got any proper employment. It is all in his Stasi file, Mr Drayton.'

'What happened when the wall came down?' Drayton asked.

'He became involved in the politics of unified Germany, but he never stopped fighting for full exposure of the Stasi's crimes and its accountability for them. In 2006, he and I worked together on a computer project, to develop software to help with the reconstruction of files that had been shredded by the Stasi in the weeks after the wall came down. Shredded by hand, most of them. There were so many, it would have taken decades to put them together. You see he was determined that the truth would come out. It became almost an obsession.'

'Did the software work?'

'Up to a point. It certainly sped things up, though there were still glitches, and funding was hard to come by, as at times was political support. There were a lot of ghosts in the files. Still are.'

Then Heinz stood up and said, 'Now if you don't mind, I have things I need to do. Does that sound to you like the résumé of a Stasi stooge?'

It didn't. Nor of a cybercrime mastermind. But then again, they never did.

'And there's one more thing,' Heinz said, stopping at the door. 'You recall that at our last meeting, I showed you a diagram of a Stasi investigation?'

'I remember. It looked like some sort of crazed game of snakes and ladders. A spider's web.'

'It was the result of a six month investigation by seventeen full-time spies and dozens of informers, including the target's wife, as well as friends and neighbours. A map of all his interests, connections and movements. His network. The map was found in the Stasi files eight years after the wall came down. It turned out that the man's wife, who was from Ukraine, had been a long-time Stasi informant. The discovery ended their marriage, and she returned to Kiev, taking their two small children with her.'

'That must have been hard on the guy,' Drayton said.

'It was Mr Drayton. Very hard. And do you know the name of the man, the target of that Stasi investigation? The computer scientist turned playwright?'

But before Drayton could say anything, Heinz answered the question for him.

'It was Herr Wolfgang Schoenberg.'

Heinz waited for the words to sink in. Then he said, 'I do hope that answers your questions. Good Day Mr Drayton.'

He walked out to the long corridor, leaving Drayton sitting alone at the bare desk in the cold interrogation room.

* * * * *

Drayton was in a taxi, returning to his apartment, when he spotted the email. Tun Zaw hadn't needed much encouragement. This time he'd hacked the computers of Bagan's military base and read the regional commander's messages. 'I thought you might find this rather interesting, Mr Chuck,' he wrote in the tone of massive understatement that Drayton was beginning to get used to.

Drayton smiled, the boy's computer skills were coming along just fine. He noted down details from the message and its attachments.

Now he needed to find Milo, and this time he didn't want company.

He closed the curtains in his apartment, turned on the lights, switched on the television, turned up the volume, then placed his smartphone and laptop on his bed, no longer wanting to carry anything connected, through which he might be tracked. He waited at the rear entrance of his apartment block until he heard a tram approaching, walking out quickly as it rumbled past, jogging after it and then boarding at a stop further along the street. He could see no sign of the Mercedes. They could make what they wanted of his visit to the Stasi museums, and he smiled as he thought of Cullen trying to figure out that one. But now he needed to be on his own.

He stayed on the tram until the end of the line and then descended to the U-Bahn, taking a series of random trains, walking down the carriages, getting on and off at the most crowded stations, in and out of coffee shops, always on the move. Surveillance was among the darkest of dark arts, especially in the cyber age. He knew that better than most. You could never be certain. The best you could be was reasonably confident, and only when he reached that point did he take a train to Neukölln.

It was dark by the time he emerged from the U-Bahn onto the crowded sidewalk of Karl Marx Strasse. Street performers surrounding the U-Bahn entrance: classical, sounding roughly like 'The Four Seasons', but only roughly. Then something Chinese. A Latin American trio. From a distance the sound merged into one discordant shriek, mixed up with the street hubbub of countless dialects. A bar boasted of 'The best fucking burger in town'. Next to that was a Turkish shisha place. Then a place full of clanging slot machines. A store selling traditional Arabic clothes next to a sex shop and a punk place with anti-fascist T-shirts in the window. The only thing they had in common was the graffiti, crawling up their walls.

He had only the vaguest idea of where he was going. Milo had described it as his local bar. A rooftop place that accepted Bitcoin. And even if he found the bar, there was no guarantee he'd find Milo there.

He went into the place selling the best fucking burgers, but the barman hadn't heard of any rooftop bar nearby. He tried a bistro, the Karl Marx Bistro, where a server said there was a cocktail bar on top of a new boutique hotel. Drayton took the directions, but it didn't sound very Milo. In a cramped cell phone shop he bought two old Nokia handsets and two pay-as-you-go SIM cards. He asked two girls standing at the counter, topping up the credit on their phones, if they'd heard of a rooftop bar nearby. One mentioned a new Italian place. Good food. Good atmosphere. She thought that was on a roof. But that didn't sound very Milo either. The other girl then described a bar on top of a shopping mall, which was pretty skanky. That was more Milo.

The entrance to the bar at the shopping mall was via the top tier of a multistorey car park attached to the mall, through a heavy metal gate and up a further steep ramp. It was mostly outdoor, worn wooden benches arranged over several tiers and looking out over the rooftops of Neukölln and Kreuzberg. Big dog-shaped silver balloons floated above the benches beside strings of colourful flags and an old green motorbike and side car with crazed-looking mannequins.

It was a young crowd, some with kids playing in sandpits. Just about everybody seemed to be smoking. There was a strong smell of weed, lots of laptops, big speakers blasting out some heavy blues that Drayton didn't recognise. All very cool, all very Milo, except there was no sign of the man himself.

Drayton ordered a beer, a big cloudy wheat beer, and took a seat near the edge, where he could look out over the neighbourhood, but also with a clear view of the entrance to the bar. He took his time, sipping the beer, playing with the old Nokia, or at least as much as you can play with a phone like that. A young guy with a beard that looked like some sort of habitat for rare nesting birds told Drayton he liked the phone, looking at it as if he'd never seen anything quite like that before.

'That's so cool,' said the kid before walking off.

Drayton ordered another wheat beer and put the phone away.

He spotted Milo approaching from the entrance, more of a shuffle than a walk, and looking like he hadn't brushed his hair since the last time Drayton saw him. He ordered a beer and then took a seat at a table in the corner of the roof, opening his laptop and then disappearing into the world beyond his screen.

Drayton took a seat on the bench opposite him.

'Hey Milo. How you doing?'

Milo raised his head from his computer, looking annoyed, not liking the interruption. Then, seeing Drayton, annoyed became puzzled, as he tried to compute what was going on, a look that seemed to Drayton like the facial equivalent of the spinning wheel on a computer screen. Milo's beach ball of death look.

'Chuck? I mean, it's you. Like. You're here.'

'Evidently, Milo. Well done. Where should I be?'

'Well they said you'd gone. You know, back to the States. When they did the thing, Friday.'

'Tell me who "they" are, Milo, and about the "thing" Friday.'

Drayton ordered more beer, because that made listening to Milo a little easier, the young German giving him a rambling and convoluted account of the shutdown of the office. He said he'd gone there as usual on Friday to find computers and desks being removed. Plain clothes security, 'cop-looking', in Milo's words, some of them American, were all over the place, saying it was being closed while an investigation takes place. 'Sent me home, saying, you know, that they'd be in touch. It was a full-on raid.'

'Where are Schoenberg and Norgaard?'

'I don't know. Their phones are unobtainable. The whole thing is really weird.'

'It's worse than weird, Milo. Somebody's trying to kill our investigation.'

'Why would they do that?'

'If I knew, I wouldn't be sitting here, Milo. Tell me, did you send me an email from your work account warning about the Ukrainian hacker, Viktorya Shevchenko?'

Milo shook his head.

'I thought not. You weren't the only one using the account. Somebody broke in and was reading your emails. They sent me one in your name. Schoenberg's too.'

Drayton sipped his beer, looking warily around the bar.

'The investigation seemed to have reached a dead end,' Milo said. The Cardinals wouldn't cooperate. Cullen, Strykov and Wang were hardly talking, let alone sharing information.'

Drayton imagined them sitting round the conference table. Captain America, Muttley and Winnie-the-Pooh, eying each other like surly, sulking teenagers.

'Schoenberg was pretty sure the malware was getting in via a flaw in the fabric of computer chips, as we'd suspected.' Milo said. 'He called it, "The ultimate zero day". Things got pretty heated, especially after the Cardinals found the kill switches to stop the latest attacks. Schoenberg kept telling them that each was a variant of the zero day, parts of a puzzle, which they'd only solve by working together. They just didn't seem to get it.'

'Perhaps they get it only too well,' Drayton said.

And perhaps, he thought, that's exactly as Dmitry intended. And perhaps they were already in touch with him, negotiating exclusive terms.

Then Drayton said, 'The latest attacks, the malware had names, didn't it?'

'It did. The variations. Northghost7 crippled the Chinese oilfields. Charlie32 shutdown Boston. Treptower5 crippled the St Petersburg power grid, and it was Glienicke12 that left four British cities without water. Pretty random.'

'How random, Milo? Who does the naming? Where does malware get its name?'

'It depends. Sometimes bugs are named after the person who discovered them. Sometimes it's in the way they're spread. You know, like a cuddly name that's more likely to be clicked on. Remember the 'ILOVEYOU' virus? Another was named after a stripper, who was a good friend of the programmer who created it.'

'What about our zero days? I take it they're not strippers.'

'No, unfortunately. The names were in the code.'

'So Dmitry named his own bugs? Is that usual?'

'Not really,' said Milo.

'And we don't have any of the keys, the kill switches the Cardinals all suddenly discovered to eliminate the ransomware? Nor do we know how the kill switches were discovered.'

'We have one,' Milo said. 'The kill switch for the Glienicke12 bug was the word Weltkrieg. That's German for "world war".'

'How come we have that one. That's the malware used against the British. Did they hand over the key?'

'No. But they gave it to the German government, because the same strain of malware crippled the Berlin U-Bahn. Schoenberg didn't think that was a deliberate attack, but collateral damage. The bug just getting lost. The German government then shared it with us.'

'Glienicke. Isn't that the bridge between East and West Berlin?'

'Yeah, where they used to exchange spies during the Cold War.'

'Let's go,' Drayton said, draining the rest of his beer.

'Where to?'

'To the bridge of spies.'

* * * * *

It took them half an hour to reach the bridge, riding a red electric scooter that Milo found using an app on his smartphone. It was another of the scooter sharing apps that Drayton found such a pain, except when he needed one. He travelled on the back, Milo driving.

They parked the scooter on the eastern side of the bridge, its sweep of solid steel girders lit by a series of tall street lights. The water of the Havel River passed noiselessly below before emptying into a larger lake that in the darkness resembled a grey blanket beneath the silhouette of forest-clad hills. The beams from the headlights of approaching cars flickered and danced amid the dark green latticework of the bridge.

'What are we looking for?' said Milo.

'I'm not entirely sure,' Drayton replied, walking to the edge of the river, where a path marked the route of the Berlin Wall, and a series of information panels explained about the spy swaps and attempts to escape across the border that ran down the middle of the river, and down the middle of the bridge.

A few slabs of wall had been left as a memorial, though all that was left of the border fortifications was a tired-looking cylindrical pillbox, which had been turned into a store for what looked like gardening equipment.

Drayton crossed the bridge to the western side, stopping where a white plaque was mounted on a concrete pillar. The inscription was in German. A history of the bridge. He began to read.

'*Die von 1904 bis 1907 errichtete Glienicke Brüch wurde im Zweiten Weltkreig zerstört...*'

Milo joined him, translating. 'The bridge was built between 1904 and 1907 and destroyed during the Second World War,' he said.

But neither got any further.

Both stood looking at the inscription.

'*Weltkreig*. It's the password. The kill switch,' said Milo.

Then they began to count.

'And it's the twelfth word on the plaque,' Drayton said.

'Glienicke12,' said Milo, beginning to laugh. 'Glienicke12.'

They sat drinking coffee in a small café near one end of the bridge, Drayton searching his pockets for paper to write down what he could remember of the inscription, since his old

Nokia didn't have a camera. As he dug around in his inside pocket a folded leaflet fell to the floor.

Milo picked it up and placed it on the table.

The title of the leaflet was, 'Cold War Tours. Cold War Berlin by Scooter', and it was the leaflet Drayton had found on the floor of Digital Futures in Yangon before he had been attacked there by Yuri. He'd completely forgotten about it. It had never seemed significant.

Until now.

Several Cold War sites were highlighted by marker pen. The first was Glienicke Bridge with the figure 12 scrawled beside it in blue. The next was Treptower Park, the Soviet war memorial, along with the figure 5. Then Checkpoint Charlie, the most famous crossing point between East and West Berlin, with a 32. And the Nordbahnhof, the North Train Station, which it described as a 'ghost station', closed down and boarded up during the Cold War because it was in no man's land. Beside that was the figure 7.

'Glienicke12, Treptower5, Charlie32 and Northghost7,' Milo said. 'The names of the zero days. Where did you get this?'

'It's a long story, Milo. But this little guide might make for an interesting scooter tour.'

'Chuck, it's more than interesting. It's like, you know, this is it. I mean, LOL. You got 'em.

'*What?*'

'It's *the* code book, Chuck. It's the Cerberus code book.'

* * * * *

It was almost midnight by the time Drayton and Milo arrived back in Neukölln and to a small and smoky basement bar close to Milo's apartment. Like eager tourists exploring the city's Cold War history for the first time, they'd jumped from site to site, searching for information boards or inscriptions. They'd looked for Charlie32 on a whiteboard beside Checkpoint Charlie, close to where actors dressed as Cold War-era guards posed for photographs in front of the preserved border post. The information was in English, and word number thirty-two was 'confronted'.

Next they'd searched for Northghost7. At the Berlin Nordbahnhof there was a big information board inside the former ghost station, alongside photographs of its old bricked-up entrance, showing how it looked during the thirty years it was shut down and sealed. Word number seven was 'Teiling'. German for 'division'.

Treptower5 was harder work, since the inscription above the stained brick archway that marked the entrance to the colossal Soviet war memorial was in both German and Russian. But the Russian came first, and since this was the bug used to cripple the St Petersburg power grid, Drayton reckoned the Russian version most likely contained the key. Word number five was 'Ъессмертны'. The corresponding German word was 'unsterblich', which meant 'immortal'.

Two other Cold War sites had been highlighted in the leaflet, also with numbers indicating a specific word on an inscription. One was a memorial to Peter Fechter, an eighteen-year-old bricklayer who was shot while trying to escape across the wall in 1962. He was left to bleed to death in no man's land. The other was a strip of the Berlin Wall, preserved as a memorial. If these had also been used to name bugs, those bugs had yet to be used. Or at least nobody had owned up to having been hit by one. Drayton and Milo visited both, finding the words, the kill switches, on the information boards.

'Congratulations,' said Milo, raising his glass of beer. 'You've solved the puzzle. You've put all the pieces together. So, what will you do now?'

It was a good question, for which Drayton didn't have an immediate answer. He'd solved *a* puzzle, that was for sure, but who could he trust with that information? Dmitry had been taunting them all, the Americans, British, Russians and Chinese. He smiled as he imagined Captain America, Muttley and Winnie-the-Pooh rushing around Berlin trying to solve their little part of the puzzle, to find the key to unlock their own frozen computer systems, but each now holding them close to their chests, like playing cards.

As he'd suspected, this wasn't about the ransomware. Dmitry was demonstrating his zero day. For sale to the highest bidder. Glienicke12, Treptower5, Charlie32 and Northghost7 were like tasters. Previews of the nuclear-grade cyber-weapon he had for sale. By providing them with keys, he was allowing each of them just enough to verify its power. He knew they wouldn't share.

There could be no other explanation.

'The Americans say Schoenberg is the mastermind,' Drayton said. 'That he's behind all this, working with Dmitry. That he's been fooling us all. And that's why they closed down the Berlin Group. They say he's on the run and they're trying to find him. I went to Lake Tegel this morning. The house is empty, taped off and guarded by police.'

Milo placed his beer slowly back on the table, the remaining colour draining from his pale cheeks. 'That's impossible. Not Schoenberg. No way.'

'I hope you're right, Milo. I really do. That's why we still have work to do. Why I need you to do something else for me.'

'What sort of something else?'

'I need you to follow the money, the Bitcoin, Milo. Did you ever identify the owner of the wallet who was paying Neo, or the exchange where he was cashing out?'

Milo shook his head, looking at his beer glass, the beer as cloudy as the world of cryptocurrencies.

'I have two things that might help,' Drayton said. 'The British hacker who used the handle Razor, real name Matt Dobberman, now dead, he used something called a Pearl Delta Card, a pre-paid debit card, anonymous.'

'It's a popular way of cashing out,' Milo said. 'There are a bunch of these services offered by banks that look the other way. You pay them in Bitcoin and they top up the card in dollars, no questions asked.'

'Check it out for me, Milo.'

Drayton then pulled a folded piece of paper from his pocket, information from Tun Zaw's last email. 'I think this will lead to Cerberus,' he said. 'This is the date and rough time that ten thousand US dollars in Bitcoin was transferred, and the wallet into which it was paid. Trace the transaction.'

'Who owns the wallet,' Milo asked.

'A Burmese general, but that's not important. It's the corresponding wallet address we need, the one the payment came from. I think you'll find it belonged to Digital Futures, to Dmitry Gerasimov.

Milo put the paper in his pocket. 'Burmese generals have Bitcoin accounts?'

'It's a lucrative business, being in the army in that country, Milo, especially when you are working with Dmitry.'

Drayton then placed a newspaper on the table in front of them.

'And there's something else,' he said, pointing to an article on an inside page.

'I'd like you to hack into a Berlin government web server and put me on the guest list of this event. Is that possible?'

'I'm not sure that's legal, Chuck.'

'I didn't ask if it was legal. I asked if it was possible.'

Milo looked at the newspaper. The headline said simply 'Superheroes'. There was a photo of Efren Bell, together with some Berlin government officials and a handful of tech entrepreneurs, the superheroes of the headline, who'd won a tech start-up competition sponsored by Bell. The article said their prizes would be presented at what it called a star-studded reception at Bell's villa in the Berlin suburb of Pankow tomorrow.

'I'll need a photo. Your mug shot.'

'Well, take one Milo,' said Drayton, positioning himself against the wall, while Milo raised his smartphone and took the picture.

'My name is Andreas Fischer, and I'm technical director of AF Global Digital Solutions. Can you remember that?'

'Sure, Andreas,' Milo said, smiling. Sounding enthusiastic now.

'Talk to nobody about any of this. Tell nobody what we have done this evening, and say nothing about meeting me. You understand?'

'Like, yeah. Cool,' said Milo.

Drayton handed him one of the old Nokias he had bought in Neukölln earlier that evening. Milo rotated it in his hand, looking under it and at the back, as if he'd never seen one before.

'It's a phone, Milo. Not a smartphone, but a dumb phone. And right now, dumb phones are good. It makes calls. Sends messages if you're lucky. My number is saved in your Nokia, and I have yours in mine. This is the only way you're to contact me.'

Milo nodded, still examining the phone.

* * * * *

Drayton returned to his apartment via the rear courtyard, the lights and television as he'd left them. As he lay on his bed, exhausted from all the sightseeing, his Nokia beeped, a good old-fashioned earthy beep. A message from Milo, saying 'All done. You're on the guest list. Starts at midday.'

He slept until mid-morning, picked up his original cell phone, and then walked to the café beside Eberswalde Strasse U-Bahn station, where he ordered the gluten-free and sugar-free vegan banana bread and an orange juice. Anna was right, the bread was good, it made a great breakfast, healthy too, and he wished he'd told her that. He wished he'd told her a bunch of other things as well.

'No Anna this morning?' asked the server.

He hadn't heard the news, and Drayton couldn't find the words to tell him.

'You OK, Chuck?'

'I'm fine. I'm fine.'

From there he took a taxi to Pankow, deeper into the old East. He made no attempt to disguise where he was going, no attempt to shake off the Mercedes. Thinking they might even turn out to be helpful.

He was taking a risk, a calculated risk, by using the Fischer name, as he had in Hong Kong. But he needed to stir things up. To provoke. He needed to see where Efren Bell fitted in. After all, Bell had been guest of honour at the mansion on the Peak in Hong Kong, the mansion where Dobberman's phone had woken up the first time. And Efren Bell and Dmitry Gerasimov had a history. They'd worked together before. Then there

262

was Anna. She'd been working for him. She'd inadvertently identified Drayton to Dmitry at the party, and then she'd died. That might even be why she'd died.

An innocent caught up in something deadly.

He needed to know.

The Mayakovsky Ring was a settlement of large, imposing villas, set back from a circular tree-lined road close to the Schloss Schönhausen, the former country estate of the Prussian royal family, which the communists had used as a guest house.

Some of the Mayakovsky villas were built in traditional style, others ultra-modern. Efren Bell's was one of the newest, and from a distance it looked like the Starship Enterprise from the *Star Trek* movies, broad, with a flat roof and slightly curved. Closer-up the Enterprise became more like a layered cake over three levels, each layer smaller than the one below.

He gave the name Fischer, and was handed a name tag with his photo. The place was busy, light classical music playing in the background, servers moving through the crowd with trays of drinks. Drayton took a glass of champagne and walked into the main reception area, where Bell was being photographed with nerdy-looking youngsters. Presumably his 'superheroes', the winners of his tech competition. An older man joined them, looking a little stiff in a suit and tie in what was pretty much a tie-free zone. Somebody from the Berlin government, Drayton guessed.

Drayton bided his time, working the room, engaging in bits of meaningless small talk, the sort of mindless jargon which seemed to come naturally to the techies. The room was hung with plenty of expensive looking art, much of it with a Buddhist theme.

Bell and his superheroes climbed a wide spiral staircase to the next level of the cake, then went out onto a terrace overlooking a lawn for more photographs. After a while, they began to drift back inside, until Bell was alone with his photographer, posing for some solo photographs, the snapper telling him to straighten his back, but to keep it casual, that casual was good.

'Smart kids, your superheroes,' said Drayton.

'Very smart,' Bell replied. 'The sort of kids we need to encourage. My dream is to harness the best technical brains on the planet. The winners here are mostly data-driven start-ups. Jürgen is developing digital maps for self-driving cars that can tell you where you want to go before you know yourself. The key is to teach the map by feeding it so much data that it can anticipate your mood and correlate that with your interests and desires, with the time and day of the week as well, and then feed you suggestions for your trip. Danielle is developing virtual reality goggles that will enable football fans to see what the players are seeing while they're playing the game.'

'Cool,' said Drayton.

'It's more than that. Imagine where we can go with that technology. It means getting inside somebody else's head. Seeing things as they see them. Imagine, understanding the criminal mind. The political mind, the military, the consumer. Or even your friends and colleagues. All you need is data. Lots of data. And there's a mountain being generated all the time. It's just a question of harvesting it. That's the big race we're in. We live in exciting times, Andreas,' Bell said, looking at Drayton's name tag.

'Or scary times,' said Drayton. 'You think people will simply accept their data being harvested and used like this? I already see push-back.'

Bell shook his head, sort of smiling, though it struck Drayton as more of a sneer.

'That's pure ignorance,' he said. 'We can't be held back by digital luddites. We have to take people out of their comfort zones. It was Facebook's Mark Zuckerberg who said, "Move fast and break things. Unless you are breaking stuff, you are not moving fast enough." We have to take up that task and challenge old attitudes'.

He adjusted his long grey ponytail.

'We have to learn to trust in the future. The problem is that people don't always know what is best for them. Privacy is gone, Andreas. It's yesterday's battle.'

'Comrades, we must know everything,' Drayton said.

'What?'

'It's a quote.'

'Was that Zuckerberg too? Maybe Apple's Steve Jobs? Or was it Google's Eric Schmidt?'

'It was the Stasi's Erich Mielke, a few words of wisdom from the long-time head of the East German secret police. He was a great data harvester and terrific when it came to dealing with non-believers.'

'What exactly are you getting at, Andreas?' said Bell, the tech evangelist suddenly looking a lot less happy, like somebody had just thrown a shoe at his pulpit.

'Nice area, Efren,' Drayton said, ignoring the question, and looking out across the lawn. 'You know this whole settlement used to be a walled-off compound for East German leaders. Pretty plush for a bunch of communists, don't you think? And that house over there, beyond the end of your lawn, the old one that's now a kindergarten, that was once the home of Erich Honecker, the head of the party, the Socialist Unity Party, I think they called themselves.'

'And?'

'And none of that makes you feel uncomfortable?'

'This area is now home to some of the leading figures in the tech industry Andreas, looking to the future, not dwelling on the past. And you, you're quite the local historian.'

'Not really. There's an information board near the entrance to the settlement. And you know what? You can learn a lot from information boards.'

Bell moved a step closer to Drayton. There were now just the two of them on the terrace.

'Do I know you, Andreas? I have a feeling we might have met.' His tone was now cold and suspicious, his face empty of its trademark bonhomie.

'I don't think so Efren. Though I was at your party at the old Berlin brewery when you announced you were raising one hundred billion dollars for your Digital Pagoda Fund. Pretty ambitious. How's that going?'

'The money's flowing in, since you ask. Investors want a stake in the future. In groundbreaking technology.'

'And *secure* technology. Isn't that what you're promising?'

'Naturally. In a world where hardly a day goes by without another damaging hack or another theft of data, investors are naturally excited by the promise of security. AI-driven security.'

'And the more scary it gets out there in cyberspace, the more they flock to you.'

A woman appeared at the door to the room. 'Efren darling, you're needed downstairs. More photographs, I'm afraid.'

As he moved towards the door, Drayton called after him. 'I was in Hong Kong too Efren, at the party on the Peak. Nice spread. So, I'm quite the groupie. You might have seen me in the crowd. Apologies if I looked a little sceptical. Such a tragedy about that young woman who drowned in the harbour. On a cruise after the party. Anna Schultz, I believe her name was.'

Efren Bell stopped and turned slowly back towards Drayton. 'I wouldn't really know about that. Now, if you'll excuse me.'

'Sure, Efren. Wouldn't want to keep you from your disciples. It's just that I'm sure she said she was working for you.'

* * * * *

Drayton followed Efren Bell back inside the house, pausing near the top of the spiral staircase to look at the artwork hung on the walls. Watercolour paintings showed temples with monks carrying umbrellas, water buffalos up to their necks in mud, smiling village girls with flowers in their hair. They shared the same fuzzy lines, giving the paintings a slightly chaotic feel if you stood too close, the work of the same artist, whose scrawled signature was in the corner of each of them.

Heavily stylised photographs showed red-brick temples topped by golden spires, shot at weird angles, playing with the sun's rays and the late afternoon light that Drayton remembered from Bagan. One had been taken from a low angle beneath a temple entrance, the sun acting like a spotlight on the engravings above, highlighting the vicious faces of the snarling dogs.

Two large teak chests with a series of Buddha statues stood in a room to one side of the staircase. Most were of the Buddha sitting with various hand poses. They were old and weathered, originals or else very good copies. Drayton's eyes were drawn to a display cabinet in the centre of the room. This one contained another Buddha head, only this one was fixed on top of a stone, a four-sided stone, with words engraved on each face, like those he'd seen in Bagan. *Very valuable, and very rare*, that's how Tun Zaw has described them, only found in Bagan, and just like the one Professor Richard Pendleton had been working on before he died. Drayton raised his cell phone and photographed it, moving around and capturing each of its four sides. Then he heard a noise behind him.

'It's a Myazedi Quadrilingual stone. An inscription stone, and it's very special,' said Efren Bell, who was standing along with four men with cropped hair and dark jackets, doing a bad impersonation of bouncers outside a second-rate night club, looking at Drayton as if he definitely wasn't welcome on the dance floor.

Bell joined Drayton beside the cabinet, the bouncers remaining by the door. 'From the twelfth century. The ancient Bagan civilization. The pride of my collection.'

'It must have been difficult to get hold of.'

'Nothing's difficult to get if you want it badly enough.'

'I prefer the plain old Buddhas. More pleasing on the eye than all these squiggles.'

'You really don't understand,' Bell said, as if talking to a slightly dim child. 'The meaning of this stone. The power of it. What it represents. Back then, and today too. Today more than ever.'

'Tell me,' Drayton said.

'Most temples had inscription stones, though not many have survived. They were an expression of the power of the donor, because he had the money, but also because he was literate. In an age when few people could read or write, language was power. And this stone is not just one language, but four.'

'That's a lot of power,' Drayton said. 'Mon, Burmese, Pyu and Pali, if I'm not mistaken.'

'Very good. So you're a scholar of ancient Bagan?'

'When I'm not doing Cold War Berlin. But maybe this guy, this donor, just got a monk to write it. You, know, a ghost writer. Weren't they the literate ones?'

'You're a very funny man Andreas, but I think you miss my point. Ancient Bagan was like Europe of the Dark Ages, where education and literacy vanished and reading and writing was restricted largely to a small elite. In Europe's case, the Catholic Church. A time of widespread ignorance and superstition. Outside the elite, goblins, dragons and fairies ruled the day. Not dissimilar to today, when the only language that matters is zeros and ones. That's the language that drives everything, and yet ninety-nine per cent of the population is as illiterate as the peasants of the Dark Ages or of ancient Bagan.'

'And I suppose the superstition, the modern day fairies, goblins and dragons, that would be social media?' Drayton said. 'The ignorant masses running around and burning effigies created by fake news. That's a very bleak view.'

'We have to nurture and empower those who speak the language of the future,' said Bell. 'The superheroes, we have been honouring today. Let them – let *us* – lead the way. That's what drives everything I do. Ignorance is inevitable in an age of rapid technical change. The important thing is that technology is allowed to forge ahead, and that technologists become leaders. Ignorance should not be allowed to stand in the way of progress.'

'The vanguard of the people. Wasn't that Lenin?' Drayton said. 'The new Masters of the Universe. Isn't that what you and your friends on Wall Street used to call yourselves before you brought the world's economy to its knees? But of course, you survived the financial carnage, didn't you Efren. Cashed in big time. Clever algorithms, isn't that what you called it? And whatever did happen to your old partner. Dmitry, wasn't that his name? Dmitry Gerasimov.'

Bell ignored the question, circling the inscription stone. Circling Drayton.

'Now perhaps you can understand why I had to have this stone Andreas. Or is it Chuck? Chuck Drayton?'

* * * * *

At that moment they were interrupted by loud voices and shrieks of laugher from just outside the room, into which bounded the big, bouncy superhero called Danielle, pulling along in her wake a diminutive man with round glasses and peroxide hair, together with the photographer and several other techies.

'Efren, darling, look who's here. Its Michel Bandini. *The* Michel Bandini.'

Bell switched into warm smile mode, stretching out a hand to greet Bandini, telling him how simply wonderful it was to see him and how his art was truly groundbreaking.

'He's created the most amazing visualisation,' said a gushing Danielle. 'It represents the ebb and flow of SMS data from cell phones all across Berlin, can you believe it? All superimposed on data flows from weather beacons. It's like *unreal*. You *must* see it Efren.'

'That is *so* amazing,' Drayton said, inserting himself in the conversation, and remembering the exhibition at Anna's gallery. 'I've seen your work. In fact, it's *beyond* amazing. You *must* get a photograph with Efren. Perhaps with our guests from the Berlin government too.'

As they moved out of the room and towards the spiral staircase, Bell's bouncer-like minders stepped forward, but Bell raised a hand, ever so slightly, but enough to send a message and have them retreat. Not now, not here.

They gathered in the garden for the photographs. As they did, Drayton ducked behind parked cars, the BMWs of the Berlin government officials next to Efren Bell's OmniX, and out of the gate. Once on the road, he began to run towards the exit of the compound, moving quickly past the sprawling villas, sitting like monuments to the privilege of old communist elite, and now seamlessly colonised by Efren Bell and the high priests of tech. Had he gone too far with Bell? His plan had been to stir things up. To provoke. He'd certainly done that, and more, as looking behind him he saw Bell's men in black coming out of the villa.

He reached the gate leading to the grounds of the old palace, the Schloss Schönhausen, sitting pretty beyond a perfectly manicured lawn, looking like a picture on a tin of biscuits. He looked all around him thinking, where the fuck are they when you need them? Then he saw them, Cullen's not-so-secret surveillance team in their black Mercedes with the darkened windows, parked just inside the gate. He tried to open the rear door. It was locked, so he banged on the window, then banged again, more urgent now, because he could see Efren Bell's bouncers getting closer.

There was a muffled click as the car's central lock was disabled. Drayton opened the rear door and quickly climbed in. Two sat up front, big men, puzzled men, because a surveillance target wasn't supposed to join them in the car. That wasn't in the manual.

'Can you please drive?' Drayton said.

They looked at Drayton, then looked at each other.

'Because those two guys,' said Drayton, pointing. 'Yes them. The ones in black heading right towards us, looking less than happy. Well, they ain't coming to visit the Schloss. You get what I'm saying?'

But they didn't get what Drayton was saying, and for a while just sat looking straight ahead, weighing up the situation, because the target they'd been told to watch from a distance now filled their rear-view mirror, and he was telling them what to do. That wasn't in the manual either.

Looking at the back of their heads, Drayton could almost see the cogs turning.

The men in black getting closer, bouncers on a mission.

'Look, if they hurt me, that is not good for your boss, Ric Cullen. Because he won't get the information he wants. And that is very bad for you. And it's especially bad for me. So can we please get the fuck out of here.'

They were just a few feet away now, reaching inside their jackets, reaching for guns. That definitely *was* in the manual, because the car's engine burst to life, and with a screech of tyres, the Mercedes accelerated away. Drayton looked behind to see the men running back towards the compound. They wouldn't be far behind.

The Mercedes moved quickly through the Pankow traffic, weaving in and out and almost colliding with an oncoming tram. It then turned and drove beside an elevated railway line back towards the centre of Berlin.

'Thank you. Now I'd like you to call Cullen and tell him we need to meet and we need to meet now.'

Once again the men in the front took time to process the request. They had still not spoken a word to Drayton. The driver, who seemed to be in charge, gave an almost imperceptible nod of his head, and the one in the passenger seat pulled out a cell phone and made the call. He spoke with a southern American drawl, cupping the phone in an attempt to keep the call private, but Drayton still picked up some of the muffled words.

'Yes, he's in car now, sir ... I don't know ... No real choice ... That's what he said ...'

Then he hung up.

Drayton looked at the photographs he'd taken of the inscription stone in Bell's villa. Then he emailed them to Tun Zaw, along with a two word message, 'Look familiar?'

He pressed 'send' just as they turned into a narrow cobbled street with tram lines running down the centre, and from there into a courtyard, stopping beside rubbish bins and several bicycles, chained to a fence. The driver pointed at a side door leading into a tenement block. There was a café on the ground level.

'In there. Follow the stairs. Above the café.' The driver said.

Drayton did as instructed; the stairs leading to a dark first floor corridor. A woman emerged from an unmarked door and gestured for him to come inside and through to a stuffy inner office with bare white-washed walls. The only furniture was a table in front of the window, chairs either side, and an old metal cabinet. It looked a lot like the interrogation rooms at the Stasi prison. Drayton took the chair in front of the window.

Five minutes later Ric Cullen entered the room, closing the door behind him. He sat down in front of Drayton. 'So what's the urgency?'

'You're wrong about Schoenberg.'

Drayton told Cullen about the inscription stone in Efren Bell's villa, showing him the photographs, and about how that led to Myanmar, to Professor Richard Pendleton. And to Dmitry.

'He's working with Dmitry,' Drayton said. 'They go back a long way. And every time Dmitry breaks into the computers of another hospital, or a dam, or a water company, it sends investors flocking to Efren Bell's Digital Pagoda Fund with its promise of a future you can't hack.'

'That's a very interesting theory,' Cullen said. 'You're saying that one of the world's greatest technological visionaries, who is also an American, is a cyber-crook.'

'I don't see any other explanation.'

'Well, try this. He likes Buddhist art and he's a rich man. Rich men aren't always picky about where they buy their art from. And as for Dmitry, don't you think that's a little far-fetched?'

'Efren Bell knows the origin of the stone.'

'So you're now an expert on antiquities, are you Drayton?', Cullen sneered, tossing back Drayton's phone. 'Maybe there's another explanation. That your judgement is being clouded by hatred. By revenge. Maybe even jealousy. That it's all gotten very personal because you're blaming Efren Bell for your girlfriend's accident.'

Cullen stood, the sudden movement tipping over his chair. 'Is that it? You demanded this meeting just to slander Efren Bell? We need Schoenberg. That's the priority. And your time is running out.'

'There's one more thing,' said Drayton, as Cullen made for the door. 'You asked if I found anything at the office of Digital Futures in Rangoon. I did.'

Cullen turned, picked up the chair with one sweep of his thick arm and sat back down.

Then there was a knock of the door. The woman entered holding a cell phone. 'I think you'll want to take this, Ric. It's urgent.'

Cullen left the room, and Drayton opened the window to get some fresh air.

Then he listened, listened hard.

The sounds were chillingly familiar.

First he heard a clanging and screeching, getting louder and then fading, followed by the ringing of a bell. A tram was passing below the window and around a bend in the track. Then a sound that was like faint bursts of static. Below the window, a woman was sweeping the sidewalk. Then a deep rumbling, as a truck passed along the cobbled street.

Finally, from the café below there was the sound of jazz. It was Brubeck's 'Blue Rondo à la Turk'.

* * * * *

Drayton lowered himself out of the window, stepping first onto a narrow ledge and then onto a striped awning that covered the outside seating area of the café below. The awning strained under his weight. He felt for its frame under his feet, keeping close to the wall, inching towards the edge from where he hoped he could lower himself to the ground.

Then one foot slipped onto the fabric of the awning, which began to rip, tearing from one corner. He felt himself sliding and then falling, his arms swinging for something to grab hold of. For a moment he managed to grip one of the awning's metal supports, until it started to buckle and bend, but at least it broke his fall before he crashed onto a table below and then to the ground.

And then he ran as fast as a throbbing ankle would carry him, sticking close to the buildings and following the tram tracks until they reached a wider road of expensive shops and restaurants. A little ahead of him was the old Checkpoint Charlie border crossing, surrounded by a clutch of kitschy souvenir shops and the usual throngs of tourists.

Dobberman's smartphone had been in that room when it last came online. The sounds were unmistakable. Somehow it had got from Bangkok to the mansion in Hong Kong and then to Cullen's Berlin office. Perhaps there was a rational explanation. That Cullen had somehow got hold of it as part of his own investigation.

Cullen also knew about Anna. Perhaps there was an explanation for that too, but he wasn't inclined to hang around and ask.

A side road led to series of low kiosk-like shops, painted bright yellow. One was serving coffee and sausages, another selling tickets for a hot air balloon promising a bird's eye view of Berlin. There were cars parked in front and out the back of the kiosks, which Drayton recognised as old Trabants, the box-like pre-fabricated car built in the old East Germany.

Then he spotted the OmniX with its darkened windows, two men climbed from the back, the men from Bell's villa, walking quickly towards him. He made for a crowded shop with a big sign, 'Trabi Safari', above its entrance, where he inserted himself among the tourists poking through shelves of model Trabants, as well as keyrings, mugs and T-shirts, all with images of the old car.

Drayton lifted a small green Trabant from one of the shelves, rotating it between his fingers, all the time looking beyond the little car and out of the window, through which he could see his pursuers waiting by a neighbouring café, biding their time.

The crowd in the shop began to thin, the tourists leaving through a rear door towards a wet and pot-holed car park where several Trabants were lined up amid deep puddles. From behind the shop's counter, a man with a scraggy beard and long earrings looked up from where he was feeding an old black dog and told Drayton it was his last chance.

'We have just one car left,' he said. 'The next safari leaves in five minutes, following the course of the wall. Come join us. Self-drive your own Trabi, man. What do you think?'

Drayton started to say thanks, but no thanks, but then felt a hand on his arm, and a familiar voice interrupted him.

'We'll take it,' said Vika.

* * * * *

Vika was wearing a silver wig and a pair of big round sunglasses. She handed Drayton a yellow 'I love Berlin' baseball cap and lurid red-rimmed shades as they walked out the back towards a line of eight Trabants. They were parked one behind the other, bumper to bumper, with a small electric vehicle at the front, preparing to lead the convoy.

'Put them on,' Vika said, as Drayton hesitated at the glasses. 'When the cars pull out, they'll be looking for a single, straight-looking guy.'

Vika chose a light blue Trabant in the middle of the pack, and when Drayton went to climb into the passenger seat, she said, 'The other door, Drayton. You're driving.'

A bubbly guide, speaking heavily accented English, moved down the line, helping to start each car. He told Drayton to keep his foot on the pedal, to pump the gas while he turned the key. The engine came to life with a roar, before spluttering and cutting out.

'Jesus, Drayton. Have you never driven a car before?' said Vika.

'Never a car like this.'

He tried again, and this time he pumped so hard on the accelerator that the roar quickly became a scream. The guide told him to ease off, and this time the spluttering was punctuated by a series of pops before the Trabant settled into a steady but shaky chug, sending up clouds of smoke from its exhaust. The guide explained the controls, which didn't take long. Three pedals and a spindly gear stick protruding from just below the steering wheel. He wished Drayton good luck, and said to just follow the car in front.

The car radio then came to life with the guide talking from the lead electric car, joking about the Trabants. 'This is a socialistic car. So the radio is one way. I can talk to you, but you can't talk back to me. Let's go.'

The chugging and gasping convoy pulled out of the compound, engulfed in stinking exhaust fumes, and onto the road in front of the yellow shops. Drayton struggled to keep the engine alive, pumping the accelerator while wrestling with the gearstick that initially refused to move from first gear. The steering wheel was heavy and the brakes like mush.

'For fuck's sake,' he said, as the car jolted and shook.

'Don't knock it,' Vika said. 'My grandmother had one of these. There was a fourteen-year waiting list. I think they've got personality. It's cute. She used to say that the headlights were like two big innocent eyes staring at you. She said they were the only eyes she could trust.'

'Well, yeah,' said Drayton, not finding it quite so cute and the personality more than a little prickly. 'And in any case. What happened to you? Why did you run from Hong Kong?'

'Not now,' Vika replied. 'And I didn't run. Drive.'

Through the crackly radio, the guide was giving a running commentary on the sites they were passing. A stretch of the old wall preserved as a monument, which Drayton recognised as one of the places he'd visited with Milo. Then the solid marble and limestone façade of the German Finance Ministry, which had been Hermann Göring's Ministry of Aviation under the Nazis, before it became the headquarters of the Soviet military administration and then home for Communist East Germany's Council of Ministers.

So many ghosts.

'Beware of bicycles,' the guide said. 'But especially be aware of big capitalistic cars driving fast.' Because at that moment one big capitalistic car in the form of the OmniX was driving fast. Very fast. Right behind the convoy, pulling out and alongside them before being forced back by an oncoming bus.

The Trabi convoy turned east, heading into the heart of the old East Berlin, taking a narrow cobbled street, along which the little cars bounced and rattled. The guide said something about the suspension, but it was drowned out by static. Drayton didn't need to hear. He could feel every bump, every stone, and in his spindly rear-view mirror he could see the big black OmniX, lurking behind the pack of Trabants like a hungry predator waiting to pounce.

Vika was right, the men in the OmniX couldn't be sure in which car Drayton was travelling. There were three Trabants with solo male drivers. Numbers six and seven, immediately behind them, and another, two cars ahead. And the Trabants were low and dark. It was tough to identify clearly those inside.

The convoy spluttered past a statue of the whiskered authors of the communist manifesto, Marx and Engels looking suitably pensive for a group of snap-happy tourists, who turned their cameras on the passing Trabants.

'Trabis are made out of a kind of fibreglass, a combination of resin and cotton waste that came from the Soviet Union,' the guide was saying. 'So they are a triumph of recycling. Except pigs would sometimes eat them. They had to position the petrol tank as high as possible because they had no fuel pumps.'

None of which made Drayton feel any better.

'Oooh, that is an aggressive capitalistic car...' said the guide, his voice trailing away as the OmniX swung out parallel to the convoy and accelerated beside it. It then turned in sharply and rammed a Trabant with the single driver, just behind Vika and Drayton. The little car jumped and span, then bounced across the sidewalk, coming to a standstill just in front of Karl Marx. Another metre or so, and it might have landed in his lap.

The tourists shouted and ran as the men from the OmniX struggled with the twisted front door of the Trabant before pulling out the driver and throwing him face down on the lawn in front of Engels.

Drayton swung his Trabant sharply to the right and down a side road, accelerating as fast he could, crunching the gears as he tried to find fourth.

'That's reverse Drayton. Not a good idea. And why the fuck have you come this way. We were safer with the convoy,' Vika said.

'Car number six, are you OK? And number five, you've gone the wrong way,' said the despairing and fading voice of the guide from the radio, until his voice was drowned out by static as the signal was lost.

But Drayton wasn't listening to that or to Vika, because the OmniX was back on the road. They'd seen Drayton turn off and were accelerating fast after him.

Vika had her laptop open now, and was working the keyboard hard.

The Trabi's engine screamed and its tyres screeched as it slid around another corner, crossing in front of a tram, and then forcing a taxi to brake and swerve, hitting the side of a bus. Drayton mounted the sidewalk onto a small area of parkland, churning up the grass and mud. Vika looked behind them. The OmniX was following, right up onto the grass.

'Hold on!,' Drayton said, as the Trabi bounced down a series of steps and across a piece of wasteland, an old factory complex looming ahead. He slowed, Vika glancing at him, before accelerating into the yard of the complex, the OmniX close behind.

'There's no way out,' Vika screamed.

Perhaps, perhaps not. It was Anna's factory complex, the one where she had her gallery and where Efren Bell had his vision, where Drayton remembered a narrow, partially blocked exit at the rear, too narrow and low to be much good for anything, except perhaps a Trabant. The little car rattled and its engine shrieked as it crossed the old embedded railway lines, Drayton wrestling with its wheel, as he turned down the narrow path at the rear of the complex.

'That's impossible,' Vika said, as she looked ahead of them. The Trabant scraped along the broken wall and under the slumped archway, which gave way, bricks crashing to the ground in their wake. Not even the most intelligent car in the world was going to follow through there.

Drayton allowed himself the slightest of smiles, banging the top of the wheel in triumph, as he turned out onto a wide street beside the Spree River, only to find himself stuck beside a crippled tram. Then the Trabi's engine cut out. He flooded the engine trying to start it. It came roaring back to life on the fourth attempt.

'Shit,' Drayton said, his fleeting moment of triumph evaporating as fast as the approaching OmniX, which again filled his rear-view mirror. He pressed the accelerator as far as it would go, but it was never going to be far enough.

'Let him catch us,' Vika said.

'What?'

'Let him catch us. I need a stronger signal.'

He glanced across at her. She was still working the keyboard.

A sudden heavy downpour pounded on the Trabant's windscreen, the wipers spreading the water, not clearing it, as if the little car was submerging, diving into the murky depths, everything ahead turning to liquid.

'What are you doing?' he said.

'That car is full of sensors and micro-processors. It's basically a computer with four wheels and an engine. The smartest car in the world, Bell calls it. Do you know how many computers this Trabant has?'

'I'd say zero. Roughly,' he replied, head bent forward, close to the windscreen.

'That would be right, Drayton. Apart from this one,' she said, patting her laptop. 'No contest.'

The OmniX accelerated, trying to pull alongside. Vika tapped at her computer and the OmniX's sunroof and all four windows opened. Rain swept into the car, as if a bucket had been emptied over it. The big car broke sharply and swerved. In his mirror Drayton could see them struggling to close the hatches, hammering at buttons that were no longer under their control. Another tap from Vika and even above the roar of the Trabi and the pounding of the rain, Drayton could hear loud music blasting, full volume. Heads turned all along the street. OmniX-treme audio, the brochure called it. Eighteen speakers, six independent channels of discrete audio, dedicated sound for all corners of the car. Bluetooth, Wi-Fi controlled. Perfect.

Another tap from Vika and the boot opened.

'Whoops,' she said. 'I thought that was the bonnet.'

They were now passing the East Side Gallery, the longest remaining fragment of Berlin Wall, a memorial plastered with paintings and graffiti.

The OmniX was back beside them. It swerved and rammed the Trabant, which jumped onto the sidewalk, scattering more tourists standing beside a mural of a Trabant bursting through the Berlin Wall, a caption saying, 'Test the Best'. They scraped along the wall under the painting of the old Soviet and East German leaders, Brezhnev and Honecker, kissing each other.

The Trabi bounced back onto the main road. The OmniX was waiting for them, but Vika was now driving it, the vehicle control system under her command.

The OmniX jerked and jolted, accelerated sharply, then broke hard. 'Fuck,' she said. 'I've never driven one of these before.'

But she quickly got the hang of it, and as she clicked and tapped, the OmniX accelerated away rapidly and then span. Then it reversed at speed, hitting an oncoming tram and then a truck. Drayton could see the driver wrestling with the steering wheel and stamping on pedals that no longer responded. The men in the back were waving their hands wildly, pinned in their places by seat belts that just kept tightening.

The OmniX then reversed at speed across the road, through a fence and onto the bank of the Spree. Then it slowed, Vika struggling with the signal. But it had enough momentum to reach the edge of the river before dropping into the water a metre or so below.

Vika clapped her hands in triumph. 'What did Efren Bell call them, 'the future of transport'?'

'Something like that,' said Drayton, pushing at the battered door of the Trabi, which fell away on to the street. 'Your grandmother was right. These things are pretty cute. When you get the hang of them.'

'She was a sharp woman. Now cross the bridge and into Kreuzberg.'

As the Trabant spluttered and chugged across the river, a crowd gathered on the bank below, watching the bubbling water. There was no sign of the car.

Vika directed Drayton through the backstreets of Kreuzberg until they reached a narrow lane of old tenement blocks daubed with graffiti. They entered a small courtyard.

'OK. Get out,' she said.

Drayton followed her instructions, climbing out of the car. They waited in silence, Vika checking her phone.

'There's something you need to know,' she said. 'The attack on the Mountville Memorial Hospital in Washington DC, the first time a version of the Cerberus zero day was used, it didn't get round your defences. Your system was strong. It held.'

'So how did it get through?' Drayton asked. 'How the fuck did it get through.'

'Somebody let it in. Somebody killed your defences. Somebody on the inside, at the hospital.'

Drayton steadied himself against the door of the Trabant, hardly noticing the white van pulling into the courtyard and parking just behind. 'But how …' he began, his voice trailing away as a group of masked men rushed at him from the back of the van, pushing him hard against the side of the Trabant.

The last thing he remembered was a hand across his mouth, the sharp prick of a needle in his neck, and Vika's words trailing away.

'I'm sorry, Drayton,' she said.

* * * * *

The hours passed in a haze of muffled consciousness. Voices in a language Drayton didn't understand. Hands firmly guiding him. A siren. More voices, raised this time as he was pushed and pulled through a jostling crowd. Echoey announcements, like at an airport. Or possibly a railway station.

Whatever they'd injected him with wasn't enough to completely knock him out, but sufficient to dull any real sense of where he was or what he was doing. He was easier to transport that way. He wanted to shout, but couldn't get the words out; wanted to struggle, but his limbs didn't respond.

They sat him down for a while on a hard wooden bench. He could smell food and then a cigarette. They gave him water, helping lift and then tilt the plastic bottle into his mouth, but he could barely swallow, and it spilt down his front. There was another tinny announcement, one they'd been waiting for. They helped him to his feet, the world around him a fuzzy kaleidoscope of shifting light and colour.

The walk was shorter this time. He was helped up steps and then along a narrow corridor and into a small compartment, where his guides left him, closing and locking the door. He lay on a long soft bench and slept. A deep sleep at first, but then he vaguely registered the door opening again and the heavy panting of a dog right beside his ear. Later there was shouting and banging, angry drunken shouting. A woman's voice roaming the corridor outside.

Drayton wasn't sure how long he slept, but when he woke it was with a start, in response to a series of sharp jolts. It was only then he realised he was on a train. A slow train and an old train. His head was heavy and it ached, as if he had a hangover, a bit like the morning after his Mekong whisky session with Bret, only without the whisky. But he could now see and hear, and his limbs were once again taking instructions. He looked for his telephone and watch, but both had been taken. At least he was alive, as far as he could tell. And if they'd intended to kill him, surely they'd have done it by now?

He switched on a light above his bench. The bulb twitched and flickered, before settling down into a barely discernible glow. The compartment was small and musty. There was a second bench above his, but it was empty. A heavy floral carpet covered the floor. The walls were a kind of wooden laminate.

There were hangers behind a curtain, as well as a table and a sink. A banana, roll and a bottle of water had been left on a table beside his bench.

There was a time when the compartment would probably have been described as comfortable, but it was a time well past. The charm was as faded and worn as the floral carpets. Was he somewhere in East Europe? The Balkans maybe? It had that feel about it, and he looked for clues in the notices screwed to the walls.

A plastic blue notice marked the emergency exit. 'In case of wreck,' it began in English and then repeated in five other languages. German, French, Spanish, Russian and Ukrainian. A notice on the door, warning to open with care, came in six languages. It was a well-travelled train. That was good.

He then saw another, this one above the window. Some sort of warning. Only this time he couldn't be sure what it said, since this was in only one language. It was written in Cyrillic. Russian, he assumed. And that wasn't good.

He pulled up the blind that covered the window, but there were no clues in the gloom. Just a slight glow, the first light of dawn beyond a thick and formless wall of trees. The train came to a standstill. Nothing moved beyond the track. A silent darkness engulfed them. Then the train creaked and strained and began to move again at a steady rhythmic pace.

He tried to open the door to the corridor, but it was locked. He rattled the handle, and then moments later it was opened from the outside, where a man and a woman were standing in the gloom of the narrow corridor. They were middle-aged and a little dishevelled, looking like slightly shabby academics, university types who'd spent too long in sunless offices.

'Good morning, Mr Drayton,' said the woman, with a strong East European accent. 'I hope you slept well.'

'It's amazing what a little medication can do,' Drayton said, with heavy sarcasm. 'Where are we, exactly?'

'Exactly, I'm not sure,' said the man. 'But we will be at our destination soon enough. Everything will then become clear.'

Drayton sat back on his bench, and began to eat the roll and banana, sipping the water. The woman watched him for a while and then apologised, saying that it was a very old Soviet-era train with no food car. 'I am sorry for the inconvenience.' She sounded like a mildly regretful flight attendant doling out the pasta because the beef was all gone.

Then she closed and locked the door again.

Drayton watched as dawn gave form and then colour to the trees, and then to fields and small villages of low, squat wooden houses, with dirt roads running between them. A long tractor-like vehicle spluttered down a muddy path close to the track, pumping out smoke in dense bursts. The driver waved, but was then blocked by a sudden blur of green, a seemingly endless train heading in the other direction. The roads became bigger, and the villages replaced by grey factories and drab apartment blocks. They were approaching the outskirts of a bigger town, a city perhaps, with signs in Cyrillic and sidings with engines belching more thick smoke. The train began to slow.

The door opened again, the woman telling Drayton they would soon be leaving the train. 'In a few minutes we shall be in Kiev,' she said.

CHAPTER NINE

Bowl of Fire of Glory

Kiev, Ukraine

As the train edged into Kiev station, the man and woman gestured for Drayton to join them in the corridor, which was an obstacle course of bodies and bags. A train attendant, his stained white shirt hanging over an enormous beer belly, was trying to coax somebody out of a compartment two doors away. But he faced a barrage of missiles and abuse. He backed away to avoid a flying shoe, water bottles and a banana skin.

But there was no real power behind the missiles, and Drayton recognised the rasping voice as that of the drunk who'd roamed the corridor. Her partner was at the compartment door with the attendant, wearing the slightly jaded look of man who had seen it all before.

On the crowded platform, Drayton made way for several policemen in thick hats and coats, reinforcements to remove the comatose woman. Their weary looks suggested it was a regular ritual for them too. Drayton thought about grabbing one of the cops by the arm, shouting, 'I've been kidnapped,' and demanding protection. But he missed the moment, and anyway his kidnappers had tightened their grip on his arms, leading him through the station's cavernous main hall and out into a chaos of kiosks, taxi touts and hustlers.

The man made a call, and moments later an old white van pulled up close to where they were standing.

Drayton thought about running. His shabby academic-looking kidnappers hardly looked like athletes who could chase him down, but where would he go? And who could he trust? He could head for the US embassy. But would that be a refuge or a prison? He'd been pleased by what he'd unearthed in Berlin. It had felt like progress. But now he was more uncertain than ever.

Vika's final words about the attack on the Washington hospital played again in his mind. *Somebody let it in. Somebody killed your defences. Somebody on the inside.* He hadn't failed, he'd been betrayed. It was an answer he'd been seeking for weeks. Weeks of guilt gnawing at him. It should have been a moment of enormous relief, but it just raised more questions. And the moment was over in seconds, as she'd pulled the rug right out from under him, delivering him into the hands of his captors. Delivering him to Kiev.

The wide highway from the airport was lined with grey, Soviet-era apartment blocks. For a while they followed signs for Kiev city centre before turning off towards the north east, where the road became narrower and was lined mostly with fields. The traffic was lighter and the road rougher until there was little else on the road apart from their white van. Drayton, sitting in the back, began to doze, but was woken by loud voices, demanding voices. The man sitting next to him put a hand on his shoulder, while the woman, in the passenger seat, got out of the car. They were at some sort of barricade, a checkpoint, the loud voices those of soldiers cradling Kalashnikov rifles. They peered in through the window and then examined the woman's documents, which seemed to satisfy them because moments later the barricade swung open.

Beyond the checkpoint, thick forest lined both sides of the road, with no other vehicle to be seen. Drayton said he needed to take a leak. The woman looked at the man, who looked at the driver, a young, thick-set man with cropped hair, who nodded and pulled to one side of the road, close to a narrow and overgrown path.

'Stay close to the road, and don't leave the path,' said the woman.

Drayton followed the path until he was out of sight of the van. He was finishing up when he heard a sound behind him. He turned to see a fox standing in the path, looking at him, without any hint of fear, before turning and walking further down the path. He followed until it returned to the thick forest. He thought the light amid the trees was playing tricks on him because in their midst was the vague outline of a building, or at least what was left of one, the crumbling remains of a house, or maybe a shop. It was hard to say, since it had become part of the forest, overwhelmed and encased by the trees and undergrowth.

Drayton pushed open a faded red door. The floor was littered with old bottles. There was a plate and a shoe, the rusting remains of a cabinet, a broken chair, a ladder with most of its rungs missing, disintegrating books. A doll was propped against the wall. He went out the back, where there were more buildings reclaimed by the forest. It looked to Drayton like it had been abandoned some time ago, but the scattered possessions suggested it had been abandoned in a hurry.

He then heard the sound of feet on broken glass behind him.

'The village was called Zalissya. It was evacuated soon after the disaster.' said the woman from the van. 'We must return to the path. It is dangerous to leave the path.'

She gestured towards a rusting triangular sign.

Drayton stood looking at the sign for a while, not immediately sure what to say or how to react. The sign was tilting and faded, but still clear enough to make out the red symbol on a yellow background.

The symbol for radiation.

They returned to the van without speaking, and as they drove on Drayton looked at his hands, felt his legs, prodded his teeth. He wasn't sure of the signs of radiation poisoning, but was certain it must be bad. He pulled at his hair, which he fully expected to start coming away in clumps.

Why the fuck had they come to Chernobyl? A thousand square miles of nuclear contamination. They'd set up the exclusion zone for a reason, to fucking exclude people, and now they were driving into the heart of it.

They turned onto a path, narrow and rutted, just wide enough to take a vehicle, deeper into the heart of the forest. The branches of trees whipped and scraped at their windows and roof, like angry giants warning them to keep out. Ahead loomed a rusting gate embossed with big red communist stars, beside an abandoned guard house. An old and faded Soviet mural of a soldier with fist raised in the air covered one wall, while the rusting hulk of a military vehicle was almost hidden by tall grass.

'We walk from here,' said the man.

This time Drayton did as he was told and stuck to the narrowing path. The sun flickered though the tall trees that surrounded them. Then the wall of trees became thinner and Drayton was aware of a faint whistling and jingling high above them.

The area ahead had been cleared of trees, and Drayton shielded his eyes from the sudden light, reflected and intensified by an enormous wall of metal. The trees had been replaced by a metallic curtain through the forest, stretching as far as he could see. He craned his neck to make out the top, high above the tree line. As his eyes adjusted, he saw that it wasn't solid, but an interlocking web of metal, like a giant fence. It was like nothing he'd seen before, and the sounds were caused by the wind whipping through and around the mesh-like structure.

'It's rather impressive in its own sort of way,' said a voice to one side of him. The man was standing with his back to the sun, so his face was at first in silhouette. Though the voice was familiar.

'I'm sorry Drayton, but if we hadn't extracted you from Berlin, you would be dead by now.'

It was Wolfgang Schoenberg.

* * * * *

Schoenberg was carrying a yellow Geiger counter about the size of a cell phone, but a little thicker. He told Drayton that the background radiation was no higher than in the city, and much less than flying in an aircraft, waving the thing around as if to make the point. He said the really dangerous concentrations were in the soil, which is why it was wise to keep out of the forest.

'What is this place?' Drayton asked.

'During the Cold War, the West called it the Russian Woodpecker, since it made continuous click-like sounds that interfered with Western radio broadcasts. The signals from here were so powerful that even commercial aircraft and telephone circuits could pick them up. There were some pretty crazy theories back then, that it was a Soviet mind control weapon. Even a UFO, trying to call home.'

'So if it wasn't ET, what was it?'

'A radar. An incredibly powerful radar. One of three built by the Soviet Union for detecting incoming ballistic missiles, supposedly to give them early warning of a nuclear attack. In the end the nuclear fallout came from up the road, when the Chernobyl reactor exploded.'

Then Schoenberg placed a hand on Drayton's shoulder. 'I'm sorry Chuck. About what happened to Anna. We are dealing with brutal and desperate people. I'm truly sorry.'

It was rare for Schoenberg to call him by his first name, rarer still for him to lower his guard and reveal a more human side.

Drayton looked away, uncertain how to respond. Then he said, 'What did she die for Wolfgang? What is this really all about? What brings you here, to this place? Surely not Cold War nostalgia, there's plenty of that in Berlin.'

'Right now, it suits our purpose,' Schoenberg replied, all business again.

'And what exactly is your purpose?'

They began to walk, following the course of the giant metal curtain, which towered above them.

'It all began here in Ukraine. In Kiev, with Viktorya Shevchenko and her brother Thomas. They were good, the best at finding bugs that nobody else could, zero days. They worked with a diverse group of hackers. Neo, Grom, Ghoul, Razor, Dim sum, Fisheye were among them. The handles you're familiar with by now. And Dmitry Gerasimov. There were tensions with the Russian from the start. Dmitry had his own business, selling hacking tools, cybercrime for hire, and wanted to sell the zero days to the highest bidder or else use them himself, instead of selling them back to the companies.'

Then Schoenberg stopped because something moved in the forest.

'The exclusion zone has become one of the world's greatest nature reserves, untouched for more than thirty years. Albeit, a rather toxic one,' he said.

They began to walk again, keeping close to the radar.

'Our merry group of hackers made a discovery that would change everything,' Schoenberg continued.

'The flaw in computer chips?'

'It was a series of design flaws in one of the world's most common computer chips, used in industrial and military control systems worldwide. It was like nothing they'd found before. At first Vika and Thomas didn't appreciate the power of what they had. Their instinct was to make it public, warn the chip maker and perhaps gain a reward. Dmitry recognised its power straight away. He saw its potential as a weapon and as a way of making money, a lot of money.

Schoenberg's Geiger counter started to beep. 'Best avoid the bigger metal pillars. Hot spot,' he said.

'This isn't the forest. You said the danger was in the forest.'

'Mostly it is, but not always.'

They walked on, keeping clear of the pillars.

'Dmitry sold details of one of the flaws to the GRU, Russian military intelligence, and the GRU used it to attack the Mountville Memorial Hospital in Washington DC, to kill the Russian double agent being treated there by gaining control of the drug infusion system he was wired to. They succeeded, and fourteen others died. But you don't need me to tell you that.'

'I know my defences didn't fail, they were disabled. I wanted to destroy the bug before it reached its target. It was allowed in.'

'Somebody wanted to capture the bug alive,' Schoenberg said.

'I need to know who.'

'I think you already do,' Schoenberg replied, cryptic as ever, measuring every word.

'And isn't that what this is all about?' Drayton asked. 'Capturing the bug alive, as you put it. The motive for all of them, to get hold of it for themselves? But what's the point if the Russians already have the zero day?'

'They have *a* zero day. The problem for them, and for Dmitry, is that once a zero day has been used it's no longer a zero day. It becomes obsolete. It can be patched. We now know Cerberus is a series of flaws. Dmitry needed access to more of them. The hackers were split. Dim sum and Fisheye left Kiev, they wouldn't cooperate, but he won over Neo, Razor, Grom and several others with promises of big money. Crucially he needed Vika and Thomas, since they had done the critical work.'

Schoenberg was walking with his hands behind his back now, looking straight ahead, as if he were a professor or perhaps a barrister building an argument, the jury at some distant point in the thick forest.

'So why? Why did Vika go to Myanmar and help Dmitry?'

'She had no choice, Drayton. Dmitry was holding her brother. Dmitry had him kidnapped and would have killed him if Vika hadn't cooperated. He was being held by separatists and their Russian backers in eastern Ukraine.'

'And Myanmar, that was just convenient?' said Drayton. 'Dmitry could provide the military with hacking services in exchange for protection while he ran his other businesses and while they tested an updated version of their zero day on a guinea pig called Richard Pendleton. It was a field trial against the military grade chip in his pacemaker. As soon as Dmitry had the data he needed, Vika, Thomas and the other hackers were expendable. As was the professor.'

They reached the end of the giant wall of meshed steel, and were standing close to the edge of the toxic forest.

'Dmitry started an auction. He wanted to sell Cerberus to the highest bidder,' said Schoenberg. 'The bugs – Glienicke12, Treptower5, Charlie32 and Northghost7 – are variations of Cerberus. Cerberus-lite, if you like, giving Cullen, Strykov and Wang a little glimpse of what he has to offer. He knew the Cardinals would never work together, but each would want to get hold of the bug for themselves. And suddenly this monster of the cyber underworld is no longer such a snarling dog. To the great cyber powers it has become a kind of Cinderella, to be wooed and courted. They all want her hand.'

'So who tipped off Dmitry that we were on to Neo?' asked Drayton.

'It could have been any of them. But I suspect that was our Russian friend, Strykov. He assumed, wrongly, that Dmitry was his man, since they'd worked together before. And of course the Russians were holding Thomas.'

'And what about Efren Bell?'

'This is where it gets a little more complicated.'

'Is that possible?'

'You see, Bell is a man consumed by vanity.'

'Yeah, tell me about it.'

'He and Dmitry go back a long way, as you know. They never lost contact. Dmitry quickly blew his part of the money they made from the 2008 crash, and Efren Bell has bailed him out at least twice. The Russian has a hold on him. He knows how the money was really made. He knows it was a scam, and Bell doesn't want those old accusations resurrected. Not now that's he's the darling of the techies.'

'So, Dmitry's blackmailing him?'

'Not exactly. Bell wants to raise one hundred billion dollars for his Digital Pagoda Fund. He's selling investors a dream of secure systems, powered by AI. Every time Cerberus strikes, the money comes pouring in. And Dmitry plays to Bell's vanity, showering him with Buddha artefacts.'

'Cullen says you are Cerberus, by the way,' said Drayton.

'How very flattering,' the German replied.

'Cullen had in his office the phone that belonged to Razor, the English hacker Matt Dobberman. It was in Dobberman's hand when he was murdered,' Drayton said.

'Perhaps you will soon have another chance to ask him about that yourself,' the German said. 'And about the hospital.'

The mesh and wire whistled above them as a gust of wind blew across the clearing. Schoenberg looking up and then back at Drayton.

'I think it's time you met the rest of the team,' he said.

* * * * *

The radar was embedded in thick concrete, which also formed the roof of what used to be a bunker-like control room below. They entered via crumbling steps, the remains of a thick metal door hanging on one hinge. Schoenberg told Drayton to watch his feet, since there were holes in the floor, and the only light came from a series of narrow slit-like windows. Drayton could feel something glass-like crunching beneath him, piles of old computer components, transistors and circuit boards mainly.

Then a vast room of empty computer racks, a corridor with peeling walls, twisted metal littering the floor, on one side another room with drawings of ballistic missiles hanging on the walls, the descriptions below in Cyrillic, a classroom, perhaps. Then another corridor, long, narrow and dusty. Schoenberg coughed. His Geiger counter burst to life with a series of beeps, but then faded away as they left the hot spot behind them. For a while, neither of them spoke.

Light streamed from a half-open door ahead of them, a faint hum growing louder as they approached, the hum of air conditioners. Drayton shielded his eyes from the sudden harsh light. It took a while for his vision to adjust and the room to come into clearer focus. Clean white walls, a pair of sofas, desks with computers. Somebody turned from in front of the computers and waved. It was a familiar face.

'Hey man, what took you so long?' said Bret. 'The beer's in the fridge.'

Fisheye was wearing a back-to-front baseball cap and a black T-shirt, the logo a picture of an entry card, the sort used for secure access to buildings, and a caption saying, 'ACCESS ALL AREAS'. Then in smaller letters below, 'The dog ate my fucking pass'. Images from surveillance cameras were spread in a mosaic on the screens in front of him, an open beer beside the computer. No headphones this time, but music from the computer speakers: 'I'm in with the in crowd', a jazzed-up version.

Then a hand on Drayton's shoulder. 'Hey, that was a great performance up on the Peak. Really enjoyed it,' said Raymond. Dim sum smiling, a big smile. 'Glad you found your way out of Hong Kong.'

'Thanks,' said Drayton. 'But your pantomime robots really stole the show.'

Then Drayton was distracted by more familiar voices, having a familiar conversation in the corner of the room, voices slightly raised.

'It's like the best way. To circumvent the two-tier security via a dedicated backdoor into their system,' said Milo Müller.

Then Holger Norgaard told Milo to please speak English. To please speak plain fucking English. Both looked across the room and waved.

Then Norgaard was at Drayton's side, an arm around his shoulder, his voice lower, close to Drayton's ear. 'Man, I'm sorry, she was a good kid. Anna was the best. We gonna make them pay for that.'

More computers and sofas lined the walls of an adjoining room, some bunk beds too. A tall skinny kid with hair looking like it had been arranged by a shot of electricity turned towards Drayton and raised his hand. But Drayton wasn't really paying attention to him. He was looking at the girl sitting on the top bunk with a laptop on her knee.

Drayton shouldn't really have been surprised. But he still wasn't sure what to say.

Vika spoke first.

'Glad you could make it,' she said. 'Welcome to mission control.'

Schoenberg spoke next, a little hesitant.

'I do believe you have met my daughter,' he said. 'And my son, Thomas. Vika's brother.'

* * * * *

So this was Thomas. *The* Thomas. Celebrity hacker and most recently prisoner of Dmitry, until somebody sprung him from his prison in eastern Ukraine. And Thomas was the son of Schoenberg, the sister of Vika. Heinz at the Stasi Museum had told Drayton that Schoenberg had had two children, and they'd been taken to Kiev by his Ukrainian wife after the marriage broke down, after it was discovered that Schoenberg's wife had been a Stasi informer.

And Drayton remembered the photographs on the table in the living room of Schoenberg's Lake Tegel house. The two fresh-faced youngsters. Vika and Thomas. Now it made sense. And like their father, the children had opted for a career in computers, albeit with a rather different trajectory.

'How did you get out of eastern Ukraine?' Drayton asked Thomas.

He didn't really expect an answer, and never got one, though the glance from Thomas towards his father told him enough. Then Thomas was back at the computer again, in the world beyond its screen. His world.

He was tall and wiry, and was wearing baggy camouflage cargo trousers, and a creased grey T-shirt that looked as if it had been slept in for several days. Maybe it had. But what Drayton noticed most about Thomas was the way he hit the computer keys, with purpose, with intent bordering on aggression. He'd seen that before, that and the look on his face, the intense way Thomas navigated the screen in front of him. It was the look and style of the sleep-deprived gamer, on a second or third day without rest, hunting down monsters or aliens. Except for Thomas the monsters were all too real.

'Hey guys, I'm ready,' shouted Bret, his words punctuated by a crack and a hiss, as he opened another can of beer. They all gathered around his computer screens, arranged as Drayton remembered them from the boxing school in Bangkok and showing video images from surveillance cameras he'd hacked. Vika fetched some more beers from the fridge, handing one to Drayton.

'What you got?' she asked Bret.

Bret clicked and enlarged a video window showing grainy footage of a solid ten-storey building, heavy traffic moving slowly along a road in front.

'Winnie-the-Pooh checked in this morning. His room's on the eighth floor, on the corner, a suite with a river view. He arrived with two others. Big guys. State security, I'd reckon. Came downstairs once around lunchtime for a coffee and cake. Other than that, he's not left his room.'

He clicked between more video windows, more hacked surveillance cameras. The lobby, the café, the hotel entrance, a lift. Then back to the wide shot of the hotel, which he said was from a camera monitoring a square beside the Dnieper River, across the road. He said it was a Chinese-owned hotel, built in old Kiev style, but a copy. He said the Chinese had been buying up a lot of property close to the river. It was the logical place for Wang Yang to stay. Home from home.

'Captain America prefers a church view,' he said, opening another set of video windows. The first was from a security camera monitoring a hotel driveway and entrance, where a sleek BMW had just pulled up and a dark-suited concierge was holding the rear door open for an expensively dressed woman. At the top of the frame, Drayton could just about make out a series of golden cupolas beyond the hotel driveway. Then Bret switched to a camera inside, following the woman to the reception desk.

'Ric Cullen checked in late last night. Captain America. Man, I so love those names,' Bret said, smiling at Norgaard. 'They so look the parts. He took a top floor room with a bird's eye view over Saint Sophia's Cathedral.'

'Interestingly,' said Raymond, interrupting. 'He didn't check in under his own name. We accessed the hotel's reservation system, and no Cullen. No Captain America, either,' he said, sharing the joke. 'He's using the name Christopher Johnson.'

'And the Russians?' Schoenberg asked.

Bret opened another window, this one showing a square with a tired, peach-coloured building beyond trees. 'Igor Strykov's staying here. He arrived about an hour ago with a couple of heavy-looking characters. I mean straight out of central casting. Request a pair of Mafiosi thugs and you couldn't have come up with a better match.'

'Why would Muttley stay there? What is that place?' Vika asked.

Thomas said it was a safe house of the GRU, Russian military intelligence. 'Kiev is crawling with Russian spies.'

'They certainly have some pretty heavy dudes coming and going,' Bret said. He switched to a security camera above the building's entrance as a shaved head moved below it, keyed in an entrance code and then entered the building.

'When does Efren Bell arrive? And Dmitry?' Schoenberg asked, standing slightly back from the others, his hands behind his back again. Schoenberg the quartermaster.

'We're expecting Bell this evening,' said Norgaard. 'On a flight from Berlin. He usually stays in a villa just outside town, overlooking the Dnieper, owned by a Ukrainian tech tycoon he's done business with. It's a bit of a fortress.'

'I'm still working on getting eyes inside the place,' said Raymond. 'Tough, so taking a bit of time, but we should be able to crack the Wi-Fi. We have a tracker in the car. It's an OmniX, which he gifted to the tycoon last year. You familiar with those cars?'

'Yeah,' said Drayton, smiling at Vika. 'Came across one in Berlin. Didn't think much of the handling.'

Then Milo said, 'Dmitry arrived this morning on an overnight flight from Hong Kong via Munich. We're not sure where he's staying.'

Vika looked uneasy. 'He's lived here. He knows this town. He has people who owe him.'

'But, why?' Drayton said. 'Why would they all come here?'

'They've been summoned,' Schoenberg said. 'Each of them received a private message to travel here urgently.'

'It was sort of an offer they couldn't refuse,' Norgaard said, smiling, that slightly mischievous smile Drayton usually found quite appealing. Though not now. Because he could sense where the conversation was going.

'And who summoned them? Who sent this offer they couldn't refuse?' Drayton asked, not liking the looks he was getting, which seemed to be building to a punchline he wouldn't find funny.

'The invitation came from you, Drayton. *You* summoned them.'

* * * * *

Schoenberg told Drayton it was the only way they could get all of them to come to Kiev, and only by getting them all in one place could they be exposed to the world.

'You see, you have something that all of them want, Drayton. The code book. "Cold War Tours. Cold War Berlin by Scooter".' He said. 'The annotated copy that is. Each cardinal has only a part of the Cerberus puzzle, and they want the rest. They believe that guide is the key to piece together the zero day for themselves. None are aware that any of the others are here in Kiev. Intriguing, don't you think?'

'Very,' said Drayton. 'But not in a good way. Not for me.'

'Don't worry,' said Schoenberg, a hand on Drayton's shoulder. 'They'll see it as purely commercial. As far as they're concerned, you've gone rogue and are simply doing it for the money. Except perhaps for Dmitry. He is of a rather more violent disposition, and may be out for revenge.'

'Which means what?'

'Which means,' said Bret, 'that he probably wants to string you up by the balls to the highest cupola in the city.'

'But that won't happen,' Schoenberg said, trying to sound reassuring. That smile again. 'Because he has another reason to do business with you.'

'Which is?'

'You've frozen his money,' said Milo, interrupting. 'You asked me to check out a debit card called Pearl Delta, the one Dobberman was using. And the payment to the military in Burma. Well I tracked them both to a Pearl Digital Bank, which is part of Pearl Digital Holdings.' Milo was gabbling now, as he always did when he got excited. 'That's were Neo's payments came from, it's where he cashed out, using the debit card, and it was the source of the Bitcoin payment to the Burmese general.'

'Basically Pearl Digital Bank is Dmitry's banker,' Norgaard said. It's a cryptocurrency exchange and it also issued his wallet, receiving Bitcoin for ransomware keys and paying the hackers' wages.'

Then Milo said, 'We've hacked and frozen the exchange, locking it with our own ransomware.'

'And Dmitry thinks you're the guy with the key,' Norgaard added, with a triumphant flourish.

'That is *so* cool,' Bret said.

'I'm not sure Dmitry will see it that way,' Drayton said.

'There's an added twist,' Schoenberg said.

'I was afraid there might be,' said Drayton.

'Pearl River Bank has protection from elements of the Chinese government. It acted as banker to top Communist

Party officials and their families, looking to discreetly move assets in and out of the country. That also ensured protection in Hong Kong. They will be less than happy with Dmitry's carelessness.'

'Sure sounds like I've been busy,' Drayton said.

'We have a plan. A performance, if you like,' said Schoenberg. He paused, waiting for a kettle to boil, then poured water into a mug, on top of a tea bag; Earl Grey. Slowly, methodically, as always. 'The plan will be orchestrated from here.'

He sat on a desk in front of the others. 'You see, you are standing in a powerful computer centre. The Russian Woodpecker holds a lot of secrets, some of them not so distant. After the Soviet Union collapsed it was left empty and rusting. But not forgotten. I was part of a technical team that came here in the nineties and reconfigured the radar. We were monitoring radiation levels, but we also overhauled its transmitters and receivers and turned them towards Russia. It became a powerful surveillance tool for NATO. Most recently the capabilities here have been bolstered by fibre optic lines to monitor what is going on beneath the new steel and concrete sarcophagus covering the Chernobyl plant. The connection speeds are phenomenal.'

Then, step by step, he outlined the performance, going over each of their roles. Bret in charge of the cameras, Raymond hacking connected devices to get closer still, Milo and Norgaard a mobile unit, Thomas doing a bit of everything.

Vika was doing the tracking. She opened four windows on her laptop, each showing a map, and each with a blue blob, the kind of blue blob that had been Dobberman in Bangkok before that blob was eliminated.

'Winnie-the-Pooh's still in his hotel, Muttley's not yet left the GRU safe house, Captain America is sightseeing in Saint Sofia's Cathedral.' She leaned towards her screen. 'Efren Bell's car hasn't yet left his villa, but we are expecting it to collect him from the airport this evening.'

'How did you install the trackers?' asked Drayton.

'In Bell's case, by hacking his car,' she said. 'That was the toughest. The others were quite straightforward. Norgaard?'

'Igor Strykov's got exotic tastes,' said the Norwegian. 'He couldn't resist downloading an app from a local escort agency offering some imaginative services and laced with Vika's spyware. As for Wang, Western food disagrees with him. He has to have Chinese, and loves Kung Pao chicken. He'd eat it all the time in Berlin. So we spiced up the online menu of his hotel, a virus or two along with the peanuts and chillies. When he ordered from his smartphone he got a whole lot more than fiery chicken.'

He looked at Drayton and said, 'Sorry, not an original idea, I know.'

He said Cullen was tougher. 'In the end we arranged for his smartphone charger to be replaced with one of our own, which transferred the spyware during charging.'

'Nice one,' said Bret.

But Thomas didn't appear to be listening. He seemed distracted.

'We've got no tracker on Dmitry,' he said. 'That worries me.' He and Vika knew better than any of them what Dmitry was capable of, and Thomas looked uneasy, irritated by the air of self-congratulation in the room. After all, the performance hadn't yet started.

'Don't forget where we are and who we're dealing with,' Thomas said. 'This is Ukraine. It's the front line in a new kind of conflict. Russian hybrid warfare, a testing ground for cyber weapons, and Dmitry's been involved with the GRU. He's dangerous and this is home territory for him.'

There was a moment of silence, an awkward silence, before Schoenberg began to speak again, saying that at times Dmitry had been useful to the Russians, the Chinese, the Americans, and to Efren Bell.

'They have all regarded him as their asset, and he's become a master at playing them off against each other. By tomorrow morning, they will all be here in Kiev, unaware of the others, and waiting for Drayton's further instructions. Each is trying to acquire the most dangerous zero day ever discovered. Each believes that ownership of Cerberus is the key for the development of deadly cyber weapons, against which there is no defence.'

Schoenberg sipped his tea, running a thumb and forefinger over his short moustache, the faintest of smiles. 'What we are planning is the biggest exposé since Edward Snowden revealed to the world the extent of NSA snooping.'

'Snowden leaked stolen NSA files. What exactly are we after here?' Drayton asked.

'We're not stealing anything,' said Vika.

'Snowden's passé, my friend,' said Norgaard, pausing, sipping his beer, licking his lips as he placed the can back on the table.

Then Bret said, 'My friend, we'll be live streaming to the World.'

'Well,' said Schoenberg. 'Let the performance begin.'

* * * * *

Drayton had a thing about plans. They rarely worked. Not for him. From his experience, the more carefully something was laid out, the more likely it would get screwed up. And it was his balls that would end up tied around the highest cupola in Kiev, as Bret had so eloquently put it.

So it was no great surprise that the following day he almost fell over Dmitry, as the Russian exited through a hotel door surrounded by a group of shaven-headed men doing a bad impersonation of extras from a second-rate mafia movie. Drayton was on his way in through the same door and had nowhere to hide. Dmitry seemed to look straight at him or possibly through him, a look that was cold and indifferent.

It seemed inconceivable that Dmitry had not seen him, but the Russian never broke his stride or his conversation, climbing with the extras into a black van with tinted windows, which accelerated quickly away from the hotel and through the square below.

The hotel was a solid Stalinist relic overlooking Independence Square. Service with a snarl, the austere lobby a major thoroughfare for pimps, hookers, hoodlums and just about every other variety of Kiev low-life, which Vika said made it ideal as a base for her and Drayton, since nobody else in their right mind would stay there.

Well, whatever mind Dmitry was in, he'd been there.

Drayton found Vika in the square below talking to a group of older women wearing headscarves and standing beside a makeshift shrine made from bricks, tyres and flowers. Several photographs of young men were propped against the tyres. Two of them looked little more than boys. Vika said the youngest was seventeen and had been killed in sniper fire during the protests.

The entire square had become a memorial to the Maidan uprising, the 2014 revolution that kicked out the president, a Russian place-man whose family had plundered the country. More than one hundred people died around the square, which was now lined with simple shrines of photos, flowers and candles. Billboards carried the almost medieval images of burning barricades, slingshots hurtling rocks at the advancing riot police. Others had copies of Facebook posts that supposedly triggered the revolution – the Facebook revolution, they'd called it. The days before social media was tamed and then co-opted by thugs, dictators and marketing consultants, and a promised enabler of democracy became its biggest threat.

Drayton watched the women refreshing flowers on the shrine, he was startled by a hand on his shoulder and turned to find himself looking into the cold, sunken eyes of an unshaven man, unsteady on his feet and grasping a hand full of braided wrist bands in yellow and blue, the national colours of Ukraine. Drayton gave him several small denomination notes and took one of the wristbands.

'He's messed-up,' Vika said. 'A veteran of the war in the east. You find them all over the city.'

'I need to talk to you,' Drayton said, leading her away from the shrine, and telling her about Dmitry.

If she was surprised she didn't show it. 'If he didn't notice you, that's good. And even if he did, it just means he knows you're already here. He still needs to do business with you.'

'We should tell Schoenberg. Tell the others.'

She looked at her watch. 'Let me deal with that. The messages will be going out soon. I see no reason to change our plans.'

Drayton retreated to the hotel's lobby bar, where he sat on a fading leather sofa that once-upon-a-time had springs. He ordered a beer, and watched the grotesque theatrics of the lobby, all the time keeping one eye on the door, not in the least bit sharing Vika's breezy indifference to the presence of Dmitry. He looked at his watch. In just under two hours, at midday, messages would go out in his name to Wang, Cullen, Strykov, Dmitry and Bell, giving each a time and place to meet him. And then the performance would begin. When he'd left the Chernobyl radar, Schoenberg had called him the catalyst, the lead player. From where he sat, Drayton felt like bait, and now the biggest and nastiest predator of the lot knew where to find him.

He picked up his cell phone, which had been returned by Schoenberg, and began to compose an email to Tun Zaw. The Burmese kid was smart and keen, he'd already showed that, but what he was now asking might be too much. But at the same time, it might just save Drayton's balls from the cupola. He pressed 'send', drained the rest of his beer and then headed to a metro station beneath the square.

His destination was Arsenalna, just one stop away, near the bank of the Dnieper River. He'd once seen a documentary about the station, named after a nearby weapons factory. It was the deepest in the world, and that's how it felt at the bottom of seemingly endless escalators. It had been built to double up as a bomb shelter, to survive a nuclear war. The walls of the platform were lined with advertisements for computers and cell phones, the tools for the next conflict.

Drayton followed a path close to the river, leading to a vast hillside statue made of stainless steel. The Motherland Monument was built by the Soviets. It held a sword in one hand, in the other a shield carved with hammer and sickle, the state emblem of the Soviet Union.

Drayton looked for inscriptions.

The wall in front of the statue contained plaques to the various 'hero cities' of the Soviet Union. Alongside that, an outdoor exhibition of weapons. There were information boards, but none were ideal. He climbed a nearby hill to a giant bowl containing an eternal flame, which turned out to be not so eternal. A man standing nearby told him it was only lit on special occasions, after opposition groups occupied the bowl and used the flame for frying eggs in protest against the Soviet symbolism. Drayton walked around it. It was called the Bowl of Fire of Glory, and an inscription circled its rim. He noted down the words, and then sat on the grass close by, working his phone, another message to Myanmar.

He heard distant church bells. Midday. The messages to Wang, Cullen, Strykov, Dmitry and Bell were now on their way. He had just enough time to return to the centre of the city for the first of his meetings, the start of the performance, feeling rather less anxious than he had an hour or so earlier.

*****

Act One. Starring Chuck Drayton and Wang Yang. And hopefully nobody else. Setting: the coffee shop in the ornate lobby of the Chinese-owned Dnieper Palace Hotel. Schoenberg hadn't exactly described the meeting in those terms, but that's how it felt to Drayton as he took a seat, his back to the lobby, as Bret had instructed. In the ceiling above his left shoulder, a security camera watched from its dark bulbous-shaped housing, squeezed between a sparkling chandelier and several fire sprinklers.

He glanced behind him. At the camera, then the lobby, empty except for a bored-looking doorman in dark uniform and white gloves, who was watching a large tourist boat manoeuvre awkwardly beside the river bank across the busy road. Drayton was ten minutes early. He picked up a magazine

311

from a white carved chest, on which also sat a large pot of orchids. Were they obstructing the view? He didn't want to leave anything to chance, so moved them slightly, feeling stupid and self-conscious as he did so. He sipped a coffee, then removed his cell phone from the top pocket of his jacket. He replaced it, upside down, making sure the microphone was unobstructed.

Then he waited.

Wang was five minutes late. Winnie-the-Pooh bounded to the table, sitting opposite Drayton, face to the lobby as Bret intended. He refused a coffee and came straight to the point.

'How much do you want Drayton?'

Drayton stuck to his prepared script, telling Wang the zero day was more powerful than anything yet found, that it would give China a cyber edge, for spying, for developing weapons. That it was valuable. But Wang interrupted him, impatient.

'I know what it is and what it can do. I asked you how much you wanted.'

Wang's tone surprised Drayton. It was unlike the Wang of the Berlin Group conference room, where he'd played the role of wooden apparatchik, full of empty clichés, as if he was addressing the central committee of the party. All with a poor grasp of English. But the Wang sitting in front of him now was polished and fluent.

'Ten million dollars in Bitcoin, to this wallet,' Drayton said, handing Wang a card with the digital address of the wallet. 'Once the money is in the wallet, you will receive a key to a digital vault that contains the code book.'

Wang stood and began to walk back to the lobby. Then he turned, and as if as an afterthought, he said, 'There's another key, Mr Drayton. To unlock a certain cryptocurrency exchange.'

'That will be an additional ten million, Mr Wang.'

'We will be in touch. Good day, Mr Drayton.'

Drayton watched Wang's short legs powering his rotund body across the lobby, two tall body guards falling into formation behind him as they headed to the lifts. The way Wang had mentioned the crypto exchange had been casual, almost calculatingly so, yet Drayton suspected that to certain people in Beijing, that key, a key to a Pandora's box of dodgy party transactions, mattered as much as the zero day.

Drayton sat in the coffee shop for another five minutes until a coach pulled up in front of the hotel, tourists returning from visiting Kiev's churches. As they spilled through the hotel's revolving doors, he left his seat, pushing through the crowd and out of the hotel. He walked briskly down an underpass to the riverside and then into the dingy departure hall for river ferries. He stood near the door, watching the area in front of the hall. Only when he was sure he wasn't being followed, did he leave and quickly hail a taxi to take him to the next act.

* * * * *

Act Two, starring Drayton and Igor Strykov. Schoenberg's choice of location for the meeting with the Russian showed to Drayton that the German did have a sense of humour, though he doubted Strykov would see the funny side. They were to meet in the shadow of what used to be a statue of Lenin. Now all that was left of it was a graffiti-covered plinth topped with Ukrainian flags where the great man had once stood. Facing it and spray-painted in yellow on a nearby wall was the face of a smirking cat. Drayton sat on a bench to one side of the plinth, his every move followed by the security camera of a nearby bank. He checked the position of the cell phone in his pocket and then looked up the narrow tree-lined path beyond the plinth, sitting sharply upright as several figures in dark overalls began to move towards him. It was difficult to see clearly because the bright sun was behind them. But he was sure they were armed and making no attempt to conceal their weapons, which they waved around almost casually. They stopped at a bench the other side of the plinth, and then they began to paint; their weapons were paintbrushes and tins of sticky emulsion.

'I hope you realise Drayton that you won't leave this city alive.'

It was Strykov, standing behind him.

Like Wang before him, he had taken on a new persona. Gone was the mischievous, wheezing laugh, the image of almost bumbling bonhomie that had earned him his nickname. This Strykov was blunt and threatening.

'If Dmitry doesn't get you then my people probably will. As soon as you sent that message you signed your own death warrant,' he said.

'I don't think so,' said Drayton.

'No? And what makes you think I'm interested in your proposition?'

'Because you wouldn't be here if you weren't, Igor. And I'm guessing you're a little pissed because Dmitry, who's been so useful to Russia in the past, isn't playing with you any more. Such terrible ingratitude, after helping take care of Thomas, too. I'm also guessing that you know the power of what I'm selling, the key to unlock the most powerful zero day that has yet been found.'

Drayton, speaking loudly and clearly, as Bret had instructed, then told Strykov the price and how he was to pay.

The Russian didn't answer. He looked at the plinth on which Lenin once stood. 'Ukraine is not a country. It never has been. We could end this charade in days if we chose. The clowns that run this so-called country underestimate Moscow at their peril. And so do you, Drayton.'

He began to walk away, Drayton calling after him. 'And Strykov, the deadline for payment is the end of tomorrow. There may be other interested parties, as I'm sure you can appreciate.'

The Russian kept walking without looking back, crossing the road in front of the bank. The security camera watched as he climbed into the back seat of a waiting Mercedes and was driven away.

Drayton quickly crossed the road and into a hotel beside the bank. He crossed the lobby and followed a long corridor leading to a bar and restaurant at the back. He left through a rear entrance and climbed into the back of a waiting car, driven by a man in a baseball hat and sunglasses. He ducked to the floor as the car pulled away. It dropped him five minutes later at the entrance of a metro station.

'Good luck,' said Norgaard from the driver's seat.

Drayton took a series of random trains before emerging not far from where he'd started, and a short walk from the golden cupolas of Saint Sophia's Cathedral. Ready for Act Three.

This was the scene Drayton was least looking forward to.

He arrived early at the Cathedral and killed time by walking around the grounds, watching a team of gardeners picking weeds. The more he looked at them, the more he became convinced they were looking at him between each aggressive stab at a weed. Were they really gardeners, or some sort of advance guard for Ric Cullen, set to pounce upon him at any moment, stoving in his head with their trowels?

He climbed the steep stairs of the bell tower, Startling pigeons sheltering behind giant bells, frantic flapping wings echoing around the tower. He was breathless when he reached the top, where a platform ran along the inner edge of the square-shaped tower. The city spread endlessly in front of him, its old heart giving way quickly to sprawling Soviet-era estates of grey housing blocks. All punctuated by golden cupolas, the Dnieper River running through its heart. Behind him, the hollowness of the tower, the ground barely visible below. High on the opposite wall, the familiar bulbous housing of a security camera.

He heard the footsteps before he saw him: Cullen making easy work of the stairs, as if he was out for an afternoon stroll.

He was quickly at Drayton's side. 'So let me see your back. Because do you know what? You've just painted one big fucking target on it Drayton. I knew you were stupid, but not this stupid. Hand over the code book while you still can.'

He pushed Drayton hard in the chest. 'How does it feel to betray your country?'

'I'm not sure. You tell me.'

'Which means?'

'Which means, who are you really representing here Cullen? Or is it Christopher Johnson? Isn't that the name you're using? Tell me Cullen, you ever heard of a British hacker called Matt Dobberman? Used the handle Razor. He was one of Dmitry's boys, until he was murdered in Bangkok by one of Dmitry's thugs.'

'What the fuck you talking about Drayton?'

'Dobberman's cell phone was in your office. In Berlin. Tell me about that Cullen.'

For a moment they stood in silence.

'Sometimes things can be messy, Drayton. Sometimes we have to compromise to keep America safe. To defend our country. Not that I'd expect you to understand a fucking thing about that.'

'Messy. Like doing business with a murderer who's holding the world to ransom.'

Cullen took a step closer, his face just inches from Drayton's. 'You really have no idea what you're dealing with Drayton. No fucking idea. You're playing a fucking dangerous game.'

'A dangerous game. Like at the Mountville Memorial Hospital, that sort of dangerous game? My defences didn't fail at the hospital, did they Cullen? You disabled them. You let the bug in. You deliberately let the fucking bug into the hospital systems, and you killed fifteen people. How does that feel, Cullen?'

Cullen hesitated, taking a step back. 'The deaths were unfortunate. We needed a live copy of the code. We couldn't let you destroy it.'

'And did you get your live copy?'

'The bug was coded to self-destruct when it reached its target.'

'They usually are, Cullen. Any adolescent hacker could have told you that.'

Cullen clenched his fists, looking as if he was bracing to strike. 'I could easily send you toppling over the edge, Drayton, and what a mess you'd make when you hit the bottom. Lying amid all the pigeon shit. Think about that.' Drayton held firmly to the flimsy handrail, bracing himself. But Cullen just pushed past and bounded down the stairs, never looking back, taking them two at a time, with military precision.

* * * * *

Act Four. Setting: the Kiev opera house. This time featuring Chuck Drayton and Efren Bell, with a supporting role from

Vika Shevchenko, wearing a dark wig, long dress and dark glasses, all with such panache that at first Drayton didn't recognise her.

'Have you ever been to the opera before?' she asked.

'It's been a while,' Drayton said, without too much conviction. 'What's it about, this Rigatoni?'

'Rigatoni's a pasta, Drayton. Tube-shaped, slightly curved and usually with ridges down the length. Rigoletto is a mix of drama, betrayal and tragedy, which I imagine sounds rather familiar. Shall we?'

They entered the opera house through a pair of heavy wooden doors, a poster for the performance on one door, showing a big, slightly hunched man with a bit of a snarl; a warning sign on the other said that the place was monitored by security cameras.

It was austere but grand, in an old Soviet style. A bit like his train to Kiev. Ornate ceilings with chandeliers above spartan corridors. Thick carpets, and walls hung with old paintings and fading photographs of past performances. Everybody dressed as if they were heading to Sunday service at the local church, smart in a conservative sort of way.

Drayton and Vika climbed several sets of stairs and then ordered two glasses of wine from a dour barman in a corner café with windows overlooking the entrance, from which they watched Efren Bell arrive, alone as he'd been told, climbing out of the back of a chauffeur-driven OmniX.

The auditorium was steep-sided and horseshoe shaped, Vika and Drayton's box at the top of several tiers, with a bird's eye view of the theatre below.

'Second tier, third box along, on the far side,' Vika said, handing Drayton a pair of opera glasses, which he trained on the wall of boxes opposite them, where Bell was taking a seat, looking at his cell phone, then putting it in his pocket as the lights went down and an orchestra began to play from a deep pit in front of the stage.

Drayton lost track as soon as the opera started. A colourful and crowded party scene unfolded with lots of extravagant posturing, the actors prancing around the stage and singing at each other, one with a growl-like sub-woofer of a voice; others so screechingly high that he thought the opera glasses might shatter. He guessed that was the point, or rather the skill, because the really extreme notes were greeted with spontaneous applause. The first act ended with the big, slightly hunched man from the poster, the one with a name like pasta, alone on stage and collapsing in despair.

'He's been cursed,' Vika said, as the curtain fell and the lights came on for the first break.

'I know how he feels,' Drayton replied, standing and making to leave the box.

'Good luck,' Vika said. 'You have around ten minutes.'

Vika stayed in their box, watching Bell through her opera glasses, watching to see Drayton enter his box as arranged to offer Bell the deal. She looked towards the ceiling of the theatre, looking for the telltale bulbous node of surveillance cameras. She couldn't immediately see any, but knew they were there and knew where Bret would now have them focussed, for the next part of their performance.

Vika watched as Bell made a call, or possibly received one. He looked at his watch, played again with his phone, looked at the curtains behind him, then at the theatre in front. A bell rang, the opera would soon be starting again. Where the fuck was Drayton? A second bell rang. Then there was movement behind Bell. The curtains parted and he turned and stretched out his hand in greeting.

But it wasn't Drayton. Instead it was Dmitry who entered the box, shook the outstretched hand and sat down beside Bell just as the lights went down for the start of the opera's second act.

* * * * *

Drayton got no further than the corridor just outside his box. They grabbed him from behind, two men, big men, built like fridge-freezers. They hooked his arms and pinned them to his sides. He tried to pull free, but their grip was too tight, tried to hold his ground, but they lifted him until his toes were sliding across the floor.

Efren Bell's black OmniX was waiting for them outside a fire exit. Drayton was pushed into the back seat, fridge-freezers either side of him. Ken Tsang, sitting up front, demanded Drayton's cell phone, which he put in a small black pouch, the sort designed to block signals, to prevent tracking.

The OmniX moved quickly along a wide thoroughfare, weaving through light traffic. It swung around a square at speed, banking sharply past a squat temple, its cupolas wrapped in scaffolding, before ducking into a narrow alleyway.

A fading metal door opened onto a steep staircase to a basement corridor lit with garish blue and red bulbs. Drayton could hear thumping music, heavy base, getting louder as they walked. He was pushed into a small room, the door locked behind him.

The windowless room was pitch-black, and Drayton swore as he hit his knee hard against something blunt and metallic. He ran his fingers along a cold wall, feeling his way to a light switch. A ceiling light flickered and faded, but it was sufficient for him to see that he was in a small office or store room, its

320

walls lined with metal cabinets and empty shelving. A desk and chair stood at one end. Boxes against one wall, drinking water mostly, from which he took a bottle. Others were full of flyers with a picture of two naked women wrapped around a pole. It had been taken through a fish tank with baby sharks, and at the top was the name, 'Day Zero Gentlemen's Club'.

That had to be where they'd brought him.

Drayton wasn't sure how long he waited in the room. He took some more water, slept for a while on the floor, read and reread the flier, slept some more. Thinking. Schoenberg's performance had gone pretty smoothly for the first three acts, but had veered badly off script, Dmitry not liking the role he'd been assigned, wanting to write his own ending, and Drayton suspected it wasn't a happy one.

He woke abruptly from a nightmare, where he was being lowered into the tank of sharks, the naked women on stage looking on and cheering. There were voices outside his room. A key in the door. The two men who'd grabbed him from the opera told him to get up and follow them, further down the corridor, to the room with the music. It was the main part of the club, lights pulsating to the beat, a low glass ceiling above perhaps a dozen tables. Most of the tables were littered with glasses and taken by groups of men, their eyes as glazed as the ceiling above them. A group of pouting, near-naked women with gravity-defying silicon enhancements and stilt-like high-heels, gyrated around poles on a small stage at the front.

Drayton was led to an enclave just beyond the bar and close to the fish tank, which was much bigger than it appeared in the flyer. The baby sharks seemed to be taking a good deal more interest in the pole dancers than the drunken punters at the tables.

'Sit down Drayton,' said Dmitry. 'Did you think seriously that I was going to pay to get back my own code book?'

'Yes, as a matter of fact,' Drayton said. 'That and the key to unlock your cryptocurrency exchange. The Chinese can't be happy about that. I thought we could do a package deal.'

Dmitry laughed, a cynical threatening laugh that suggested to Drayton that negotiations were not about to begin.

'You're in my city now, Drayton. You know I could have had you killed at the opera or maybe at your hotel. I could do it right now, at this table.'

He took a gun from inside his jacket and lay it at his side. He flicked back his hair, which had flopped over small eyes drilling into Drayton.

'At the end of the day, the code book is an irritation. So is the bank. They won't damage my business. What I have to offer is too valuable to too many people. Mostly it just pisses me off. You piss me off. And I don't like being pissed off. It hurts me. And it's very bad for you.'

Dmitry paused for effect. Then he said, 'And it's also very bad for Vika.'

He pulled a cell phone from his pocket. Tapping on the screen a few times before turning it towards Drayton to show a grainy video image. It was Vika, tied to a chair and gagged. She was in what looked like a cave with white-washed walls, broken by the fuzzy gold outlines of faces and a cross. Dmitry said something to the phone in Russian and a man stepped forward and slapped Vika around the face, knocking her over. The picture followed her to the ground, where she was wriggling and kicking like an angry wild animal trying to free itself from its shackles.

'So the deal I am offering you Drayton is very simple,' Dmitry said. 'The code book and the cryptocurrency key and you and Vika live. If not, Vika's body will be dragged out of the Dnieper River a few hours from now. What's left of it, that is.'

He placed the gun under a drinks menu as a server came in with an expensive bottle of whisky and ice.

'This city has a tragic history Drayton, past and present. The hills around the Dnieper River are riddled with caves and tunnels, a thousand years old. It's where monks hid from Mongol invaders, where they lived and were buried. Those were brutal times, with very imaginative means of torture and death. They put a lot of thought into how to make their enemies suffer.'

He turned the phone back towards Drayton. Vika back seated, blood trailing down her face.

'My employees can be very imaginative too,' the Russian said.

He poured the whisky, pushing a glass to Drayton.

'You know,' he said. 'Branding using red-hot irons was used as a means of torture long before they marked the butts of cows.'

He spoke into the phone again. Then the screen was filled with by a man holding three lengths of metal – branding irons – their ends glowing bright red, a different shape on each. One was a ₿, the symbol for Bitcoin, another was @, as used in email addresses. A third was the head of a snarling dog.

'Vika has always liked the digital world, so it would be rather appropriate don't you think. Perhaps to complement her tattoos.'

Vika was still writhing and kicking, defiant as ever, but now firmly pinned to her chair. The man with the branding irons took a step towards her, a crucifix on the wall behind her glowed under the light from the branding irons. Another step closer and a series of fading icons came to life, bands of gold illuminated around the heads of stern-looking saints.

Dmitry propped the phone against the whisky bottle and turned to Drayton.

'So, the code book and the key.'

Drayton was silent for a moment, staring at Dmitry's screen, the look of utter panic on Vika's face. Then he said, 'I need my phone. If you want the keys, I need access to my phone.'

Dmitry looked at Ken Tsang. The money man had joined them at the table, but looked like he'd rather be elsewhere. Dmitry nodded and Tsang removed the pouch containing the phone from his inside pocket. Drayton powered up his phone, moving his finger quickly around the screen, scrolling and tapping.

Then he said, 'You've got it.'

Dmitry looked at his phone, a new message contained two links. He clicked on the first, which opened a document on which was written a single word, 'FireOfGlory2010'. He clicked on the second, a file which demanded a password to open it.

'So where's the fucking code book and key?'

'Inside the file,' Drayton said.

'The file's locked. What's the password?'

'Well here's the thing, I've forgotten it.'

Dmitry's face started to redden. He was sweating. He took a sip of whisky, a long sip, his hand shaking slightly. Then he reached for the gun under the menu, thrusting the barrel into Drayton's ribs. With his other hand he grabbed Drayton by the hair and pushed his head hard against the table.

'So, Drayton the cyber guy forgets passwords?'

'It's easy to do,' Drayton said, talking, struggling to get the words out.

Dmitry eased his grip slightly.

'You see the password was complicated.' Drayton 'And in Russian. Not one of my languages. But you've go clue, 'FireOfGlory2010'. Just like the clues in Berlin.'

'Fire of Glory, the eternal flame?' said Ken, who until then had been sitting without talking, Ken the fidgety money man watching Dmitry the attack dog.

'Well, maybe we should see what Vika thinks about that,' Dmitry said, picking up his phone again, trying to reach the cave, but failing to get a connection.

He left the table, Ken Tsang following him.

Drayton, left with the two fridge-freezers, called after them, 'If you're trying to crack the password, take care. You only get two attempts. Get it wrong twice and it will delete the file. You know how it goes.'

Dmitry returned ten minutes later, sitting opposite Drayton. Ken Tsang sat beside the American. 'You get it?' asked Drayton.

Dmitry grabbed for Drayton's hair again ramming the barrel of his gun hard into his neck. Then he abruptly sat back, looking over Drayton's shoulder to where the fish tank appeared to be boiling. The bubbles that usually rose in a steady stream as they aeriated the water had turned into a torrent. Gushing to the surface. The sharks were in a frenzy, darting back and forth, round and round. Then the water burst over the top of the tank, one shark leapt out and slid down the bar. The girls at the poles screamed and bolted from the stage. Another shark landed, snapping and wriggling on the table in front of Dmitry. He lifted his gun and shot it once, then twice. It jumped and then continued to wriggle, though

ces. Ken was wriggling too, since
rough the shark and hit him in
dly turning red. The dwindling
stage looked around in dazed
s part of a show.
g, spotting the bulbous glass
began to wonder.
was soon back in front of him, where Ken
his head slumped on the table, his face next to the shark's,
a dazed grimace on both. Then the music was turned up so
loud it was painful. The lights began to flicker. Everybody
began to shout, but it was impossible to hear above the music
that was now just a distorted blast. The fire sprinklers came on
next, a fine haze engulfing the club. Then the power went out.
There was silence at first, and then a rising chorus of shouting
and screaming.

Drayton felt a hand gripping his arm. The barrel of the gun
in his ribs again.

'Move,' said Dmitry.

* * * * *

Drayton was again squeezed in the back of the OmniX, between
the fridge-freezers. But Efren Bell's all-singing all-dancing car
refused to do either, and the driver appeared to shrink under
Dmitry's angry gaze, as he tried desperately to start it. After
what seemed to Drayton like an age it sprung to life, and they
left the alleyway onto deserted city streets, bathed by the first
light of dawn, and took a broad highway beside the river.

Every traffic light was red. 'Come on! Come on!' Dmitry
snapped. 'Ignore the fucking lights.' But it wasn't only the
traffic signals that were against them. No matter how hard the

driver pressed on the pedals, the car moved lethargically along the highway. The driver muttered nervously about a problem with the accelerator, while Dmitry pounded the dashboard with his fists. '*Fucking* car!'

The Motherland statue eventually appeared through the gloom ahead of them.

Dmitry marched Drayton at gunpoint through a dark tunnel lined with Soviet-era engravings of heroic soldiers and workers, looks of grim determination etched on their larger-than-life faces. Drayton looked at Dmitry, who for the first time seemed uneasy or maybe uncertain. Though Drayton knew that made him no less dangerous. He jumped as pigeons flew from behind one of the engraved soldiers, their flapping wings amplified in the enclosed space of the tunnel. He saw Dmitry raise his gun, and wondered for a moment if he was going to shoot the pigeons too.

The eternal flame, the Bowl of Fire of Glory, sat at the top of a bank just beyond the end of the tunnel. The Motherland statue loomed over them from another nearby hill. They climbed the bank to the bowl. It was early, but two gardeners were already there. One, an older man with heavy coat and broad hat drawn low over his face, was watering the lawn, using a very old watering can. The other was younger and broader, and was sitting on the rim of the bowl surrounding the flame, pulling out weeds from a little ornamental garden. He was wearing a hard hat with a light on the front.

Dmitry read the Cyrillic inscription surrounding the bowl. 'Вечная слава героям!' Eternal Glory to the Heroes!

'There are just three words, Drayton. Three fucking words.'

He opened his phone. Three words. He'd try them all.

'Go easy Dmitry. The words might be combined. FireOfGlory2010. I might have run the second and the first words together. Maybe the zeros are spaces. Or maybe I added them up. You know, two plus one equals the third word. And you get only two chances, just two chances.'

Dmitry moved towards Drayton, pulling the gun from his pocket. But then he looked around. The sound of footsteps on gravel, approaching on a walkway the other side of the flame.

It was Cullen. 'This had better be good, Dmitry.'

'What the fuck are you talking about?'

'You said it was urgent,' Cullen said. 'That you had the code book, that you wanted to do a deal for the zero day. So I'm here Dmitry. Not happy, because this isn't the way we do business. Never was and never will be. I don't like to get summoned. So talk to me.'

'What summons? I said fucking nothing.'

'So why the fuck did you message me, telling me to come, right now.'

'I didn't fucking message you.'

Then Cullen saw Drayton. 'What the fuck's he doing here? You said you'd got rid of him.'

They stood looking at each other. Then at Drayton. But before Dmitry could answer, they all looked back down the slope where, gasping and wheezing, Igor Strykov was climbing towards the flame.

Muttley paused for breath close to the top and shouted. 'Dawn is bad Dmitry. I don't do dawn. And you know what, I don't do ultimatums either. So what the *fuck* is this about?'

'What ultimatums? What the fuck do you mean?' Dmitry said.

'You seem to forget Dmitry that you wouldn't be in business if not for us,' Strykov said. 'And we can terminate you pretty fucking quickly. You're forgetting where your loyalties lie. So where's the fucking code book? The zero day?'

Then he saw Drayton.

And then Cullen.

They stood looking at each other, until Cullen broke the silence. 'So go ahead Dmitry, do a deal with the GRU, the Keystone Cops of the cyber world. The zero day won't be secret for long, because Russian military intelligence leaves a digital trail like an elephant through the fucking savannah.'

Strykov laughed, the wheezy Muttley laugh. 'And what does that make the NSA, Ric? Security like your old mum's ancient desktop, leaking like a fucking sieve. Half the bugs on the dark web have been stolen from Fort Meade by half-baked hackers with junior diplomas in computer science.'

'He's got a point there Ric,' said Drayton.

'Who the fuck asked you?' Cullen snapped.

'And suppose the Keystone Cops are already *inside* your systems, Ric,' continued Strykov. 'Water, the power grid, Wall Street. The lot. Sleeping bugs, back doors, through which we can leap in and shut down the lot whenever we like. Maybe we don't even need Dmitry here.'

'Don't you think we know what you're trying to do, Igor, probing our systems?' Cullen fired back, taking a step forward. 'And suppose we've found those bugs and turned them, so the minute you try and activate them, the lights go off right across fucking Russia.'

Strykov stepped forward too, and the two men stood just a couple of metres apart, squaring off like gunslingers in a third-rate spaghetti western. And for a moment Drayton wondered whether that's how it would end, with them pulling guns and blasting away, especially when Strykov reached into his coat, and Cullen said, 'I wouldn't do that if I were you, Igor. Do you think I'd really come here alone, without back-up?' Glancing towards the row of old weapons, field guns and tanks mostly, that formed an exhibition in front of the Motherland statue.

'Sitting in the tanks or hiding behind them?' Strykov said sarcastically.

'Maybe both. Can you afford to risk that?'

Then Strykov nodded towards several buildings at the top of the river bank. 'Can you?' He pulled out a packet of cigarettes from his inside pocket. Another wheezy laugh.

'Maybe we can do a deal,' Cullen said. 'You and I.'

'Not a bad proposition,' Drayton said. 'Are you talking about a kind of bug timeshare, or buying out Igor here from his current employer?'

'Kill him.' Cullen said to Dmitry. 'Kill Drayton. Kill the son of a bitch.'

Dmitry had his gun by his side, thinking, weighing up the order a good deal more deeply than Drayton found comfortable. Drayton began to back away, glancing left and right for somewhere that might provide cover, seeing nothing useful, but spotting a familiar rotund figure approaching.

'Hey!' he said, waving, as crunching along the gravel path came Winne-the-Pooh. Wang Yang suddenly stopping and taking in the scene in front of him.

'Just like a reunion of the Berlin Group. Come and join the party,' Drayton said.

Wang had been a faithful servant of his own party for longer than he cared to remember, the consummate apparatchik, with a vocabulary to match. Innovation did not come easily, and he seemed to be struggling to compute the scene in front of him. For a moment Drayton thought he might just turn and walk away, and he probably would have done, had he not been carrying fresh and tricky instructions.

Drayton turned back to Dmitry. 'So everybody's here. Ideal. You can auction your zero day. Will it be Russia, China or America that gets the world's most powerful cyber weapon? It's your call. They're all eager buyers.'

Wang knew a thing or two about auctions. He'd hacked a few in his time, big ones. New York, London, Paris. Looking to trace the assets of a comrade or two who'd fallen out of favour, but almost drowning under all the dirty Chinese money he'd discovered; there was hardly a senior comrade who was not looking to park his cash in fine and not so fine art, perhaps a mansion or two, as long as it was well out of China. The information had been quietly buried. And now his masters had told him to give priority to the key to Dmitry's cryptocurrency exchange, ordering him to obtain it at all costs. And what a political hornet's nest that could be.

'This is not the appropriate forum,' Wang said, before muttering something about resolving differences in a mutually beneficial way, which always sounded slightly absurd, more so in the shadow of that snuffed out eternal flame.

'I think what Mr Wang is trying to say, Dmitry, is that he'd like a quiet word about your bank, since certain party leaders could face embarrassment if their dealings are exposed.'

Which made Strykov laugh. Wang biting back, 'I don't need any lecture from a Russian about corruption.' The Russian then calling Chinese hackers 'amateurs', thieves grabbing industrial secrets. Wang calling Russian hackers 'gangsters', destroying things, fucking things up, for what? Cullen gesturing to Dmitry, as if to say, 'how can you possibly deal with these people?' Strykov calling Cullen an arrogant thug, 'which goes for the people you work for.' Cullen saying Russia is like the fucking mob. Strykov saying, 'how flattering', and hinting he had stuff, personal stuff, on Cullen. The American saying, 'You really wanna go there? Wait to see what we've got on you.'

'So who's it gonna be?' said Drayton to Dmitry.

They all looked at Dmitry, who said nothing.

'Except you can't deliver, can you?' said Drayton. 'Because you don't have the code book. You've brought them all out here for nothing. No wonder they're all so pissed about getting out of bed so early.'

Then they all looked down the hill, back towards the city, where the sound of sirens, distant at first, was getting closer, flashing lights approaching.

Dmitry turned back towards Drayton, raising his gun, but Drayton was no longer where he'd been standing. In the few moments they'd been distracted by the sirens he'd backed up and hauled himself into the bowl, where he was now lying on his back close to the extinguished flame, his legs poised to kick should anybody appear over the rim after him.

He lay there for several minutes and when he climbed back out, Wang, Strykov, Cullen and Dmitry had gone. Several police cars were at the foot of the hill, having responded to reports of vandals at the monument. Drayton told them he'd seen nothing, no eggs – fried, poached or scrambled.

The gardeners agreed. They'd been there all the time, managing to remain all but invisible. But not the watering can and the hard hat, which followed every bit of the action.

* * * * *

The cave monastery was on a steep slope beside the Dnieper River, golden cupolas peering out from above high walls. The OmniX was parked beneath trees in a small courtyard, looking from a distance like a dark hunched animal. Dmitry was a blue blob on the screen of Drayton's smartphone, his location transmitted from a tracking device installed on the Russian's phone when he'd clicked on the links Drayton had sent him.

The blob moved closer to the river and then stopped. Drayton followed it as far as the heavy door in the monastery wall. Steps beyond the door led to a small shrine with white-washed walls, candles flickering in front of several icons and a golden cross. The eyes of the saints seemed to follow him as he walked, the light from the candles giving them a piercing glow. An archway led to more stairs, much steeper this time. He took a candle from the shrine, swearing as hot wax dripped onto his hand. Then he slowly descended into the cave beneath the monastery.

He followed a long tunnel with white walls and arched ceiling, small shrines cut into the walls. Coffin-like boxes lined low shelf-like recesses. One was draped with what looked from a distance like a heavy black shawl. Drayton cupped his hand around the flame of the candle as a sudden breeze swept along the tunnel. Light jumped and bounced off the walls and ceilings. The black shawl rose, ghost-like, in front of him and then took on the shape of a man, tall and thin with long black hair and beard, a heavy crucifix around his neck. A priest, whose dark eyes, buried deep in his thin expressionless face, following Drayton as he passed.

Then Drayton froze, because up ahead, their bodies almost filling the tunnel, was the cause of the turbulent air. Dmitry and one of the fridge-freezers were approaching, and approaching fast. Drayton turned. The priest was still standing, watching. To run would just draw attention to himself. There was another recess to his left, a slightly bigger one this time, with a coffin beneath an icon. He snuffed out the candle and stepped into the recess, draping himself over the coffin as the priest had done. His face to the lid, lips touching the glass top, his body turned away from the tunnel. He heard voices, Dmitry barking something at the priest, who replied in little more than a whisper. Drayton tightened his grip on the coffin, bracing for the blow, and with horrible vision of being bludgeoned, branded and stuffed into the box beneath him, alongside whatever grisly monk remains it contained.

When the blow came, it was more of a tap. Then a gentle hand on his head. It was the priest, looking a good deal more benign close up, a candle fully lighting his face. Dmitry and the fridge-freezer had gone. Drayton stood, and the priest beckoned him to follow, relighting Drayton's candle. The tunnel dipped steeply and then took a sharp turn to the right before reaching a junction. The priest pointed to the right. Drayton peered into the darkness, but could see nothing. When he turned back the priest had gone.

Drayton followed the priest's directions, the tunnel narrowing until it reached a metal door. There was another shrine beyond the door. Inside, slumped against the wall amid the icons, crucifixes and a pair of coffins, sat Vika, bound, blindfolded and gagged, but still alive. She began to wriggle and grunt as he entered the room. He leaned down beside her, first removing the gag and blindfold, then using the flame from the candle to cut through the ties around her ankles and wrists.

'So what the fuck kept you?' she said

Before he could answer, there was movement outside. Drayton leapt to his feet, looking for somewhere to hide. Then he rushed towards the door, but it was already swinging open. First he saw the cold blue eyes, then the glint of something hard and metallic, crashing down on his left shoulder. He fell to his knees, pain searing through his upper body. The man kicked him in the chest and he fell backwards, hitting his head hard on the stone floor. His vision was blurred, the room spinning. There were two men standing over him now. One with a metal bar. The other with something else metallic, only this one was glowing bright red on its tip, and the tip was getting closer to Drayton's face. He could feel the heat, the intense heat of the branding iron with the glowing snarling dog in its tip. Dmitry laughing as he pushed it towards Drayton's forehead.

Then there was a scream and another sharp movement. Something swung above Drayton's head sending Dmitry crashing hard against the wall. It was a leg, Vika's leg. And it was followed by several more crunching blows from her fists and shins. Dmitry slid down the wall, blood dripping from a gash in his head. The branding iron had been knocked out of his hand, landing on one of the coffins

Drayton rolled away, his vision still fuzzy, but clear enough to see Vika facing Dmitry's henchman. She twisted and turned as he lunged at her, then sent her arms and legs smashing into his ribs. He lunged again. She ducked, side-stepped, and then hit him hard on the back. He landed on the heavy coffin, which tipped over and fell on top of him, spilling its contents of dust and bones. He was pinned beneath it, writhing and screaming. At first Drayton thought the bones had freaked him out, that he was spooked by all the monk remains. Then he saw the branding iron, lying on his chest, burning rapidly through his skin.

Vika pulled Drayton to his feet and out of the door. It was pitch-black in the tunnel, and they felt their way along the cold, damp walls towards the distant flickering of candles. She asked him if he'd come this way, but his head was throbbing and he couldn't think straight. And everything was beginning to look the same. He leaned heavily against her for support, surprised by her strength.

They reached another cave, this one more a mini-church. Two priests were praying. Vika spoke to them in Russian, then one, little more than a boy, came over and put Drayton's arm over his shoulder, taking his weight, helping him along the tunnel to where a narrow concealed doorway led out to a path overlooking the river.

Drayton slumped against a fence, a sharp drop-off beyond. Vika sat down beside him and wiped blood from his forehead.

'I told the priests you'd had a deeply spiritual experience, so overwhelming that you fell and hit your head against the floor,' she said, smiling now.

But Drayton wasn't smiling. He was no longer listening, because behind Vika, Dmitry had emerged from the caves. He was unsteady on his feet, but he had his gun in his hand. He stopped in front of them, not saying a word, raising the gun, pointing it at Drayton, squeezing the trigger. Drayton instinctively closed his eyes, looked away and braced himself for the impact. There was a sharp and loud crack. Then two more. Then another. But no pain. Drayton opened his eyes to see Dmitry staggering towards the fence, blood oozing from his chest, a gaping hole where his forehead used to be. He felt for the fence, then another shot and he tumbled over it, Drayton watching his body as it rolled and bounced down the steep rocky hillside and into the river below.

Then he turned back and he saw Thomas, gun in hand, embracing his sister. They were both crying.

* * * * *

Bret said it was the most awesome fucking video he's ever streamed. 'No shit, the scene at Dmitry's club was *so* crazy. Man, I *loved* the deranged sharks. And the stuff at the eternal flame... The look on the faces of those dudes when they saw each other. *Crazy.* And you weren't too bad yourself.'

He slapped Drayton on the back, then quickly apologising when Drayton winced.

'Two ribs, yeah, and a few stitches?'

'Three ribs broken and eight stitches in the back of my head,' Drayton said, showing Bret the needlework.

They were sitting around a long table in a Kiev restaurant, which had a rustic feel, with lots of kitschy art, servers in traditional dress. The table was laden with food. Fish, meats that Drayton didn't recognise, dumplings, salads, alongside plenty of beer and wine. Drayton was sitting on one side of the table between Bret and Holger Norgaard. Vika, her brother Thomas and Milo sat opposite. Schoenberg and Raymond at the two ends of the table.

'By the time we were streaming the video from the eternal flame, there were two million people watching. Two fucking million. Can you believe that?' Bret said.

'I still don't get how you were able to find where I was and set up the show so quickly,' Drayton said, cracking another beer, which seemed a more effective painkiller than the multi-coloured horse pills he'd been handed by the hospital.

'Well, you and then Vika getting grabbed at the opera, that wasn't in the script, so that was a bit worrying,' Norgaard said.

'Yeah, for me too,' said Drayton.

'The strip joint they took you to, that was the address Dmitry gave on his application to that Yangon club.'

Drayton laughed. 'How'd you get in?'

Raymond took a sip of Coke, cradling it as if it was priceless champagne, relishing the moment. 'Through the fish tank. The thermostat in the tank was wireless controlled. No security. Once in there, not only could we control what was going on in the tank, but we could control everything else on the wireless network – the sound, lights, sprinkler system.'

'And the surveillance camera,' Bret said, with a grin as wide as the hapless sharks.

'But the sound wasn't great,' said Milo. 'Until Dmitry gave you back your phone and we activated the mic.'

And Schoenberg said, 'That's also when we learned about the flame. It didn't give us much time. We disabled the OmniX for as long as we could without them getting suspicious, and then we slowed it down, changed a few traffic lights too. That gave us time to set up the surveillance and send out the invitations to the Cardinals.'

'The watering can and hard hat. Very retro,' Drayton said.

'It was the best we could do at short notice,' Bret replied.

'Nobody really noticed you. They were so wrapped up with each other.'

Bret was looking at his phone again. 'They've gone fucking viral man. I mean tens of millions of streams. And that's just on YouTube. We also put out some edited highlights, together with profiles of Winnie-the-Pooh, Muttley and Captain America, based on your original meetings with them.'

'So,' said Schoenberg, pushing back his chair. 'You took out your own … What shall we call it? An insurance policy, I think that would be the best word, Drayton. I'm glad you did. It was smart. Perhaps you can share it with us.'

Drayton took another large sip of beer. Everybody watching him. 'I had a bad feeling, after I almost bumped into Dmitry at the hotel by the square. It was impossible that he didn't see me. I knew I needed some kind of back-up plan. I had on my cell phone the code book and the key for the cryptocurrency ransomware. Both in plain text. So I locked them in an encrypted file.'

'FireOfGlory2010?' said Milo.

'That was the clue. That was how we ended up at the eternal flame.'

'So what was the password?' Vika said.

'Fried eggs. Two words.'

'What's that got to do with eternal glory?' said Raymond.

'Not much,' said Drayton, teasing them. 'Except that In December 2010, a Ukrainian artist fried eggs on the eternal flame as a protest against old Soviet-era memorials.'

'Fuck, you kiddin' me?' said Bret.

And Milo said, 'That's, like, so cool.'

Even Vika looked impressed. 'And in the strip joint, when you sent Dmitry the links to the files, that's how you got the tracker on his phone, how you were able to follow him to the caves?'

'That's right. And more. When he clicked on that link, the spyware was able to grab everything on his cell phone. Contacts, emails, messages, photographs. Everything.'

'Well, that's too bad,' said Thomas, joining the conversation for the first time. 'His phone went into the river with him. We're too late.'

'It was all grabbed before he took his dive,' Drayton said, pulling a memory stick from his pocket and tossing it to Schoenberg. 'Should make for interesting reading and give us a pretty full picture of who else he's been doing business with.'

'Who downloaded it, given that you were rather busy?' Schoenberg said. 'If you don't mind me asking.'

'A young friend,' said Drayton. 'A friend who also supplied me with the tracker and spyware. A friend in Myanmar.'

There was silence around the table for a moment. Then clapping. Schoenberg and Norgaard laughing. Bret punched the air and went to slap Drayton on the back again, before thinking better of it. Thomas still looked a little sullen, but maybe marginally less so that before. Vika ordered champagne. Milo giggled.

Like a presiding judge, Schoenberg brought the table to order and began his summing-up.

'Dmitry Gerasimov and Ken Tsang are dead. We've shared the code book and technical details of the Cerberus zero day with the chip maker and with those attacked by it. As for Ric Cullen, Wang Yang and Igor Strykov, I think their careers are probably over. Cullen faces some uncomfortable questions in Washington. He's facing criminal charges over the hospital. My one big disappointment is Efren Bell. There may of course be something on this,' he said, tapping Drayton's memory stick. 'And we have a record of the cryptocurrency payments in and out of Dmitry's wallet, with Milo matching names where he can. But he does seem to have got away.'

'Not completely,' said Drayton, passing along the table a copy of that day's *International New York Times*, a picture of Bell on the front under the headline, 'Tech tycoon faces antiquity smuggling probe'.

'Antiquities?' said Norgaard.

'Old stuff, you mean?' said Milo.

'Yeah, Milo. Even older than last year's iPhone.'

Schoenberg looked at the newspaper. 'It says he's being investigated for receiving stolen Buddhist artefacts from Myanmar. They've seized as evidence a twelfth century inscription stone from his Berlin villa.'

They all looked at Drayton.

'Dmitry was testing his zero day on Professor Pendleton, the archaeologist, holding him hostage through his pacemaker. But he was also forcing him to steal some particularly valuable artefacts, some for Bell, and none more rare than that stone, which Bell had always wanted. Well, it seems as if the professor had the last laugh. The inscription below the head was written in ancient Burmese languages. Pendleton knew that language and added a few words of his own saying, "This head has been stolen and the owner is a thief." The Berlin police were tipped off by Pendleton's Burmese assistant, who also provided them with a full translation.'

'This assistant,' Vika said, 'he's not the same person that dabbles in computer code by any chance?'

Drayton didn't answer, just smiled, and then Milo said, 'I mean, doing the guy for stealing this old stuff still seems petty after what he's done.'

'They take antiquity smuggling seriously in Germany,' Schoenberg said.

'And anyway,' said Norgaard. 'Think of Al Capone. They got him for tax evasion.'

'I think his Digital Pagoda Fund is dead after this,' said Schoenberg. 'Investors will run for the hills.'

Vika stood to leave. A hand briefly on Drayton's shoulder. A few whispered words in her father's ear, a kiss on his forehead, and then to nobody in particular, 'See you guys around.'

Bret followed her out, saying he felt the need to kick the shit out of some punchbags. Then Raymond, saying he had work to do in Hong Kong. When Drayton looked back across the table, he saw that Thomas had already left.

That left Schoenberg, Milo, Norgaard and Drayton.

Schoenberg said the Berlin Group was back in business and with more work to do than ever. 'I need you all.'

'Let me think about that,' Drayton said, standing to leave, shaking Schoenberg's hand. High-fives with Milo and Norgaard. 'I might just go offline for a while.'

Then he sat back down beside Schoenberg. 'There's something that's been niggling me, Wolfgang. When you first rang me, to bring me to Berlin, you were already working with Vika and Thomas. They were feeding you information about Dmitry. But then Thomas was kidnapped, and Vika disappeared. You feared she was dead. Is that right?'

Schoenberg said nothing, slowly rotating the wine glass in front of him.

'Isn't that why you sent me to Myanmar, to find your daughter? To find Vika. You were communicating with her throughout our little travels, after she took over the email account. You knew what we were doing. Everything. Then when things got a bit crazy, veered off script, there was one crucial thing you could always rely on, that I had no great loyalty to my old employers, not after I was scapegoated for the hospital attack.'

Schoenberg refilled Drayton's glass, and topped up his own, his face breaking into the familiar half-smile that gave nothing away.

He raised his glass.

'*Prost*. Enjoy your break, Drayton. And keep in touch.'

Drayton walked to the river, where he sat at a scruffy beer bar and ordered a cold bottle. *Let the performance begin.* That's what the German had said when they were all gathered at the Chernobyl radar. Perhaps the performance had started a lot earlier than that – when the German first called him in Washington, summoning him to Berlin.

He took out his phone and opened a banking app from which he transferred one thousand dollars to an account in Myanmar. He then sent a message to Tun Zaw.

'Thanks,' he wrote. 'Good job. Your computer course is covered. And some. Stay away from the dark side.'

Tun Zaw replied almost immediately. 'Need anything else?' he asked, sounding eager. Then he wrote, 'Did you ever find our daughter?'

It took Drayton a few moments to remember. That's how he'd described Vika back in Bagan. 'Yeah, I found her,' he replied. 'She's off travelling again now. You know, you might even get to meet her. You have a lot in common.'

Then he wiped his phone, drinking another beer as he watched the progress bar as it deleted all his data. When it was finished he walked to the water's edge and threw the phone in. For a split second, it seemed to hang in the air, twisting and turning, life-like, as if it was struggling, before falling like a stone and hitting the water.

It floated briefly. A pair of seagulls swooped low and then hovered overhead, thinking it might be something tasty or useful. It turned out to be neither, and they quickly flew away.

Drayton walked on. He wasn't sure where he'd go next. But as his phone sank into the Dnieper, he was reasonably confident that only he would know.

BEIJING SMOG

A CYBER THRILLER

IAN WILLIAMS

Chapter One

The Cyber Guy

The hotel described itself as an intelligent building, the smartest hotel in Beijing, full of sensors to make stuff happen without pressing buttons, but the way Chuck Drayton saw it, the place was retarded.

He called the front desk, which tracked down the general manager, a German called Wolfgang, and he told Wolfgang they needed to work on the intelligent bit.

"Not just once, three times, man. I was up half the fucking night." Wolfgang said he was sorry to hear that and he'd be straight up, meeting Drayton five minutes later in the executive lounge on the thirty-fifth floor, where the American was standing beside one of its big windows looking for a view. The first thing he told Wolfgang was that the view sucked. He said that it reminded him of one of those over-priced Chinese landscape paintings they sold in the hotel shop, mountains shrouded in mist. Except the mist was smog, thick smog, pierced here and there by the dark shadows of grey skyscrapers and apartment blocks.

He said he could feel his life expectancy shrinking just looking at it.

Wolfgang ordered coffee and said, yeah, but don't you think it's kind of moody, and he apologised again for what he called the hiccups with the technology. He said it was a new hotel and they'd had teething problems with the sensors that were supposed to detect movement in the room and switch stuff on and off.

"There was no movement, Wolfgang. I was asleep," Drayton said. "Then suddenly the curtains open, the TV and the lights come on. I went to sleep last night thinking I'm in a hotel, then next thing I know I wake on the set of *Paranormal Activity*. You get what I'm saying?"

Wolfgang said he got what Drayton was saying and apologised again. He said it was definitely a hotel, and offered a complimentary dinner, lunch, drinks – whatever the hotel could do to make things good; Drayton said he'd take the lot. With a final flurry Wolfgang said he would deal with the matter personally, right now, and excused himself to go and find someone to yell at.

The German had sweat dripping down his forehead as he left. He looked stressed, and Drayton suspected his wasn't the first complaint about the hotel's IQ.

Drayton made a note in his iPhone, a reminder to speak later to the US Embassy security guys, who'd recently given the place full clearance as safe for American diplomats, and tell them that giving a green light to a hotel with a mind of its own, a forty-floor poltergeist, might not be the way to go.

Then he looked again for the maestro. Where the fuck was he? They'd agreed to meet in the lounge at two and travel together to the concert, scheduled for late afternoon, but it was now nearly a quarter to three.

He found an internal hotel phone and called down to the maestro's room, but it went straight to voicemail, meaning that the guy was either on the phone or had it on do-not-disturb mode. Maybe he'd taken a nap and overslept, though the maestro didn't strike Drayton as the type that took naps.

He decided to go and bang on his door, but the maestro's room was on a different floor to Drayton's and the smart lift wouldn't take him there since it wouldn't accept his smart key to get access to the maestro's smart floor. And since the smart lift didn't respond to yelling or to banging on the lift's smart console, Drayton went back to his room and phoned down again for Wolfgang.

A woman on the front desk said Mr Wolfgang was in a meeting, but she had a message from Mr Abramovich.

"He says he'll meet you at the concert and that he's taking the car," she said, and Drayton said that was just great and could she call him a taxi? The woman said sure, only there weren't many around right now and the traffic was terrible.

Drayton hung up and opened a taxi-hailing app on his iPhone. He could see taxis. They looked like rows of termites on his screen. Usually it didn't take long for one to respond, changing colour from white to black when they accepted the fare. Only today the termites weren't nibbling, stuck in little white clusters.

He refreshed the app, but the termites were still stuck. He could barely make out the road below from the window, but at that moment the smog cleared just enough to see what had paralysed the termites. The receptionist was right. The traffic on the ring road was at a complete standstill.

Maybe the maestro hadn't travelled too far, and could still turn around, bring the embassy car back and collect him. He picked up the maestro's business card from his desk: "Alexander Abramovich, composer, conductor and cultural ambassador". Drayton called the cell phone number on the card, an American number, and after three rings the maestro picked up.

"This is Abramovich."

"Mr Abramovich, this is Chuck Drayton. I was surprised to hear you left without me. It's very important we stick together."

But before Drayton could get to the bit about turning the car around, the maestro interrupted him, saying he'd had to leave earlier than planned because of the traffic, and wasn't going to be delayed by Drayton's petty squabbling with the hotel. He said he had a concert to conduct, that this wasn't just music, it was diplomacy, and that you, Mr Drayton, still had a few things to learn about that.

"And another thing," the maestro said, "I want my laptop back."

"Can we talk about that later?" Drayton said, not trusting the telephone line.

"I want it back, Mr Drayton, and you have until tomorrow to return it to me."

"We still have a few tests."

"Fuck your tests, Mr Drayton. I want it back. It was nothing. I overreacted. And anyway, I no longer want to pursue it, and I no longer need you. What I'm doing here is too important to be undermined by your cyber stupidity and paranoia."

Drayton wanted to yell, you were hacked, you moron, and I just hope your pretentious bullshit about cultural diplomacy is being read by somebody who cares more than I do. But the maestro had already hung up.

Drayton decided he'd have to take the metro, and he hated the metro. The nearest station was just around the corner from the hotel. That was the easy bit. When he got there the entrance was packed, and he was swept inside on a human tide, which carried him down two escalators and to a platform on which there was barely room to breathe. The platform had markings, little lanes, for getting off and on the trains, which was encouraging, but meant nothing. As the train approached, the crowd on the platform steeled itself like a team facing off with hated opponents in a grudge football match, and when the doors opened both sides charged. Drayton was carried onto the train by the weight of the crowd behind him.

He'd now almost certainly miss the pre-concert reception at the National Centre for Performing Arts, Beijing's modern egg-shaped arts centre, usually just known as that, the Egg, where Abramovich was performing. Drayton reckoned that at this rate he'd be lucky to get there for the concert itself. Not that he was too bothered, since he found the guy, this maestro, insufferable. He had an ego the size of Tiananmen Square, maybe bigger.

And the loathing was mutual.

The guy's laptop had been hacked soon after he'd arrived in Beijing, there wasn't much doubt about that. He'd opened the machine in his hotel room to find it had connected itself to the internet, the cursor roaming around the screen and doing its own thing, like it had a mind of its own. The laptop was hyperventilating, fan whizzing around and doing all sorts of stuff, but without the maestro at the controls.

He was a childhood friend of the US Ambassador, so he'd taken the machine straight to the US Embassy, yelling and ranting, saying the laptop contained sensitive plans, emails and notes as well as semi-finished compositions. The Ambassador said he'd have specialists look over it, do the forensics, look for digital fingerprints. That had calmed the maestro down a little, but still he ranted, like the future of world peace was at stake.

Like it was all the fault of the embassy.

The first thing Drayton did when he was put on the case was to make sure it wasn't, that nobody at the embassy had been poking around the guy's data. Abramovich had just been to North Korea, part of a tour that started in Russia and would take him on to Vietnam. The way Drayton saw it, the guy had kept some pretty unsavoury company in Pyongyang and Moscow. But nobody at the embassy put their hand up.

He'd hit it off badly with Abramovich from the start, calling his concerts the Tyrant Tour, thinking he was being funny, making a joke of it. But the maestro had called him an idiot, saying that America had lost the moral authority to lecture anybody about anything. He said he was using music to build bridges. That bridges were needed right now because there was a clown in the White House, a dangerous clown, and that he, Abramovich, was the real American diplomat.

Now, a week later, he and Abramovich could barely stand the sight of each other, and Drayton was seething because thanks to this jerk he was stuck on a train that was beyond crowded, four stops from the Egg, four stops too many as far as Drayton was concerned, the crush getting worse at every station.

He didn't think he'd ever be able to get off, but salvation came in the form of a bunch of what he took to be students, who'd clearly done the journey before and lined up in a wedge-like formation as the train pulled into Tiananmen West station, the closest to the Egg. Doors opened, and a dozen heads were lowered, shoulders tensed, before the wedge drove its way off the train; at its arrow-like point a lanky kid with his arms outstretched in front of him was holding an iPad to slice through the crowd. Drayton followed in their wake, thinking it was the smartest use of an iPad he'd seen all week.

Only they swept out of the wrong exit for the Egg, and he had to double back against the tide and into another dark corridor, this one lined with posters and with another barely penetrable crowd. Then he found himself face to face with the maestro, or at least a giant poster of the man, looking grim, about to fire up an orchestra, baton in hand, his chin raised, eyes wide open. Which was pretty scary. The caption said, "A Concert for Resilience and Hope".

Drayton paused for breath under the poster, thinking he could do with both if he was ever going to make it to the hall.

At least the forensic guys still had the maestro's laptop. Abramovich had started to have second thoughts twenty-four hours after he'd handed it over to the embassy, seduced by all the bullshit receptions, as Drayton saw it, Chinese officials telling him they were honoured. Privileged. That this was a special moment. An historic occasion for Beijing, for China-US relations, for classical music, they'd said, raising a glass. And the maestro lapped it all up, all the fawning, as if it meant something.

Drayton had trailed along, one reception after another. One Chinese official had told him they were excited to have in Beijing America's greatest living conductor, and a true statesman, performing with a Chinese orchestra for the first time, and Drayton didn't have the heart to say he'd never heard of Abramovich before the guy had arrived in Beijing.

But it all played to the maestro's ego, and he'd said to Drayton that maybe he'd made a mistake, that maybe he'd just been tired and nothing really was going on with the cursor and stuff. And anyway, he said, it really wasn't worth making a fuss over.

Drayton had tried to change the subject, asking Abramovich, "What's with the Leningrad thing? Why are you playing that? It's Russian."

The maestro said that was the point, that music has no boundaries. He said his grandparents on his father's side were Russian, that he'd inherited a passion for Russian classical music, but it was really all about the message.

"On one level the *Leningrad Symphony* is about the defence of that great city during the Second World War, Mr Drayton, but Shostakovich saw it essentially as a tribute to human resilience."

"And this *Shostakooooovik*, he's Russian?"

"He's Russian, Mr Drayton. But if it makes you happier, after the break I'll be conducting the *New World Symphony*, written in New York, and a reflection on America. Neil Armstrong took a recording to the moon. Is that American enough for you?"

Drayton said he liked the sound of that, but why couldn't he put the music by the American guy first?

The maestro said the American guy was Czech, his name was Dvořák, and would Drayton please excuse him. With that he headed back towards a podium, where more tributes were flowing, telling his assistant along the way to please keep that moron from the embassy away from him.

Which would have been just fine by Drayton, but he still had a job to do, and this was bigger than Abramovich. Much bigger.

He continued his slow progress down the corridor and into the Egg, though this time without the help of the student battering ram.

Eventually the corridor opened onto a vast concrete-walled lobby area, the Egg's main glass doors up some steps to one side, the ticket office and cloakrooms on the other. A wall of metal detectors blocked the route down to the main concert halls, though security staff in badly fitting uniforms, frisking people at random, seemed mostly to ignore the madly pinging machines.

No sooner had Drayton been through a metal detector when a group of perhaps twenty police and plain-clothes security agents, some with barely concealed weapons, entered through the main doors. They swept down the steps, shouting to clear out of the way, and forming a cordon around a short balding man with thick-rimmed glasses. The short man just looked straight ahead, walking briskly, or as briskly as people could be cleared from his path. What Drayton noticed most was the way the man's big glasses framed a child-like face. Most people backed away instinctively.

The short man and his escort barged through the metal detectors, since there was no way round them, and the pings turned into one manic high-pitched wail, which lasted well after they'd moved on.

"Who's that?" Drayton asked one of the Egg's security men, who was looking at his metal detector like it might blow up at any minute.

The man just shrugged. Didn't know, and cared even less.

Much to his surprise, Drayton had arrived with twenty minutes to spare before the concert, so he found a bar and ordered a beer, a local Tsingtao, which was lukewarm but went down so well he ordered another, thinking all the time, *who was that guy?* Maybe the maestro was the real deal after all. Drayton hadn't really got a good look, since the guy was dwarfed by his bodyguards, but there was a stern, serious look on that baby face, that was for sure.

A buzzer, a five-minute warning, sounded, and Drayton made his way to his seat, in an elevated section at the back of the hall. The place was packed, but he really wasn't in the mood for this.

The lights went down, and an announcement asked valued customers, out of respect for the artists and the law, to kindly refrain from any recording, videoing or photography.

As the orchestra entered the stage, dozens of smartphones were raised in the air to record, video and photograph. They were joined by still more, as the maestro entered, clad in black jacket and black bow tie, bowing deeply to the smartphones, spotlights highlighting his shiny balding head and round rimless glasses.

Attendants who'd been showing people to their seats scrambled into action. Each had a small laser pointer that they trained on the offending devices, moving the beam up and down. The laser beams were soon dancing all over the auditorium.

The orchestra looked like they'd seen it all before. If the maestro was surprised, he didn't show it. He looked serious and solemn. Just like his poster. And just like the music he was about to conduct.

The smartphones were lowered, driven away by the lasers, or maybe because they already had what they wanted and were now posting online with captions saying, "Hey, look where I am".

Drayton loved those small acts of defiance.

The maestro lifted his baton and the symphony began with a rousing melody from the string section, which Drayton hadn't expected and rather liked. But it didn't last; the Nazis were on the march and so was the maestro, waving his baton as if the defence of Leningrad depended on him alone, the music growing in intensity.

The first movement seemed to go on forever, and as it reached a climax, Drayton felt exhausted, drained. Then he felt a sudden trembling that seemed to rise up through his chair. Those sitting nearby felt it too, and they looked around like maybe the Führer's Panzer tanks had entered the hall and were about to take out the maestro. It stopped, but then started again, which is when Drayton realised he was sitting on his phone, which he'd switched to vibration mode and stuck in his back pocket. Somebody was trying to get hold of him.

The first movement ended, and as throats were being cleared, noses blown and smartphone messages checked, he ducked for the aisle, winding his way towards the exit, his body bent forward like a stressed orangutan criss-crossing the floor of its cage.

"No re-entry once the music starts again," said an attendant, one eye on Drayton, one on the lookout for smartphones.

"That's fine by me," Drayton said.

The security detail, the Praetorian Guard for the little guy, was now huddled in small groups outside the main hall. Other plainclothes security patrolled past the doors of the hall with curly earpieces and big bulges under their jackets.

Drayton reached a quiet corner of the foyer between a pillar and a big gold artwork, a grotesquely contorted head of a buffalo mounted on a wooden plinth, when his phone vibrated again, a call from an unknown number. He took the call, but said nothing, waiting on the caller to speak first.

"Chuck, it's Dave."

"Hey Dave, what's up?"

"We need to talk. We have a breakthrough."

Drayton said that was great, but he was still at the Egg, at the concert, baby-sitting the maestro.

"Fuck the maestro," said Dave. "We have what we need."

Drayton said he could be at the embassy in twenty minutes or so, and Dave said, "No, don't do that. I'll meet you in

Tiananmen Square in front of the portrait of Mao. It's more secure."

Drayton left by the main entrance of the Egg. He raised the collar of his thick black overcoat, with matching scarf and thick woollen beanie hat, strapped on a pollution mask and stepped out into the frigid gloom. Police cars were lined up in front of the Egg's titanium and glass dome, with more armed men, and Drayton wondered again who the little guy was and why he needed that level of security.

It took him ten minutes to walk to Tiananmen; he thought the giant square was atmospheric in all the smog. The blurred outlines of the Great Hall of the People to his right. National Museum to his left. Tall street lights, smudge-like, lining the edges. The closer ones had halos of haze, but in the middle distance they faded to nothingness.

He stopped close to the portrait of Mao Zedong, at Tiananmen Gate, hanging above a tunnel into the Forbidden City, the old Imperial Palace. Guards stood rigid in the foreground, and crowds jostled for photographs in front of them, selfies mainly. Drayton took one himself, on his iPhone, and then looked back down the square trying to spot Mao's mausoleum, but it was lost in the smog. He decided he'd pay the old despot a visit at some point, see him in the flesh.

There were a lot of people mingling there. Drayton guessed that was why Dave had chosen this place, figuring there was anonymity in the crowd. But it was sometimes difficult to tell what was going on with Dave, a guy who thought his job was so secret he didn't even have a second name. At least not one he wanted to tell Drayton.

He reckoned it was probably a turf thing too, the Beijing spooks wanting to keep control, wary of the upstarts like

Drayton from the Shanghai consulate. It was stupid really, but Drayton never felt particularly welcome at the embassy.

He was beginning to wonder if he'd ever find Dave when he felt a hand gripping his arm, and Dave said, "Hannibal Lecter, I presume."

"Yeah, you like it? I figured it might add a year or two to my life expectancy."

Drayton's big black pollution mask was an all-encompassing studded contraption that covered half his face. He imagined it did make him look pretty scary, that he should keep away from kids, though he thought it more Darth Vader than Hannibal, the Hollywood cannibal. But it seemed to do the job, keeping out the filthy air, though at times Drayton found he was struggling to breathe at all through its multiple filters.

"This one's pretty useless," Dave said, pointing to his own mask. "Maybe worse than useless."

He was wearing a simple white surgical-style mask with the words PM2.5 Mega Blocker printed on the front.

"I think it refers to the tiny bits that do the most damage," he said. "Someone at the embassy bought a whole bunch of them online, while we wait for fresh supplies from Washington."

Drayton said they had plenty at the consulate, smirking beneath his mask, scoring an easy point for Shanghai, which Dave ignored.

"There're a lot of fakes online," Drayton said.

"Yeah, tell me about it," said Dave.

And then he said, "Let's walk", and they headed east away from the square along Chang'an Avenue, the wide thoroughfare running across Tiananmen's northern end.

"I'm really sorry you got landed with this guy, this Abramovich," Dave said. "Sounds like a real pain, but hey, you're the Cyber Guy."

357

They walked for a while in silence before Dave said they'd got the forensic results back from Fort Meade, and the National Security Agency had confirmed the maestro's laptop had been infected with malicious software, malware that allowed somebody else to take remote control and read his files, messages and emails.

"They were having a poke around when he got back to his room and he saw the cursor dancing all over the screen."

"Why the maestro?" asked Drayton, and Dave said there was some interesting stuff on his computer, that he'd had some quite high-level contacts in China and in North Korea. In Russia too, where he met the President.

"He had some less than flattering things to say about us, the American Government, that is," said Dave. "There was a lot of gossipy stuff, emails, notes to himself, and a pretty full address book. The guy does have some decent contacts."

"I can imagine. And you happened to just stumble upon all this?"

"Well, we were inside his computer. We had to look to see what might be of interest to the hackers."

"Or to you."

Dave ignored that and said, "The key thing, Chuck, is not whether this guy had anything interesting on his computer. It's the pattern, the fingerprints. It's what it tells us about their capabilities. The hackers didn't cover their tracks very well, and Fort Meade says it's consistent with other attacks we've seen against US companies and business people, hoovering up information wherever and whenever they can."

At that moment, a pair of police cars raced out of the gloom of Chang'an, their sirens wailing, lights flashing. Both men instinctively turned away, raising the collar of their thick coats. Drayton pulled down his black woollen beanie hat to just above his eyes.

"You know that building?" said Dave, pointing to the fuzzy outline of the Beijing Hotel, overlooking Chang-an. Then without waiting for an answer he said, "It was from one of those rooms on the left that the famous images were taken. Tank Man. The guy standing in the street facing off against a tank during the 1989 Tiananmen Square massacre. It was right here."

Drayton said yeah, he remembered the photo. He said he'd read that Tank Man had never been identified, that nobody had ever figured out who he was, and he asked Dave whether he thought that could ever happen again.

Dave said from what he could make out, the Communist Party leader seemed in control, locking away his rivals, saying they were all corrupt. And Drayton said the guy was making a lot of enemies. That maybe it was a sign of weakness.

Dave just shrugged, and Drayton said the maestro wanted his computer back, that he was making threats.

"He can have it back," said Dave. "In fact the sooner the better. We've installed a little something of our own in case the hacker returns for another look around his laptop."

"And what little something is that?"

"That's not important right now, Chuck. What matters is that the hackers have left quite a digital trail, and we're close to pinpointing where these attacks are coming from."

"That does sound like a breakthrough," said Drayton. "Where are we talking about?"

And Dave said Drayton needed to get back to Shanghai, just as soon as he could.

* * * * *

By that time at the Egg the final movement of the *Leningrad Symphony* was building into a frenzy, and so was the maestro. His face was contorted, grimacing, his arms waving manically as he drove the orchestra on, marshalling the defences of Leningrad.

The little man with all the security was dabbing his eyes, overcome with the emotion of the music. He was seated alone in a box high on one side of the hall, with carefully arranged curtains making him all but invisible to the rest of the audience below.

He was an elderly man, who'd trained in what used to be the Soviet Union. He was hard, uncompromising and feared. Sentiment was not something he was known for, but he did have one private weakness – for Russian music, especially at its most intense and moving. And none more so than the *Leningrad Symphony*, even if it was conducted by an American.

He saw it as more than just a tribute to the resilience of a city. It was about determination and resolve. It was about strength. All of which he felt he needed now more than ever, to uphold the leadership of the Communist Party which he'd served for almost fifty years. To defend it against the enemies he saw everywhere.

As the music reached its climax, the smartphones came back out, as did the laser pointers. The phones stood firm this time, like the defenders of Leningrad, determined to capture the stirring finale of the symphony.

One laser beam, this one directed from high above the stage, seemed to wander away from the main area of the hall and the main concentration of smartphones, climbing up the steep sides of the hall and into the darkened area behind the curtain. It came to a halt squarely on the forehead of the little man in the box, who seconds later toppled backwards off his chair as a single bullet followed the beam to its target.

Acknowledgements

Writing about computers and hackers, even as a work of fiction, runs the risk of descending into techno-babble. I am tremendously grateful to those who read early drafts of this manuscript and helped me keep it grounded and comprehensible. Thank you Philip Beresford, Barrett Feldman, Patrick Garrett, Jerry Harmer, Ian Harris, Graham Williams, Serena Williams and Simon Williams. And a big shout out to Darrell Newman, who knows more about computers than I ever will and handed me the ultimate accolade, 'it sounds like you actually understand this stuff'.

A big thank you also, to all those who helped me during my field research in the Far East, Berlin and Kiev. This was invaluable in bringing alive the political context in which hackers ply their trade, as well as understanding the way spies, criminals and corporations (often with considerable overlap) are competing for control of cyber space. They are too numerous to name individually and in any case many, in sensitive positions, prefer me not to do so.

Zero Days is a work of fiction, but I have endeavoured to make the hacks and the general cyber skulduggery as real and as plausible as possible. There is little in the book that is not possible now or will be in the near future. I am very grateful to friends, fellow-students and teachers at the Information Security Group of Royal Holloway University. They helped and inspired me to make sense of the dark cyber world, and during the course of my study there, induced in me a permanent but healthy paranoia towards computers and the internet.

I am grateful also to Clare Christian, Heather Boisseau, Julia Pidduck, Anna Burtt and the rest of the great team at RedDoor for all their hard work on this book. They understood the importance of *Zero Days* and have been enormously supportive throughout.

About the author

Ian Williams is an award-winning journalist who has reported from across the world. He covered business for the *Sunday Times* before becoming a foreign correspondent, based first in Russia and then the Far East for *Channel 4 News* and then the American network NBC. Ian has travelled and reported from across China, and more recently covered the Russian annexation of Crimea and the conflict in eastern Ukraine. In 2017 he published his first novel, *Beijing Smog*, a satire on modern China. He has taken a strong interest in the dark cyber world, the world of hackers and cyber spies that are at the heart of his new thriller, *Zero Days*.

ianwilliamsauthor.net
zerodaysnovel.com

Find out more about RedDoor Press and sign up to our newsletter to hear about our **latest releases, author events,** exciting **competitions** and more at

reddoorpress.co.uk

YOU CAN ALSO FOLLOW US:

 @RedDoorBooks

 Facebook.com/RedDoorPress

 @RedDoorBooks